UPRISING

TWISTED LOVE
(BOOK TWO)

UPRISING

TWISTED LOVE
(BOOK TWO)

ELLIE SANDERS

Never was there a story of more woe, than Juliet and her Romeo
—Romeo & Juliet, William Shakespeare

TRIGGER WARNINGS

This book is a dark modern, retelling of Romeo and Juliet. There are a lot of triggers so please be aware of this before embarking down this road as it's labelled 'dark' for a reason.

Ideally, I'd prefer for you to dive into this book blind so as not to spoil the twists and turns but I know some people like a warning. Below are the main triggers.

For a full list please visit www.hotsteamywriter.com

Triggers include: familial abuse, emotional abuse, sexual assault, rape, physical violence, physical assault of a child (hitting), forced pregnancy vibes, human trafficking, organ trafficking, drug use, torture and murder.

There are also a lot of extremely explicit sex scenes so if this is not your thing, then this book / duet is not for you.

Reader discretion really is advised because you have been warned.

PLAYLIST

Tears and Rain — James Blunt
Everybody's Fool —Evanescence
In The End — Tommee Profitt, Fleurie, Jung Youth
Nightmare — Halsey
Rise — Coryyx
Carry You — Ruelle, Fleurie
Beautiful Crime — Tamer
We Must Be Killers — Mikky Ekko
You Are The Reason — Calum Scott
I'm Kissing You — Des'ree

ROSE

It's early. Too early to be awake.

And yet we both are.

We're lying here, as the rising sunlight streams in through the gap in the curtains. Neither of us are talking. All I can hear is his breathing, all I can see is that beautiful smile of his as he watches me back.

I'm transfixed.

Lost in this moment in time.

He raises his hand, strokes my cheek, grazes it with his fingertips and I turn my face so that I can kiss his palm.

He's so beautiful. Even now, even after all this time, I still can't believe he is mine, that we are here, like this.

He doesn't speak. He just lies there, wrapping his arms around me and I shut my eyes, lost in the safety of that feeling. In the protection of him.

I can smell him. That deep intoxicating scent of the man I love.

"Rose…" He murmurs softly.

"I love you." I whisper it back, needing him to hear it, needing him to know it. To feel it too, to feel everything I am feeling in this moment.

He smiles again. "I love you too. I've always loved you."

I blink, realising that my tears are falling. I don't know why I'm crying right now. I don't know why I can feel this pain because Roman is here, and I know I'm safe with him, that I'll always be safe with him.

"It's time to wake up." He murmurs.

I shake my head. I don't want too. I don't want to come out of this. I think, if I could, I would stay here fast asleep and dreaming forever.

He cups my cheek, kisses my lips, but it's not enough, this kiss isn't nearly enough.

"Rose." He murmurs again.

"Don't leave me." I say back.

His eyes show his pain, reflecting what my own body, my own heart is feeling.

"You have to take care of Lara." He says.

"But we were meant to do this together." I reply. "I can't do this without you."

"Yes you can."

"Roman please, please, don't leave me, don't go…"

He shakes his head slightly. Opens his mouth to say something only I'm being shaken awake. And this moment, this dream, whatever it is, it's gone.

I BLINK OPENING MY EYES. THE FRESH AUTUMNAL AIR HITS ME FROM where Darius likes to sleep with the balcony doors open. It chills my skin, leaves me in goosebumps, but he either doesn't notice or doesn't care.

His hand reaches around pulling my face so that I'm forced to look at him.

"You were muttering." He says. "In your sleep."

I drop my eyes, averting his gaze. It's not the first time I've done that. But it's not even like I have any control over it, after all, who decides what they dream about?

"Do you want to know what you said?" He asks.

I don't reply, don't respond. It feels like a trap. But then everything with Darius feels like a trap. If living with Paris was like being on eggshells then living with Darius is like being suspended on a glass platform that may shatter at any moment, while a volcano is threatening to erupt beneath your feet the entire time.

"You said his name." He states.

I don't play dumb. I don't act like I don't know what man he's referring too. I just blink, waiting for the inevitable consequence of the heinous crime I've committed.

He grips my face harder, pinching my cheeks together to the point that it really hurts. "You keep saying his name."

I gulp, my body trembling before I can stop it. "Darius…"

He doesn't let me say anything further. I don't know if it's his anger or his lust driving him right now but he grabs me, forcing my legs apart, and shoves himself inside me.

I let out a cry screwing my face up at the horrific intrusion.

He's not gentle. He's never been gentle. I think he gets off on the power, on the control of it.

He starts pounding into me, grunting as he does and his sweat begins to cover my skin in a way that makes me want to puke.

I used to shut my eyes. I used to pretend that it was Roman, that this was us, but nothing about this is even close to what we had.

There's no consent, there's no pleasure, and there's definitely no love.

All I can do is lie here and take it, take each awful moment, telling myself over and over of the one thing I do have. The one thing that matters in all of this.

Lara. My daughter.

And in a way it does make this more bearable, though it doesn't make the pain and the brutality of it any less.

I stare up at the chandelier far above us. Letting my focus on it try to override the pain of what my body is enduring. It's ridiculous to have such a thing in a bedroom. Sometimes I wish the mechanism holding it would snap and the thing would fall down and crush us both.

But that wouldn't help Lara.

His hands find my throat, he wraps them around tight enough to restrict my airway while ensuring he doesn't leave any noticeable evidence. Instinctively I grasp his hands, trying to stop this piece of tyranny but he's too strong to fight.

"I'm sick of hearing his name." He spits. "Sick of you saying it."

"I'm sorry." I gasp quickly. It's hard to even speak through his grip but I know he hears me.

He tilts his head, then thrusts brutally into me and I let out a cry as I feel myself tear. "Sorry isn't good enough."

"I'll be better." I state, not that I have any control.

He narrows his eyes, yanking me around, twisting us so that now I'm on top, held up by his hand still wrapped so tightly around my throat.

I stare down at him as he takes in my body. The look on his face, the way he smirks as he enjoys my nakedness makes me sick to my stomach, but there's nothing I can do. I'm his to do as he wants, and this is what he likes best.

"Prove it then." He says. "Ride me like the good whore you are."

I want to refuse. Everything in me makes me want to lash out, to fight back but we both know I can't. He has all the power here so I'm forced to do it, to act like this is what I want, that he is what I want. I throw my head back, shut my eyes, fighting the tears as my body rips more with each movement.

"I'm the one you love." He growls. "Me."

"Yes." I whisper back. I'll say anything, agree to anything in this moment and he knows it as well as I.

He shoves his thumb on my clit. I jerk as he does it but I keep on rolling my hips. Keep on the pretence.

"Come for me Rose, come on my cock." He says pushing so hard it hurts.

I screw my face up, I can't come. I've never come. Not once since he started touching me. Maybe I'm too broken now, maybe I'm just not good enough at pretending but each time he tries to force this all it does is end the same way, with him hurting me more.

He pushes, rubs, does everything he can to try to force my body into giving him what he wants.

I try to pretend, I try to moan, but even that sounds wrong. And besides he can feel it, he can feel from how my body is wrapped around his that I'm not giving him what he wants.

"You will come for me." He growls. "You're going to come around my cock like the little slut you are."

I nod, pretending more, pretending harder.

I have to do this. I have to do all of this for Lara.

He grips my throat, pulling my face down level with his. He's close now, I can see it, I can feel it too in the way he's fucking me, he always hurts me more just before he climaxes, as if that little extra pain is what gets him off.

"Come you useless fucking slut." He spits.

But I don't.

Even as he groans, even as he pumps himself into me.

And then he slumps back into the pillows and I pull myself off of him, feeling every bit the used piece of trash he wants me to feel.

ROSE

We're sat in the oversized dining room, eating breakfast. Or at least Lara is eating while I act like this is all normal.

I tried hiding away, hiding us both away, keeping out of the main part of the house while Darius and his cronies seem to be everywhere but he soon put paid to that. He wants me on display. He wants everyone to see his beautiful trophy wife-to-be. Afterall, I'm part of his election plan, I appeal to the masses, make him more likeable, more electable.

And he's ensuring he maximises my potential at every opportunity.

Lara's grown more quiet. Her whole demeanour has changed in the last two months since we moved in here. Since her father died.

I don't know how to help, and worst of all, I don't think I can help because we both know what this is, we both know that neither of us want to be here, that we're essentially hostages but I refuse to act like that around her. I want her to have as normal an upbringing as possible.

But nothing about this *is* normal.

And nothing I do right now can change that.

I glance at the armed men. All five of them stood around the room. They're for my protection or at least that's what Darius tells the press while we all know what their real job is. To watch me. To keep me under-control. To ensure I don't say or do anything to undermine Darius or reveal my true situation.

Because the press caught wind of that little shootout. They even had pictures of it. Of me, being held at gunpoint. Darius put a good spin on it of course, stating that I was kidnapped and held to ransom. It also gave him a convenient excuse for justifying why we're rushing this wedding. Why this whole whirlwind romance is being expediated.

It makes sense after all. It's natural that I would be jittery afterwards. That after the loss of Paris and then this new trauma, of course I would want some happiness, of course I wouldn't want to wait.

And Darius, my loving, kind, considerate fiancé, is naturally so concerned in giving me everything I desire.

The masses soak it all up. They love every minute of it. It's a true love story for the ages. Either they're too insipid to see what it is or worse, they really think I'm a gold-digging whore throwing myself from one rich Blumenfeld into the arms of another.

But Darius's approval ratings have never been so good and that alone all but seals my fate.

I glance at the ring on my finger. It's nothing like the one Roman gave me. But then none of the circumstances are the same. Roman gave me something of worth, Roman was someone of worth. Darius all but jammed the ring on my finger, after ensuring he bought the biggest damned diamond he could get.

It's flashy. Garish. In truth not unlike the one Paris got me, so perhaps it's a Blumenfeld thing though I don't want to dwell on that any deeper than I have to.

"Can I get down mummy?" Lara says, in that timid new voice of hers. She's lost her laughter, lost her smile. All her confidence is shattered.

I look at her plate and it's only half cleared. She's lost her appetite too but I can hardly fault her for that. It's hard to eat when you have five sets of eyes watching every move you make. Every scoop, every slice of the blunt knife.

I nod holding my hand out and she takes it quickly. Without a look at the guards I lead her from the room and out onto the veranda. They follow but they stay by the door, at least giving us a little distance.

When we're far enough away I crouch down and give her a hug. I keep hugging her as if this one act could heal all the harm I've done. Could cure all my failures.

Because I have failed her.

I've fucked up so badly that I don't know how to fix this. I thought rescuing her from my father would be a good thing, but all I've done is thrown us both into the lion's den.

She hugs me back so urgently.

"I'm so sorry." I whisper for what feels like the billionth time.

"It's not your fault mummy." She says sounding far too mature for her years.

I sweep her hair back, stare at her face, seeing every miniscule part of Roman that's reflected in her.

"This won't be forever." I whisper. "I will get us out."

"I know mummy. I know you will." She says hugging me again.

I pull her in, shut my eyes so tightly, I won't cry in front of her - I make sure of that. I keep my tears, my desolation, all of it for when I'm alone. I have to be strong for Lara. I have to make sure she believes in me. I have to give her hope. Something to cling to. Even though I have no idea how I'm going to make it a reality.

"Rose."

We both tense at his voice.

Reluctantly I let my daughter go and stand turning to face the new monster controlling my life.

"Her tutor is here." Darius says fixing his gaze on my child the way a man would a piece of trash that had blown into his path.

I bite my tongue. Darius has been more than clear that I'm not allowed to spend all my time with Lara, that seeing as she's old enough to go to school she should at least be tutored.

But I know she hates the tutor. I know he's a prick to her and I wonder if he's done that on purpose, if Darius chose him on purpose. Because I see it, the way my fiancé looks at my child, the way he sneers at her.

He sees Roman in her.

He sees her father and I know he wants to punish her for that.

"Mummy…" Lara whispers.

I turn to look at her, showing in my face that if I could I would stop this.

She nods, giving in, reminding me of all the times I've done the same. All the times I've been forced to relent to the will of everyone else around me., forced to break myself for the wants of others. I feel such a flash of anger as I register it, that my child is enduring this, that all these arsehole are doing this to an innocent girl simply because of who her parents are.

And then she walks past us both, to where the tutor is standing in the hallway with his arms crossed, already scowling.

I want to launch myself at him. I want to smack his horrible face, beat him so hard for the way he treats my child but I can't. I can't do a damned thing.

Darius walks up to me, taking my hand. He's all smiles, all charm.

"The journalists are here." He says.

My stomach turns at what that means. More photos. More fake moments. Darius has been more than keen to capitalise on our relationship if you can call it that.

Every time a bit of bad press happens, every time there's a story criticising him, or in some way not helping his election campaign he makes sure something leaks about us, some new loving tale of devotion and the polls respond accordingly.

I give my best fake smile. I have to be more convincing on these days. I have to be the Rose Capulet everyone has read about.

The true sunshine princess of Verona Bay.

The girl every woman aspires to be.

With the life every person wishes they had.

The journalists practically fan girl when they meet me. I know I'm a big name, I know I should be used to it after the way everyone at the Clubhouse used to act but it grates worse than ever.

Darius of course laps it up.

He gives a great spiel about how he knew Paris was physically abusive and that he'd tried to step in, to protect me, and then when Paris had died, how he'd comforted me, made sure I was okay. And all the while he's smiling at me, putting on that charm offensive that he does so well.

If I didn't know what he was really like, I'd believe every word.

They ask questions, probing questions. I let Darius take the lead but I'm also sure to add my own parts, to look as if this is everything I've ever wanted because I'm not stupid enough to risk anything right now.

Not when he essentially has a gun pointed at my daughter's head.

"Let's take some photos." The journalist says.

Darius nods. "How would you like us?"

"Natural." She replies. "Our readers want to see the real couple. Just pretend we're not here and we'll snap away."

I meet Darius's gaze. We both know we can't do that.

But I can see the way his eyes glint, the way his lips curl, that this amuses him. I wonder if that's why he keeps this up, keeps the articles and magazines and all of it. Because it's just another form of torment for me. Just another way to prove that I am powerless. Helpless. Completely and utterly at his mercy.

He leans in, his hand cups my cheek and it's so hard not to flinch, not to recoil from his rancid touch.

"I love you Rose." He says.

Only the words sound wrong. The way he says it sounds wrong too. He doesn't love me. He doesn't love anything about what makes me *me*. He's locked me in a cage, trapped me in his web.

I'm a thing to own.

A possession he's laid claim to.

I might as well be a jewel locked up in his safe.

And we both know he would rather see me dead than free of him.

"I love you too." I reply, keeping that gaze, playing the part and all the while I'm imagining it's someone else's face.

The man worthy of my love.

The man Darius murdered in order to get me.

3

ROSE

His hand cups my face.

I can feel the warmth of it against my skin.

I lean into kiss him and he lets out a soft groan as he deepens it.

"Rose." He murmurs.

I nuzzle into him, push my body on top of his, feeling how hard he is beneath me.

The covers are up over our head. It's hot underneath them but I'm not complaining because I'm surrounded by his smell, practically engulfed in it.

"Roman." I murmur.

He sweeps my hair back and kisses me again.

I can feel my lips curling up into a smile. I can feel my heart twisting with emotions that I up until now feel like I've not felt enough. Not allowed myself to enjoy enough.

His hand moves to cup my waist, I shift enough that my legs are either side of him, that if he wants he can take me.

And then I blink, opening my eyes, wanting to stare into his as he does it.

Only his face isn't his face.

His skin isn't his skin.

It's rotten, hanging off his skull and his eyes... he doesn't have any eyes left. They've completely decomposed already.

I shake my head, my heart stopping in my chest.

"What's wrong?" He asks.

I don't know how to reply. How to answer that. He isn't him anymore. He's dead.

I try to get off but my movements are only resulting in crumbling his body to dust.

Roman is dead.

He's not even recognisable as a person.

He's not even any sort of remains you can mourn over either.

I'm covered in bits of him.

Covered in what's left and I can't get it off.

I can't get free.

I WAKE SCREAMING. DARIUS TRIES TO SHUT ME UP AT FIRST, TRIES TO silence my cries, before he realises that I'm too hysterical, too panicked, to simply stop.

And then he's pulling me into his chest, burying my face into that awful smell of him.

"Sssssh." He murmurs. "It's just a nightmare."

I don't reply. What can I say to that when every waking minute with him is a living nightmare?

He cups my cheek, pulls my head so that I'm forced to look up at him.

And slowly, he wipes the tears that's he's ultimately responsible for.

There's a look you could mistake for love in his eyes. One he always seems to get when he's more gentle. Though those moments are so rare and far between.

Sometimes I wonder if he wants to acknowledge to himself what this is. Sometimes I wonder if he's telling himself that I'm not his captive, that I chose him freely. That every second spent with him is something I enjoy, that I relish.

He leans in claiming my lips and it's such an odd response in this moment that I don't even push him off. I just lie limp in his arms.

He pushes his tongue into my mouth, I grimace pulling back but his hands wrap around my head forcing me to take it, forcing me to accept his kiss.

When he finally breaks off I slide out of the bed, ignoring the groan he makes at the revelation of my naked body, and then I walk into the ensuite. I can't lock the door, he's removed every lock on this floor, and he's made it clear all the ones on the lower level are out of bounds to me.

That I'll be punished if I even attempt it.

But I do shut the door.

It's all I can do. The only privacy I get and I know it'll be short-lived.

But in this moment I'll take it. I'll take every fleeting second I can. I need to breathe, I need to think, I need to wash away the horrific image of Roman's rotting face from my memory and just have a few brief seconds to myself.

Only as I get in the shower and the water starts cascading down I hear it, the creak of the hinges, the sliding of the glass door. All tell tale signs that my peace is already gone.

He gets in behind me, and immediately slides his hands around and across my body, laying claim to me once more.

He fondles my breasts, rubs shower gel over them, staring at me in a way that makes me so close to puking.

"I love your body." He murmurs. "You're so beautiful. So per-fect to look at."

I don't reply. It's all I can do not to throw up over his feet.

And then he pushes me against the tiles, shoving himself inside me, and begins fucking me. I wince, screwing my face up. I'm so not turned on that every thrust is like a dagger.

He groans grabbing at my breasts, squeezing them like it's some sort of stress relief. He's too lost in his own pleasure to notice how much I am not into this.

"You're so tight, you're gripping me so good."

I hate his voice. I hate his dirty talk, I hate it all. I want to shout out that I'm not gripping him, that I'm not enjoying this for a minute, that what he's doing is excruciating to me, disgusting too.

Only I don't dare.

I can't say those words. I can't do anything but grit my teeth and take it.

He runs his fingers down, massaging my clit as I try not to jerk.

"Come for me Rose." He murmurs.

I shut my eyes. Thank god he's not actually pleasuring me in this moment because I don't want to. I never want to come for him. I never want him to think that I'm enjoying this. Even the few times he forces me to pretend we both know that's what it is, a pretence.

I never want him to believe anything else.

I never want to give him that satisfaction.

And as he starts digging his hand into my hip, groaning harder, I brace myself for more insults, more degradation as he gets closer and closer to his climax.

THE BLACK LIMOUSINE PULLS UP OUTSIDE THE HOUSE AS DARIUS GRIPS my hand so firmly in his that I think he's actually trying to crush my knuckles.

"Remember." He murmurs.

As if I won't.

As if I could forget.

We get in. He sits beside me, and I stare out the window but I can feel the way he's watching me.

This is a risk, taking me out in public, at least he clearly thinks it is.

But for me it's just another torture session. Another show of how much power he has and how much of a prisoner I am.

Only today is worse.

Much, much worse.

We reach the chapel and it feels like some sick reversal of when Paris died and we held his funeral. It's hard to believe that was almost six months ago. It's hard to believe that at the time I thought that was my absolution. My chance of escape.

The car comes to a stop.

Someone opens the door and Darius gets out before walking around, and ever the gentleman in public, he holds his hand for me to take.

I'm quick to do it, quick to get out, and the cameras are even quicker to snap a photo of the new golden couple.

I'm wearing a birdcage veil. I had to wear something. I had to conceal my face in case my grief broke through because how could I justify why a Capulet was crying over the death of a Montague?

Darius leads me inside. My heels click on the stone floor as we walk past all the onlookers and down the aisle, right to the front, to where seats are reserved for him as the Governor.

I sit down beside him. The only reason I'm here is because I'm his fiancée. Mercifully, my parents are a no show and that at least is something because I think if I saw them, if I saw their fake faces, and their pretending to care I'd lose my shit and scream from the pulpit about what's really going on.

A murmur goes through the crowd.

I look and my heart sinks. Sofia is walking, with Otto holding her arm. I can see she's trembling but I can see the gaunt look on her face too.

No doubt everyone thinks it's from grief but I know it's got nothing to do with the loss of her brother and it's all about the monster twice her age that even now is sucking the very life out of her.

She's wearing a long sleeved dress, it hugs her body, showing how much weight she's lost in the last two months. But it tells me something else too; that he's still hurting her, that under that fine fabric she's covered in bruises, covered in marks from that bastard of a husband.

I drop my eyes. I can't look at her right now because I think it might send me over the edge.

I feel like I failed her too.

I should have found some way to protect her, to save her for Roman's sake.

Darius squeezes my hand as if he can sense where my head's at and I heed the warning of that action.

The service goes by in a blur. I don't pay attention, I just zone out, trying to focus on my breathing but it's so hard when the eulogies start and people who barely even interacted with him stand and talk about what a good person he was, like they knew him, like they understood him.

The official story is Roman's car was crushed by a falling tree killing both him and his friend Benvolio. By all accounts it was a complete accident. Something no one could be blamed for unless you wanted to take it up with god that is.

I'll admit, if I believed in god, then I would be taking a lot more than just this travesty up with him. I'd want to know how it is that such a man as Darius, such a man as my father is not only clearly pardoned for their sins, but rewarded for them too.

Darius gets up. I watch as he makes his way to stand in front of everyone and as he begins talking my stomach turns.

"Roman Montague." He begins. "He was the ultimate prodigal son, a man redeemed and returned to us…"

I clench my fists, I do everything I can to maintain my composure.

"...For so many of us we saw the light in him, the good."

He glances at me and I swear he's smiling. I swear he's laughing inside at this moment. Mocking me, mocking all of us.

"...He will forever be remembered as a loving son, a devoted brother, and beacon to those who fall from the path, who lose their way but want to come home."

My eyes dart to Sofia's, she's sobbing so hard it looks like everyone around her doesn't know how to react. Otto is gripping her hand, acting like he cares, but under the guise I can see that glint that tells me he's finding this as hysterical as Darius is.

"...He had so much hope, so much potential, he wanted to change the world, to redeem himself and yet his life was cut so tragically short before any of those dreams could come to fruition."

I wince. I drop my head but then force myself to look at him. I want him to feel it, I want him to realise that this moment here, this is just another piece I will have vengeance for.

I meet his gaze and I'm certain he feels every moment of that glare I give him. I'm certain he feels the full force.

And before I can stop myself my tears are falling. Not just one, not just a few, but my cheeks are wet and it's all I can do not to sob. I drop my face, stare at my feet hoping nobody sees but most all praying that he doesn't.

As Darius sits back down I don't look at him.

I can't.

But I'm trembling, fearful, and yet so absolutely furious.

They did this. They murdered Roman and now they're all stood around acting like it's some tragedy. Like an awful act of nature.

As soon as the service is done and I can get away with it, I slip out, away from the group of people gathering around us. I murmur about needing fresh air but that's not what I need.

I need Roman.

I need him so much it hurts.

He's dead. He's gone.

I walk not paying attention to where I'm going. I can see a door ahead. I know it can't lead outside, it could just be a cupboard but I open it and walk in, anxious to get away from all the stares around me.

Only my eyes widen when I realise where I am.

It's his coffin. I'm here, in the room where it's been placed ready for the undertakers.

I stare at it stepping forward. Perhaps this was fate, perhaps this was my moment to say goodbye, to get some sort of closure. Only I don't want too. I don't want to admit that he's gone. To accept it and alongside that, accept that me and Lara are stuck were we are.

That we did lose.

That all three of us lost.

How did this happen?

I put my hand on the casket. It's closed. I guess after what they did to his body they couldn't exactly have an open one could they?

The wood is smooth. Cold. A sob escapes me and it's all I can do not to throw myself on top of it and properly give into my despair.

I don't look around, even as I hear the footsteps getting nearer. Even as I hear them coming right up behind me.

But I know who it is. My jailor back to ensure I don't do anything to jeopardise his little plan.

The air feels tense. I grit my teeth, compose myself, I know he can't do anything right now while we're in public and that at least gives me comfort.

"Weren't reconsidering your options were you?" He murmurs.

"No." I reply. Like I have any options.

"Good." He says stepping even closer. "Because you realise how pointless it would be? I have the entire city's police at my disposal. If you even think of running, if you even try, I'll have you dragged back to me within the hour and what would happen to your precious little brat then?"

"I'm not going to run." I say. At least that's not my immediate plan because I don't stand a chance right now and I'm not stupid or desperate enough to convince myself otherwise. I have to bide my time. Play the long game.

"No?" He muses. "After that little outburst I wondered if you'd forgotten yourself?"

"In what way?" I ask turning to look at him.

His face changes, for a second I see what almost looks like sympathy.

"Rose." He murmurs, like he cares.

I look away, I think I hate him when he's like this more than when he's just a straight up brute.

He steps closer, wiping my tears before I can stop him. "You have to get over this." He says. "You have to move on."

I bite my tongue so hard I can taste the blood. How can I move on when the man I love is dead? How can I move on when I'm sleeping in the bed of the man who killed him? Did he really think I'd be able to stand here, to pretend that none of it matters?

He takes a deep breath. "You're only making this harder for yourself."

"I'm not." I whisper.

He snarls back. "Yes you are. The man is dead. It's over."

"Roman." I hiss. "His name is Roman."

He grabs me, pushes me back, shoves me with such force that I almost fall over my feet and his hand is the only thing keeping me upright.

"I told you before." Darius says tightening his grip just a tiny bit more. "I told you to stop saying his god damn name."

"I hate you." I spit.

He smirks turning me around, pushing me onto the coffin face first. "Like I care." He replies.

"I wish you were dead. That you were the one lying in this casket." I cry.

He lets out a laugh, but as he does I can feel it, the way he's pulling on my dress, raising it.

"No." I gasp.

He leans in, pushing me flat onto the wood. "No?" He taunts. "You don't get to say no."

"Darius."

"You loved Roman so much huh?" He says as he yanks my underwear aside.

I kick out, try to get free but all I end up doing is allow him to twist one of my arms to the point I think it might break and the pain of it is enough to stop any of my further struggles.

He unzips his trousers, I can hear the sound of it, the sound of him fumbling. My breath increases tenfold, I'm crying even more, and then he rams himself into me, groaning as he does.

"Fuck your cunt is so good."

"Get off me."

He laughs. "I don't think so Rose. I'm going to fuck you right here, right over his corpse, and you know what? There's nothing either of you can do about it."

He shoves my head down, clearly he doesn't care what I look like after this, what state he leaves me in. The mesh of the veil sticks into my skin, catching my eyelashes. And then he starts fucking me so hard the coffin really does begin to shake.

"Please Darius, please stop." I whimper.

Only he laughs harder. "You can't stop me." He says. "Your precious Roman can't stop me either."

I can't shut it out. I can't even pretend this isn't happening. He's fucking me like he's determined to break the casket beneath us.

"How does it feel huh?" He taunts. "How does it feel knowing that Roman can't save you? That he's not coming to help? That he's never coming back?"

I don't reply. I don't say anything. I know he's trying to break me, and I won't let that happen, no matter what he does, no matter how horrific this gets, I'm not giving in, I'm not.

"You're mine Rose. All mine." He says, lowering his head so that his lips are right by my ear and I can feel the heat of his breath on my skin. "I never want to hear you say his name again. I never want you to even think it. He never existed, no other man exists except for me. Have you got that? Have I made myself clear?"

He tightens his grip, his hands twisting in my hair as I yelp.

"Have I?" He repeats.

"Yes." I whisper.

He lets out a groan, picking up speeding, fucking me over and over until finally, mercifully, he comes.

He pulls out, wipes himself on a handkerchief and then tosses it at my still sprawled and defeated body.

"Clean yourself up." He says. "You've got five minutes to make yourself presentable."

And then he walks out leaving me there, leaving me alone, as his come begins to drip out.

I know I have to face them. I know that I have to walk out of this room, look this entire city's elite in the eye and act like none of this just happened.

I have to do it. For Lara's sake.

I take in a deep breath, steeling myself. Every time he does this, every moment he violates me, it's not breaking me, at least not in the way he thinks.

It's crushing my heart, that's true. I can't deny that fact.

But what need do I have for a heart now that Roman is dead?

I can be cold, I can become just as ruthless as all the rest of them, and I am, I will be, I will become everything they are and more.

Because this is how I will save Lara. I will store up every insult, every injury, every degradation and I will serve it back on them tenfold.

And the best bit is they don't even realise what they're doing, what they're creating.

Because this is how villains are made.

And this is what they are making of me.

I will finish what Roman started. I will have my revenge. I just have to bide my time, as he did, and when I serve it, I will ensure there is no chance they can outmanoeuvre me.

I will ensure every one of them is lying dead at my feet.

4

ROSE

I stand staring at myself.

I look like a statue.

I feel like one too.

Emotionless. Hollow.

The seamstress pins the fabric, takes it in a tiny bit more around my waist. I haven't been to the Clubhouse in forever, haven't worked out, and all that muscle I used to have is shrinking now. I look like I'm wasting away, all my strength, all of it is going and soon I'll be nothing more than skin and bones, I guess that will make me a better punchbag for Darius when he loses his temper.

Lara sits staring at me and I don't know what to say, how to answer the confusion in her eyes.

I'm wearing a wedding dress. One designed for me but not one of my choosing.

None of it is to my taste, it's too flamboyant, too attention seeking. But Darius wants all the attention he can get, he wants it flashy, he wants me to look like a million dollar bride. And my mother was more than happy to ensure that this dress did all that, starting with the price tag.

I clench my fists, fighting back the bile. I'd given anything to rip this damned fabric off my skin, to grab Lara, start running and never look back.

"It's beautiful." The seamstress says stepping back, admiring her handiwork.

Lara tilts her head. "It's too stuffy."

I let out a laugh. It catches in my throat and for a moment it feels like we're both trying not to cry. She steps up to me taking my hand and whispers so quietly no one can hear. "Daddy always said you were most beautiful without all the fancy clothes."

I let out a low breath, giving her a hug. I like that she remembers him, that she remember us, the three of us.

"I agree with daddy." I whisper back before planting a kiss on her head.

She looks up at me and she grins like it's our secret and I guess in a way it is. We're fellow conspirators now. Only I have to be careful, because she's a child, she's not as astute as me and I won't let her suffer any of the consequences if this blows up.

"It's perfect." Darius says strutting into the room, cutting through our brief moment of peace.

Lara shrinks into herself, stepping back, all but melding into the curtains to avoid his overbearing presence.

I grit my teeth, put on a smile as if I'm happy to see him, and he walks around me obviously taking in my body.

"The skirt should be tighter." He says.

The seamstress frowns. "Any tighter and she might have difficulty dancing."

Darius shrugs like he doesn't care.

I gulp as he reaches out for me, as he pulls my body into his. "Rose has a beautiful body. I want everyone to see it." He says as he grabs my arse, pushing my hips into him like I'm grinding against his cock, as if my child isn't right here.

"Darius." I murmur, trying to sound bashful and not re-proachful.

"Governor." Someone says from the door.

We both turn and I see Ty stood, arms crossed, obviously avoiding my gaze.

"What is it?" Darius says.

"They're ready for you." He says.

Darius lets out an annoyed growl. "I'm busy. They can wait."

Ty looks at me then looks back at Darius. "Ignatio has urgent business he needs to discuss."

I tense more at the sound of my father's name. I know Darius can feel it, I know he revels in the fact that I fear my father as much as I do.

He releases me with a smirk.

"Better not keep my father in law waiting." He says before planting a kiss on my lips and then he struts out of the room with-out a backward glance.

I turn away, hug myself, forgetting for a brief moment that the seamstress is still here, that I'm still being observed.

"Rose." Ty murmurs making me jump. Evidently he didn't follow on after Darius when he left.

"What do you want?" I say.

We haven't spoken, haven't said anything since that awful din-ner two months ago, since the night everything fell apart and Ty just sat there, watching it, doing nothing.

He looks over at Lara then back at me. I don't know if he understands who she is, I don't know if my parents have taken the time to explain that particular part in the story.

He pulls a face looking over at the woman with the pin pot still in her hand. "Take a break." He says to her.

She hesitates for a second then clearly decides better.

"Rose...." He begins as soon as she's gone.

"What do you want?" I say more forcefully.

"This wasn't meant to be like this." He says. "None of this..."

I screw my face up. "What are you talking about?"

He scowls walking over to the window. The Governor's House as the most incredible view over the Bay. The only good thing about being here is staring out, watching the waves, watching the sunsets, imagining that I'm free to actually enjoy them.

"Sofia." He murmurs so quietly I almost don't even hear it.

"What?" I say.

He shakes his head. Runs his hands over his face. "Forget it." He says.

I grab his arm, wrenching him around.

"Sofia what?" I ask.

He flinches. "She's not in a good way."

"No shit." I spit back. We both know Otto is treating her like his own personal punchbag. That he's still making her pay for the supposed crime that she 'wasn't a virgin' after all.

But deep down I fear it's more than that, because he married her, less than a week after they murdered Roman, Otto forced her into matrimony and now if she dies he can inherit the entire Montague fortune.

Somehow it feels like that's what he really wants. That all of this, all the violence, is just a short term diversion from his end goal.

"I want..." He trails off looking at Lara like he can't trust her not to blab.

"You want what?" I say hoping he hears the venom in my voice. Like I give a shit what he wants.

He narrows his eyes, shakes his head, and walks away.

ROSE

The sun is shining so brightly. On days like this it's hard to believe summer is really over but the oppressive heat is gone and you can see from the way the sun is lower that the days are getting shorter.

We've been out in the rose garden for most of the afternoon. Darius has been holding a political rally, gearing himself up for the elections.

I swear my face hurts from all the fake smiling I've been doing. And my body aches from how much I've had to hold myself back from snapping, from dropping my mask, and revealing what's really going on.

Within touching distance of me is the Chief of Police, the Head of the Militia, and every other arsehole Darius has said he will use to hunt me down if I do anything to wreck his little plan.

And Darius is the midst of everyone, right in the centre, schmoozing and working the crowd as they surround him like some sort of hero.

I take another sip of my drink. Some days I need the alcohol just to take the edge off everything but it's a fine balance between calming my nerves and ending up drunk, which is something I cannot risk under any circumstances.

A few wives chat away to me. We all make polite small talk. Most of them are twice my age and I can tell from the looks they give me when they think I don't notice that they can't quite figure out what it is between me and Darius. I guess they're on the side of me being a gold digger. That I'm so enamoured of the Blumenfeld name that I'd marry any one of them available and happily spread my legs for all the diamonds I get in return.

The thought turns my stomach and I make an excuse of needing the bathroom.

I can't stand it.

I can't stand what everyone is saying about me. What everyone is thinking of me.

I walk back into the house.

The wind picks up and if you look carefully you can see the leaves starting to turn, you can see the way autumn is truly setting in.

I imagined spending Christmas with Roman, spending our first Christmas together as a family. I wanted the three of us to go buy a tree, to decorate it together.

I wanted me and Roman to go ice skating. In public. As a real couple. I wanted to buy Lara so many presents. To really spoil her.

I wanted so much that I will never have now.

He's dead. I'll never hear his laughter again. Never see him smile.

I take a deep breath trying to hold in those emotions as the wave of grief hits me because I can't fall apart here, too many people are watching. Too many people are around me.

It's safest when I'm alone. When I can fall apart in the dark and no one sees. No one knows.

"Rose?"

I turn at the voice behind me. I don't recognise it.

It's a woman, a journalist judging by the way she's dressed, with a no nonsense blouse and dark blue chinos. Even her mousy brown hair is cut short, like she doesn't want the time or hassle of dealing with anything too fussy.

"I'm Katie Matthews, from the Verona Tribune."

"What do you want?" I ask.

She gives me a polite smile. "Just a conversation."

I gulp. You don't simply have a conversation with the press and I highly doubt this little tete-a-tete isn't being monitored. Darius wouldn't run the risk of it, of me being able to converse freely.

"If you want a statement on something…" I begin.

"I don't care what the Governor has to say, it's your opinion I'm interested in."

I narrow my eyes. She doesn't look like the type of reporter who cares what I think, the fashion editors, the gossip columns.

She steps nearer glancing at the guards who are stood, far enough that they can't hear but within eye shot of me.

"I saw something the other day." She says quietly. "Witnessed something between you and the Governor, if you will."

I frown. What does that mean? Darius and I are always damned good at putting on the right show in public.

She moves to stand in a way that her back is to the guards, blocking their view of this. And then she pulls her phone out flicking across the screen and plays what feels like my entire destruction.

I freeze.

It's me and Darius. In *that* room. With Roman's coffin.

I look at her.

How the fuck did she get this?

I look back at the video, I think it's more horrific seeing it than the memory of what he did and thank god the audio is down so I don't have to hear myself, I don't have to hear the pitiful noises I know I was making as he was forcing himself on me.

"He assaulted you." She states, like I wasn't there.

I shut my eyes. My heart is thumping so loudly.

She knows. This journalist knows.

"Rose, I saw enough to know what's going on, I heard enough too."

"You know nothing." I snarl.

"Why are you doing this? Why are you even with a man like him? He's twice your age."

I look up glaring at her. I don't need her pity and I certainly don't need her contempt. But I have to shut this down now, before it grows legs and Lara is put in danger. I grab her arm, pull her through to the balcony on the other side. I know the guards won't follow me there. They prefer to lurk inside. Besides they know there's no escape, no way to get down from the height of it to the ground so there'd be little need for them to step in.

"You have no idea what you're talking about…" I begin once we're further out of earshot.

"Is he blackmailing you?" She asks pocketing the phone. "Has he got something on you to force you into this relationship?"

I grit my teeth.

She needs to stop. She has to stop. She's going to get Lara killed.

"You can't print this. You can't…" I say.

"Do your parents know?"

I let out a laugh then. "Why do you think I'm even in this situation?" I say before I can stop myself.

Her face reacts to that. We all know what my parents are. They're not as good at hiding their true nature as the rest of us. "I can help."

"No you can't." I snap back.

"Rose, I can do an exposé. Don't you see, whatever he has on you, I can let everyone know that this relationship is not consensual."

"I don't want that."

"Why ever not? He's hurt other women you know. He's sexually assaulted a lot of other women. You could put a stop to all of this."

"I can't." I whisper feeling even more like a failure. I know there are other women out there, I'm not an idiot, Darius didn't become who is over night, he didn't turn into this monster just for me. No, I know he's been this way for years and I know the way I'm acting, the way I'm doing nothing, is allowing this to continue, allowing him to continue hurting others as well as myself.

"Why not?" She snaps more forcefully, as if she thinks I'm simply making some excuse.

"Because he has my daughter." I hiss before I can stop myself.

Her eyes widen. She stares at me. "What daughter?"

Fuck I'm an idiot. It feels like I'm losing control, like everything is spiralling.

"Please." I say. "You can't print that, you can't print anything. He'll hurt her, he'll hurt me."

She scans my face trying to figure out if this is some sort of rouse. "You're going to marry him?" She says incredulously.

"I will do whatever it takes to protect my child." I state.

She stares at me. "Okay, okay, I won't print this, not yet, but…"

"But what?" I ask. Of course she wants something. Everyone wants something. Nobody in Verona ever does a good turn unless there's something in it for them.

"Is there anything I can do?"

I screw my face up confused. "Excuse me?"

"To help?"

"Help with what?" Darius asks.

We both turn, my face draining of every ounce of blood as Darius looks between us. He wraps his arm around me in a way that could be both a loving gesture and one of control.

"What do you need help with sweetheart?" He asks me, all smiles, all charm and my heart rattles in my chest like a panicked bird that knows it's about to be slaughtered.

I give my best smile back at him and he squeezes me tighter.

"I…" My voice is too caught up in my panic to even come up with anything. My heart is thumping so loudly I'm sure he can hear it.

"I'm from the Gazette. We were talking about doing a feature." Katie says. "Once you're married, we'd love to get an full page spread about what it's like being the first lady of Verona."

"So why would you need to help Rose?" Darius asks.

Katie looks at me and smiles. Clearly hoping I'll jump in.

"I was saying that I'm a little swamped with all the wedding planning at the moment to consider it." I state.

A micro expression crosses Darius's face. We both know that's a lie. I'm not involved in any of the wedding planning. My mother is doing it all. Forcing it all. Neither Darius nor she trust me to do any of it thank god.

"But this feature would be after." Katie says sounding every bit like a pushy journalist after a scoop. "We could include some shots from your day, and perhaps even ones from your honeymoon, if you were willing to share them?"

I wince. Honeymoon? God, I hadn't even thought of that particular torture.

"That sounds like a good idea." Darius says.

"Perfect." Katie replies. "I'll make a note to touch base when you're back. We can pick out the photos you'd want published together, make sure you approve of them."

"Perfect." I repeat trying not to sound like a damned robot.

And then I stand there, with Darius's arm around me watching her leave.

"What was that about?" Darius growls as soon as she's out of earshot.

I turn to face him. "I..."

"You're swamped with wedding planning?" He scoffs.

"I had to say something. She caught me unawares. She asked how it was all going. I didn't realise she was a journalist and then..."

"And then what?" He tightens his grip as he speaks, making his displeasure more than abundantly clear.

I gulp. "I acted like a standard bride, that all I wanted was the perfect day. I started wittering on about favours, seating plans, whatever I could think of."

He looks like he's not buying it but there are enough people still around for him not to be able to make a scene.

"Let's go back to the gardens." I say putting my hands on his chest. We're being watched. I can feel it, half the room beyond seems to staring through the glass at us as if this is some sort of movie playing out.

He grunts. "Fine, but you're not leaving my side for the rest of the evening."

I give him a placating smile. I can do that, I can act exactly as he wants if it spares me a beating later.

6

ROSE

I hate these nights the most.

More than when Darius is fucking me.

More than when he's hurting me.

I hate being here, looking at them, hearing their voices, just breathing the same damn air as them.

Darius is sat beside me. He always likes to sit beside me when they're here.

We're not even in the main dining room, we're in the smoking room, where it's more intimate, and if anything that makes it worse.

We ate dinner while Darius and my father discussed his campaign, and now that I've been made aware of it they don't hold back from discussing their other businesses too. The ones the press don't report on. The ones I can barely stomach even thinking about.

It turns out Darius runs the gangs now, he controls all the drugs coming in and out of the city and he controls all the flesh trade too.

So much for law and order. He's the biggest crime lord in Verona and yet he's also the judge, jury and executioner.

I wince at that. At how much power he actually has. And what it would take to beat him.

No wonder he outmanoeuvred me. Outmanoeuvred us. Roman and I didn't stand a chance.

My mother smiles at me. She's had surgery on her nose, she took the opportunity to augment it after our fight so now that it looks more perfect than ever.

Every time I look at her I'm dying to curl my fist up and break it all over again.

"So I've changed my mind about the flowers." She says.

I blink in response. Does she really believe I give a fuck what flowers I have?

"I think we should do roses. Red roses. Every table can be scattered in red petals and it will contrast beautifully with the blush of the bridesmaid dresses."

The bridesmaids I didn't choose. All women I've barely spoken to. But then why would I? This isn't my wedding. This is a show, a performance for the masses. We're getting married in the damn cathedral. The President has an invitation as does several billionaires and the entire city's elite.

It's going to be livestreamed so all of Verona can feel like they're there, watching their Governor, that they're part of his family, one of us.

Just the thought of it, of standing before all their thousands of eyes, of having those cameras constantly on me while I have to not breakdown even once is why I think I can't even accept that this is happening.

I'm too afraid. I'm too desperately hoping that something, anything might happen to put a stop to it.

But I know nothing will, short of my own death, I will be walking down that aisle and Darius will be the one, grinning, holding his hand out, forcing a ring onto my hand as I pretend this is what I want, this man is who I want.

I let out a snarl. I can't hold it in anymore.

Darius tilts his head.

My father's eyes practically sparkle. "I see you haven't put a leash on her then." He says.

Darius reaches across, putting his hand on top of mine, sending a message to me, a warning. "It's a work in progress." He says. "But we're getting there aren't we Rose?"

I gulp meeting his gaze and nod. I can't speak. My voice seems to have dried up and my head is screaming at me to get a damn grip and stop being so bloody reckless all the time.

I'm putting Lara in danger.

My father lets out a laugh at that. "Maybe you should take a leaf out of Paris's book? He was always good at keeping her under control."

My fists clench. I want to snap back a retort. I want to dive across this table, claw his bloody face off.

But Darius doesn't react. He just leans over, takes a sip of his bourbon and chuckles. "There's a time and place for such methods. I'm hoping my Rose is beginning to prefer the carrot to the stick."

My father meets my gaze and smirks more. "I guess we'll see won't we?"

Darius nods, moving his hand to my thigh, all but laying claim to my leg and then they continue on, talking about a new 'shipment', new 'stock', they have coming in that needs to be tested.

My stomach turns. I know what stock they're talking about. It's not clothes, it's not products. It's people. They're selling people.

"So I was saying…" My mother waffles on.

I let her distract me. I let her high-pitched, nonsense fill my head and calm that spinning fear inside me. I don't want to think about it, to think of others in a worse situation than me, to know that they are being kidnapped, forced into doing things they don't want, forced into the sex trade and god knows what else just so Darius can continue lining his pockets. But then that's exactly what I am being made to do too. I may not be walking the streets, I may not be forced to service multiple men but I'm as a much a sex slave for Darius as they are to their pimps.

She smiles at me, holding her glass of sherry that catches the light enough that it casts a red hue across her pearl coloured dress.

I don't know how she does it. I don't know how she acts like this isn't happening and then I remember, what she said, all those months ago, about the good of our family, about ensuring our name lives on.

"We're so proud of you Rose." She says. "This union, this marriage will ensure our legacy continues."

I gulp. That is all she cares about isn't it? Our legacy. The bloody Capulet name.

"About that…" Darius says breaking off from his conversation. "I know Rose didn't take Paris's name when they married but I insist this time…"

My mother glances at my father. He frowns for a second, clearly weighing it up. He wants everyone to know a Capulet is the wife of the Governor but he needs Darius's favour.

"You want her to take your name?" He says.

Darius smiles. "She's my wife. Why would she not take my name?"

I don't say anything. None of this concerns me after all. I'm an object being sold here. A ware being passed from one owner to the next.

"Fine." My father says. "But any children you have will bear both your names, both Capulet and Blumenfeld."

My stomach churns just like it did every time Paris used to bring up the idea of children.

"Naturally." Darius says so smoothly it feels like someone is walking on my grave.

They're sealing my fate right now. The three of them. They're here, literally picking at the pieces that make my corpse, deciding which bits of me they want and which bits aren't worthy to keep.

And from what I can tell it's the same shit as last time.

The only parts Darius wants is my name, the bits he likes to fuck and my womb. The rest of me is surplus to requirements.

ROSE

We're in his house, in his bed, curled up. I don't know what the time is. I don't care.

I only know Roman is here, that he's with me, and in this moment that's all that matters.

He leans in and kisses my lips gently, softly.

I feel the lingering imprint of that kiss so deeply in my soul as he does it.

"Rose." He murmurs.

Even the way he says my name does something to me.

I blink, feeling a wave of sorrow, a wave of guilt. My tears are falling hard down my cheeks.

He brushes each one aside with his thumb but more fall.

Only they keep falling. They don't stop.

"I'm letting you down." I whisper it.

"No." He says.

"I am. I'm betraying you."

He shakes his head.

"I can't do this, not without you."

"You can Rose, you're so much stronger than you realise."

I sob then. I'm not strong, I'm weak. So weak. I keep ending up in this same shitty situation and every time I'm out manoeuvred. Beaten. Pathetic.

He pulls me in, holds me to his body, and I can smell him as I bury my face into his neck.

"Forgive me." I say.

"There's nothing to forgive." He says back.

"Yes there is." I sob. "Because it should be us."

"I know."

"It should be us." I snarl. My anger surging, every pent up emotion I've been trying to numb suddenly there, boiling, erupting up inside me.

"It will be one day."

"How can it?" I gasp. He's dead. He's gone. There is no 'us' now. There is no anything and there never will be.

He tilts his head. "Maybe not in this life. Maybe we will have to wait until the next…"

I let out a whimper. I can't spend my life without him. I can barely manage one day, how can I live for years like this? For decades?

"Love like ours doesn't die Rose. Love like ours never dies."

"But you did." I say. "You died. You left me, you left me and Lara."

I know it's unfair to be angry at him, to see this as his fault but he promised, he promised he would save us and yet here we are.

But then I promised too didn't I? I promised to marry him and here I am about to marry another man instead.

My body slumps as that realisation hits me. "I let you down." I murmur.

He shakes his head, cups my cheek. "You've never let me down."

I stare back at him, no longer capable of words. This man changed my life, this man is my life. My soul and his are connected, joined, one and the same.

And yet he is gone.

He is gone.

And I am here, stuck in this world, stuck in this hateful place, knowing I will never wake and see his face, that I'll never see his smile, never hear his laughter or feel his touch ever again.

"I can't do it." I gasp. "I can't do this. I can't live without you."

Only he doesn't reply. He just fades away, leaving me with my tears and my pain and the knowledge that when I awake the man beside me will no doubt punish me for daring to speak his name again. For daring to utter it.

I'm woken by the alarm. Darius grunts, turning it off, clearly he drunk enough last night to ensure he didn't have to hear my usual cries. I guess he didn't want to sour the moment with the thought that I was still pining after another man, still wishing it was Roman beside me and not him.

He rolls over grinning at me. His pearly whites almost glowing against the morning light.

"Show time." He says.

I fucking hate him. I hate that smile, I hate the way he speaks, most of all I hate the way his smell seems to wrap around me like a vapour from the pits of hell.

He didn't let me sleep alone. He refused to honour that tradition. I guess it doesn't matter because it's not like we're honouring any of the others. There's no love. No consent. This is a forced marriage in every sense of the word.

He gets up, walks to the dressing room and comes back fully clothed, though thankfully not in his wedding suit.

"Tell me you remember." He says.

I meet his eyes, wanting to argue, wanting to show defiance.

"Rose." He half snaps. "Tell me you understand what the consequences are if you fuck this up."

I grit my teeth and nod. I'm not a fucking child. I know exactly what the consequences are. He's made that abundantly clear.

"Tell me then." He persists.

"You'll hurt Lara." I state, my voice as hollow as I feel, as powerless too.

His lips curl, he kneels onto the bed. "Not just Lara." He states. "I'll punish you both."

I let out a shudder. I don't care if he harms me, he's done it so many times now it feels like the pain doesn't even matter anymore, but I won't let him do that to Lara. I won't let her get hurt because of my actions.

He plants a kiss on my lips as if he hasn't just threatened both my life and my child's. "Hair and makeup will be here in an hour." He states like I don't know it.

And then he walks off.

And I stay here, staring out the window, staring off as the memories, as his face, as the longing, as all of it haunts me.

When I do get up, I'm barely out of the bathroom and my mother is there, all smiles, with a bottle of champagne and glasses already filled and bubbling away in her hands

"Might as well start the celebrations now." She says. She's so happy she's practically vibrating with joy right now.

I grunt in reply. I'm not celebrating. I have nothing to celebrate.

She tuts, taking my hand and all but wrapping my fingers around the stem. "Drink Rose, it will steady your nerves."

I blink back at her. Is she an actual idiot? Does she really think that I'm nervous? That I'm some sort of blushing virginal bride? It's not nerves I feel. It's uncontrollable, unimaginable fury.

I'm so close to tossing the champagne in her face, to smashing the glass into her eyeballs.

Only the knock at the door breaks off the glare I'm giving her.

The makeup artist walks in, all smiles, and with that the charade begins.

I'm perched in a chair, everyone chats away happily around me. I don't speak. I don't do anything but stare at myself in the mirror as if I still can't believe all of this is real. My mother flits back and forth, she laughs, she drinks glass after glass.

She really is having the time of her life.

My makeup is finished long before any outsiders get here. It's intentional to keep up appearances because when the cameras arrive we wouldn't want any record of the bags under my eyes, of the bruises marring my skin even if they are faded. No, I have to be flawless from the get go.

My bridesmaids arrive right on time. They smile at me, they simper appropriately but we are all aware of the part we're playing today. They're tick boxes. They get to live off this for the next few years, live off the fact that they were part of this particular piece of Verona history.

My hair is styled, in long flowing waves that pin against one side of my head so that a pearl and diamond piece of jewellery can slide in.

I slip into my dress and walk slowly back out to the ooos and ahhhs of everyone around me. My mother especially relishes this moment as she looks on at the fine creation she imagined now brought so artfully to life.

It's so tight now I feel like I can't even breathe. I take shallow breaths but it doesn't help.

I slip my shoes on, they're ridiculously high but exactly what I'd be expected to wear and then my mother pops the long cathedral veil onto my head.

"Perfect." She says.

"Am I?" I reply.

She looks at me smiling. "Today you are." She states and I can see it, that flash of something in her eyes.

I'm doing what she wants, giving her what she wants, of course I'm perfect today.

I drop my gaze, my eyes searching the room for the face I know I won't see. The person who's been banished to her room. Locked away, with only an iPad to entertain her.

Lara.

Darius has made it clear under no uncertain terms that she is not allowed out today. That she is not even to be seen. Not that I argued with him because I didn't want her to see me like this, to see me doled up, to see me marrying another man, betraying her, betraying Roman with seemingly such little resistance.

I let out a sigh, swallowing the lump in my throat.

"It's time." My mother says, handing me the bouquet, all but ramming it into my hands.

My heart sinks further as I realise she's right. I can't put this off any longer.

We walk down together with the bridesmaids chattering merrily as they walk ahead.

At the very bottom of the stairs my father is there, just like the last time I was in this situation. He runs his eyes over me before holding out his arm for me to take.

I can't do it. I can't play this part.

So I walk past him, towards the waiting car.

Only he grabs me back snarling. "You don't learn do you?" He says.

I can feel it, my body trembling, my heart fluttering more rapidly. More panicked. I hate that he's touching me right now. I hate that today is going to be everything he's dreamed of; all his ambition coming to life.

He takes me out to the car. I clamber in and once he's seated we sit in stony silence the entire way, down the streets, down past all the masses of faces that are out staring at us, waving, throwing roses.

By the time we get to the Cathedral I'm shaking so much I can't stop my hands from moving. My father stares at them then at my face with that hard look on his.

And I see it, that warning.

That message in his eyes that he will hurt me, that he will hurt Lara, if I fuck this up.

The door opens, he walks around holding his arm out as the crowd cheers so loudly. I don't hesitate then, I take his arm and we walk up the stairs that now feel like a mountainside and into the hushed silence beyond.

There must be over a thousand people in this building. Over a thousand sets of eyes that snap to me.

Someone crouches down at my feet, rearranging my dress making sure I am the picture perfect bride everyone expects and then that god awful lilt begins.

I can smell the flowers that fill the space, I can hear the sniffles of people. My footsteps seem to echo so loudly, above the music that's playing so merrily.

I look ahead and I can see him, stood at the very end. He's smiling.

Roman.

My heart lifts, for a second I want to pull myself free, to kick off my heels and run down the aisle, tossing the flowers and to throw myself into his arms.

But then I blink and it's not him.

It's not him at all.

He's dead. He's gone. I'm all alone now.

Roman's face changes, his beautiful features mar into those of Darius's. Those soft lips become chapped. That stubble becomes clean shaven, and those eyes, Roman's dark eyes turn pale watery blue.

I wince, my breath hitches again, thank god the veil is covering my face because I need it now, I need every little bit of help I can to get down this aisle.

My father sets a quicker pace. I know he can tell that I'm too jittery. I know he knows that I want to run, to scream, to escape so badly. But we both know too that that's not an option.

The bridesmaids walk behind me in a way that feels like they too are guards, bringing up the rear, ensuring I make progress, ensuring I cannot get away.

By the time I'm halfway up the aisle I swear the music has finished and it has to be repeated.

Why is this aisle so long? Why is this Cathedral so long?

Darius stands there, his eyes fixed on me as if he can will me to his side.

I'm afraid I'm making noise, I'm afraid that I'm whimpering like a dying animal but my father isn't showing any sign of it so I guess that too is in my head.

I stare at the tiles beneath my feet. Some of them aren't tiles at all. They look like grave markers. God, I'm walking over dead bodies to get to Darius and if that's not a marker for what this relationship is and how it started then I don't know what is.

When we finally reach the front Darius takes my arm from my father's hold.

"You're so beautiful." He murmurs.

I don't reply. My throat feels too tight, my airway feels so constricted, I don't think I can even formulate words.

The bishop stands in front of us. He clears his throat, instructs everyone else to take a seat and I so desperately want to join them.

I think my legs might collapse, I think I might just fall here, in a heap, in front of everyone and this charade, this entire thing will come out and everything I've endured to save my daughter will be for nothing.

"Dearly beloved, we are gathered here today to witness the union of this man and this woman…"

I zone out, I'm looking at Darius, seeing that smile on his lips but I can't hear the words, I can't pay attention.

I shouldn't be here.

I shouldn't be stood, at an altar with this man. Not after everything he's done to me. Not after everything he's done to my daughter.

This was meant to be Roman.

Roman and me.

We were the ones meant to be standing before an altar, declaring our love, declaring our lives for one another.

This man, holding my arm, forcing me into this, he means nothing. He is nothing.

Roman is gone. Roman is dead. I'll never see his face again.

"Does anyone know of any lawful impediment why these two cannot be wed?" The bishop asks.

I stand there wishing, hoping, screaming in my head of all the reasons why but no one speaks. No one says a thing. The only noise made is from a man coughing and he looks around embarrassed as he does so.

The bishop continues. Darius speaks his vows. He talks of love, of honour, of respect, as if he understands what any of those words truly mean. As if he has any intention of adhering to those vows.

It's so hard not to scowl then. Not to drop that perfect mask painted across my face.

I want to say it then, to shout, to scream out what this really is, that he has my daughter, that I don't want him, that none of this is what I want, but even as that idea sets in my head all I can think of is Lara.

Of what Darius will do to her if I don't obey him.

"Rose..?"

I blink. What the hell did they say?

"Do you promise to love Darius, to honour him with your body, to honour him with your words, to respect and obey him?"

I gulp. "Yes." I say somehow finding enough movement in my voice to get the word out.

"And will you forsake all others, will you commit yourself for the rest of your life solely to this union, solely to this man?"

"Yes." I agree again. Like I have any fucking choice in the matter.

A ring is all but shoved onto my finger. I don't remember putting one of Darius's but as he says the words 'man and wife' and Darius lifts my veil planting a less than chaste kiss on my lips, it's like something latches onto my heart. Like someone is squeezing it so tightly I can't breathe, I can't even pump blood around.

I let out a whimper but no one hears. No one even notices. They're too busy soaking up the dream that Darius is selling them. The romance of our love that he's created in their minds.

I try to take small breaths but even those aren't getting in.

Roman is gone. Roman is dead. I have to save Lara.

"Please sit for the sermon." The bishop says pointing across to the two chairs at the side clearly placed for us.

Darius leads me to them. I sink down feeling like my legs are collapsing. I just have to hold on, I just have to keep this up a little bit longer.

But as the bishop starts droning on, as he reads some part of the bible out, I don't think I can. My hands move, I don't mean too, I don't even register it but they're there at my throat. Clutching.

I can't breathe.

I can't fucking breathe.

My head goes dizzy. It feels like I'm actually having a heart attack and then I'm falling, off the chair, and those tiles that have laid here for hundreds of years are coming up so fast and I know when my face collides with them that it's going to hurt.

It's really going to hurt.

ROSE

"There's nothing medically wrong." The doctor says, looking from the papers to me as I'm laid out on the gurney, still in my wedding dress, though someone was kind enough to remove my killer heels.

"What do you mean nothing wrong?" Darius snarls. "She collapsed. You don't just collapse."

The doctor sighs looking at the sheet again. "I've run her stats, I've checked her heart, her lungs, everything is normal."

"If it's normal then why the fuck was she faceplanting in the middle of our wedding?" Darius says.

I shut my eyes, relieved for once that he's taking his anger out on someone other than me.

I can feel the weight of his ring, it's tight around my finger like he intentionally got it made a little too small so I'd constantly feel the reminder of it.

We're still married. That still happened.

I didn't pass out or whatever it was in a timely manner enough to stop it. All I've done is cause more drama, more trouble for myself. But that's typical of me isn't it? I've never been able to act in anyway that's not resulted in it backfiring on myself.

"I can't give you an explanation Mr. Blumenfeld because medically speaking there isn't one."

"What does that mean?" My father asks. He's been stood in the room, in the corner, observing the way he always does, waiting for his moment to strike and clearly he's decided this is it.

The doctor looks across at me. "Are you stressed right now Ms. Capulet?"

"Wwhat?" I stammer.

"It's Blumenfeld." Darius says. "She's taken my name now we're married."

The doctor inclines his head. "Mrs Blumenfeld." He corrects himself and it's so hard not to turn my face up at that. "Are you under any undue stress, is there any situation in your life that is making you feel like you're losing control?"

I gulp looking at Darius. He's stood right there. The living, breathing epitome of everything the doctor just described.

"Of course she's stressed." My mother says quickly. "She's a bride on her wedding day. She's got half the world's press here, watching her every move, how could she not be stressed?"

"Are you saying she's had some sort of panic attack?" My father sneers.

"Not exactly." The doctor replies. "Stress does things to the body, it's more than likely that your fiancée suffered some sort of cardiac event but we cannot see it on the charts because now that it's passed there's no spikes, no changes to her heartrate."

"You mean she had a heart attack?" Darius says.

"No. We can see if that was the case and that's not what happened."

"Then what did happen?" My father half shouts as I flinch. There's a vein in his neck that's protruding so much I think *he* might just have a heart attack. Though that would certainly make this day a little better if he did.

I'd even welcome that as a wedding gift. My father dead. Yeah, that would be the best one I receive.

The doctor looks at me for a moment before addressing my father once more. "With all due respect I don't think you raising your voice is helping your daughter right now."

"With all due respect you can fuck off." My father snaps.

"Enough." Darius says. "Ignatio, Carla, I think it best if you both leave."

They splutter. "She's my daughter…" My mother protests.

"And she is my wife." Darius snaps back before practically pushing them out of the room and shutting the door.

When he comes back he fixes his gaze on the doctor. "I want the Head of Cardiology in here."

"Mr Blumenfeld, I can assure you…"

"I don't give a fuck what you can assure me, I am the Governor, this is my wife. I want him in here or I will sue this hospital for everything it's got."

The doctor blanches, nods, and all but sprints for the door.

And then he turns on me.

I flinch more. I'm expecting a full fucking tantrum now. He walks up to me, sits in the chair, and takes my hand.

"Rose." He says more gently than I expected.

I don't know what to say. What to do.

I can see under this calm demeanour that he's raging. I ruined his perfect plan. His perfect wedding.

"Talk to me."

I gulp. "I didn't mean to…"

He brushes my hair back. It's somehow still all styled, I can feel the clip digging into my skull and I so dearly want to rip it out and hurl it as hard as I can.

"If you're sick we'll deal with it."

"I'm not sick." I don't know why I even say it. It would be better if he thinks I am. He might even stop hurting me so much then.

The door opens. We both look as a man closer to Darius's age walks in.

"Mr Blumenfeld." He says holding his hand out. "I'm Doctor Strauss, I'm head of Cardiology."

Darius takes his hand, shaking it in a way that makes me think the two of them are having some sort of contest over who can crush each other's knuckles the most.

"I've looked through your wife's notes on the way down. I can't see anything of concern from the ECG, or the scans."

"She collapsed." Darius says. "Healthy people do not just collapse."

"No." Strauss agrees.

"Could she be pregnant? Would that be it?" Darius asks.

My head whips, my stomach does a full three sixty. Is that what he's thinking? Is that why he's not acting like I'm a criminal right now?

Strauss shakes his head. "No, we tested for pregnancy and it came back negative. Besides your wife has an IUD, it would be incredibly rare for her to be pregnant with such a device fitted."

I think my heart stops. My breath catches in my throat. How the fuck do they know that? It's not in my notes. I know that.

I panic as Darius turns his head, fixing his eyes on me. "An IUD?" He repeats.

My mouth goes dry. I can feel my fear multiplying.

His hand lands on mine and he squeezes, demonstrating in that moment all the anger that he will unleash upon me as soon as he is able to. "If we wanted it removed, how would we go about that?"

"Gynaecology can do that. You can make an appointment..."

"We're here now." Darius states.

"No." I gasp and Strauss looks at me before looking back at Darius.

As he opens his mouth Darius cuts across him. "I'm the Governor of this city. I decide what funding this hospital gets, it would be a real shame to see that cut, wouldn't you agree?"

Strauss narrows his eyes for the tiniest of seconds before nodding. "I'll see if I can get someone now."

"Thank you. You've been most useful." Darius says in a tone that makes the bile rise up in my throat.

I'm so fucked now. So utterly fucked.

As soon as the door shuts he gets up, putting his hands either side of the headboard, all but encasing me. "You have an IUD?" He growls.

"I..."

"When were you going to tell me that?"

"Please..." I whisper. "I don't want another baby. I don't want..."

"I don't give a fuck what you want Rose." He slams his fist into the wall creating a crater from the impact as I shrink further up. "You'll do as you're told. How hard is that for you to understand?"

I can feel my chest tightening again. Maybe it was a panic attack, maybe that's exactly what it was, my heart, my body, all of me physically reacting to the awful situation they're holding me in. That they expect me to accept as normal.

When the gynaecologist walks in, I lose the pretence. It doesn't matter now. Darius knows enough to make me pay for this and I'm not going to let my fear stop me from fighting now. From taking the chance that one person around me might just have a conscience.

It's clear the man has been prepped. That he understands exactly what this situation is because he doesn't speak to me, doesn't even look at me, in fact he's doing everything he can with his body language to pretend that me as a person doesn't exist.

Darius is the one to yank my dress up. I try to fight him and he backhands me before asking the doctor if they have a sedative.

Thankfully the doctor decides that's not an actual request but he doesn't do anything, he just watches as Darius half rips my wedding dress because it's so damn tight, and then they strap my legs into the stirrups, tie them in when I resist, and as I'm half screaming and Darius is trying to cover my mouth to keep my quiet while simultaneously holding me down, the doctor is there, between my legs, taking away the one tiny bit of control I had in all this.

When it's out Darius holds it up in his hands, taunting me with it. It's tiny. Almost insignificant to look at.

"Having my child will make everything better." He states. "Because then you won't want to escape me anymore. Then you will give in. And then you will be loyal."

I hang my head. I can't reply. I can't do anything but let the tears fall again.

ROMAN

We're back at the ball. Only it's not quite the same as it was. She's in my arms and we're dancing, laughing, showing the world what we really are.

My heart feels lighter than it's ever been.

I swirl her around, admiring the way her dress both covers and hints at her beautiful body beneath.

When I catch her in my arms she all but blushes.

"Rose." I murmur before leaning into catch her lips.

She wraps her arms around my neck, deepening it, letting out a soft moan that I feel in my soul.

"I love you." I whisper as we break apart.

"I love you too." She says before glancing around and then letting out a nervous sound.

"What is it?" I ask.

"Everyone is watching us." She says.

I smirk glancing around. Yeah they are. They're all fixated on us. A Montague and a Capulet. Two people forbidden from loving one another and yet we do.

"Let them watch." I say. "Let them see what we are to one another."

She bites her lip. "Aren't you afraid?"

"Of what?"

She jerks her head and as if by magic her parents are there. Darius is there too. The three of them are scowling. Making their feelings more than abundantly clear.

"They can't hurt us Rose." I say. "No one can hurt us now."

She shakes her head as her eyes fill with tears. "That's not true."

I move to grab her, to hold her tighter, but it feels like she's pulling away.

"Roman." She gasps.

"I've got you." I half shout.

Only I haven't. She's slipping through my hands. She's fading away.

I snatch at her, snatch at the fabric of her dress. But she's gone. She's vanishing right before my eyes.

And the three of them are stood, laughing, mocking me as I watch her disappear further and further from my reach.

I WAKE GASPING. CHOKING. THERE'S A TUBE DOWN MY THROAT. There's a machine beeping almost manically like it's about to explode.

I grasp at the plastic, try to yank it out but a nurse is suddenly here, telling me to stay calm, removing it in one swift practiced motion.

I shake my head, swallow, registering the tightness of my throat, registering the uncomfortableness.

I feel weak. Dizzy. Like my body hasn't moved in a long, long time. The nurse starts checking my vitals, shining a light in my eyes, but clearly she doesn't find anything of concern.

I try to flex my fingers, to wiggle my toes and though they respond my muscles feel so stiff.

"Roman?"

I look up seeing Ben stood at the door wide eyed.

"What happened?" I ask before looking around. I'm not in a hospital. I can tell that much, and yet there's hospital equipment all around me. Hell, I had a damn tube down my throat.

"What do you remember?" He asks.

I frown, scrunching my face up. I was with Rose.

Fuck Rose. I asked her to marry me. She said yes. She…

"Rose." I say looking at him.

And the face he pulls says everything.

"Where is she?" I growl. My voice sounds hoarse, I can hear the strain from lack of use. Fuck, how long have I even been out?

I shift and I can feel something. There's a tube in my cock. They put a damn tube up my cock?

"What the fuck?" I say lifting the blanket seeing where the catheter is coming out. Apparently I've been pissing like that then?

The nurse thankfully removes it as well, and though I don't watch, I can feel as it slides out. Fuck, I never want to experience that again.

And then my eyes snap back to Ben. He moves further into the room, sinks into the chair, he looks broken, he looks like he's been to hell and back.

"What the fuck is going on?" I ask.

"They took her. Her and Sofia." Ben says. "And Lara too."

"Who?"

"Darius." Ben replies. "They raided the house, killed everyone they could find."

"Darius has my daughter?" I repeat not quite registering everything he's saying.

"He has Rose as well. And Otto has Sofia." Ben states.

I clench my fists, my anger surging. "How the fuck did this happen?"

"They laid a trap and we fell right into it."

I'm out the bed before I know it. My adrenaline is spiking and in truth my body is too weak to hold me but I'm lashing out, smashing the shit out of the concrete wall.

Darius has Rose? Darius has my daughter? I shut my eyes and I can see it, the fear in Rose's face as if I was there, as if I was witnessing that awful moment when she realises I failed her.

Ben grabs me, pulling me around and in my fury I almost punch him in the face.

I blink, heaving, trying to calm myself. My legs are shaking worse than ever. Christ I'm weak. Pathetically weak. I realise as he holds me that he's the only reason I'm not faceplanting onto the floor.

"Where am I?" I ask.

"We're in the tunnels." Ben says.

"Tunnels?"

"From the old city. It's the only safe place we could find."

I know of the tunnels. I know of their existence. But as far as I knew it was off limits to everyone except the Storm Crows, a motorcycle gang that would soon as gut you as anything else.

When I state that fact Ben gives me a look I do not like.

"What?" I ask.

"It is off limits." He says. "We made a deal."

"Who?" I ask.

"Me and Holden. We were the only ones to survive. Everyone else is dead."

"Why the fuck would the Storm Crows make a deal with us?"

"Because our Governor has a lot to answer for and you're gonna help us with that." A man growls from the doorway.

My head spins. I turn looking at him, taking him in. He's covered in tattoos. His body is practically made of ink. His long hair is pulled back into a top knot. I can see he's wearing the infamous leather jacket that all his biker gang wear but on him it looks less like a jacket and more like a form of armour. He grins at me and I see it, that famous golden tooth.

"You're Koen?" I say.

He nods.

I guess it's hard to mistake him for anyone else. He's younger than I imagined. I don't know why but with all the rumours swirling about him I always thought he'd have more years on me. But he barely looks a decade older than I am.

"Tell me then, why would you help us?" I ask.

He stalks in, putting his hands on the end of the bed frame. Even his fingers are inked. "I heard you were taking out the factories. I heard you were stopping the organ trade."

I nod.

"Let's just say we have a similar objective." He states.

I narrow my eyes. Like fuck I'll take that as an answer.

"You think it's just street kids their selling?" He growls.

"They took someone important to you." I guess.

He nods. "My sister."

"What does it matter?" Ben says. "Darius has a chokehold on this city. If any of us want to actually survive here we have to cut the vipers head off."

"I thought that was what I did when I killed Calvin." I state.

Koen's eyebrows raise. "You killed Calvin?"

I shrug. "Someone had to." I state. "So tell me, what are we going to do? How the fuck are we going to bring him down now?"

Koen grins. "All in good time pretty boy. For the moment you need rest."

"Fuck that." I reply.

"He's right." Ben says. "You can't just wake up from a coma and go all guns blazing."

"Coma?" I say looking between them. "What the fuck?"

Ben takes a deep breath, all but pushing me onto the bed and I don't fight, I let him because in truth I'm in very real danger of collapsing.

"You've been out for over two months." He says.

"What?" I gasp.

"You nearly drowned. They put a bullet through your chest. I had to drag you out of the wreck, had to get you far enough away that they wouldn't spot us."

I remember it now. I remember that. I remember being on the phone to Rose too. Her saying how scared she was, telling me to take care of our daughter, effectively saying goodbye.

"Rose." I murmur. "Where the fuck is Rose?"

Koen tilts his head. "She's not your Rose anymore mate. She's the Governor's wife now."

It's like a dagger to my heart. Like someone has just buried it so deep they've hacked at my soul. She married him? Why the fuck would she do that?

I shake my head not believing it.

I told her to wait, I told her I was coming.

And then I realise why she's done it. He has Lara, he has our daughter. Of course she married him, of course she did whatever she had to, to protect Lara. It's the same twisted situation as before.

Only I promised I'd save her.

I promised I'd get to her.

And yet all the while she's been in danger I've been out. Unconscious. Bloody useless.

I snarl, slamming my head back against the wall.

"We'll get her back." Ben says. "We'll get all of them back."

I look at Koen, at where he's still stood assessing me. "How many men do you have?" I ask.

He smiles. "More than enough for what we need."

"You're sure about that?" I retort. I don't know whether to find this man's confidence reassuring or not.

I was confident. I was so fucking certain. "I spent six years planning how I was going to get my vengeance and yet Darius still fucking beat me." I state. "What makes you so sure you can do better?"

His eyes flash. I can see he's pissed. He steps up putting his hands on the end of the bedframe. "I don't fuck around so when you're ready I'll show you what we're working with."

"I'm ready now." I spit.

He shakes his head. "You can barely stand. You've been pissing into a tube for the last few months. Do you even know what day of the week it is?"

I open my mouth to reply only I don't, do I?

He gives a grunt before turning on his heel.

"Fucking prick." I say before I can stop myself.

Ben looks at me but doesn't comment. He just sinks into the chair and starts telling me every horrific thing that's happened since I've been out.

ROMAN

My body really is weak. I can see how much muscle I've lost. How much I'll need to get back to ensure I'm strong enough for what's ahead.

My chest bears the scar of where I was shot. I run my fingers over it, feeling the raised skin and how tender it is. It's barely an inch above my heart, how I'm not dead I don't know but I take that as a good omen. That even God wants me to survive, to continue this fight.

Ben took me on a tour through our new home and it's surprisingly better than the name suggests. It's not even tunnels, at least the bit we're in isn't. Apparently the Storm Crows set about expanding it, widening the space, turning it into a network that stretches for miles.

It's like some huge military style bunker, as if they're preppers all ready for the apocalypse.

We've been given our own area too. Holden and Ben watch me warily as I look around the space, but I'm not complaining. It's cleaner and warmer than I imagined. Hell, take away the fact there aren't any windows and it's not that bad.

I've let them talk, let them explain all the little details, like how they get the food here, how the plumbing is fully functional. In truth I don't give a shit about any of it, only I don't voice that opinion. I'm happy for them to carry on the conversation because it means I don't have to. I don't have to try to smile and pretend that any of this is okay.

I need time to process, time to think, but right now we're in what could loosely be classed as a canteen. All around are long tables with benches either side and at one end I can see all the counters where no doubt you have to queue to get your dinner.

"The food's not great." Holden says.

"But it's better than starving." Ben says.

I look between them and smirk. I can't tell if they're trying to soften the blow of all this, manage my expectations or some such shit.

"How many people are here?" I ask.

"Maybe a thousand." Holden shrugs.

"A thousand?" I repeat as my eyes widen.

Ben glances around before leaning in. "They're not all Storm Crows. Some are just unfortunates that have fallen foul of the Governor and now they're here, hiding out."

"This is like some den of thieves." I say. "Like something out of Robin Hood."

Ben laughs. "Maybe."

"Koen makes sure everyone has a job." Holden says. "That everyone pulls their weight. If you don't have a useful skill then he gives you something to do like cleaning."

"He's like a lord." I mutter.

"And this is his kingdom." Ben says.

I don't know if I like it. I don't know how this sits in my head. But then where else can I go? Where else can any of us go? I glance around, watching the few people milling about. There are kids here too, whole fucking families.

"Do they all know what Darius is like?" I ask.

Holden nods. "Yeah, most of them stay out of the main fighting but the men and some of the women are happy to get stuck in and fight back when needed."

"And what does that look like?" I ask.

Ben winces. Holden tilts his head. "In truth it's just been little skirmishes. Nothing big. I think Koen is goading them, poking the dragon before he does something that really rocks the boat."

"And how do we know who's a Storm Crow and who's just hiding out for safety?" I ask.

"Tattoos. All the Storm Crows have tattoos."

"So no one else does?" I can hear the disbelief in my voice. That can't be a way to decipher it.

They shrug. "You get used to it. But we're all in the same boat. It doesn't matter if we're part of his gang or not, we all get treated the same."

That makes me pause. There's no hierarchy? No Storm Crows lauding it up?

"What's he like then, Koen?" I've heard things about him. Enough things to make me want to consider better options, that is if there were any.

"He's fair. But he has a short temper. Someone tried to sell us out a few weeks ago and he found out..." Holden grimaces. "Let's just say what they did to him will haunt me for years."

"So he's not afraid to get his hands dirty." I murmur. I'm not surprised. He and his brother used to run the streets before Darius and Calvin came in on their 'Safe Verona agenda'.

I take a deep sigh. I need some space to think. I need some time to process this.

"You okay?" Ben asks.

I shake my head before looking up meeting his gaze. "Can you do me a favour?"

"Anything." He replies.

"I need…" I pause. How do I explain what I need? What I'm asking for? When I get the words out Holden is giving me such a look and Ben, Ben is looking like he wants to talk me out of it.

"I need to see it." I state.

"Roman…" Holden begins.

"Just do as I ask." I reply.

Ben gets up, jerks his head for me to follow and I do, ignoring the stiffness in my knees. I need to exercise too. I need to really start working my muscles.

If I were in a hospital I know I would have started rehab by now. I'd have a dedicated physio helping get my body back to strength.

I guess I'll have to figure that out for myself.

But right now that can wait. All of this can wait.

I STARE AT THE SCREEN. I KNOW I'M TORMENTING MYSELF, TORTUR-ing myself but I do it anyway.

I can't stop rewinding it, playing it back, seeing her face as she gets out of the car, seeing how the veil covers her beauty, how her father holds her arm and he walks her inside, away from the crowds, with the cookie cutter bridesmaids following close behind.

I guess this was how it was for her and Paris too. Him march-ing her down the aisle, ensuring she can't pick up her skirts and try to escape.

Her dress clings to her. It's too fussy, too elaborate to be any-thing my Rose would have picked so I'll put money on it being her mother's choice. And I can see why. It's the kind of thing you'd expect an actual movie star to wear. It must have cost millions. It's encrusted with diamonds, turning every step she takes into a flash of rainbow light.

She's holding a bouquet of pure red roses. Again, I'd put money on that being her mother's choice.

I stare at the ring on her finger, the huge rock that Darius clearly picked out as a warning to every other male in the vicinity to back the fuck off like he's laying claim to her. Like he has that right.

I wonder where my ring is. If she has it somewhere, if she manged to keep it safe or if Darius stole that too.

A snarl leaves my lips. I can see her sad face beneath the veil, beneath the mask she's projecting, I can see it. I can feel it too, as if our love somehow connects us. She doesn't want this, she doesn't want any of this and yet she's sacrificing herself right now for our daughter.

I think in this moment I love her more.

I love her and I hate myself.

Because I did this, I let this happen. Maybe I was too cocky, too sure of what I was doing to stop and think that Darius might just be planning his own coup.

The damned Cathedral is packed. Darius has been sure to make this a media sensation and no doubt the polls will reflect this because the timing is perfect too. Right before the campaigning starts. And who could resist such a tale? Who could resist re-electing a Governor so firmly focused on family values, on love?

The camera angle changes. Rose's eyes seem to dart about and I see it, the fear there. She's petrified right now.

When Ignatio hands her over, the way Darius looks at her, the words he murmurs, words I should be saying. Words he has no right to say to her.

She doesn't reply. I wonder if it's because she can't say anything that wouldn't show what a sham this really is.

And the worst bit comes. The vows. She agrees to honour him, to respect him, to love him for the rest of her life. My heart nearly stops when I hear her utter the word 'yes'.

I don't know what I expected. I knew the outcome. I know this happened weeks ago and yet hearing it, seeing it, it's like a dagger to my heart.

"She collapses just after they're announced." Koen says.

I turn my head looking at him, at where he's leaning against the doorframe. We're still unsure of one another. He might have given us safe haven but I don't understand what he gets from it.

I grunt in reply. I know she collapsed. I know the feed cuts out initially citing technical difficulties before the true reason is revealed.

That she passed out.

That she had to be carried out to an ambulance.

But what I don't know is why.

I'm petrified that she's sick, that he's hurt her in some way that has caused this.

And the other thing I don't see in any of this is Lara. I don't see her anywhere.

Clearly Darius made sure my daughter was out of the picture for his big day. No doubt he didn't want any reminders of me to ruin it for him. But I can't stop wondering where she is, if she's with them, if he's locked her away the way Ignatio did, and worse, if he's hurting her as well.

Koen takes a seat opposite me. I try not to bristle. Not to show that right now I want some god damn space.

"It's time we had a talk you and I." He says.

"Really? Now?" I reply glancing at the screen again. Now is not the time. I'm too on edge, too wound up about everything to think calmly, rationally.

He smirks leaning forward.

I should watch my mouth really. He's a gang leader. He could turf me out, skin me alive, and no one down here would bat an eyelid by the sounds of it.

"Your friend made some promises." He says. "While you were off in La La land."

"What promises?" I ask.

He grins again. "Money."

Of course he did. Of course Ben said we'd pay. "We don't have any." I state.

He lets out a laugh. "Now that's not true. We all know the Montagues are rolling in dough."

"Not right now. Darius took everything,"

He shakes his head. "Yeah but when we take it back that's when you pay up."

I narrow my eyes realising what this is. He's speculating. Putting a bet on me, like I'm a horse at the national.

"How much?" I ask.

"Twenty million."

"Twenty million?" I repeat. Fuck me, where did Ben pull that number from?

"We'll waive your expenses. Your accommodation, food, clothes etc."

"Very noble." I retort.

He grins. "I like you Roman, you've got more bite than your mate does."

"Ben has bite. You just haven't seen it yet." I say.

"Nah? Guess he saves that for your sister huh?"

I raise my eyebrows, what the fuck does he know about Ben and Sofia?

"He doesn't shut up about her." He states. "He tried to get me to rescue her."

"And you refused?" I say. God, what is Sofia going through right now? What awful things is she enduring because of my fuckups?

He shakes his head. "I would have, she's a pretty thing, at least she was till Otto Blumenfeld got his hands on her."

I clench my fists. I haven't dared to contemplate what Otto is doing because I know if I do, that *will* send me over the edge.

"Why didn't you help?" I ask.

"You have no idea what it's like now. Fucking Capulets own the streets. Darius is ensuring it's his way or the highway. We can't step foot above ground without one of their cronies shooting our head off."

"Then how are you supposed to help me?" I snarl.

He leans forward, gripping the arms of the seat and his leather jacket creaks with the movement. "We help each other. You have contacts. We have men. We start a war, a real war, a guerrilla war. The way they do in the favella. We make sure we have areas, zones, the cops won't dare to go and piece by piece we take this city from them."

"And how are we meant to do that when you get your head blown off every time you go above ground?"

"Get me the guns." He says. "Then I'll show you how."

I don't know if he's crazy or not. I don't know whether I'm crazy, to be here, to think that he can help. But what choice do I have? I won't just hide here and leave my family to their fate.

"I'll get you guns." I murmur. "But I need a car, a phone, and clothes."

"Whatever you want, we'll have it for you."

The way he says it is so confident, as if he has the entire world at his disposal. I can't decide if I like it or hate it. "How far do these tunnels stretch?" I ask.

"Under the entire city." He states.

"So we can pop up anywhere?"

"Anywhere you like."

"Do you have plans for it all?" I ask. I need to get my bearings. I need to see where we are in terms of the buildings above.

He gets up. "Follow me. It's about time you learnt where the command room is."

"Command room?"

"You'll see." He says walking out, no doubt expecting me to follow. And I do. Like a dog, hot on his damned heels.

ROMAN

He wasn't kidding when he called it a command room. It's like something out of a movie. One wall shows dozens of screens all with a CCTV feed.

"We usually have the main locations up but we can switch to specific ones if needed." Tia says.

I glance at her, she looks like the cross between a computer nerd and some weird cosplay character the way her hair is dyed bright orange and big thick framed glasses perch on her nose.

"Can you hack into them, can you block the feed so they can't get it?" I ask.

She shakes her head. "No, the technology they're using is too advanced. We haven't figured out how to get past it. All we can do is see what they're seeing."

I grin, sounds like I can teach them this at least.

"Where is the map?" I look at Koen.

He's staring at a screen as if transfixed. I give him a nudge, probably not the best thing to do and he gives me a look that says he might just rip my fucking head off.

"What is that?" I ask looking at the building he seems obsessed with.

"It's the new Barn."

"What?"

His face goes so hard. "They built it especially. We got some guys inside, they were live streaming to us what's inside before they got found and well…" He makes a gesture like he's blowing his head off which I guess says enough. "The place's got state of the art medical facilities, holding bays, they literally gut and cut them right there and there's an incinerator on sight to ensure there's no body left at the end."

"Fuck me." I murmur.

"They learnt mate. They learnt after you burned the last one down."

"How did they do that so quickly?" Surely such a thing would take years to build, to construct?

He lets out a sigh. "You'll be surprised the things you can do when you have enough money."

Yeah he's right about that. Look at Darius, look at all the Blumenfelds, the things they've done, they things they've gotten away with just because they're rolling in it.

"Let me see the maps." I say.

He grunts pulling his eyes away, and walks over to where a door is. "We keep the maps in here. Keeps it tidy."

I smirk. An MC President who likes to be organised? That's a new one on me though I make a point of keeping that to myself.

The maps are good. More than good. He must have stolen them from somewhere, that or he has an actual cartographer squirrelled away somewhere. I tilt my head seeing how the tunnels beneath line up with the glittering city of Verona Bay above.

From my reckoning we're right under…

"Liberty Square." Koen says. "Which is why we have to travel at least a few miles before we come up above ground."

I raise an eyebrow questioningly.

"The Square and everywhere around Parliament are heavily guarded. It's like a Nazi regime up there."

"Fucking fantastic." I mutter.

He pats me on the back. "We can do this. If we follow my plan. If we do this right."

"Meanwhile my sister and daughter and Rose are enduring god knows what." I snarl back.

"Yeah?" He says. "Better they are where they are then they're locked in a cage waiting to have their heart cut out so the coke-head daughter of a multi-millionaire can continue her life party." He sneers.

My fists clench. I know he's right. On some level he is. But he's not the one that has to live with it, to know that they're suffering and I'm stood here, not doing a damn thing to stop it.

"You get used to it." He says.

"What?" I ask.

"The guilt."

I huff. I don't think I will. Even if I do win this, even if we save them, how the fuck am I going to look them in the eyes?

We walk back out and once again I stare at the screens in front of us.

"Do you have the Governor's house?" I ask.

Koen gives me a look but they bring up the feed anyway. On the big screen.

It looks like a damned fortress. I can see people inside, figures moving about. Did I think I'd spot her? Did I expect to see Rose stood, staring out the window? I don't know, but my heart sinks when I realise she isn't there, she isn't visible.

Koen goes to say something but I cut across him.

"How about I show you how to hack the feeds?"

"What?" Tia says.

I grin at her. I need to do something. I can't just stand here, driving myself nuts. I walk over to one of the computers, nudge the guy aside and pull up a screen.

Tia stands over my shoulders and as I start to do it she gasps every now and then.

I can feel Koen staring into my back. Maybe I need to prove a point too. Maybe it's about time he saw me as more than just a rich pretty boy and someone of substance, someone just as capable, just as ruthless as he is.

ROMAN

I know this is a mistake. That a voice in my head is already screaming at me to turn back. To go back.

To run back to the tunnels and hide.

Only I won't do that. I have to at least try and do something.

Besides I used to sneak into the Capulet mansion all the time. I used to creep right up their immaculately kept lawn and devour their sweet little princess while they all were complete oblivious. So how hard can this be? Walking the streets, stalking them, making sure to keep my head down when I pass every amber streetlight.

I came up not far from Liberty Square but it's still a good ten minute walk to the Governor's House.

When I get to it I know exactly where to go. The same weak-spot in their defences I found last time. The same corner where the cameras have a blind-spot and anyone can climb up and in without them realising, as long as they keep their movements contained, controlled, precise.

Only I don't feel controlled.

I feel anything but.

My hands are shaking. My body already feels like I've run a marathon. Sweat is beading along my brow despite the cold air around me.

Christ I'm weak. Really weak.

I need to start working out. I need to start building my strength back but that's going to take time.

Time I don't have.

Time my Rose and my daughter do not have.

I take a deep breath, steel myself for this moment and hope the adrenaline alone will be enough. My hands press against the brickwork, finding those almost familiar indents where my fingers can get a holding.

Slowly, cautiously, I haul myself up. When my body raises high enough that I can pitch over the top I pause, holding my balance on my stomach, seeing how much this house has changed.

It's crawling with men. All armed. All in body protection. As if Darius is expecting a full-scale assault at any moment. My body begins to shake, my weight threatens to pull me back down, back on the wrong side of the wall.

And then I see the movement. The glimpse of it. A flash of fabric too fine to be worn by a man.

She's walking, gliding through the house. She looks more like an apparition than a real person.

"Rose."

I whisper her name, wanting her to hear it. Desperately, deliriously needing her to turn her head, to look from the hallway through the overly stuffed room and see me.

Sense me.

Christ, just look at me.

My heart thumps in my chest so loudly it's like I can't hear anything else. The gun at my side is all but calling to me, begging me to unclip it and start shooting. To kill every one of these fuckers that's stood between us.

She's so close. She's within actual touching distance and yet there's an army of men blocking my path.

A shout goes up.

I know I haven't made the noise. That it didn't come from me.

A spotlight suddenly illuminates where I am and as if my body already knows what to do I fall back, from the wall, landing in a heap the other side.

My hands are grazed, my arms are scuffed. I feel like my ankle is twisted but I don't have time to stop, I have to move, have to run.

I spring up and my bones groan in protest.

Shadows are moving towards me so fast. It's like a stream of darkness pouring out and as I step back they start shooting, clearly not caring who the fuck the intruder is.

I grab my gun, shoot back, though it's more as a response in this moment than anything else.

More bullets come at me.

I pick up my feet running as fast as I can and the bastards follow me.

My chest feels so tight. My legs feel like actual lead. I have to get away. I have to escape because if I die here I'm condemning them, condemning Rose.

How I don't get shot I don't know. How I manage to dodge every bullet must be some sort of miracle.

They're hot on my heels. Shouting. Hunting me down like a dog.

Only there's nowhere for me to go. Nowhere I can hide. It's too exposed here. I'm too out in the open. The entrance to the tunnel is at least a mile away from where I am and there's no way in hell I'll make it in time.

I pump my arms harder, forcing myself onwards.

I'm not going to make it.

I can't physically keep this up.

I turn the corner, duck behind a car, take a moment to try to catch my breath only someone grabs me from behind and I spun around and slammed into the bumper.

Koen's face comes right up against mine and I can see how angry he is.

"You fucking idiot." He growls.

My eyes glance back, seeing the militia getting closer.

Koen looks too then mutters something I know is not meant for me.

More gunshots ring out but this time they're coming from our direction to theirs.

I can see them, the two men perched, holding position just back from me.

Koen grabs me, half dragging me to a van and he all but throws me in before the others jump in behind me.

Around us the motorbikes seem to roar into action.

"Get moving." Koen shouts as the militia begin to pepper our vehicle.

The tyres screech as we drive away. I lay sprawled on the damned metal floor like some sort of kidnap victim.

When I pick myself up Koen lands a punch right to my face. I groan, landing flat on my back.

And then he lands another one.

And another one.

Blood streams out of my nose. My eyes are stinging with the tears.

Only I don't just lie there. I clench my fists slam them back into him, making contact with his ribs. He groans but clearly even my punches don't have the impact they did.

"You think this is a game?" He snarls as everyone around us just watches. "You rich entitled prick. You think you can just sneak around and all the rules don't apply to you."

"What fucking rules?" I growl.

He tilts his head, his eyes are screaming bloody murder and for the first time I realise exactly why everyone shits themselves around him.

"Darius owns this city. I told you that. I fucking told you." He snaps. "And you still think you can swanny on up to the Governor's house and what, just ask for him to hand over his wife?"

"I had to…"

"I don't give a fuck what you had to do." He growls. "This isn't about you and your hurt ego."

That hits a nerve. I slam my fist into his face and he barely even registers it.

"You think that's what this was?" I shout. "You think that all of that was about me? It has nothing to do with me." I'm losing it, all my control, all my anger, my rage, all of it is pouring out of me. "Rose is in there. My daughter is in there. You think I'm just going to sit by and play it safe while they're in danger?"

"It's about more than them." Koen replies.

"No, it fucking isn't." I say. "Not to me."

He sits back, his chest rising slowly as he watches me. "You put everyone's lives at risk. Everyone who lives in the tunnels, every single one of us, all because you wanted to play the hero."

"I wasn't playing the hero." I growl.

"I don't give a fuck what you tell yourself, how you convince yourself you were right, this is my war now. My fight. We do this my way or you can fuck off out and I guarantee you'll be dead before the sunsets. Darius will make sure of that."

I draw in my breath trying to steady the rattle of it. He doesn't understand. How can he? He doesn't have children, I doubt the man even knows what love feels like. What any of this feels like. Rose is back there, Darius has his hands all over her, and I *still* have done nothing to stop it.

Nothing to help.

We sit in silence until we come to a stop and when we do I know exactly where we are. The doors open and both Ben and Holden are stood waiting for us.

Ben shakes his head at me like he too is disappointed, like he too expected me to just stay here, safe and sound.

"Roman." Holden says quietly but I don't say anything. I just get out, ignoring the shaking of my legs, and I walk past them all, needing space, needing thinking time.

I'm not some errant boy. I'm not some entitled twat who thinks he can swarm in and take on Darius the way I believed six months ago. I know it's not the same situation, that everything has changed, and yet I can't just stay here, doing nothing.

I had to try. I had to.

ROSE

The camera's flash in my face.

People are screaming, cheering, celebrating like they've all just won the damn lottery.

We're stood to the side, waiting to be announced, but the noise is deafening.

All around I can see the banners, the ribbons, Darius's face on posters that people are waving about like he's some sort of deity.

Right after the wedding we went into campaigning. But that wasn't before we had a 'mini moon' and Darius ensured the press had a lot of photos of us, all loved up.

He hasn't let me out of his sight for a minute.

He's kept me here, right by his side, like I'm some good luck charm in this election and I guess, considering he's won, this proves it.

I'm in a slinky dress, one he once again picked for me, and his hand is holding me to his waist.

All around us it feels like an actual party. People are patting Darius on the back, congratulating me, and all I can do is just keep that fake smile plastered on my face and wait for it to end.

Someone walks up to the microphone, the crowd hushes for a second and then he calls out "Your new Governor."

Darius grips my hand tightly and walks me out with him.

The crowd goes wild. Wilder than before. Flowers are thrown, confetti seems to pour down in the blue and red colours that Darius had every poster, every leaflet, every ribbon printed with.

Darius grins, wrapping me in his arms and kisses me, plunging his tongue so forcibly into my mouth I have to grip his shirt to stop myself from reacting.

The crowd wolf-whistle. They roar with approval.

And I have to fight the very real need to choke.

"Ladies and Gentlemen." Darius says after breaking off. I keep my eyes focused just behind Darius, as if I'm looking at him, when in reality I'm looking right past him.

"My beautiful wife and I would like to thank you from the bottom of our hearts." He says.

More cheers. More fucking noise.

"I'm so honoured to be re-elected as your Governor, to be able to serve all of Verona as I have done, and to continue to turn this city into the glittering home we all love and cherish…"

It sounds like bullshit. As I listen to him drone on about his duty, about his intentions, it all sounds like absolute crap but I keep that sweet smile on my face, I laugh at the few jokes he makes and when he leans in and kisses me again I'm sure to kiss him back.

I'm not stupid. I won't fuck this up. Not today. Not in front of the hundreds of cameras that are trained on us.

Darius grabs my arse, gropes it as if that's all I am, a piece of meat, and again enough of the crowd seem to enjoy that moment while internally I swallow another insult.

He thanks them one last time and then we walk away, from the blinding lights, from the thousands of people watching us, back to the muted space behind the stage to where Carter is waiting at the back entrance.

He catches my eye and it's all I can do not to shudder. He's half the reason I keep out of the main house, half the reason I hate it as much as I do because he switched teams, got a promotion, he's all Darius's man now. Although I suspect that's got more to do with keeping me in place, ensuring I can't escape. Maybe my father and Darius put their heads together to come up with that particular plan.

He's murmuring about protests, about a few streets that have turned to riots, but he's quick to gloat that the militia have already put out the fires and arrested the troublemakers.

"Good." Darius says nudging me to the waiting limousine.

I get in and Darius is right behind me with his hands on my hips as if I need help. His leg presses against mine as he sinks into the leather of the seat. And then to my horror Carter gets in as well sitting opposite us in a way that feels more than threatening.

The door slams shut. I jump at the sound and my eyes dart between them.

Carter grins at me.

And Darius puts his hand on my leg in what is an indecently high place.

The windows are blacked out. No one can see in so at least in this moment I don't have to keep the falsities up. I try to shift away, to pull my body further into the corner but Darius yanks me back with an annoyed growl.

"Why is he travelling with us?" I ask. I can hear it, the fear in my voice.

Darius tuts glancing at me. "We have things to discuss Rose."

I fold my arms, staring out the window, trying to pretend neither of them are there as the city whizzes past. We're a good half hour from the House. Darius made sure he hired the best venue in the Bay for his victory speech.

"I'd recommend going street to street." Carter says still with his eyes fixed on me. "Make an example of them."

Darius leans back shutting his eyes, rubbing them with his thumb and forefinger. "Fine. Do what you think is best."

"We should also make a plan about how we're going to continue this charade."

My head spins. I look between them. Are they talking about us? About me and Darius? Surely not.

Darius lets out a laugh. "It doesn't matter. I'm in now so there's nothing they can do."

Carter shakes his head. "We'll need to keep an eye on the press…"

"All in hand." Darius replies looking at him. "No one is going to print anything we don't like. I've made sure of that."

"And the polls?" Carter asks.

Darius lets out a chuckle. "They'll say what we want from now on, just like the votes did."

I gasp. Is he saying what I think he's saying?

He casts his eyes over me. "Don't look so shocked." He mutters. "You think I'd leave it to chance? You think I leave anything to chance?"

"You rigged the vote." I half whisper, as if I'm afraid to confirm it, as if I'm afraid of what these two will do to me if they know I know.

Carter grins leaning forward. "What else did you expect Rose?"

I can't believe they've done it. I can't believe they got away with it. But they have haven't they?

"But all those people…" I stammer. There were so many of them, all cheering, all celebrating like this was real.

Darius grins squeezing my leg. "People can be hired, bought. You saw what I wanted you to see. What I wanted everyone to see."

I don't understand. He told my father I'd help him win this election, that marrying me would help his popularity but if he was just going to cheat anyway, then why put me through any of this?

"Don't worry your pretty head about it." Carter says patting my knee.

I jerk, almost kicking him from our proximity. "Don't you dare fucking touch me." I snarl.

Darius digs his hand hard into my leg in response making me yelp.

"I'm getting bored of your constant protests." He states.

"Why did you do it?" I ask. "Why did you force me into this if you were going to ensure you won anyway?"

He grabs my face, pulls me so that I'm staring into those watery eyes of his. "Because I can Rose. Because I can do whatever I want. Have whatever I want. And what I want is you."

I shake my head with the little movement he allows and the pair of them laugh harder than ever at my expense.

ROMAN

The place is a ruin. A complete and utter ruin. I stare out almost in disbelief at what they've done to it. The Montague House.

Being here is a risk. One I don't need to take.

And yet it feels necessary.

Koen gave me enough men, bikes, and supplies to at least give us the ability to shoot our way out if this does go tits up but he made it more than clear what his feelings on this excursion are and exactly who he would hold responsible if it does end badly.

I can't tell if he simply agreed because I didn't go behind his back or if this is an easy way to be rid of me.

Ben opted to stay behind. I don't think he could bring himself to see the destruction and in truth I think Sofia's situation is hitting him hard.

I blink, shaking away the rush of anger, and guilt, and every emotion I feel at the knowledge of where she is right now and what Otto is undoubtedly doing to her.

Holden walks beside me.

In silence.

I can hear the birds singing from what was once a loved and tended garden. For a moment I wonder how it's possible, how anything can feel joy when the world has ended, when everything worth living for is gone.

I let out a low breath, dropping my gaze, staring at the bits of debris strewn around our feet.

This house has stood for over two hundred years. It was one of the finest buildings in the entirety of Verona. And now, now it's a wreck reminiscent of a war torn city not the glittering streets of Verona.

Someone set it alight. Torched the place after they'd murdered everyone inside and stole away my sister and child.

I can see the blackened out interior through what was once the great hallway, only the walls have collapsed inwards. Half the building seems to have crumpled in on itself and that great beautifully carved oak staircase is now nothing but ash.

Darius had a story put about that arsonists did this. That this was another tragic accident to befall our family but I seriously wonder how the population of Verona can swallow all these lies.

How they can believe it all.

Holden bends down, picking something up, brushing off all the dirt and grime and I realise it's a photograph, torn, seared at the edges. I take it from his hands, study it and my heart clenches more as I see it's me, me and Sofia. And our parents too.

God, what would they think of me if they knew about this? If they knew how far we'd fallen. If they knew how much danger my sister is in right now and that I'm stood doing nothing to save her.

I guess it's a good thing my father died when he did. He didn't have to see the ignominy of our situation. But then he contributed to it as well. He was the one that started the whole organ trade, after my mother passed, after he grew bitter and greedy in his later years.

And then he was too weak to stop the Capulets from gaining ground, taking over.

I shake my head, clench my fists. I don't know what I expected to see coming here, I don't know what I expected to feel either but I had to see what I'd done, just as much as I had to watch that footage of Rose's wedding.

These are my fuckups. My mistakes.

And right now everyone I care about is paying a damned high price for my ineptitude.

I turn leaving the others to follow me back.

I've seen enough. I need to plan now, I need to channel this anger into something useful. Something of worth and not this deep festering emotion that gives me nothing.

Holden catches up with me and we walk, both hands in pockets with our heads bowed.

As we get nearer the bikes there's a yapping. It's barely noticeable but the closer we get the louder it grows.

And then I turn as I realise what that sound actually is.

"Bella." I murmur.

She looks like shit. She's running full pelt, her little legs all covered in mud and dirt. Her fur has grown so long it's mangled into itself and you can barely see her bug eyes through it. She has twigs and leaves caught up in her body.

I bend down scoop her up. She's so thin I can feel all her bones. How the fuck she's still alive I don't know but I hold her close, let her nuzzle into me the way she used to do to Rose.

She stinks but I don't care. It doesn't matter how filthy she is. This was Rose's pet. She loved this little dog.

Some of the men look at me like I've lost my marbles but I just ignore it getting onto the back of the nearest bike, tucking her into my jacket to keep her as safe as possible.

She'll need a bath. And a groom. And we'll have to sort out getting her decent food seeing as she's allergic to everything.

But she's alive.

This poor little creature somehow managed to avoid all the death and destruction around her.

WHEN WE GET BACK TO THE TUNNELS I GIVE HER A BATH. SHE FIGHTS hard, splashing me and Ben with water as we try to get all the muck off.

We towel her dry and again she squirms, grumbling, clearly hating every minute.

I don't even know what I'm doing but I start cutting away at the mange and as I do I can see how red, how angry her skin all is. I guess that's from the allergies, from having to eat whatever she can find.

"It's okay pup." I soothe not that she seems to care.

"I heard a rumour…" Tia says walking up behind us and we both look up.

"What rumour?" Ben asks.

"That you decided to get a pet." She says smirking.

I shake my head. "That's not it. It's Rose's dog. Somehow it survived."

She pushes me gently aside, picks up the scissors, and starts cutting like she knows what she's doing.

I raise an eyebrow at her and she lets out a chuckle. "My mum had cockerpoos. You learn very quickly how to groom them or they cost you a fortune."

I grunt back because I'm not sure what else to say.

But Bella seems to calm down, seems to understand that she's less likely to lose a limb now that someone skilled has taken over and when she's done, when she finally resembles the creature Rose used to adore, I scoop her back up into my arms.

"We need eggs and rice for her." I say.

"She's too good for tinned food?" Tia teases.

"She's allergic to all food. To everything but eggs and rice."

Tia smirks more. "Sounds like she's more high maintenance than her owner."

I don't bother to reply. I guess that's exactly what Bella is and yet what does it matter? I head to the canteen. I don't know when the poor thing last ate but I need to fatten her up, besides I've got a feeling she'll be a good distraction at night, when everyone else is asleep and all I can think about is Rose and Lara.

About what they're doing. About where they are. If they're in pain. If they're cold.

No, Bella will help.

And when I get Rose back she'll be even more happy to see her dog is safe and sound.

ROSE

I wake to the sound of screaming.

For once it's not me. Not my voice in the dark.

I throw off the covers, spring from the bed, my head telling me to get to Lara, to check she's safe.

But when I get to her room she's tucked up, fast asleep, somehow miraculously, completely undisturbed by all of this.

I huddle in the darkness watching her but then I hear it again.

Another scream.

I could stay here, I could stay with my child and ensure whatever this is doesn't find her but somehow I know this doesn't involve us. That whatever this is, this is Darius's secret. Perhaps the very thing Roman was blackmailing him about.

If I want to fight him, I need to know what's going on. I need every weapon in my arsenal.

So I grit my teeth and force myself out, out of the room, down the long hallway and barefoot I creep down the ridiculous wooden staircase.

As I descend further into the main house I can hear it, voices, men's voices, and the whimpering of someone injured, someone hurt.

My heart picks up. I don't know what this is, what the fuck is going on but I don't turn back now, I keep walking, placing one silent step in front of another.

As the moonlight trails into the rooms I can see shadows, people moving about. I squint seeing it's just the guards Darius has on near constant patrols, keeping the place secure. I swear this house has more of them than Fort Knox.

And then hands come up behind me, a hand grips my face and I scream into the palm as I'm pressed into their body.

"And what are you doing out of bed?" Carter says.

I flinch more. Struggle harder. And he shoves me forward, forcing every step I take.

My eyes dart about as we make our way down to where Darius's home office is.

I can see a light under the door. I can hear the voices getting louder. This is where it's all coming from and my fear escalates as Carter opens it and forces me inside.

Half a dozen sets of eyes snap to me but mine find the ones belonging to a girl who looks barely more than a teenager, stripped, bleeding, obviously terrified in the centre of the room.

And then Carter is shoving me forward while simultaneously releasing his arms so that I fall onto my knees in front of all of them.

A few smirk. A few take the opportunity to leer at me and I realise then how stupid it was to be creeping around in just the slip I was sleeping in. I didn't even put a robe on. I was too concerned for Lara's safety to consider it at the time.

I pull myself up, bringing my arms up to obscure my body as best I can but they've all been treated to a nice view of me.

"Rose." Darius says.

I gulp looking above the petrified girl's head to the man stood right behind her.

"Why are you here?" He asks, as if I've walked in on a business meeting and nothing nefarious at all.

I shake my head, my eyes darting back to the woman who's now silently pleading with me to help. Only I don't know how I can.

"I caught her lurking down the corridor." Carter says.

"I wasn't lurking." I snap back.

Darius's lips curl, he steps closer, and me and this mystery girl both tense even more.

"What were you doing then?" Darius asks.

"I heard a noise. A scream." I say.

Darius grins. Yanking the girl's head and she whimpers as she's forced back right into his crotch.

"Did you now?" Darius replies. "Did you wonder what all the commotion was? Did you want to come join our little party? Join in the fun?"

I shake my head as all the men snigger.

I don't know what the fuck this is but all I want to do is scramble to my feet and get the hell out of here.

As I try to get up Carter grabs me. "Not so fast." He says.

"Let me go you piece of shit." I hiss back.

He lets out a laugh. Darius laughs too before fixing me with a look.

"You're not meant to be out after dark Rose." He says. "I made that very clear didn't I?"

I nod. He did make that clear. That was the one rule he had when he forced me to move in here. That and I had to do what he wanted, whatever he wanted, without complaint. Not that I've been following through on that front.

The girl starts crying like this is all suddenly too much.

"For fucksake." One of them moans.

"We already told you we're sick of your tears." Darius snarls tightening his grip on her hair.

"Stop." I say and his eyes snap to me.

"What did you say?" He asks

"Let her go, whatever this is, just, stop it." I plead.

He pushes her hard, making her face plant onto the parquet flooring. He jerks his head for Carter to release me and then he's grabbing me, gripping my arms so tightly in his.

"You're hurting me." I gasp.

He laughs and that smell of the alcohol on his breath tells me if I didn't know already exactly how he's going to treat me, especially in front of all his boys.

"Do you know what this little bitch has done?" He asks me.

I shake my head. Of course I don't know. I've never seen her before in my life and yet whatever it is, it can't justify what they are doing.

He grins more. "She broke the rules too."

"She blabbed her big mouth." One of the other men say.

"About what?" I ask.

Darius pulls me in, pulls me so my face is nose to nose with his. "Do you really want to know the answer to that one Rose?"

I don't know if I do. Maybe it's easier being ignorant. Maybe it's easier hating the monster Darius is in my head than understanding the true one he is in real life.

He watches my face, watches my expression as if he can read the thoughts going through my head.

"Let's take a little trip." He says.

"Where?" I ask as my stomach drops, as I tremble more.

He glances at the woman still sprawled at our feet. "Perhaps we can kill two birds with one stone." He says kicking her enough to make her yelp.

"Darius…" I gasp but he's already frogmarching me from the room, leaving everyone else to follow behind us.

ROSE

I'm forced into the Mercedes. I'm still barefoot, still wearing nothing but the silk slip I was sleeping in. Darius makes a point of enjoying how my body is responding to the cold and it takes everything I have not to glare at him.

I guess the girl is shoved into one of the cars behind us but Darius makes sure it's just us in this one. Just me and him and his driver.

I huddle into the leather seat. It's freezing cold. I dare to glance at the dashboard and see it's the middle of the night. For some reason that makes me even more afraid.

"Darius." I whisper, putting my hand on his.

He tilts his head smirking. "Trying to play nice now, is that it?"

I shake my head. "This is a misunderstanding."

He lets out a laugh. "I'm not that stupid Rose."

"What do you mean by that?"

"You think I don't know you were snooping? You think I don't know you're trying to figure out a way to escape me?"

I gulp shaking my head.

He grabs my jaw pulling my face right into his. "Perhaps after tonight you will realise exactly what this is."

"What, what is?"

"Your situation." He spits before shoving me back.

I don't reply then, I just shut my eyes trying not to fall apart.

It feels like we drive for ages. Darius doesn't say a word. He just keeps his eyes fixed on me while I sit, wishing I was anywhere other than where I am. I don't know who is back at the house. I don't know how long we're going to be out, wherever we are. What if Lara wakes and I'm not there? What if no one else is there?

My heart starts to race. I have to get back. I have to make sure that come morning, whatever happens, Lara is none the wiser about any of this.

When we do come to a stop the silence around us is deafening.

Darius grabs my arm hauling me out of the car and I yelp as my feet find the sharp stones imbedded into the ground.

Behind us I can hear the other men, the taunts, the laughter, and the crying of the girl as she's dragged along too.

I look up, I stare at the massive building in front of me.

"What is this place?" I whisper.

"You're about to find out." Darius says.

All around the perimeter are armed men. Dressed in black. With helmets and masks that seem to obscure their faces, twisting them into more monstrous manifestations than what they already are.

I shudder when I look at them but Darius ignores them all, walking past them as if they don't exist.

Inside it's barely warmer than outside.

The concrete floor soaks away what tiny bit of heat is left in my feet and they feel like ice blocks.

As the girl takes in the building she starts whimpering more, pleading, begging them not to do this, whatever this is. I think she knows what this place is, I think she understands exactly what's going on while I'm still stuck, petrified but ignorant all the same.

We walk further in. My eyes dart about looking for some clue, looking for anything that will tell me what this place is and when we do come to a stop I gasp in horror.

In front of me are glass kennels like the ones a vet would have. Only they're bigger. Much bigger. And inside, trapped inside are people.

I let out a cry. Darius tightens his grip but clearly this here is what he wanted me to see. Only I still don't get it.

Why would he be locking people up like this? Surely we have prisons for criminals and none of these people look like they belong there. Some are children for fucksake.

"Do you know what this is?" Darius half whispers.

I shake my head.

"This is the main source of my wealth. Your father's wealth too."

"How?"

He grins. "What price would you put on a life?" He asks.

I frown, shaking my head more in confusion. What sort of a question is that?

"If Lara was sick, if she was dying, what would you do to save her?" He asks.

"Anything." I say fiercely.

He nods. "Say she needed a new heart. They're tough to come by. Hard to get a good match…"

My eyes dart to the people staring back at me. What the fuck is he saying right now?

"There's a good market for it Rose." He continues. "A very good market."

"For what?" I ask.

"Organs."

My stomach lurches. I think I'm going to puke. I try to pull my arm back but he yanks me hard into his chest.

"No you don't." He says, gripping my face, forcing me to stare back at the people he is all but selling like spare parts. "Look them in the eyes." He states. "Each one of them pays for your lifestyle, for those jewels you have, those pretty dresses…"

"I don't want it. I don't want any of that." I spit.

He lets out a laugh. "That's not your decision to make."

"Why did you bring me here?"

"Because it's time you understood." He replies. "Time you stopped this pathetic attempt to fight me and just submitted."

"I don't want you." I say back. "I've never wanted you. And I never will."

He tilts his head smirking. "No? You're bold with your words tonight. So perhaps it's time for another reality check."

He clicks his fingers and the girl is brought out in front of us. She stopped wailing now but she's making awful whimpering noises instead.

"I had a mind to use her. I'm sure she'd fetch a good price. Her heart, her lungs, even her skin is worth something." He states. "But then you've been a little bitch haven't you?"

"What do I have to do with it?" I gasp.

"Everything." He replies producing a gun from his belt pointing it at the girl and before I can do anything he's pulling the trigger, blowing her head off right in front of me.

For a second it's like time itself stops. Like my head can't process what the hell has just happened. Her blood covers my face. Covers my skin. I blink and it's there, in my eyelashes, in my mouth. I can taste it. I can taste the copper hint of it on my tongue.

I scream. I scream so loud as everyone around me seems to laugh.

Darius smacks me over the head with the butt of the weapon and the force of it silences me. But I crumble to my feet with my tears streaming down my face.

He just murdered someone, just killed them for no reason whatsoever that I can tell.

He grabs me by my hair hauling me back up only I'm too afraid now to even attempt to fight him.

"Let this be a lesson to you Rose." He spits running his hand other over me, smearing the girl's blood further. "It's about time you understood that I am not fucking around. I own this city. I own everyone in it and most particularly I own you, do you understand that?"

I nod, whimpering.

He's worse than I imagined. So much worse.

He yells for someone to clean up the mess and then he starts to drag me back out only I can't walk, I can't even stand and he's forced to carry me because my feet no longer work, my body no longer works either.

But as we leave I see him.

In the shadows.

Lurking.

And just like the last time he witnessed something horrific, he's not doing anything or saying anything.

Clearly he knows, clearly he's well aware of where our family's wealth is from, but apparently he's made his decision. Ty is happy to stay, enjoying the Capulet party for all he can get, irrespective of who else gets killed along the way.

ROMAN

It's not her screams that rip right into my soul. It's her eyes. That fear, that pain, but most of all that betrayal.

Because I'm stood here, watching, witnessing everything he's doing to her, every horrific violation of her body and yet I'm not moving.

I'm not stopping it.

He's groaning, grunting, clearly enjoying every minute as he lavers her skin with his disgusting mouth.

"Roman."

She whimpers my name as if she knows already that I won't help. That I can't. That in this moment I'm as trapped as she is.

Except I'm not am I? I'm just stood here. Doing nothing.

"Roman." She screams it this time, as her tears roll down her cheeks.

He's got his hands in her hair, twisting his fingers in amongst the strands, as his body pins hers to the bed.

"You're so fucking perfect." He groans. "My perfect wife."

I feel the bile rising in my throat as those words hit me. She's his wife. His.

"Roman." She gasps. "Why won't you do something? Why are you leaving me like this? Leaving us…"

His hands grab around her throat cutting off the words as he picks up his pace. I want to yell. To scream, to hurl myself at the monster assaulting her and yet I don't.

"Roman." She's crying now. Sobbing. "What did I do, what did I do to deserve this?"

I can't answer. I can't reply. I clench my fists as if that's the only movement I can make.

And as I watch, as I do nothing, he continues his assault. He continues hurting her.

And I continue as I am.

Observing.

Witnessing.

Doing nothing to save her.

I stand in the shadows. Hide in them.

Though it feels so much different this time.

I used to revel in this. I used to enjoy being someone who could disappear, who could leave without a trace.

But now, now I feel like I don't exist.

And in a way I don't.

Darius held a memorial for me. They buried a god damn coffin with my name engraved on it. God knows what was inside. God knows what shit they buried in my name.

To this entire city I am dead and nothing about that notion gives me comfort despite the fact that right now it is useful.

I see him approaching. I see the way the light changes as he makes his way through the entrance to where I am.

When he sees me he freezes for a millisecond as if he cannot quite believe this is real and I'll admit I'm still surprised that this is even happening myself.

"Tyrone." I say quietly.

He nods his head curtly. "Roman."

"What do you want?"

He frowns glancing behind, as if he expects an army of assassins to spring out, as if he's worth going to that much the effort to killing.

"I want to help." He states.

I raise an eyebrow. "Excuse me?"

"I want to help you."

"Why?"

"Because Rose deserves better. And Sofia…" He trails off looking at his feet like he can't admit what he's wanting to say.

"What the fuck about Sofia?" I snarl.

He looks up, and I see it, something akin to the fury inside me. "Sofia won't make it to Christmas if we don't do something."

I snarl, clenching my fists. Otto dares to hurt her? Dares to lay a finger on her? It's hard to contain my rage, it's hard to know that this too is my fault, that I set this in motion when I agreed for the whole fake dating charade to go ahead and yet I'm doing absolutely nothing to stop it.

"What of my daughter, what of Lara?" I ask. I need to know she's okay, I need to know that Darius hasn't laid his filthy hands on her as well.

His eyes widen. He looks like this is complete news to him. "How is she your daughter?" He says.

I tilt my head. "She's mine and Rose's." I state. "She's our child."

He blinks, his eyes darting from side to side as if he can't quite digest that information. "How?"

"What does it matter?" I snap. The logistics don't matter. She's my daughter, that's what counts, and I have to protect her. Though I'm doing a shit job of that so far.

"You were…" He trails off shaking his head. "She was pregnant, that's why she went away." He says putting it together. "I never understood why she was so heartbroken by Tybalt. They never even liked each other. But she wasn't was she? They were hiding her, hiding that secret."

"She was pregnant." I confirm.

He slumps against the wall. "How the fuck did I not see it?"

I let out a bitter laugh. "No one did."

"But her parents knew." He states it like a fact. Like he understands it all now. Like suddenly it makes sense to him.

"They blackmailed Rose with it." I confirm. "Used Lara to make Rose do whatever they wanted."

"Including marrying Darius?" He says.

I shrug. I don't think that was so much her parents as Darius himself seeing as he has them both in his possession. I've seen glimpses of them, fleeting shadows as they've moved through the house on the CCTV. None of them have ever been clear enough, I've never been able to see their faces, to truly see them.

"How the fuck did I not see any of this?" He growls.

I don't reply. I can't answer it. The man's clearly been oblivious for so long while I thought he was part of the conspiracy.

"They're selling people." He states. "I was there, at one of their compounds. They had children. Fucking teenagers. They steal their organs, sell them on the black market."

"I know." I reply. "I was trying to stop it."

"Darius took Rose there." He continues.

That gets my attention. "Why?" I ask.

He shrugs. "I think to make her comply more. She's been fighting him. At least trying to."

I hate the way he states it. The way it just sounds like a fact of life. And I hate the fact that this is happening to her and there's nothing I can do.

"Look, I'll do what I can, whatever I can." He says. "Darius trusts me, Ignatio trusts me too."

"I don't know if I do though." I reply.

He shakes his head. "I know I should have seen this, I know I've been a prick but I want to help, not for your sake, but for Rose's. And Sofia's."

"Why do you care about Sofia?" I ask. He's mentioned her name twice now, and the way he looks, I don't like it. I don't like that fear in his eyes.

He lets out a low breath. "I don't have to justify myself..."

"Yeah you fucking do." I growl.

He steps up to me, almost facing off. And I see it, that same arrogance that Tybalt had.

"I care for her." He says. Like that answers it.

"Care?" I repeat.

He lets out a growl. Like he doesn't have to explain himself further.

"You love her." I say realising what it really is.

His eyes flash. He looks like bloody murder right now. "I don't..." He pauses. "I don't even know her, not really, I just..." He looks away then looks back with cold fury. "In other circumstances, in another world, Sofia would be mine, just as Rose is yours and no one would even question it.

Fuck me. He does love her. I stare at him for a moment completely dumbfounded.

"Does she know?" I ask.

He lets out a sigh that I can't interpret. Either she's oblivious and that's his pain, or worse, she knows, that they love each other and he's in the same shitty situation as me and Rose right now. Forced to endure the knowledge that another man has what is ours. That another man is hurting what is ours.

"Fine." I say, clearing my throat. "I need you as a spy. I need you to help sabotage them from the inside."

"Whatever you need I can do."

I grunt. And then it hits me, the one thing I really need, the one thing Rose needs more than anything in the world right now.

I dig my hands into my pockets, grab the scrap of paper that's there and scrawl onto it.

"Give this to Rose. Make sure she gets it and no one else sees."

He takes the note, does the decent thing of not reading it and pockets it.

"I'll do what I can." He says.

"No, you make sure she gets that. And you get a Juliet rose, you put that on top of it."

He meets my gaze and nods.

"I'll be in touch about everything else." I say before turning on my heel.

I need to be smarter this time. I need to plan it better. I can't come at them the same way, I can't think I can take Darius out from the shadows.

I'm going to wage a war. I'm going to set this entire city on fire. Set off an uprising. And the only way it will end is when I have Darius's head on a spike.

18

ROSE

It's been a long day. A horrifically long one.

But then that's my life now.

All smiles in public and pain in private.

The only good moments are the few hours I get with Lara. Where we both try to pretend we're not where we are. Where we both try to act like we're not desperate to escape.

Since Darius got re-elected it feels like one constant rotation of public outings, meetings, cutting ribbons, acting and playing the part of First Lady.

I don't know why but I thought this would be easier, that it would get easier, once the wedding was done, once Darius was in for another term. I guess I was kidding myself, self-soothing in a way. I wanted to believe that once this season was passed everything would return to quiet, to me just hiding away, inside, away from all the gossip, and the stares and the exhaustion of people.

But I don't have that. It seems I will never have that. Now that he's put a ring on my finger, and after the incident almost immediately succeeding that, it seems Darius is determined to flaunt me at every opportunity. I'm a circus pony, a performing monkey. He dusts me down, covers me in glitter, and parades me about for all the masses to stare at, for everyone to admire.

Even my time with Lara now is being limited though no one has spoken the words. No, they're too clever for that. But too often I'm being hurried away, called away, made to attend some appointment that apparently supersedes the needs of a desperately lonely, desperately heartbroken six year old.

But what's the worst are the other times, when Darius wants me. When we're alone. He seems to have gone into overdrive now, as if knowing that there's no physical impediment to me getting pregnant is spurring him onto ensuring I am as soon as possible.

And I don't know how to stop it. I don't know what I can physically do to ensure that never happens. I can only hope that my body is so broken that biologically speaking it puts my own survival ahead of the need to reproduce.

And the only sign that's happening is that I haven't yet had a period, which means I'm not ovulating. Though I don't know whether Darius is in tune enough with women's bodies to understand that little nuance. From the way he's fucking me, I'd say not.

With every test he makes me take I grow more and more fearful that the result will be positive but so far, somehow, I'm till dodging this. It's the only way I can fight him now.

I've stopped answering back. I've stopped fighting in any meaningful way. I'm too traumatised by what he did, by the fact that he murdered that girl as if it was nothing.

I knew he was a bastard, I knew my father was capable of such acts but I guess I was kidding myself that Darius wouldn't be. I thought he'd simply outsource it, that he wouldn't sully his own hands with such acts.

I guess I was wrong there too.

And that thought, the fact that he will willingly pull the trigger makes me so much more fearful for Lara because it will only take one time, one instant, one moment where I've pushed him too hard and he decides the best way to punish me is by murdering her.

I can't let that happen.

I have to do everything I can to ensure that doesn't happen.

And that means submitting, in every way, giving him what he wants.

My heart sinks as I think about it, as I realise this is my life, it's so much worse than it was with Paris. At least Paris gave me some freedom. At least I had Bella, and I had hope.

Here I have nothing except my daughter. She's the only shining light in all of this.

But she's also the very thing I have to get out of here, I have to protect her because sooner or later Darius is going to snap, he is going to lash out, and it's going to be her face he slams his fist into.

I tuck her in, read a bedtime story. Darius is out somewhere tonight, out with Otto, and the rest of his arsehole cronies. He left Carter to stay and watch us and though he's not come up to our level, I can hear him pacing about below, making enough noise to let me know he's there, just looking for an excuse.

"Mummy?" Lara whispers.

"Yes baby?"

"Why doesn't god love us?"

"What?" I frown.

"Mrs Bates used to say if I was good then god would be good to me. But I don't think I've been naughty. And I don't think you've been naughty, so why is he punishing us?"

I steel my breath. How the fuck do I even answer that? I don't believe in god, I've never even mentioned the 'g' word before so I don't know where this is coming from. "Who is Mrs Bates?"

"She used to look after me, in the house, before Daddy came and took me away."

I feel my shoulders sag. "It's not that simple baby."

"In what way?" She says. "I'm good. I am good. And I know you are too…"

I hug her, trying to hide the tears that are threatening to spill. "It will be okay baby. I promise you. This is just the bad part in the story, the bit where you think the monster is going to win, but it won't last forever."

"It is lasting forever mummy. It is." She sobs.

I hold her tighter. I don't have any other words of comfort. I don't know how to explain how fucked up this world is and in all honesty I don't think I want her to understand it yet. It's better she's ignorant of the worst parts. Better she retains some sort of innocence for as long as she can.

"It will get better." I say over and over, sweeping her hair back, soothing her until she's fallen asleep and I pray her dreams are better than her awake hours.

And then I walk back into my room, ready to spend the rest of the night crying and grieving in the darkness until Darius comes to bed and I have to play pretend again.

As I go to wash off the smear of makeup from my face, I freeze staring at the table in my dressing room. There's a rose placed on the top of it.

The stem is short. Someone cut it right by the bud as if they needed to sneak it in.

My heart starts to race. I blink trying to figure out if this is some sort of hallucination.

Only it's still there.

It's real.

I walk up to it and I realise it's not a Juliet rose, but it's so damn close I doubt the average person could tell the difference.

I look about, glance behind me. Is this a trick? Is this some new form of torture that Darius has devised? Did he find out this little titbit about Roman and now he's going to torment me, to twist this memory into something awful, something tainted?

But there's no one here. The room is silent, the house feels empty even though I know Carter is right below me, making sure the captive wife is where she belongs.

I pick it up, take in a deep inhale, and a tear escapes, sliding down my cheek.

"Roman." I whisper his name.

It feels like his ghost is here. It feels like he's haunting me. That his spirit is lingering about, refusing to leave the earth because of what happened to him in those last awful moments of his life.

I drop my gaze and then spot what else is there.

What was underneath it.

It's a scrawled up note. Half torn paper with ragged ends.

I pick it up, unfold it, and let out a whimper as I see the handwriting. Handwriting I'd recognise anywhere.

It is Roman. It's his writing.

'I'm going to save you both. Do whatever you have to in order to survive Rose. Whatever. Stay strong. I love you.'

My heart's racing now. I stumble out of the room, out past the bedroom, and onto the balcony. Was he here? Was he in this house? How the hell did this note even get here?

Roman's alive. He's alive.

I crumble to the floor. My legs giving way as my grief, my pain, all of it hits me. How is he alive? How is this possible? I saw his coffin? I saw…

But I didn't did I?

Reality hits me like a tidal wave. I didn't see him. All I saw was a wooden box. I never saw Roman, I never saw any proof that he was actually inside.

"Roman." I gasp again. Wishing he was here. Wishing he'd climb up over the balustrade. I wouldn't even need him to hold me, to touch me, just seeing him would be enough. Just seeing him here.

It feels like something switches inside me. Like a fire comes back to life for the briefest of seconds.

Roman is alive. I know in my heart. I know that's why this grief, this pain, none of it has left me.

And if he is alive then all of this, every awful moment is simply borrowed time.

One horrific hiatus before Roman comes and it finally all ends. Just as he always promised me it would.

But why would we still be here if he was? Why would we both be suffering like this? That thought cuts through me and I hang my head as more tears fall.

It *is* a trick.

It has to be.

Roman isn't alive. He's not coming. No one is coming.

If I want to fight this, if I want this to end then I've only got myself to do it.

And it has to ends. Somehow, someway I have to get us out, because Lara cannot continue living like this.

And in truth, I don't think I can either.

ROSE

I'm sat with Lara, eating breakfast, or at least trying to.

She picks at her food. Clearly a habit she's learnt from me.

I try to encourage her, try to get her to take just one more mouthful. She doesn't looks starving, mercifully, she doesn't look sick, but I know she's not eating as much as her body needs and with the stress of this, it is going to catch up to her. It's just a matter of when.

"Just one more mouthful." I half plead.

It's pineapple and yoghurt. Her favourite. Or at least it used to be.

"If the brat doesn't want to eat then leave her to it." Darius snaps.

We both tense, both unaware that he was close to us, unaware he'd even come into the room.

Lara looks up at me, and her eyes fill with tears. But as if in defiance she picks up her spoon and scoops a piece of fruit onto it before putting it in her mouth.

My lips curl before I can stop them.

"Good girl." I say reaching out and squeezing her arm. It's all I can do now, the only fight I have, and it feels as pathetic as it is.

"Send the child to her room." My mother says and I stiffen more.

She's here? My head turns and I narrow my eyes. The pair of them are stood, in the double archway watching us like we're the criminals.

"Who is that lady mummy?" Lara asks so quietly.

"That's your grandma." I say back.

"She's no granddaughter of mine." My mother snarls. "Not with who her father is."

My fists clench, I swear I'm so close to hurling the contents of the bowl right at her perfectly done up face.

"Go to your room." Darius says staring at Lara. "Your tutor will be here soon so you can wait there."

Lara drops her head, slumps her shoulders, and slowly gets down from her seat. On instinct I pull her back, pull her into my arms and hug her so tightly. I won't let them break her the way they're breaking me.

I'll take whatever punishment they delve out right now because Lara's wellbeing is worth it.

"I love you." I whisper into her ear. "I love you so much. And Daddy loved you too."

She blinks, her eyes filling with tears but then Darius is there wrenching us apart.

"Stop pandering to her all the time." He says before giving her enough of a shove to be gone.

"I'm not pandering." I snap back before I can stop myself. "She's my daughter. I'm not going to just leave her to you jackals."

My mother shakes her head muttering while Darius grasps my face in his hand.

"I can't wait until you start popping out my children." He says. "Because then you can focus all that maternal spirit you have into nurturing them."

My stomach twists. I think that's part of my fear, that if I do get pregnant what will I do then? I can hardly blame an innocent child for the horrors of what their father is.

"Are you done?" I say.

Darius narrows his eyes, clearly my response isn't to his liking and I wonder what my mother will do if he decides to make a point by using his fists. Will she simply stand there? Will she willingly watch her child be beaten?

I guess I already know the answer to that because she sold me like a prized cow at market. She doesn't care what happens to me now. She's got the result she wants. What happens after is irrelevant.

"Let's go Rose." She says.

"Go where?" I ask looking between them.

Darius smiles. "I thought a day out would be good for you. You used to like shopping so I spoke to your mother and we agreed it."

"I don't want to go out." I reply. It's not exactly true. I'd love to be out, to be free of these damned walls and the prison Darius has constructed around me, but I sure as hell don't want to go shopping with my mother. And I don't want to leave Lara here, alone, and without my protection.

My mother huffs looking at Darius. "I see she's in one of those moods this morning." She says.

"When is she not?" Darius replies like I'm some spoilt child misbehaving all the time.

My mother walks up to me, yanking my arm. "I would have thought, considering your circumstances that you would make yourself more amenable."

"What does that mean?" I snarl.

She gives me a look of contempt. "You're lucky he even tolerates having her around."

"Excuse me?"

"That bastard child of yours. You should be grateful she's even here. The least you could do is show Darius how much you appreciate his efforts."

I screw my face up before I can stop myself. What effort has he made? When I glance back, he's there watching every move I make still. Yeah I am going to pay for this later. He's going to make sure of it.

Only, when I return it's clear he's got another thing on his mind.

He pulls me into the bedroom and I know where this is headed, only I can't decide whether having him fuck me is worse than a beating. They both hurt. They both fracture a bit more of my spirit and yet I think him violating me is worse. Enduring the feel of him, hearing the way he moans as if this is a thing of pleasure, I don't think I'm ever going to get that horrific sound out of my head.

"Strip."

I don't bother fighting it. It's far easier not to.

I slide my jeans off. Toss my clothes. Making sure my eyes are on the carpet because I don't want to see the excitement in his. And in a way this is how I protest. The only way I can. I may not say the words, I may not physically try to stop it, but he won't have me, not in any way that makes him think I want him back at least.

"Get on the bed."

I do it. Even though my underwear is still on. I lie back, shutting my eyes preparing myself for that disgusting feeling of his skin on mine.

The bed sinks with his weight as he climbs on beside me. He runs his hand over my stomach, across my ribs.

"Your skin is so smooth." He murmurs.

I grit my teeth. It's not a compliment. Not from him. I wish my body were made of scales, of spikes, I wish I was covered in warts, that I reflected on the outside how he makes me feel on the inside.

He slides my underwear off, tossing it to where my top is.

And then he grips my jaw. "I got you something." He says.

My eyes open. I look at him and then at the object in his hand. I think my words fail me. All I can think is 'fuck'.

"You won't come for me." He says planting a knee between my thighs, stopping them from shutting. "So I had a little think about how to rectify that."

I gulp staring at the vibrator in his hand. I don't *want* to come for him. That's the point.

He leans over, pouring enough lube across my vagina that I could swim in it. I screw my face up but as always there's nothing I can do.

He turns it on, his eyes glinting more as it starts to buzz.

"Let's see how long you can resist this?" He murmurs.

I shake my head. I know it will work. I know he's going to beat me in this and for once I just want one small part of me, one minuscule bit of what makes me *me* kept to myself. I don't want him to take this from me.

To take the last of my pleasure. To steal that too.

"Darius." I plead.

He leans in, placing a hand right by my head to hold himself right above me. "Beg me to make you come."

"That's not what I want." I say back.

He lets out a chuckle, running the damned thing between my lips and I jerk like I've been shocked. "It feels good doesn't it?"

I shake my head more violently.

He does it again, pressing harder this time. "Admit it Rose, admit that you like it."

"I don't. I don't want you. I hate you."

He grabs my throat, pushing the toy right against my clit at the same time. "We'll see how you feel when you're gasping my name."

I shut my eyes but the pulsing is so strong. My body is throbbing as my blood seems to flush to where it's being stimulated. I don't even remember the last time I did come. No, I do, it was with Roman, on his mouth, on that morning before everything went south, when we thought we'd have a lifetime of this, a lifetime of each other.

Roman is gone. I'll never feel his touch, his love again.

I whimper as he steals that memory too. As he tarnishes it.

He starts circling, tiny little movements that feel so horrifically good.

"There's a good girl." He says repeating the words Roman said to me so many months ago, when he too was forcing himself on me, only I wanted him, I wanted him so much.

And I don't want this.

"Please Darius, please don't…"

He snarls, rubbing it up and down, stimulating my clit in a way I know is making my body scream for more.

"I want to watch you come." He says like I give a shit what he wants. "You're my wife and you're going to give me this."

I grip the sheets, I physically try to do everything I can to tell my body to stop this.

"Stop fighting me." He says. "Stop fighting and just enjoy it."

I can't enjoy it. Even as this pleasure builds and builds. I shake my head as much as I can with his hand holding my throat. My tears are streaming. I know I'm going to come. I can feel that coil building tighter and tighter and I'm biting back the moans I so desperately need to let out.

"Come you slut." Darius says as his spit lands on my face.

My back arches, my legs kick out, I fight so hard to keep myself from doing it but I'm toppling over, screaming, coming like it's my salvation. Only I'm not thinking of Darius, I'm not acknowledging that it's him doing this to me.

"Roman." I scream his name. I know I do.

And I see his face too as if it's imprinted on my mind, tied so intrinsically to my pleasure that I cannot achieve it without him.

But as I come down, as I blink, meeting those furious blue eyes, I see his fist curling tight before it makes impact and then there's nothing but darkness.

ROMAN

"**D**addy."

The scream tears through me.

It echoes in my head, echoes around the dark room.

I can see her in his arms. I can see the way he has a hand wrapped around my daughter's throat.

"Daddy." She cries harder.

I'm try to raise my hand. I try to move but it's like my body is made of stone. Like my feet are stuck to the very floor.

"Your daddy doesn't love." Darius taunts.

Lara cries harder. I can see all those tears pouring down her reddened cheeks. She's staring back at me with such a look of betrayal. "Why don't you love me daddy?"

"I do." I shout. "I love you so much."

Darius smirks, tightening his grip around her waist. "Then why aren't you stopping this Roman?"

"Lara." I gasp.

I feel helpless. I feel pathetic. I feel like the complete failure I am right now.

I try to do something. I try to move but my body won't respond. I'm just stood here.

Darius throws her to the floor. She lands in a heap. And then he's crouching over her, curling up his fists and slamming them into her tiny body as she curls up so small trying to protect herself.

"Your daddy won't save you." He taunts. "No one is going to save you. No one even wants you."

She whimpers harder and he raises his leg bringing it right down onto her stomach.

She's too small to take such a beating. Her body is too young. He's going to kill her if he continues this.

I try to shout that, I try to do something, but I'm paralysed.

"Daddy." Lara screams again. "Daddy why won't you save me? Why?"

WE'RE OUT PAST THE PERIMETER OF THE CITY. IT TURNS OUT THERE'S an entrance we can actually drive out of and that's what we've done.

Me, Holden, Koen, and a bunch of his soldiers.

I get the feeling he doesn't quite trust me yet.

Though maybe after today he will. Maybe he'll realise we're not all empty words and no action.

The rain is coming down like a constant spitting of water. I can feel it on my skin, I can feel it soaking into my bones. It's a standard autumn day here, all the oppressive heat of summer is forgotten about in the sopping wet dullness of autumn.

When I shut my eyes I still see it, those images, of Rose, of Lara, of my nightmares about what Darius is doing to them. It's harder not to react, to stand here, acting like every moment I'm asleep I'm not reliving it over and over.

I'm torturing myself. I know that. And yet part of me needs to. I need to feel this pain, to understand it, to in some ways share the horror of what they are experiencing, what I let happen.

The engines rumble loudly as they approach. Around me the others shift. Do they think this is an ambush? Do they think I would cross them?

I look across at Koen, meet his black eyes and then step out, step towards the headlights as they get nearer.

The door of the closest one opens. Boots hit the ground and then I see that same old gap toothed grin.

"Fuck me." Terry says. "You're actually alive?"

"Can't get rid of me that easily." I reply.

Terry smirks running his eyes over me. "Nah, but you look like shit mate."

Of course I look like shit. I've spent months in a coma completely out of it, while my body has started to waste away and then I've woken to find everything I hold dear, everything worth something in this life has been taken from me. Again.

"So do you but I guess somethings don't change."

He narrows his eyes before he's embracing me with a laugh.

"Fucking prick." He says slapping my back.

"Terry this is Koen. Koen Diaz."

His eyes widen as he looks across at the MC President then they shoot back to me.

"Fucking hell Roman, I see you've changed your friends then…"

"I've been forced to." I say. But that seems hardly fair. "We're working together now." I state. "We have shared aims."

Terry gives Koen another look but shrugs it off. "I take it these are for them then?" He mutters.

"They're for us." I reply nodding my head, following over to where the trucks are.

The backs are dropped, Koen is quick to inspect them, to open up the crates to see exactly what we're dealing with.

"Very nice." He murmurs holding an assault rifle that glints even in the dull light.

Terry stiffens a little. "Roman, they're fucking gangbangers." He mutters.

I narrow my eyes. "Maybe they are." I say. "But I'd much rather they have these than Darius."

He tilts his head like he's weighing it up. "Fine." He says, like he's gifting them and we're not paying him thousands to buy them. "Let me know when you need more."

"What else can you get?" Koen asks.

Terry hesitates like he doesn't want to answer that. "You mean beyond guns?"

Koen smirks. "Come on, we're not idiots, these are military grade weapons. If you can get your hands on these you can get other things…"

"Such as?"

"Drones, tanks, the good stuff." Koen grins.

Terry looks at me and then back at him. "The fuck you want with stuff like that?"

"Darius has all of that at his disposal and more." I state before Koen can reply. He's right, I should have thought of it, I should have realised that what we have even now is not enough. "If we stand a chance of doing this we need to match him."

"There's a big difference between getting you guns and getting you tanks. I can't exactly fit one of those on the back of my truck can I?" He snaps.

"But you can do it?" Koen asks.

Terry squirms just a little. "For the right price. It won't be cheap."

"Money isn't an issue."

That makes me pause. How much does this man have? How much is he making even now, while Darius has all but chopped the legs of all his business enterprises.

"I'd need some time." Terry states.

"How much time?" I growl. I'm not angry at him just sick of everything taking time, meaning more precious hours of what I know for me are unbearable and for Rose are unimaginable.

"A few weeks."

I shake my head. "We need it sooner than that."

"I can't do sooner Roman, not without putting a fucking great target on my back." He snaps. "Besides you'll need time to figure out where the hell you're gonna be hiding them."

"We have that sorted." Koen says. "Get us the tanks, get us everything you can and in the meantime..." He fixes his gaze on me. "We'll have a little fun."

Fun? He thinks this is fun?

He stalks off back to where his men are finishing packing up our vehicles. I stare after him for a moment.

"You sure you know what you're doing here?" Terry says quietly.

"We don't have any choice." I state.

"What will you do after? If you beat Darius, then how will you stop the Storm Crows from taking over?"

I let out a sigh. That's a problem for another day. As selfish as I am I don't really care if that is the outcome. My priority is beating Darius, saving Rose and Lara and my sister. They're my concern not how this glistening gold city and all its inhabitants may have to adapt if Koen takes over.

"When that day comes, then we'll deal with it." I state before turning and leaving. I don't want to think about it more. I don't want to dwell on it.

I need to focus on the now. On the immediate. Get my family out and get my vengeance.

Nothing else matters beyond that.

ROSE

I hear a whimper.

It's quiet. Far off.

But I know that voice anywhere. I know it as well as my own.

I storm through the house, pushing one door open and then another, not caring if they slam, not caring what noise I make.

When I find them I freeze.

Lara is there, with blood streaming from her nose and tears down her cheeks.

And her tutor is standing over her, arms on his hips, with such a look of contempt.

"You brought this on yourself." He says. "I told but you don't learn…"

"What?" I half snap. Instinct already telling me what is going on though my head is racing to catch up.

He looks up, meets my gaze and blinks.

"What is this?" I repeat.

Lara runs to me, burying her face in my stomach, smearing that blood all over me. I wrap my arms around her, holding her for a second and then squat down to see why on earth she's bleeding.

It's her nose. It's streaming with blood. Her face looks red and puffy from crying but I can see it, the hand mark where someone has hurt my child.

I look up accusingly at the man still daring to be here. Still daring to act like this is okay.

"She had a nosebleed." He shrugs like it's not even a big deal.

I raise an eyebrow at him. It's such a blatant lie and he thinks he'll get away with it?

"He hit me mummy." Lara whispers. As if she's afraid to tell the truth, afraid in this moment that I'll let it go, that I won't protect her.

My anger surges, I can feel myself shaking as my adrenaline pumps through me. I put my arms on Lara's shoulders, manoeuvring her out the way of this.

"You hit my child?" I say.

"It was an accident." He says but I hear that smug arrogant attitude. He's not even trying to be convincing. He really thinks I'm just going to let this go doesn't he.

"You hit my child." I scream it.

And then suddenly I'm seeing red. All reason, all logic is gone. I don't think about the consequences. I don't think about anything but making this bastard pay.

I launch myself at him and as we collide, we fall onto the floor, but I land on top. I land on him.

"You dare hurt my daughter."

I'm punching him, one fist and then another. I don't stop. I don't relent.

He tries to fight back but in this moment I'm too powerful, too full of rage and fury and pent up emotions that have been locked, trapped, encaged for so long that now that it's out it's like an explosion.

"How many times have you hurt her?" I shout. "How many times have you dared to lay a finger on my child?"

He can't reply. He groans out as I deliver blow after blow.

But I'm not stopping. I won't stop. This bastard has dared to touch Lara. Dared to beat a six year old. He's an adult for fucksake. He's a grown man.

This moment here is for Lara, this moment here is for her to see that I'm not just sitting idly by, that I will protect her, that I will do everything I can to ensure she is safe.

And I'll admit part of this is for me too. I have to prove that I have some power, I have to prove that I am protecting her, that I've not just brought her to the wolves and let them feast on her corpse.

"You bastard." I yell delivering a perfect right hook.

He lets out a whimper. A pathetic noise that if anything makes me hit him harder.

"You absolute bastard." I land another punch breaking that hook nose of his. I guess that's karma isn't it?

But my hands are a mess now, they're covered in blood and I'm not so sure some of it isn't mine. I know I'm crushing knuckles. I know I'm breaking my own fingers but I don't care. I hate this man. I hate every minute that he's forced my daughter to endure.

"Rose."

I don't look around. I just continue beating him.

And then I'm dragged off, hauled up by my arms, and I swing a punch delivering a perfect fucking uppercut to Darius's jaw.

He jolts. His face registering the pain.

And then my stomach twists.

I freeze, panting, as it feels like an entire bucket of ice cold water is dropped on me.

Darius narrows his eyes, rubbing where it's already bruising. He looks down at the man still sprawled on the floor.

He's not making any sounds now. He's not even whimpering anymore.

One of the guards nudges him with his boot. He doesn't move. He's just lying there, like a useless piece of shit with his face so marred it's hard to believe he even had one.

"He's dead." Someone else says.

A smile creeps across my lips at those words. Dead huh? That's a shame. A real fucking shame.

Darius grabs me, hauling me by my throat till my feet barely touch the ground.

"Why the fuck did you do that for?" He growls.

"He hurt my daughter." I say back though my voice is constricted from the angle he's got me at.

He drops his hold, studying me, like he doesn't know how to react to that.

Maybe I am crazy now. Maybe he has broken me but not in the way he intended. "I will kill anyone that lays a finger on her."

He tilts his head like he's realising what he's creating. Like it's dawning on him that I'm not a broken little creature huddled in the corner now. That I'm twisting, turning into something dark too.

I step back away from all of them and pull Lara into my arms.

And then I face off against him once more. "If any of your men, any one of you dare even look at her with contempt, I will rip out your eyeballs and gut you."

"You won't do shit." Darius snarls.

"You want to push me on that?" I say. "You really want to see how far a mother will go to protect her child?"

He lifts his chin, no doubt feeling that punch I delivered and he walks out shouting for someone to clean up the damned mess.

"Mummy." Lara whispers as soon as he's gone.

I squat back down, check her face. My hands hurt now, they're absolutely throbbing but I don't care, Lara is my first concern. She always will be.

Her nose has stopped bleeding but her face is still smeared with dried blood.

"Let's get you cleaned up." I say leading her away from all the arseholes still around us.

WE'RE IN A BATHROOM. I LOCKED THE DOOR DESPITE THE FACT I'M not allowed to.

I put her up on the marble counter and fill the sink with warm water.

"Why didn't you tell me?" I ask gently. I know it's not the first time he's done it. All my instincts tell me that.

She sniffles. "I'm sorry mummy."

"Don't apologise baby." I say cupping her cheek. "You have nothing to apologise for."

She nods but I still see it, that confusion. She's too young to understand all this. Too young to be in this situation, dealing with all the shit Darius keeps throwing at us. I need to get better at protecting her. I need to be a better mother to her.

"If anyone ever hurts you, if anyone ever says anything to you, you tell me okay?" I say.

She nods again.

I let out a sigh, dropping a towel into the water, and carefully start dabbing at her skin, ignoring that searing pain from my fingers all the while.

It doesn't look broken. I think he just backhanded her but it was enough. It was more than enough.

"You killed him mummy." Lara says.

I pause meeting her eyes. I can see she's trying to process this, trying to get her head around what she's just witnessed.

"I thought killing people was wrong but you killed him and daddy killed Mrs Bates when he rescued me."

I remember that. I remember us sat in Lara's room, watching her sleep that first night after he found her, and Roman confessing it.

He shot her because she wouldn't let Lara go. I feel a wave of pride in that. It's unfathomable. Ridiculous even. He'd done that to protect our child. He'd done what he knew was necessary.

But I remember him holding my hand, squeezing it, and us both for that brief, beautiful moment, just able to enjoy being parents for once.

I'll never be able to hold his hand again. I'll never be able to touch him again.

"Killing people is wrong." I say. I can't deny that. And I won't let her grow up with a warped sense or morals. "But I was angry and he was hurting you. I needed to set an example to everyone here. I need them to understand that no one can hurt you."

"They hurt you mummy." She says and my heart breaks at that. That she sees it, that she knows.

My tears drop. I hang my head because I don't want her to see but I'm so distraught in the knowledge that she *has* seen. She knows. It's another thing I haven't shielded her from. Another part of her innocence chipped away.

"I know baby." I say pulling her in, wrapping my arms around her. "But it doesn't matter."

"Yes it does." She says more forcefully. "It does matter."

"I will take everything they give because it protects you Lara, do you understand that? I love you so much, I will never let them hurt you again."

"I don't want you too." She sobs. "I don't want you to get hurt."

"I know."

"It's my fault they're hurting you." She states.

I grit my teeth meeting her gaze. "Why do you think that?"

"They say it. The guards. They tell me that no one wants me here. That my daddy is dead and I should be dead too."

My stomach lurches. My anger rages again and I think for a minute I might just go on an actual rampage. Except I can't, I have to focus on Lara, on comforting her. Now is not the time for more violence.

"They're lying Lara. Every one of them is lying."

"But daddy is dead." She cries.

"You can't listen to them. You can't believe what they're saying." I soothe her.

"I want my daddy. I want to go home." She sobs harder and this time I don't try to hold it in, I don't pretend.

I cry with her.

I stand there, holding my child, crying for so long I think we both run out of tears.

I'm a murderer now. I'm as bad as Darius and my father and all of them. And yet I know, if the circumstances repeated, I would do it again. I wouldn't hesitate.

They've made me into this and I refuse to feel any shame, any guilt. I'm not a victim, I won't be one. I will survive by any means possible and I will do everything necessary to ensure Lara survives.

22

ROSE

I'm sat in his damned home office, with the doctor strapping my fingers up.

Turns out I did break bones. Three of them to be exact. And I've severely bruised the knuckles on both hands as well.

But I'd do it again.

Even now.

If one of the arseholes around me even thinks of saying something to Lara I swear to god I will start throwing punches again and I won't stop until they either put a bullet in my head or they're dead themselves.

And I think Darius can see it.

I think he can tell that this has gone too far.

He's pacing, his eyes fixed on me, but his face shows that he's trying to figure out next steps. Trying to make some sort of plan about what to do.

Good. I hope I've unnerved the bastard. He thinks I'm just some weak willed woman. He thinks that after all the abuse I've endured that I'll simply shrink into myself, that I won't react to it too.

I watch him with a curl of my lips. I'm enjoying his obvious discomfort. It's nice to see the shoe on the other foot though I know it won't last for long. That he will make me pay for this. He'll have to assert his control over me.

The doctor finishes strapping the three fingers on my left hand, leaving only my index and thumb free and then he moves to my right, examining the middle and ring finger before he pulls out more supplies.

He mutters, like he's never seen such damage on a girl before. Like Darius hasn't hurt me worse than that.

I don't reply. I keep my gaze on Darius. But with my now spare hand I reach out for Lara, keeping her close. Ensuring he sees it too.

He made his point back when he murdered that girl and right now, I'm making my point.

Someone walks in breaking this standoff between us. As I look I realise it's Ty and I narrow my eyes. He's here more and more these days. Lurking in the peripheries. I wonder how he's fitting into all this. What new part my father's given him.

His eyebrows raises when he sees my hands but I can tell he's already heard what's happened.

As if that tips the scales Darius steps towards me. I tense up, ready for this next round of fighting.

"You killed the tutor." He says.

I smirk more. Maybe this is the part I have to play from now on. Maybe I need to become more deranged, more psychotic to deal with this. More fucked up.

"How is she going to study now?" He asks like that's my primary concern.

"I don't give a fuck about her studies." I state. She's six years old for Christ sake, I doubt it even matters considering the circumstances we're in.

He snarls slamming his fist into a lamp sending it smashing to the floor. "So what, you think I'll just let the brat run riot is that it?"

"You dare…" I begin pulling my hand free from the doctor. I'll fucking have him for that comment.

He grabs my throat, even as my fist lands into the side of his head.

"Stop." Ty says.

I don't look at him. I don't look at anyone except the monster who has me in his grasp.

"Mummy." Lara whispers.

"You're scaring her." Darius taunts. "Look at your daughter, look what you're doing to her. Do you really want her to think that this is who you are Rose? That you're some psycho bitch?"

I let out a laugh. Like hell his manipulation will work. "Lara knows who I am." I say. "She knows I will fight every one of you to protect her. That I will die protecting her."

He raises an eyebrow squeezing just enough to make my eyeballs bulge.

I don't know what the doctor thinks but he certainly doesn't say anything, he just stands there watching this interaction, like all the guards are, unmoving, uncaring by all accounts.

"Send her away." Ty says.

My eyes dart to him, my panic seems to soar. What the fuck?

Darius turns his head but his grip is still so tight around my throat. "Excuse me?"

Ty doesn't look at me, he keeps his gaze on Darius. "There's a boarding school on the outskirts of the city. Send Lara there, that way she's out of your hair and she gets the education you so clearly want her to have."

My heart twists, I screw my face up. What the hell is this?

"No." I say.

Darius drops his hold stepping back with that grin on his face he gets when he comes up with a plan he knows is going to work.

"Get me the details." Darius says.

"I already have." Ty replies pulling out a leaflet, handing it to him like this is already a done deal.

I stare at it in horror. This can't be happening. They can't separate us.

"Mummy?" Lara says and I move going to grab her but Darius is quicker. He snaps his fingers and the guards are there, pulling us apart, wrenching me from her before our hands even touch.

"No." I scream.

"You think there wouldn't be consequences? You think you could just kill the tutor and I wouldn't punish you for it?" He snarls.

"We agreed." I gasp. "We agreed that Lara would stay here, with me."

His lips twists. "But you've not kept up your end of the agreement, you've not been playing ball have you Rose?"

"Don't take her from me. Please Darius." I cry.

But he just grins harder.

I look at Ty, at my cousin who's created this situation, he meets my gaze and for a second I swear he mouths the words 'trust me' behind Darius's back.

Only I can't.

He's done nothing to prove he's on my side. Nothing to show that.

I go feral, I lash out, I completely lose it as Lara is dragged from the room. Darius follows after her saying he wants her packed up and at the school within the hour and that she can stay away for the holidays too.

I'm screaming, fighting, doing everything I can to stop this but my hands are as useless as my actions.

I think even the guards can't face it and instead they leave me here, broken, slumped on the floor, whimpering like a broken bird that knows they'll never find freedom, that they'll never fly again.

They're stealing my daughter again. Taking her away and I can't even say goodbye.

I bury my face, cover my head with my hands, rocking my body back and forth. Telling myself over and over that every hurt they're delving I'm going to deliver back tenfold. I will make Darius pay for this if it's the last thing I do.

"Rose."

I stiffen, looking up at the judas stood before me.

He squats down cupping my face and flinch from the contact. "Trust me Rose." He says.

"Why should I?" I snarl.

He lets out a low breath glancing to the doors, to where we both know the guards are stood still listening.

"I'm doing this for both of you." He says so quietly.

"You're doing this aid your own advancement." I snap back. "You're doing this so that Darius will give you something in return."

"What can he give me?" He asks. "What could he possibly offer me when the one thing I want is trapped the same way you are?"

I screw my face up. What the fuck is he talking about? Who is trapped?

"Rose." He says gently. "Look at it this way, Lara will be free of this place, free of all the abuse."

I know that's true. I can't deny that. But she'll also be far from my protection. What will happen when she gets to that school? Where will she sleep? How will she adapt to such an alien surrounding? She's never even been around other children.

"She's my daughter." I gasp.

"She can't grow up like this, she can't live like this." He says as if he understands my child's needs better than I do.

But he's right there too. She can't stay like this, not after what she confessed, not after seeing the way everyone is treating her.

But I don't want to lose her. I only just got her back.

"I can't…" I sob feeling like my heart is ripping in half and that same awful breathlessness threatens to overtake me.

"She'll be safe, she'll be with people who love her." He states.

I screw my face up. What the fuck does that mean? How can anyone at that school love her better than her own mother? He's making it sound like I'm the one being selfish here, that I'm the one hurting her.

"Let her be free Rose, let her go, and focus on saving yourself."

I hang my head. I can't save myself. I feel too broken now, All that confidence, all the twisted darkness that was festering in me barely an hour ago is lost now that I have don't have Lara to protect.

He picks me up, holds me to him and hugs me, whispering so quietly. "This will end. I promise you."

"You don't know what you're talking about." I reply. How can it end? I have no way of ending it now beyond killing Darius and then killing myself.

And what would that mean for Lara? She'd be at the mercy of my parents then.

I can't do that. I won't do that. That's not a viable option. Not a viable outcome for Lara.

"Roman is coming." He states.

My heart stops. My body freezes. I clutch him like my life depends upon it. There's no way he just said that. No fucking way.

He looks at me, meeting my gaze and nods only enough that I can see.

"He's alive Rose." He states, more mouthing the words than actually speaking them. "He's alive. And he's going to save you."

I let out a sob. A wail. It sounds as pathetic as I feel right now. How is he alive? How is this not all some trick.

"If he was alive then I wouldn't be here." I reply. "He wouldn't have left us like this. He would have stormed this building, he would have killed everyone to get us out, he…"

He shakes his head. "We can't do that. It's not possible. So we're bringing him down a different way this time."

"We?" I repeat as if the word makes no sense to me.

"I'm helping him. Helping Roman."

I scoff. This is a joke. No way would Ty help Roman. He hates him. He hates all the Montagues. He always has. And more so since Roman killed Tybalt. He's never forgiven Roman for murdering the brother that he looked up to like an idol.

"I am Rose. Do you think I'm happy to just sit here and watch all of this? Do you think I'm as fucked up as Darius is, as your father is?"

I don't reply. But I can see he can tell what I want to say. That I did think that. That I believed that.

"I'm helping Roman." He states.

"How?" I want facts, I want substance. Not just words.

My pain is turning to anger again. If Roman is alive, then why the hell has he left us here all these months? Why hasn't he reached out? Why am I only hearing this now? I can feel myself shaking and it's hard to tell if it's from anger or pain.

"I'm passing information. I'm his spy."

I scan his face trying to see the lie in those words.

"We're going to show the entire city what Darius is." He continues. "We're going to dismantle his entire power structure and then we'll cut off his head."

"Why can't you do that after?" I snap. "Why can't you get rid of Darius first and then…"

"Because Roman tried that already. That's what he was doing last time and look how that turned out."

I look away. My body trembling to the point that it's uncontrollable. I don't know what to think. I don't know how to process any of this right now.

"Trust me Rose, trust Roman, trust what we're doing."

"I want to help." I say.

He shakes his head. "No, it's too dangerous."

"Seriously?" I reply. "You think I just want to stay here, waiting, enduring everything Darius does to me?"

He shuts his eyes. "No." He says again.

"I can help. I have to help, I have to do something or I really will go mad. Besides, I know things you don't. Darius tells me things."

"What?"

I grit my teeth. Admitting this is shameful but I've been shamed so much it doesn't matter now. None of it does. "He taunts me with things he's doing, uses them as proof that I can't beat him."

His eyes flash bloody murder. "Alright." He says. "Tell me what you know, but Roman can decide what to use of the information you give."

I nod, my stomach fluttering like he's actually giving me something.

And then we hear it, someone approaching. Ty loosens his arms, clearly trying to let me go, but I grab him back.

"Wait." I say. "If you want to help, truly help, then get me something, anything that will mean I can't get pregnant."

"What?"

"You heard. Darius is fixated on it. I need to make sure that doesn't happen."

He physically shudders as if what I'm asking is repulsive and maybe in a way it is. Maybe it's shameful to speak it but I won't let him trap me, I won't let myself become more connected to Darius than I already am.

"Okay." He says.

"And tell Roman, tell him that I love him. Tell him…" My voice falters as the door opens. God I have so much I want to say, so much I need to say.

"I will." Ty mouths before letting me go.

I drop my gaze, returning to the broken thing they expect me to be.

And Ty walks away leaving me alone with Darius once more.

ROMAN

I should wait.

I know I should.

But I'm not going too.

Not now.

Not when I've waited so long.

Not when she's waited so long.

Not when she's right here within my grasp and I can actually do something. I can actually save one of them.

I walk down the hallway. I can hear the chatter of children around me, I can see them too, playing in the fields, it looks like they're in the midst of a game of football.

Holden is beside me. Ben is behind because this building is too old and narrow for us to walk three abreast.

We planned this out, planned this exact school, I just didn't expect Ty to be able to set it in motion so quickly. Apparently Darius was more than happy to ship my child off and I don't want to think about what it will do to Rose to have separated them.

When we reach the headmaster's office I rap my knuckles on the door.

A curt answer comes through the wood and we walk in.

He's sat behind a huge antique desk, not unlike the one my father had. He frowns taking the three of us in.

I know ordinarily three men wouldn't be able to walk into a school unchecked and I can see he's disarmed by it.

"Who are you?" He asks.

I draw myself up. Sliding a photo across the desk.

"This girl was just sent here, correct?"

He glances down then looks at me. "I can't confirm…"

"You will." I snap back. "This girl is my daughter."

He shakes his head. "No, the girl is…"

I cut across him again. "I'm not here for a conversation."

"If you think I will hand her over…"

"You will." I state.

He narrows his eyes. "We have a duty of care. The parents of this school expect their children to be safe here."

"I'm not disputing that." I reply, pulling out a seat, sinking into it. I'll try a different tactic, see how this works if he wants to be difficult.

I place the gun on the desk.

He physically jolts as he takes it in.

And then I pull out the photos. The all too explicit images of him and his secretary. They'll ruin his marriage, ruin his career too. He gulps staring at them.

I don't say the words but we both know what this is. That I'm blackmailing him.

"Get my daughter." I say. "Have her brought here and if she doesn't recognise me then we'll leave. No further questions. No further hassle."

He shakes his head. "I'm not endangering…"

I smirk leaning forward. "Get my daughter. Now." I growl.

He shuts his eyes, clearly he still wants to refuse me but he's also shitting himself right now and I can't say that I blame him. I wouldn't want to be faced off against me in this moment.

He leans forward, pushes a button on the intercom and mutters into it.

And then we sit there, me and him, while Holden and Ben stand behind us acting like guards. All of us silent. All of us waiting.

The door opens. I turn before I can stop myself and my eyes land on her. There's a teacher stood behind her, clearly they escorted her here.

She's got a bruise across her face. Her hair is scraped back into a tight plait. She's in a little uniform, complete with a tie done up to her neck and a little plaid skirt that's a size too big and comes down past her knees.

My eyes widen. She's grown. Even in these few months, she's changed so much.

She looks around the room with such a look of fear in her eyes before they settle on me.

And then she's running, crying, throwing herself into my arms as I catch her.

"Daddy." She sobs.

"It's okay Sweetpea."

"I knew you weren't dead. I knew you weren't."

I hold her so tight I don't think either of us can breathe. I'm no longer in the chair, I'm on my knees, on the cold tile floors, holding her like my very existence depends upon her.

The gun is still there, on the desk, all but forgotten about. Ben reaches across and takes it before the headmaster gets any funny ideas.

"Daddy." Lara sobs again.

"It's okay." I say sweeping her hair back. "Daddy's got you. No one is going to hurt you now."

"They have mummy." She replies. "They hurt mummy."

My stomach twists. I feel a flash of fury not only that they're doing that, but that Lara has witnessed it, that my child has obviously been traumatised by it.

I scoop her up, holding her the same way I did the first time I rescued her and she wraps her legs around my waist.

"Are we going home now?" She asks.

I kiss her forehead, glancing at the man who I know is no longer going to argue the merits about his precious school safety while he's banging a subordinate.

"We're going home Lara." I say walking out. Leaving Holden and Ben to follow after me.

I SIT IN THE BACK OF THE VAN. LARA IS IN MY LAP, REFUSING TO EVEN let me go for a minute.

"I knew you'd come back daddy." She says.

I give her my best smile. "I'm sorry it took so long."

She shakes her head. "It's okay." She murmurs but I can see it's not. I can see the way she is now, that old spark is dimmed. My daughter is not the same as she was.

"Who hit you?" I ask.

She scrunches her face up. "My tutor."

I raise an eyebrow. It doesn't look fresh enough to be from the school. What kind of school would hurt a child anyway?

"Mummy killed him for it." She says.

Ben chokes. I swear Holden almost swerves off the road at the way she just says it so calmly. So matter of fact.

"Mummy did what?" I ask trying to act like this is all normal. A perfectly natural conversation between a father and his child.

She looks at me frowning. "She punched him daddy. She punched him until he was dead."

Fucking hell. Rose did that? My Rose? I don't know what to think, on one hand I'm so proud of her, that she's protecting our daughter, but on the other hand, she beat a man to death in front of Lara. What the fuck?

"She said she wanted them all to know." Lara says studying my face.

"Know what?" I reply.

She juts her chin, a look of defiance so reminiscent of her mother. "What happens if they hurt me. That she'll kill them all. She said she'd rip their eyeballs out daddy."

I gulp. Jesus fucking Christ. I don't know why I'm so shocked. I know I'd do the same, I'd act the same and yet to think that my Rose is, it's unnerving because what the hell has she gone through to become like this, to act like this?

I wrap my arms around her tighter. "It's over Sweetpea. You never have to see any of that shit again."

She buries her face into me and I can feel it, her relief. But she's not relaxed entirely. In truth she feels like a rocket about to go off at any moment.

"Are we getting mummy now?" She asks.

Holden and Ben exchange a look. I feel my heart sink because how do I explain to my child that I'm knowingly letting her mummy stay in a place like that? That I'm not saving her too.

She looks between us pushing her body off of mine.

"I want mummy." She says.

"I know Sweetpea." I say as gently as I can.

She shakes her head, her eyes filling with tears as she realises we're not going to get Rose right now. "I want my mummy." She says louder. More forcefully.

I try to hug her again but suddenly she's screaming, having a full on tantrum.

"I want my mummy. I want my mummy."

She's screaming it over and over. I can't calm her down, I can't do anything as she completely loses control, slamming her fists into me, into the seat, into the metal of the frame.

"It's okay." I try to say but she's so far beyond any form of reason.

I can't reach her in this moment, I can't even get close.

ROMAN

By the time we get back to the tunnels Lara has cried herself into exhaustion. She's slumped against me, the tears still streaming down her cheeks, but she's stopped screaming now.

It's like she's given up.

I hate it. I hate the look in her eyes. I hate the defeat.

We come to a stop. I unclip the seatbelt around her and pull her out. She whimpers but she doesn't do anything, she feels like a dead weight in my arms.

"We're home Sweetpea." I say.

She looks around and then frowns.

"This isn't home." She says. Her voice sounds empty. Devoid of emotion.

I let out a sigh. I know it isn't but it's all we have right now.

She jerks in my arms. "I want to get down." She states and I let her. I won't force her to do anything she doesn't want, especially now when it feels like that trust we had has crumbled to nothing.

As she stands she looks around. Peers into the stark concrete ahead of her.

"What is this place?"

"It's a tunnel." I say. "We're safe here. No one can get to us."

She looks at me then narrows her eyes. "We're underground?"

"Yeah." I murmur.

She clicks her jaw. "Princesses don't live underground." She states. "Monsters do."

I crouch down, scanning her red, puffy, angry face. "Now we're the monsters Lara. We're the ones who are going to come up, to take back everything they've stolen from us."

She scrunches her face up. "I want mummy back. That's all I want."

"We'll get her back. I promise you." I say

She huffs and then walks away from me like she doesn't believe me anymore. Like she thinks all my promises mean nothing now. I guess I can't blame her. I didn't save her, I didn't save Rose, after everything I said, everything I'd promised them last time.

Ben pats me on the back. "She'll be okay. Just give her some time."

I grunt in reply because I'm not sure that's true. She's a child, she shouldn't have witnessed half the things she has already and with Rose gone, it feels like that trauma is just festering inside her.

I need Rose back.

We both need her back.

And my guilt for leaving her there, for removing her child and leaving her alone in all this multiplies.

WE GET HER SETTLED INTO A ROOM. KOEN'S MEN HAVE ALREADY SUP-plied a bed and some essential things. Someone even managed to get her a doll, though I've never seen her playing with one.

She sits there staring at the blank grey walls.

And then those tears start to stream down her cheeks again.

My heart twists, I want to say something, anything to make this better but what the fuck can I say? What can I do? The one thing she wants, the one thing we both need is the one thing I cannot give her.

I turn to go, to give her a little space, but a flash of movement makes me look. Makes me pause.

Lara gasps holding her arms up and Bella jumps right into her lap.

"Bella. My puppy." She says burying her head into her fur.

I sink down onto the bed beside her. She doesn't look at me, just continues cuddling the dog.

"We found her in the ruins." I say. "I don't know how she survived."

Maybe I shouldn't have admitted that. Maybe I should have kept that to myself.

Lara looks at me then. "I hid her." She says.

"What?"

"When those men came, when they started shooting at everyone I hid Bella and me in the cupboard. I didn't want them to find us. Only they got me anyway."

I lift my hand wanting so desperately to hold her but instead I stroke the dog.

She watches me as I do it. "Mummy must be missing Bella too." She says with such a small voice.

I nod. "Yeah she must be." I agree. "Can you take care of her? Can you look after Bella for mummy till she gets back?"

Lara looks at me with fresh tears in her eyes. "Okay daddy."

"There's my girl." I say cupping her face. I can feel how wet her cheeks are. She's trembling too.

"She has to have that special food remember." She mumbles.

"I know. We've got it here." I reassure her.

And then she's hugging me, burying her face into my body. "I missed you so much."

"I missed you too." I reply.

She heaves into my body, moulds herself into me as I hold her so tightly.

"I was so scared. The whole time. I was so scared." She sobs.

"I know you were Sweetpea. I'm so sorry I couldn't get to you sooner."

"Why couldn't you?" She asks.

I take in a deep breath. "I had an accident."

"Were you hurt?"

I nod. "But I'm better now."

"Did they do that to you? Did they hurt you too?"

I nod again.

"They hurt you so you couldn't save us?" She guesses.

I meet her gaze. I'm not going to lie. I want her to understand this, even if she's too young to get the full subtleties. "They planned this. They planned to break us up."

"Why?"

I grit my teeth. It's a step too far to tell her why. "Because they're bad men Lara. Bad people."

"I hate them." She says.

"Me too."

"I hate Darius the most."

I squeeze her tighter, hearing the venom in her voice, hating the sound of his name on her lips.

"He hurts mummy. He hurts her and tells her it's her fault."

My stomach drops at that. It takes all my strength not to lose my shit. "What?"

She looks at me, and I see it all the trauma there in her face. "He's a liar daddy. A nasty, horrible liar."

"Yes he is." I reply as those words sink in. As it really hits home how much Rose is suffering right now.

ROSE

We're sat, facing each other across the ornate dining table.

He's staring at me.

And I'm staring at my plate unsure how I can even manage a mouthful. My hands are practically useless, I can only just hold the fork in my right hand. I guess he'll be keeping me locked here, out of view until the bones heal because he wouldn't want anyone to get the wrong idea now would he?

But she is gone.

My daughter is gone.

The room feels empty, the house feels more desolate than ever. Like I'm living in a tomb, a mausoleum and I'm just biding my time, waiting till he does enough to kill me.

He hasn't even said what school she's at. Hasn't even said that she's okay.

But he seems happier, like some great weight has lifted. Did her presence really affect him that much? I guess so considering she was a walking reminder of everything me and Roman were. Everything I would kill to get back.

He takes a sip of his wine before letting out a long sigh.

"I don't want to be like this." He says.

"Like what?" I ask.

"This."

I look at him and then instantly regret it. All those emotions, all that hate comes flooding back. It's all I can do not to pick up the knife in front of me and gut him.

"I love you Rose." He says.

"No you don't." I reply.

He shakes his head, slamming his fist onto the table, making me half jump out of my chair. "Why are you so difficult?"

"What else did you expect?"

He snarls, clenching his fists once more. "You weren't like this with Paris. You were obedient to him."

I let out a laugh and it sounds so hollow, echoing off the walls.

"No I wasn't." I say.

He tilts his head. "I watched you, I saw how the two of you were. You were his perfect wife."

My stomach twists, maybe that's what the world saw but that wasn't how I was. I just got very good a pretending when we were out in public.

But that was before, before Roman came back, before I realised that he hadn't tricked me, that he hadn't played me. It was easy to be a robot, easy to pretend when my heart was made of stone but now, now I know what really happened, and for those few weeks we were together, my soul lived in a way I know I'll never get back.

I'll never feel that again.

And the man sat opposite me is the very reason why.

So I guess it's no wonder I can't be that anymore. He's the reason.

"I want you to be my perfect wife." He states.

"I don't give a shit what you want." I reply.

He screws his face up. "Do you like me hurting you? Is that it?"

I glare at him. Like he doesn't get off on it. Like he doesn't enjoy putting the fear of god into me.

"You stole my child." I state. "You stole her away…"

"You brought that on yourself." He says. "Besides what does she matter when we will have children of our own?"

I grit my teeth. That's not happening. No fucking way am I doing that. "I don't want your child." I half spit. I'm not simply going to replace Lara like she's some broken object.

He acts like I've not even spoken. He takes a mouthful of food and then continues on.

"We should sort a nursery. Maybe it's a bit premature but I like the idea of being ready."

"I said no."

He looks at me, tilts his head. "I'll speak with your mother. I'm sure the two of you would love another shopping trip. You can buy things for the baby, for our new family."

"I'm not pregnant. And I won't be getting pregnant."

He takes another mouthful, that smug smile on his face. "I want a boy first but if we have a girl I won't complain."

I don't reply then. I just give up. It doesn't matter what he says, none of this matters. Besides he had my IUD removed so it's not like I can stop this.

But Roman is out there, Roman is coming. I just have to play ball, pretend for as long as I can now and know that he is going to make Darius pay. I just hope he does it quickly enough that I'm not carrying his child.

He reaches across, takes my broken left hand in his and though he's being gentle enough I still fight the whimper of pain.

"I want to be kind to you Rose, I want to treat you right."

"Then let me go." The words are out my mouth before I can stop them.

He shakes his head. "That's not an option." He states. "So how about we start afresh? We used to enjoy each other's company, do you remember, we used to flirt with one another, tease one another."

I shut my eyes. I know I did flirt with him but it wasn't to lead him on, it wasn't because I wanted him in any romantic way, it was just that's how everyone behaves with him. I wasn't looking for something more. I wasn't after something more.

"Let's take a walk."

"What?" I reply.

"Now, let's go outside. Let's work together, to make this right."

"I don't want too." I reply. I want to hide in our room, cry myself to sleep. Mourn the loss of my child as well as the never ending pain of losing Roman.

Being outside, being in public means I have to pretend. I have to be all sunshine and roses when inside I'm more dead than ever.

He ignores my remark. Gets to his feet and gives me a look that forces me to mine too.

And then he's walking us to the front of the house, wrapping a coat around my shoulders, hiding my hands in sheepskin gloves, and all but forcing me out the door while the bodyguards ensure they're close behind.

The Governor's House is in the best part of the Bay. It stands with the back facing the beautiful cliffs and sea and the sprawling front looks onto the promenade meaning we're pretty much in the hustle of the city as soon as we're out past the gates.

Darius's arm wraps around me, he pulls my body into his in what would look like a loving embrace. I can smell him. I can smell the musty cologne he wears and the hint of cigarettes because he's taken up smoking again from all the stress.

But under that I can smell the alcohol too.

The nights he properly drinks, the nights he's sat alone in his office brooding are my worst. Because I know how they always end. With drunken outbursts, and violence.

Though I guess now the silver lining is I don't have to hide that from Lara anymore.

I don't have to stifle my cries or work so hard to cover the bruises. The next time he beats me I can simply hide in our room, try and recover without having to force a smile on my face for her sake.

"My grandfather had this built." He says bringing me out of my head.

"Had what built?" I reply.

"This walkway. The old one was falling to ruin, so he funded a new one. He funded a lot of the building works, turning this city into the beauty it is today."

I don't know what to say to that. The Blumenfeld's are the wealthiest family here, even my father's wealth pales in significance and I know Darius uses his influence as Governor to ensure his own pockets are suitably lined.

"You used to play here." He says.

"What?"

He grins. "I used to watch you, you'd run up and down this front while your mother tried to get you to behave."

When the hell was that? I frown trying to recall it but I have no memory of it whatsoever.

"You were only five or six, tiny then."

My stomach turns at that. I don't know why but it makes me feel more sickened about all of this.

"Why were you watching me?" I ask.

He shrugs. "I wasn't Governor, back then I was simply running the family business, ensuring the then Governor did what we wanted, what Calvin wanted. It's what got me into politics in the first place."

Fuck, Calvin, I haven't seen or heard about him in what feels like forever. No way the bastard just dropped off a cliff. No way I would be that lucky.

"Where is he?" I ask.

"Who?"

"Calvin."

He pauses looking like he doesn't want to tell me.

I stare back at him trying to read the expression on his face. What if Darius got rid of him? What if he decided to wipe the board entirely, take the whole pot for himself. I know he's capable of it. He's already demonstrated that exact point to me.

"Did you kill him?" I ask.

His grip tightens at my words. "No Rose. Your old boy-friend did."

"Roman killed Calvin?"

He snarls. "I told you I never wanted to hear his name…"

"I know." I say quickly. "I'm sorry."

He tilts his head. "Change the subject then. Tell me something I don't know. Something about you."

"What is this?" I reply. He's acting like we're on a date. Like we're genuinely interested in one another.

"Tell me Rose."

"I don't…" I begin but he just bristles with annoyance.

I take a deep breath. I don't want to tell him anything. I don't want him knowing anything more about me.

"I used to work out. I used to enjoy working out." It's pathetic, lame, he might just see right through it, after all everyone used to go on and on about my physique. There was a whole corner of social media dedicated to getting the 'Rose body'.

"You used to have a dog too." He remarks.

I wince then and my heart twists more with pain. Bella, my poor Bella. I try not to think of her, I hate thinking of her now.

"I can get you another one. A puppy." He says as if she's re-placeable as well.

"No." I say. I don't want that. I don't want another living thing reliant on me. Bella is dead, gone, Carter took great delight in telling me that fact, in telling me how he'd chased her down and gutted her with a knife himself.

I think that broke me as much as seeing Lara in the hands of Sampson. Seeing her being held like she's some sort of criminal in those first few weeks after everything collapsed around me.

"You don't go to the clubhouse anymore." He murmurs.

"How can I when you won't let me out of the house?"

He huffs. "Because I don't trust you Rose. Not for a damned minute."

I stop, pulling my arm back, folding them across myself. "You have my daughter as collateral, do you really think I would do anything that risks her life?"

He sizes me up. "Perhaps not."

"I'm not asking for the world here, just to be able to come and go more, to have some freedom. Please Darius. I'm not a bird you can keep locked up. Can't you see, you're killing me by keeping me as I am?"

He puts his hands on my shoulders. "I can keep you however I want Rose." He says.

"Then why are we even having this conversation?" I reply.

He smirks. "Fine, if I consider it, will you stop be such a bitch?"

I chew my lip. I don't want to give in. I don't want to just stop fighting but I can't escape while he has me under armed guard the entire time. I need to be smart. I need to act smart.

"I'll try." I say. It's the best I can do, the best I will do.

He lowers his face to mine. "Prove it." He murmurs.

I know what he wants, what he always wants when he says those words, when he acts like this.

I hate myself for doing it but I kiss him, trying to keep it light, only his arms wrap around me and he sticks his tongue into my mouth, invading my space as I clench my fists within those gloves, needing the pain of it in this moment as if it's some sort of release, some way to channel all that deep depressive emotion I have.

We're in public. We're in full view of what feels like the entire city.

I hate the taste of him, I hate the way he kisses me, the way his tongue pushes against mine.

And as we break apart I register it, the camera's the flashes. We'll be all over social media before we even get back to the house. I can see the headlines now, the Governor and his new bride, all loved up on a romantic stroll in the cool autumn evening.

I feel a slash of guilt at that. Betrayal too. He's just stolen my child, literally from my arms and I'm here tonguing him like it doesn't matter. Like Lara doesn't matter.

Once again I'm forced to act like the whore the world has made of me when all I want to do is disappear, retreat, lose myself in only Roman's touch. Roman's arms. Roman's love.

ROMAN

It's going to be a long week.

A good week.

A week we send a message to the entirety of Verona.

They spent so long living with their heads in the sand, deliberately ignoring all the flashing red warning lights that show what's really going on. But now they're going to realise that they're not immune from all of this, that their actions have consequences and after tonight I'm going to have each and every one of them looking over their shoulders, wondering if they're next.

We start off on the outskirts of town. Koen makes sure we have enough bikes and people to overpower any militia Darius might have lurking and by the time any reinforcements get to us we'll be long gone.

Holden heads up one team. I head up another. I know Koen has three already on route to the main substations and if they're successful we'll all witness the evidence of it.

When we get to the reservoir it's more guarded than I antici-pated but within minutes we've shot down everything that moves.

We've been strategic with our targets. We picked this one out especially and as I start planting the bombs I can't help but feel a thrill of excitement, of glee. Finally I am doing something. Finally I am making a point.

It takes a good ten minutes to ensure they're all were they need to be. We have to do this right, to blow this up in such a way that all the water fucks off down the valley and we don't end up drowning ourselves.

But that's also why we choose this one for the big explosion.

Verona has two reservoirs. Two massive artificial lakes that feed the city and ensure that even during the height of summer all the grass is green and every swimming pool is filled and sprinkler can flow.

Darius isn't stupid. He knows that this infrastructure is vital to keeping his power.

And that's exactly why I'm going to take this right out from under him.

I step back, far enough that I know the explosion won't reach me and without hesitation I hit the detonator.

The sound is like thunder. The very earth beneath me seems to shake as if this were natural.

I can hear the rush of water, the sound of it cascading down the hill.

And just as the silence settles in, I hear another explosion. And then another.

Both of them are far off. In the distance. Miles away from where we are. I turn my head staring down to the city beneath me and I can see the evidence of what Koen has done. What his teams have done.

Gone are the glittering lights. Gone are all the sparkles of Verona. It's pitch black. As if the city isn't even there. The only thing visible is the car lights, that look like insignificant specs.

But the noise, the sound of vehicles beeping turns the darkness into chaos.

I get back on my borrowed bike, luckily for us there's a tunnel entrance not far from here, and we've been amassing fuel all week to ensure our own generators keep everything underground powered.

We've been amassing water too. And food. We've really have got enough to survive a nuclear holocaust and for once I find that thought a relief.

Holden's voice comes through the earpiece. "It's done."

I pick it up, speaking into it as the ten of our group ride away. "You got it all in?"

"Every drop." Holden says.

I grin at that.

We couldn't take out the other reservoir without causing serious casualties and while this city has a lot of answer for, the only blood I want on my hands is Darius and his cronies.

But leaving the reservoir intact meant blowing this one up wouldn't have the same effect. We needed to take out both. We need to twist the knife and ensure Darius feels the pressure point tightening.

Poison seemed like a good back up plan. Nothing too insidious mind. Just enough to cause sickness, diarrhoea, the kind of things to make it undrinkable.

And ensure Verona's water supply will barely last the month.

"I'll see you back at base." I say.

We've got more planning to do. This is just the first act. The first melee.

Tomorrow night, tomorrow, we're going to really hit Darius where it hurts.

ROMAN

Maybe I'm an addict. Maybe I'm as fucked up as Darius is but watching it play out, seeing all the drama on the TV and for once Darius isn't able to hide from it, to control it, to spin it into something positive.

It took the six hours to get the electricity back and even then it's not restored the entire city. Only the hospitals, police, and government buildings have full services. Everywhere else is either still in darkness or it's being rationed.

The footage their showing is from earlier but they've got it on replay like it's the damned president on a tour.

He looks tired. He looks worn out.

I stare at his face seeing every wrinkle, every grey streak of hair. That's what Rose sees when she opens her eyes. Every day she has to look at that and smile, and pretend, and I honestly don't know how she does it.

She's got more strength than me. More resilience.

She's warrior fighting a battle that no one else seems to even notice.

She's stood beside him, holding his hand, with a look of concern that matches his.

I knew he'd parade her out. I knew he'd dust her down and flaunt her for every ounce of goodwill she can bring.

But as I watch her movements I can see she's injured. Tiny tells, tiny minuscule shifts that tell me under that beautiful cloak she's bruised and beaten.

And as she turns, I see her hand, the one clasping his, while the other is tucked out of view. Her fingers are in a cast. Two of them strapped together, leaving only her thumb and index finger free so she has to grip his hand with just them.

Did he do that? Did he break her fingers?

I guess it's telling that no one is commenting on it, that no reporters or gossip sights are even mentioning that she's injured. Clearly Darius has full control of the press now, though I expected nothing less.

I let out a snarl. Lara is beside me, staring at the screen, as if she could will Rose to walk through the glass and escape.

Maybe I shouldn't have let her watch, maybe I should have kept this from her but I didn't want to say no, besides I don't know how soon I can get to Rose, this maybe the only way Lara sees her mother over the next few months. I won't deny her this. I won't deny her anything.

She takes me hand, squeezing it as if I'm the one who needs comfort.

"Mummy looks beautiful doesn't she?" I murmur.

Lara tilts her head. "She looks sad."

I wince at that but it's true. I can see it, in her eyes, in her face, under that heavy makeup she has on to no doubt hide bruises, she does look sad. She looks heartbroken.

"Rose." I murmur her name, feeling once more like the ghost Darius made me.

I can do this. I can beat Darius. I just have to keep my control and hold my nerve. As I let out a deep sigh I see Koen stood watching us both from my peripheries.

"It's time Sweetpea." I say.

Lara nods. She doesn't even pull a face, but she gets to her feet and gives me a hug. "Good night daddy. Cuddle me when you're back."

"I will." I say planting a kiss on her head and Tia is the one who takes her hand to lead her back, to watch over her while we're out causing more shit.

"I love you Lara." I say after her.

She turns giving me what feels like a genuine smile. "I love you too Daddy."

God, I don't think I'll ever tire of hearing those words. Of seeing her face.

"You ready?" Koen says.

I get to my feet, dusting off the remainders of cake crumbs from my jeans. Yeah I'm ready. I've been ready for this one from the moment Koen showed me the place on the camera.

WHEN WE GET TO THE NEW BARN IT'S EVEN BIGGER THAN I REALISED. My stomach physically turns as I take it in. Christ how many people have been brought here? How many people have they murdered here?

Of course this place still has power. Darius has made sure his precious little money maker isn't affected.

I glance at Koen, as all his men and women. Yeah he's surprising forward thinking when it comes to this war. Or perhaps it's just we need all the help we can get.

Ben is back at the base. He's still fucked from the accident, though he's doing his best to hide it, he fucked his back up pretty bad getting me out. It's another thing I owe him for.

God, that list is getting so long I don't think I'll ever repay him.

"Ready?" Koen says.

I don't reply with words. I just cock my gun and grin.

I'm more than ready to send a message. More than ready to let Darius and everyone else in his shitty pockets know that yesterday was not it. That we're going to keep coming, keep attacking, till everyone of them is dead.

Koen sends his soldiers in first. That's how they look, how they act. I'll admit I'm impressed with how organised he is but then we're up against Darius, we have to be just as good as he is, and he's got the entire City's militia on his side.

The place is armed. Fortified. I guess he did learn something.

It takes a full ten minutes of fighting just to get in the gates.

Back at the Control Room we know they've cut all the feed, ensured no word of this can get out through CCTV, phones, radios, anything. We've created a blackout zone. Scrambled everything.

But what it means is we can't use anything either.

So we spent weeks memorising the plans, memorising which team goes where and who does what. There can't be any mistakes. We can't afford for there to be.

When we do get inside it's way worse than I expected. It's like some sci-fi futuristic nightmare. Everything is white. Sterile. To one side we know all the holding bays are. Cages essentially, by a nicer name.

And to the other side, that's where all the shit happens. Where the surgical rooms are based. Where the organ dispatch place is. Where the incinerator is also located.

We get the victims out first. Koen tells them who he is, that we're helping them, and for the most part they seem to believe us. I guess they know they're going to die anyway so perhaps they need some sort of hope.

I watch as some of the poor fuckers have tubes removed from their bodies and they hobble out.

Every organ, every bit of tissue is stolen to order. Some of these poor bastards have been here for months, waiting till there's a match. Till they're unfortunate enough that some rich arsehole needs a lung or a cornea and their genetic code means they hit the jackpot and it makes them a suitable candidate.

From what we found from Ignatio's records all those months ago some of these organs are even going out of the country. That this is an international operation. And I don't doubt Darius has been keen to spread this further, after all, there are only so many millionaires and billionaires in this country. If he wants to continue his revenue stream he has to diversify right?

Once we've got all the innocents out we turn out attention to the rest. I don't care who they are, cleaners, guards, doctors, you name it, we put a bullet in their heads. They were a part of this, they willingly helped aid this operation so they deserve everything they get.

But we make sure to document it, to take evidence. If it comes to it, we may need this to bring him down.

But just as we're pouring the gasoline, just as we're planting the explosives someone calls out. Shouts out.

I pause looking around and we all freeze as the headlights of a car illuminate the compound.

Someone is coming.

The question is, do they know we're here? Do they know what we're up to? And how much of a bloodbath is this about to turn into?

ROMAN

The men outside are smart enough to act like they belong. They do nothing to spook the vehicle as it comes to a stop.

And Koen is careful to remain out of sight because we all know his face well enough to give the game away.

When we hear the engine die shouts ring out. A few gunshots are fired but it's clear whoever is there is quickly disarmed.

I finish placing the bomb, set the detonator, and rush round to see whoever the fuck is here.

But as my eyes land on his I freeze.

He stares back at me wide eyed, as if he can't register who I am. As if he's forgotten my face. As if.

"Ignatio Capulet." I murmur.

Well, well, this evening has turned out even better than I imagined.

"You're, you're…." He splutters, fighting against the two men that are holding him in place, on his knees.

"Dead?" I finish the sentence for him with a smirk. "Not as dead as you'd like to believe."

He shakes his head. "No, you died. Darius…"

"Lied." I snap. "He pretended I was dead and you let him have Rose."

He gulps, his eyes darting as if he can work out some escape, only there is none. No mercy, no escape, no nothing but me and him.

"Get him up." I order. "Tie him up. We're taking him back with us."

The men do as I ask without question but Koen stalks up to me and for a minute I think he might argue.

I raise an eyebrow challenging him and he places his hand on my shoulder as if we're comrades and I guess in a way we are now.

"See what he knows before you kill him." He says quietly.

I grin back. "Oh don't worry about that. I'm not going to kill him. I'm going to make sure he lives, that every minute he's with us he pays for this, and for Rose, and for everything they've done to this city."

Koen grunts back and walks away to continue pouring more gasoline.

And as I stand back and watch the entire thing go up in flames I can't help but smile.

Not just because this is destroyed but with Ignatio in my possession I can finally get a piece of revenge, a piece that I desperately, deliriously need.

There's a storm coming.

I can feel it in the air. I can feel the way everything is teetering on the edge, like the very heavens are about to open.

It feels like the world is celebrating my victory. That God himself is lauding my achievements. I'm an avenging angel once more.

And this time I know exactly who I'm taking my wrath out on.

ROSE

The flash of lightning wakes me from sleep.

And then the thunder rumbles so loudly I wonder if the storm is right above us.

Autumn always brings storms to the Bay but for some reason this one feels more ominous. More threatening.

As another crash echoes around the room, I wake up enough to really register it.

And then I'm scrambling from the bed, scrambling out the door, and down the hall to where Lara's room is.

I know she hates the storms. When the first time one hit we cuddled up together, held each other in the dark and I soothed her until it was past and she was fast asleep in my arms.

But as I half crash into the room I freeze. Her bed is empty. There's not even any covers on it.

And then it hits me.

Everything hits me.

Lara isn't here, is she? In my stupid sleep addled state I'd forgotten that.

I stare at the bed. At the room that's so sterile, so devoid of life.

And then I'm sinking to the floor, with the wood so cold beneath my body.

I couldn't face coming in here, I couldn't face seeing her space, acknowledging that she really was gone. It was never much of a room. Beyond a bed, and a few pieces of furniture this was all Lara had. No toys. Nothing that made this space less like a prison. Darius wouldn't permit anything. I guess I should be grateful he didn't make her sleep on the floor like a dog. I think he even said that to me on one occasion.

I let out a whimper as my grief hits me all the harder. My daughter is gone. Stolen again.

How does this keep happening? How am I always living like this?

Another streak illuminates the space. As it does I see the drawing, the tiny marks she's dared to make. I crawl on my hands and knees to where it's half concealed behind the bedframe. My fingers trace along the ink, to the figures, to the three of them, one small in the middle, holding the hands of the two bigger ones, with the words 'mummy' and 'daddy' so tiny beneath them.

I think my heart breaks at that.

She must be scared right now, she must be awake, afraid, hearing the storm and I know no one is comforting her. No one is with her.

She's all alone.

And she must feel exactly that. That she's been abandoned. Forgotten.

"Lara." I whisper her name, wishing the wind would carry it, praying that she knows I'm thinking of her, that though I'm not physically there, I'm still holding her in my head. Holding her so tightly.

My tears fall harder, I curl up, holding my stomach, remembering how she felt when she was inside me, when I could feel every move she made, when I could protect her, at least to some degree.

I don't look up when I hear his footsteps. I don't even acknowledge him as he towers over me.

"What are you doing?" He asks quietly, as if it's not obvious, as if he doesn't know.

I hang my head further down. Will he beat me for this too? Will he make me pay for the pain I'm suffering, the pain he's once again responsible for?

He lets out a huff sinking down and I tense up at the sudden proximity of his body to mine.

He doesn't speak. He just seems to sit there, listening to my sobs, listening to my heartbreak.

"Why are you doing this?" I whisper.

"Doing what?" He replies. There's no sympathy, no consideration. His voice sounds almost devoid of emotion.

"This. Keeping me like this. Keeping Lara from me. Hurting me the way you do."

He lets out a snarl, grabbing my face, forcing me to look up at him. In the flashing light of the storm he looks even more grotesque, even more of a monster. "Why do you think Rose?" He asks.

I don't know. I can't fathom any reasonable explanation for why one person would hurt another the way he does.

"I gave you a chance remember? I gave you an opportunity to live the way you wanted, with Lara here."

"No you didn't." I reply.

His fingers dig deeper into my jaw. "What else would you have me do? I tried to be nice, I tried to treat you properly and you threw it in my face. You don't even try with me, you won't let me love you."

"Because I don't love you. Because I've never loved you. I've never wanted you." I state.

His eyes flash. "And there's your answer, that's why I hurt you, because you say shit like that. You refuse to accept this, you refuse to even compromise."

"I shouldn't have to." I snap. "I shouldn't have to do any of this. You forced me to marry you, you forced me to be here, you…"

His look silences me.

"I'm not letting you go. I will never let you go. This is your life, so you have to make a decision, do you want to be happy, or would you rather suffer this pain?"

"You're not giving me a real choice." I whisper.

"Yes I am. You just don't like your options." He replies. "If you behave then I'd treat you right, I'd spoil you the way you deserve and we'd both be happy. But you won't do that will you? You're too bloody minded, too fixated on some fantasy life you'll never get, so I have to respond accordingly. I hurt you because you deserve it. I hurt you because you make me. I take no pleasure in it Rose. But your actions have consequences so stop acting like you're the victim here."

I pull my face from his grip. Turn my head away. He actually believes that doesn't he, he actually thinks his behaviour is justified.

"You conspired against me." He continues. "You and that Montague scum. You're lucky I didn't hurt you more. You're lucky I'm not treating you the way Otto treats Sofia."

"She isn't a part of this." I state. "She was never a part of this."

He lets out a laugh. "She's a whore, just as you were for that boy. She'd been playing my cousin for months with no intention of actually marrying him."

"She's barely more than a child." I hiss. It's not exactly true, Sofia is the same age I was when Roman and I met, the same age I fell pregnant. "Otto is over twice her age."

He smirks. "She's legal." He states in a way that makes my stomach churn.

I open my mouth to argue but he cuts across me. "Enough. I'm done with this conversation. Done with explaining myself. Get back to my bed, you've woken me up so you might as well give me something in return."

My eyes widen. Really? He wants sex right now?

He hauls me to my feet jarring my arm by the way he yanks on it and he stares at where my nighty dips low between my breasts. "Remember Rose you make the decisions, you can either have enjoyment or pain. It's up to you."

I clench my fists, hating his words, hating him even more as he leads me from what was my daughter's room back to the suite at the end of the hall.

But as we walk, my stomach twists and I let out a groan, I'm cramping up. I can feel it. I'm finally having a period and the loss of Lara seems to hit me harder then. The memories of what I had, of what was stolen, of every moment that should have been joy but they turned to darkness. It twists inside me as bitterness fills my mouth.

Darius pulls me back scanning my face. I don't want to tell him what this is, what this means. Because a period means my body is ovulating again. A period means he'll be able to track it.

But as he looks at me, as he stares down between my legs, I know he knows. And I can see it in his eyes.

I am so utterly fucked now.

ROSE

Something is going on. Something not good.

I don't know what it is but Darius has been yelling, shouting, smashing shit all day. I stay out of his way. I stay out of all their way.

Carter seems to be coming and going and the few times he's seen me I swear I think he might just hurt me too.

So I hide up in the rafters, stare out, practically day dreaming for what feels like hours, watching the waves crash below as the residuals from the storm continue to wreak havoc on the sea, as my insides twist with cramping.

This part of the house is so desolate. Unwanted. Forgotten almost. I think it was once servants quarters but now, beyond the cleaners, no one else even comes here. There's no furniture. Nothing but the parquet and the view from the windows, which are like little arches springing up from the floor.

I guess I'm relieved Lara isn't here, that she's not witnessing any of this because I know every second will have petrified her.

Today I will have to play nice. Today I will have to do whatever Darius wants, because he's too close to losing control, too close to doing something really fucked up and I don't want to be the one that pushes him over the edge.

I grit my teeth, mentally trying to come to terms with that.

Darius kept me awake for the rest of the night. Kept me entertaining him, if you will. Turns out he's not put off by blood. That he didn't even bat an eyelid. Perhaps that's why he's in such a foul mood, he's tired and he usually sleeps like a log. I guess he has no conscience to haunt him for all the terrible things he's done.

I lean back, resting my head against the window frame. The coolness of the glass is soothing. My eyes feel heavy. There's a dull ache in my head. I just want some peace. I just want one moment where there's no sound. No noise. Just silence.

"Rose?"

I jerk awake, unsure for how long I'd drifted off for. My neck feels stiff, my back is at a funny angle, my fingers are still throbbing and my stomach feels on fire from where it's ripping itself apart. I don't have any meds to take away the pain. Darius took great delight in refusing that.

I sit up straight seeing Ty crouched with a look of concern.

"You okay?" He murmurs.

My eyes dart behind him, to where the door is open all the way across the space.

"He's in a bad mood." I state.

Ty nods. Only his lips curl slightly which makes me frown.

"What's happening?" I ask.

"Roman's causing shit."

"What?" I gasp.

"They took out the new barn yesterday and now they're ambushing the militia, turning half the streets into a warzone."

"How is that possible?" I ask.

He grins. "He's working with the gangs. Turns out Darius has pissed all the scum of this city off enough that they're mobilising against him."

"But Darius will just send in the militia. He'll just kill them all." I state. I know that's what he'll do. It's what he did before me and Paris got married, the last time the gangs rioted, which on reflection explains the timing doesn't it?

"Not this time Rose. There are too many of them and the militia are taking heavy losses."

"Can they get here? Can they stop Darius? Stop all of this?" My heart starts beating so fast, god, could this be it? Could it be over?

His face falls a little. "They wouldn't get close." He murmurs. "The only reason they're able to win where they are is because it's the poorer districts, the streets are narrow, it's ideal territory, but here, there's too much security, too many people this end with too much power for Darius not to ensure it's guarded."

"So how does it help then?" I reply.

"It's guerrilla warfare. Psychological. If they can take certain areas, build their own strong hold that will help, but it's sending a message, planting a seed that Darius is not a Governor they can trust to keep people safe."

I let out a huff. It doesn't matter what Verona thinks of Darius. He rigged the vote. He's got enough power to ensure he won't be toppled like that.

"It's a start Rose, we have to start somewhere."

I fold my arms, I guess he's right. Maybe I need to learn patience. Maybe that's what this situation will teach me.

"Your dad is missing."

"What?" I practically go dizzy with the speed at which my head spins.

"Don't let them know you know." He says.

"He's missing?" I repeat.

"I think Roman has him but I can't sneak out to confirm it."

I cover my mouth but I can't hide the laugh. Roman has my father? Suddenly last night doesn't feel half as bad, half as torturous. God, I hope he's hurting him. I hope he's seriously fucking him up.

"And I have something for you." He says.

"What?"

He pulls out a little plastic box from his pocket, inside is a syringe. He holds it out for me to see, but I can see he's squirming just enough to show he's not comfortable.

"What is it?" I ask.

"Contraception."

My eyes widen at those words. "Excuse me?"

He pulls the cap off the end. "It will last thirteen weeks."

My eyebrows raise. "How did you get it?"

"Does it matter?"

No. I guess it doesn't. I pull my arm out of my cardigan. "You're sure it will work?"

He nods. "I paid good money, even had the nurse show me how to do this."

I bite my lip. It feels more than awkward to be doing this, to be even having this conversation but as the needle jabs into my arm I'm so fucking grateful.

He does it quickly. Practised.

"There. Should fix that issue." He says only he's not quite meeting my eyes.

Yeah he's definitely hating this as much as me. I want to hug him, I want to show my thanks but the thought of touching a man right now after what Darius put me through last night, it physically repulses me.

"I'll keep track." He says. "Make sure you get another hit in time."

My eyes widen. If it lasts thirteen weeks does he really think I'll still be here then, that I'll still be trapped in this situation?

He gives me a look like he's just realising what he's implied. "I didn't mean…"

"It's okay." I say even though it's not. Nothing about this is okay.

"I'm sure you'll be out by then. I'm sure this will be over." He says so quickly I know he's just saying it to make me feel better.

I put the bravest smile I can on, mustering all my internal fight. "I can handle it. Just help Roman."

"I will." He says before he shuffles out, leaving me alone.

I know Darius is going to hurt me today.

That if Roman is causing chaos then he'll need to sate his anger on me as punishment, though he won't admit that's what the cause is. No, he'll twist it around, make out it's me doing this, that I deserve this beating just like I deserve every one he delves out.

But I can feel it, the tiniest bit of hope sparking in me. I can't get pregnant now. I don't have to deal with the horror of any of that.

And Roman is out there, he's fighting, he's actually doing something to bring Darius down.

I just hope it's enough. God, I really hope it's enough this time.

ROMAN

We made sure to keep him out of sight. To lock him somewhere secure. Somewhere no one could just stumble upon him.

It's not that we don't trust everyone down here but Ignatio is no fool, he has his hands in enough pies that he might just have someone here, willing to aid his escape.

I've had him strung up by his arms until I had time to deal with him. Left him in the dark. Mentally fucking with his head because he knows I'm going to hurt him and while I'm itching to cause as much pain possible I want him to suffer the way I have.

I want it drawn out. I want him to be there, in the darkness, trapped, helpless. Knowing there is no escape. No getting away from it.

When I walk in he's hanging like some limp animal in a trap and I stand, letting the light pour in behind me, letting the brightness of it dazzle his eyes.

He's still in his suit. His crisp white shirt from yesterday looks grubby. And I bet those shiny oxfords are more than pinching at his toes.

I pull the rope loose, letting him land in a heap, and he groans as his body collides with the concrete.

I know Ben is itching to get his hands on him, Holden too, but I won't let them. This moment here is mine.

It's Rose's too.

And the thought makes me pause because as much as I'd like to walk out of this room knowing the bastard will never take another breath of air, I want Rose to witness it. I want her to enjoy this moment as much as me. I want her to have her revenge too.

I grab him by his collar forcing him into the chair and tie him in place, making sure the rope is tight enough to really cut into his skin. He barely puts a fight up and I guess considering his age he must be half beaten already.

"You and I are going to have a little chat." I say.

He blinks up at me then his eyes dart to the door.

I smirk, walk over, and shut it and for a moment we're both pitched into darkness before I flick on the painfully bright strip lights above our heads.

He hisses under his breath, squinting as his eyes adjust.

And I take the moment to pick up the cane from the side. It's not the best torture device. If I wanted information I'd be far more successful with a knife, but I don't want him to bleed out. I don't want him to have any serious wounds.

I want him to stay here, to fester, to live for months, enduring every moment of pain I inflict upon him.

I lash out, striking his arm enough to make him jerk.

"You sold your daughter." I state. "You all but marched her down that aisle…"

He lets out a laugh. "You're still obsessed with her then."

I narrow my eyes. "Not obsessed." I reply. "I love her, which is more than you and that bitch of a wife have ever done."

He takes in a snort of air. "Don't act all noble with me boy…"

I lash at him again, striking his face hard enough to draw blood and he spits in response.

"What was the deal you made with Darius? What was Rose worth to you both? Huh?"

He tilts his head. "You think I had to make a deal?" He sneers. "Darius would have taken her for nothing."

"But you wouldn't have agreed to that." I state. "No, you would have wanted to ensure you had a nice slice of the pie."

He smiles. "What else was she good for?"

My anger flashes at those words. I smack him hard, hitting the same spot on his face as I did the last time and that wound increases, as does the swelling around his eye.

"She was a whore." He spits. "A worthless piece of…"

I don't let him finish that sentence. I force the words back into his mouth with my fist, feeling with more than a little delight the way his teeth crunch, the way they break.

"She's worth a thousand of you." I snarl. "She always was. You just couldn't see beyond your own greed."

"And you can't see beyond your own cock." He spits. "You got one taste of her and that's all you wanted but Rose doesn't love you. Not really. She's a Capulet, she's just like the rest of us, she wants power, money, everything you cannot provide and everything Darius does."

I punch him again, focusing all my anger into the fist that slams into his eye.

"She's not like you." I state. "She's nothing like you."

"And yet you're here and she's in the Governor's House, riding his cock." He laughs.

I'll admit that makes me lose it. I slam one fist and then another, beating his body, hitting him so hard the chair slams back into the floor and I have to physically calm myself, physically pull myself back from murdering him.

"You sold her." I state. "And I want to know what the price was."

He's panting, visibly shaking, and that beautiful silk shirt he had on is torn to pieces and covered in his blood.

"What do you think it was boy?" He says.

"You get a cut on the whole organ thing." I reply.

He grins at me, his teeth all sharp and broken from where I've punched him. "Not just that. It was never just that."

"Then what else?"

"You think too small. Just like your father did. You think only of the short term but what good is that, what good is any of it if someone like you could come in and destroy it?"

"So what else?" I ask.

He sits back in the chair, lifts his jaw as if this were a conversation in his office, that it was on his terms and not mine. "Power." He says. "Ultimate power. With my name tied to Darius, with our blood tied to his no one can come at us, no one can take us down."

"But that only lasts as long as he remains Governor." I state.

He grins then. We both know Darius can only run for two terms, that by the laws of this state he's not able to run again once this one is up. But that look, it tells me something, it tells me so much.

"He was going to change the law…" I murmur.

"Of course he was. You think he'd do all of this and risk someone new coming in and dismantling everything?"

"But the people would never accept that."

"He owns them." Ignatio states. "He owns the press, the media, every voice in the street. Every dissenting voice has either been paid off, blackmailed, or murdered."

I stare at him for a moment as if I can't quite comprehend the words.

"So why did he want Rose? Why is she even caught up in this?"

Ignatio tuts like I'm an irritation. "Come on Montague. You're better than that."

"Tell me." I growl.

"She's the perfect wife. She was for Paris. And now she's with Darius he doesn't even need to fake his approval ratings. They love him because of her."

I turn my face up disgusted. She's just a pawn they're using. A tick box to maintain their grip on their power.

"And once she's popped out a few of his children…"

"What?" I snap stepping forward. My heart is thumping in my chest, my anger is suddenly soaring.

"You think she's not pregnant already?" He smirks. "Darius hasn't stopped fucking her since Carter handed her over to him."

I can't think. I can't breathe. The room feels like it's spinning.

"When she gives him a child, when they have their perfect family then…"

I don't let him finish that sentence. I slam my fists back into him, breaking ribs, driving my anger wherever I can land a punch.

The thought of her pregnant, of having to endure that, of bearing him a child. I can't bear it. I can't even comprehend it.

As I blink I see Lara, in my head, I see all the moments that they stole from us. The moments we should have been able to cherish.

I see Rose, as I imagined her, with her belly swollen, with my hands holding her, feeling our child kicking beneath her stomach. And I'm there, holding her hand, soothing her, witnessing the birth of our child, seeing the joy in her face, seeing the tears too, and knowing that my own are falling at the incredible joy it is to be parents. That this is our first child. And that, god willing, there would be more, as many as Rose wants. It would be our family. Ours. And no one would come between us.

I can see her first steps, I can hear her first words, the first time she laughed, the first time she danced.

My daughter. Mine and Rose's.

And yet they stole that, every moment, every part of our history.

I'm stood over him, the man who ultimately is responsible for it all and my hand is itching so bad to pick up the knife on the side and slide it across his throat, to slice through his neck and watch as his blood spurts out.

But that joy, that moment, that's not mine to take.

"I'm not going to kill you." I murmur. "I'm going to keep you alive, keep torturing you, keeping beating the shit out of you. I'm going to make you pay with blood for everything you've done to your daughter. Everything you've done to Lara too."

He looks up, meeting my gaze with the one eye that can still open.

"When I have Rose, when she is safe, and only then will you die."

He doesn't reply. He just lies there, in a pool of his own blood and I turn on my heel making sure to leave him in the dark once more.

32

ROSE

The Cuckoo Club.

The name shines, emblazoned in neon red in the foyer. Of course they didn't put it out on the main street, out where any mere passer-by might see.

I've heard things about this place. I've heard enough stories of what goes on here to already feel my adrenaline spiking as it sets in what I'm wearing, how he's doled me up like a treat.

Darius keeps me close to him as we walk further in.

My nerves are on edge. I'm already beginning to tremble. Music is pumping in a heady beat almost reminiscent of sex. Everything is in a shade of red and black like that is their entire colour palate. All around are women, barely dressed, dancing, no, writhing on various stages as men ogle at their feet.

The lighting is low, enough to make it feel sultry, sexy even, but under it, it's obvious what this place is and the kind of people who come here.

I don't understand why Darius has brought *me* here though. Is this some power play? Is this some new form of humiliation? My gut tells me it's to send a message, to make a statement. Around us it feels like the city is collapsing into chaos. I know Roman is behind it, I know he's turning the screws and that soon, really soon he'll force this battle out into the open.

The city feels like a pressure cooker. And any minute it's going to blow.

And yet we are here, partying, just like Nero did, dancing on the rooftops as the embers begin to spark beneath our feet.

Men in suits seem to be everywhere, drinking, enjoying themselves. As my eyes adjust I see something else; the women aren't just dancing for them, they're...

"Does it turn you on?" Darius asks in my ear.

I jump like a bolt of lightning has hit me. "Wwhat?" I half gasp.

"Public sex?"

I shake my head quickly. No it fucking doesn't. I don't want him thinking for one minute that I am willing to do that, to be seen doing that.

He tilts his head. "So you wouldn't ride my cock right now while everyone watched?"

I can see he's taunting me but underneath it still feels like a test. He still has all the power, and we both know if he wants to he can force me into this.

"No." I snap back.

He grins more before wrapping his arm around my body. "We'll see." He mutters as he leads me further on through the crowd, towards an ominous looking door right at the very back.

Two burly men are stood obviously controlling who can and cannot go through. But they take one look at Darius and nod quickly before opening it and holding it for us to pass. Something tells me that Darius has been here before, that perhaps he frequents this place a lot.

Ahead there's a set of polished silver stairs. Faux candles and mirrors seem to be everywhere as if they're trying to feminise this space, to make it more romantic. But there's nothing here that feels romantic, nothing here that feels remotely close.

My heels click on each step.

My dress shifts, so that with every move I take, my left leg is entirely displayed. My gut twists as I realise why he made me wear this dress. I'm being paraded like a whore for him. I just hope this is all there is to it.

When we reach the top I can see it's a private room. Although one side is glass panels so they can look down to the show beneath us, it's too high for anyone to see in, there could be an actual orgy in here and no one below would be able to witness a thing.

The music is less pervasive here, we can still hear it beating away but it's not loud enough to stop any would be conversation.

The room is packed. Dozens of men's eyes snap to me. I shrink into Darius, for once wanting his presence to shield mine.

"Evening." Darius says to them, his eyes scanning their faces but it's clear their attention is on me.

I recognise a few of them. Men whose names are associated with my father, associated with Darius. This is his party. His little gang of cronies. My heart sinks as that sets in. I'm surrounded by them. No one here is going to bat an eye if Darius decides to do something.

"I see you brought your wife." Someone says back and a few snigger like hyenas about to go in for the kill.

And that's exactly how I feel. Like I'm some new born gazelle, barely steady on my feet and they're already circling, deciding where best to sink their teeth into me.

"Darius." I whisper his name. I don't know what this is, what the fuck is happening, but every instinct in my body right now is screaming at me to run, to run and not look back.

He smirks at me before all but shoving me out in front like I'm some piece of art to be admired.

I half stumble, only just managing to stay on my feet in these damned heels. And they spring up as one, swarming me, leering at me. One of them reaches out to grab me and I let out a scream that cuts through the music.

"No touching." Darius says pushing through grabbing me back. "Look all you want but no one touches Rose but me. Got it?"

I shut my eyes, I tremble once again against him. This *is* a powerplay. I can feel my tears pricking my eyes. I don't want to be here. I don't want to be anywhere near these men.

"Take me home." I plead it to Darius and he just laughs.

"No Rose, we're here to have some fun."

"This isn't fun." I state.

He laughs again, walking us both to where a vacant chair is that seems more reminiscent of a throne. He sinks into it, pulling me into his lap and I feel it then, his cock is hard. This is turning him on.

"We're going to stay and enjoy ourselves." He states.

"I want to go home." I say. I want to be anywhere else but where I am right now.

He tuts annoyed pulling at my skirt and sliding his hand under the fabric. "Then let me change your mind on that."

I snarl back, my fear turning to anger. I'm not doing this. I won't do this. I grab his hand, dig my nails so hard into his skin that I swear I draw blood. He growls annoyed but it does stop him. At least, it stops him from assaulting me because he doesn't remove it, he keeps it there, laying claim to me for everyone to see.

He nuzzles if face into my hair sighing. "You need to loosen up Rose, stop being so boring all the time." He states.

"Fuck you." I spit back.

He grins. "Would you like me too? I'd happily slip this dress off and fuck you hard while everyone here gets front row seats."

I can see it, I can see him doing that, I can see him violating me while his mates enjoy the show. He's threatened it more than once too, more than enough times for me to think he's just waiting for a chance.

"Please can we go?" I whisper.

"No." He says firmly before snapping his fingers, ordering drinks. Only, I know drunk Darius is so much worse than he is right now.

When they arrive he all but forces the liquid down my throat. I half choke and the men around us smirk.

I don't know how to fight this. I don't know how to make this end but I know the longer I stay, the worse this is going to get.

He forces another drink down my throat. Again, I nearly choke. My head is starting to buzz. I don't want to get drunk, I don't want to lose any level of control I have over myself.

"Darius." I say again.

He tilts his head, narrowing his eyes, making it clear I'm not behaving the way he wants.

"Don't make me do this." I plead.

"Do what?" He asks.

"This." I state.

He grins, his hand running up my body. "You're my wife. To honour and obey. Remember?"

I screw my face up. "I'm not doing whatever this is." I state.

He laughs, groping me enough to make it hurt. "You'll do as you're told Rose." He says.

"What if I'm pregnant?" I say back. "You've been fucking me enough, what if I have your child in me? Alcohol is bad for our baby."

His lips curl, he leans forward kissing me and for a second I think that's done it. That that thought will be my salvation. Only he pulls away and I can see it in his eyes. He's not bought it.

"Nice try." He mutters before his eyes drift off and that smirk gets bigger.

I look across to what has caught his attention and gasp.

It's Otto, Otto and Sofia. She's wearing a dress with almost the entire sides held together by straps. God, I thought my dress was bad, every step she makes flashes the curves of her body. What's left of them anyway.

And all the awful bruises too.

Her eyes dart about. I see it, that same fear I have, only her movements look off. Like she's not in full control of herself.

He sits opposite us, Sofia's made to sit in his lap the same way I am Darius's. And when I make eye contact with Otto he grins more.

"How is our dear First Lady?" He asks.

"Fuck you." I spit.

He lets out a laugh, even throws his head back as he does it.

Darius wraps his hand around my neck pulling me hard into him. "If you continue to show me up then I will have to make a statement." He mutters.

"Do it." Otto says. "It's the only way these bitches learn their place."

I want to retort. I want to say exactly where they can both stick it but I know it will push Darius too far. So instead I let my fear take over, I recoil into myself, hoping that whatever sacrifices I end up making tonight I can live with them in the morning.

Otto snaps his fingers, just like Darius did and a waitress comes running. He mutters to her and she nods before disappearing off.

"The usual?" Darius says.

Otto shrugs.

I stare at Sofia. She's got her eyes shut now, like she knows what's coming and she's trying to brace herself for it.

I whisper her name but she doesn't respond. It's like she's shut down. Like she's mentally somewhere else entirely. Christ what has he done to her? How has she become this shell of a person?

The waitress comes back, holding a silver tray. On it I can see the drink but I see something else too.

I whip my head staring back at Darius. "What the fuck is that?" I snarl.

He chuckles. "Just watch…"

I fight him then, I fight his hold, trying to stop this.

But Otto is already picking up the syringe, taking Sofia's arm and she's not even putting up a fight. Like she knows how futile it is to even try.

"He's drugging her." I scream.

Otto looks back at me, jabs the syringe into her skin and she hisses then. That's all the response she makes.

And then he's pushing the end, shoving that clear liquid into her vein.

"Don't be a party pooper." Darius murmurs.

I kick harder and he wraps his arm in a headlock around my head. "Enough." He says.

Everyone's looking, everyone is watching the Governor now and seeing how he controls me. I can see the smirks on their faces. Can hear the laughter too.

"He's drugging her." I state again.

"It's just GHB." Darius says. "It loosens her up, just watch."

I don't want to. I don't want to witness what it does.

Otto sips his drink clearly waiting for whatever length of time it needs to take effect.

And all too soon, he's putting his empty glass down, pulling Sofia around so that she's now facing him and he's undoing her dress, stripping her for everyone to see.

"No." I shout.

Darius growls clearly getting my annoyed by my lack of obedience. "Maybe we should give you some." He threatens.

I shake my head so quickly in response. I'm being a coward now. I know I am, but whatever it is, whatever it does, I don't want any part of it.

Otto carries Sofia, lays her on a padded bench and all the men start swarming around. He looks at me, holds my gaze, and spreads her legs.

"You fucking bastard." I shout.

Darius hits me then. Hard against the side of my head. I see stars for a minute, something screams in my ears and I can't tell if it's my voice or just my brain taking the impact.

"Have you forgotten yourself?" He says. "Have you forgotten what this is?"

"I won't sit by and…"

"And what Rose?" He taunts. "I have your daughter remember? It would be an awful shame if little Lara were to get injured, were to break her leg or something worse."

My fear multiplies then. "No. Darius please don't, please don't hurt her."

He yanks me around, grabs my throat, and grins. "Then get on your knees and suck my cock."

"Wwhat?"

He leans closer, and that smell of bourbon hits my face so hard. "You heard. Show everyone here what a good little slut you really are for me."

I can feel my tears falling. I can feel my stomach churning because there's no other way around this. No escape. The sounds of grunting, of moaning, is echoing behind me. I don't want to look and see what the fuck is happening, what they're doing to Sofia.

Darius widens his legs and I all but fall into the space between them. And then he's pushing my face down, forcing me into position.

"Suck me Rose. Suck me good."

I do it. I hate that I do it, but I'm reaching up, undoing his trousers, undoing the zip, reminding myself of every time I did this for Paris. Every time I was forced to and how it wasn't that bad, that I survived and that right now, right behind me, Sofia is having it so much worse.

As he pushes himself into my mouth he groans. "Fuck."

I look back up at him and all I can think is how exactly I'm going to kill him. All the ways I've going to inflict such pain on him, how I'm going to cut the skin from his bones, how I'm going to break his legs for threatening to do it to Lara. How I'm going to cut his dick off too. How I'm going to shove it so hard down his throat that he chokes on it.

He smirks like he can hear my thoughts.

Like he believes it's not possible.

And then his eyes are drifting off, to whatever horror is happening behind me.

ROMAN

If there's one thing I've learnt from history then it's if you want people to rise up, you have to make it personal. You have to make it their problem too. Bring the fight right to their very doorstep.

Tonight, that's what we're doing.

We're going to make every wealthy residence of Verona believe they're not safe in their homes, that any minute a viscous mob is going to scale their gates, steal away their gold, and butcher them in their beds.

It's revolution 2.0. It's reliving history. I want them to think the peasants are revolting. I want them to believe the masses are rising up.

They've all stood by, all allowed this city to grow fat on the glitz and glamour of it all.

I guess tonight they'll learn that their dear Governor won't save them. That all the power and protection he professes to have is nothing more than silkened words with no substance to back it up.

Ben is back at base. Once more he's stayed helping from the side-lines.

Koen has his own group of soldiers, and he's headed for the home of a media mogul. A man, he believes is responsible for the death of his sister.

I'll admit I don't envy the bastard when Koen gets his hands on him. We've already heard some of what he has planned.

Holden is taking out another family. And two more teams are also in the proximity of their targets.

This is our biggest night to date. Our riskiest too. We've got so many locations spread across the city it would be easy for one of us to get isolated, to get caught, and for the whole house of cards to collapse at our feet.

But I can't think like that.

I won't think like that.

Once we pull this off the very foundations of Verona will be fractured. When everyone wakes tomorrow they'll know that their high walls and their expensive security is worth shit. That at any moment we can come for them.

I pull up beside the Capulet House. I may have Ignatio in my keeping but that's not enough to sate my needs. I want the pair. I want the whole devious collection. The man and wife responsible for my pain. Responsible for Rose's pain. Responsible for all of it.

The gates are locked. But I don't even try them. I know they're impassable. I know that going in that route will only guarantee failure.

So I creep in through the back. The same way I did so many years ago.

And it's hard not to relieve those memories, to remember Rose and me, when we were carefree, when we were happy, when the thrill of getting caught was almost as fun as being with each other.

I want that back. I want that happiness. I want those carefree moments.

We cross the grass quickly, efficiently, shoving our bodies into the pristine granite walls. I spent hours going through the blueprints. Detailing exactly where the cameras are and where the blind spots exist. Where all the weaknesses in their defence system is.

We hacked in an hour ago and Tia is monitoring everything for us. So far there's been nothing beyond Lady Capulet sauntering to get a drink.

I wonder if she's realised her husband is missing. Surely she must do. Surely he doesn't usually disappear for days without any mention of it, without any contact?

I shrug off the thought. Soon enough she'll know the truth anyway.

We get in through the basement. We could have as easily broken in further up but I want to clear the space floor by floor. I don't want any surprises. I want this as controlled and precise as a military operation. Get in, get the traitorous bitch, and get out.

Within seconds Tia tells us someone is coming, that down the hall the patrols are headed our way. We take position, waiting out of sight until they're close enough and then we take aim, bringing them down in perfect near silent motion, with only the slight swish of the bullet through the silencers.

Once they're down we dump them in the cellar, out of sight, and then continue onwards.

It takes all of ten minutes to clear the basement and floor above. We've taken out twenty guards. All with perfectly executed precision. But as we make our way to the third floor my nerves pick up. From what we can tell this is where the she-bitch will be residing.

I nod to the men around me. They spread out, clearly room by room and we find absolutely no one.

As I make my way into the master suite I can feel it, my adrenaline, my heart racing, my hands itching to wrap around her neck.

But I pause as I hear the sound of grunting, of moans, of skin slapping against skin.

My stomach turns as I realise what this, what I'm hearing, what I'm seeing through the darkness of the night but I can't help the snigger too. At finding her like this.

"Well, well." I murmur.

Two voices gasp in shock.

I smirk flicking the light on and she's there, naked and spreadeagled, with what looks like one of the guards on top of her.

"This is a little awkward." I say.

Carla's face turns from flushed to pale as she realises who is here, stood in front of her. She makes a move to cover herself while the man on top of her scrambles off.

"You know I was wondering why you weren't missing your husband. Why you weren't making more of a fuss about his disappearance..." I say. "But I guess this explains it."

"What are you doing in my house?" She says sitting up, pulling the sheets over her sweaty breasts. Her hair is askew, she's so far removed from the pristine, stuck-up image she usually presents.

"I'd have thought that was obvious." I reply.

The man she was fucking makes a bid to take me on. He launches himself at me and I bring him down with barely a second glance.

Carla shrieks out, like she's not got her hands more than covered in blood over the years.

"Get up." I snarl. "Get on your feet or I will drag you out of here."

"You do that and Darius will…"

"Will what?" I mock. "You think he gives a shit about you? He has everything he wants. You made sure of that when you gift-wrapped your daughter for him."

"Rose was more than happy…"

My bullet cuts through the headboard, barely millimetres above her head, and she trembles, falling silent.

"Get up." I repeat.

She pulls the sheets around her, stumbling to her feet. "Let me get a robe, please."

I hate the way she begs. I hate the way it sounds. She's so entitled, she just expects me to agree and though I want to tell her to shove it, I don't want to see her naked.

"Make it quick." I jerk my head to where the door to the ensuite is. I assume there's a bathrobe in there.

She rushes in, and I hear the window sliding open which makes me laugh.

"It's too far to jump Carla." I say loudly. "You go out that window you'll break your bony neck."

She whimpers and then walks out pouting with a white robe wrapped around her body.

I grab her arm, yanking her out the room.

She yelps again, playing the victim. "Roman please…"

My anger flares as I fix her with a look.

"I wasn't involved, I'm as much a victim in all of this as my daughter."

"Don't you dare." I snarl shoving her hard into the wall. "You think I don't know what you did? You think I don't know that you were the one manipulating everything? Pretending to be me, telling Rose that I didn't love her, telling her to abort our daughter."

"I, that wasn't me, Ignatio…"

I let out a laugh. "It's not going to work Carla. You can't talk your way out of this."

She shakes her head and those crocodile tears start pooling in her eyes. "I only wanted the best for Rose. That's what you wanted too. I just wanted her to be happy, to have the best in life…"

"And selling her to Darius gives her that, does it?"

She huffs. "He's the Governor, he could give her everything she ever wanted, all her dreams."

"She wanted me." I state jabbing my finger in her face. "She loved me."

"She loves Darius now."

I don't entertain it for a second. I know it's a lie. Rose doesn't love Darius, she wouldn't be passing on information through Ty to bring him down if she did. But I can still see her, that fake smile, that way she lets him hold her. I know it's a mirage, I know it's not real. But my jealousy is there, festering. Because he's the one touching her, he's the one kissing her, forcing her to god knows what.

And then Lara's voice repeats in my head. That he hurts her. That he hurts her and tells her it's her fault.

I shove her hard, pushing her down the ridiculously ornate stairs, she stumbles, falling down the last few and lets out a cry. Around us my men are stood watching her. I know they don't feel an ounce of pity either. We were clear about her part in all this, we could show exactly how she's linked to the organ trade.

I grab the collar of her robe hauling her back to her feet and the damn thing comes undone all but flashing her body to everyone.

She squeals trying to cover herself and I allow her only the time it takes to tie the cord before I'm pushing her out the door.

But as we get outside bullets start raining down on us. Loud.

Some arsehole has a machine gun.

We duck, pulling Carla back. Whoever it is clearly doesn't care if he kills her and while I'd agree with the sentiment that privilege is reserved for Rose. She gets to decide the details, the method, how long we draw it out and make her suffer.

"Let me go. Roman please. Let me go." She pleads.

"Not a fucking chance." I growl.

We start shooting back, taking position while mentally I curse because this *will* get attention. Half the city will hear the noise and I don't doubt Darius will have the militia out.

Two of our men move out, securing more ground, providing enough cover for someone else to drag Carla out towards the vans.

But as they get close more bullets hail down on us from a completely different position.

Carla screams. The man holding her yanks her back and she takes the moment to knee him in the balls.

And then suddenly she's running, barefoot, across the gravel, screaming, hollering, her hair is awry, her robe is flapping in the wind.

I snarl springing from where I am but whoever is out there starts shooting once more and I'm so close to getting my head blown off.

"Get that fucking bitch." I shout before taking aim, shooting right at where I know the arsehole is hiding.

We hear the groan as my bullet finds him. Without hesitation I'm running again, chasing after Carla even though I know it's too late. The bitch is gone. She's slipped through my fingers.

And then we hear the sound we've been dreading. The sound we've all been listening out for.

The militia are on their way. It's over. This whole thing is over.

I give the order, ensuring every one of our men are back in the vans and then we're speeding down the streets, driving like mad men.

We have to get away, we have to get to the tunnels before they realise it's us. Before we fuck everything up.

ROSE

Someone is knocking on our door. Tapping urgently. I sit up in the darkness. In fairness it's hard to sleep, hard to close my eyes when all I can see, all I can hear is Sofia and what they've done to her, what they keep doing to her.

Darius groans before he shoves the duvet off and walks to the door.

"What?" He snaps.

"There's been another incident."

It's Carter. Even with Darius stood here I can feel his eyes searching me out and I pull the sheets up, hiding myself from his gaze.

So Roman has been busy then.

For some reason it doesn't give me relief. Not now, not in the darkness. In moments like this it makes me fear more, makes me panic.

"What incident?" Darius growls.

"Carla is missing."

I gasp before I can stop myself and Darius gives me a look that says 'shut the fuck up'.

And then he's walking out, slamming the door, making it clear that though it's my mother I'm not allowed to know the details.

But I can't just sit here.

I wait long enough to make sure it's safe and then I'm creeping out, tiptoeing through the darkness. They're not even in his office, they're just stood, in the hall, one level below where I am and their voices carry up.

"You think it's him?" Darius murmurs.

"It's not just the Capulet House, they've attacked a dozen others. All high profile, all big names, all linked to you know what."

Darius curses.

"They strung Collin King's body up over the East Bridge."

"What?" Darius growls.

"We've already dealt with it."

"I thought you had people watching Carla after Ignatio disappeared."

"We did. They got them."

"They're dead?"

"Yes."

Darius curses again and then I hear something smash. "I told you." He growls. "I made it perfectly clear that she was not to be taken. She knows too much."

"Why do you think I had men on her?" Carter growls. "I gave them specific instructions. They knew if any attempts were made then Carla was to be neutralised."

"Is there a chance she's dead? That she was shot and that you haven't found the body?"

"I think that's high unlikely."

"Fine. Do what you need to. Go street to street, I don't give a shit how much noise you make."

"We need to be savvy." Carter replies. "We need to instil calm. The last thing we need is people thinking you're losing control."

"I don't give a fuck what people think." Darius shouts. "We cannot allow them to find out. We cannot allow them to realise what she knows."

"I'll deal with it." Carter says.

"You find her, you kill her." Darius snaps.

I gulp, creeping backwards, slipping back into the bedroom, into the darkness.

I can smell his scent in the area, I can smell his body odour, and his cologne but in this moment that's not what's making me want to gag.

What does my mother know? What the hell is she aware of that means Darius wants her dead? I always thought the two of them were thick as thieves. He never seemed to show any animosity to her in the past so what the fuck has changed all that?

"What are you doing out of bed?"

I let out a whimper spinning around as Darius is stood, in the doorway, like some sort of monster.

"He said my mother was missing…" I begin.

He tilts his head. "You hate your mother."

"And?"

"Do you think I'm stupid enough to believe such a lie?" He half snarls.

"She's still my mother." I say stepping back, retreating. "I'm allowed to be concerned."

"Is that what you are Rose?" He asks crossing the room, catching me in his grip. "Are you concerned?"

I shut my eyes, my bile rising to my throat, all I want to do is shove him off, to lash out, to fight.

"Get back in that bed and shut the fuck up." He says all but shoving me onto the mattress.

I clamber in, waiting for the disgusting feel of his hands, waiting for the inevitable clues that's he's going to assault me once more.

Except he doesn't. He just stands there watching me before he turns and storms out.

I guess this really is a big deal then. That my mother is such a significant clog in this fucked up machine that he has to take action, he has to ensure she is found, and quickly.

ROSE

The room is rammed. The buzz of gossip, of laughter, of pointless conversations fills the air around me. I stare at the perfectly done up faces, at the pristine hair, at the expensive clothes and even more at the expensive jewels.

I wonder if they can see it.

I wonder how they can't.

How they're all so totally oblivious to this.

But I guess that's what money does. Money and Power. They're all so obsessed with obtaining it, with flattering those who have it, they don't want to look beyond all that gilded façade to see the horror of what created it.

Only this city is not so gilded now is it? Roman has put paid to that. And yet it doesn't seem to be enough. Even with all the power cut, even with the severe water shortage we're now facing, none of these people around me seem to give two hoots.

No one here seems to know my mother is missing. I guess Darius did another number on the press, ensuring that little fact was kept out. No, he wouldn't want anyone to know his mother-in-law, the famous Carla Capulet was MIA because that really would send a message that our perfectly built empire is crumbling into ashes.

I blink, feeling like there's something inside me actually dying. I can still hear it, the sounds, the horrific noises of what they did to Sofia.

What I failed to stop.

And I realise with a rancid feeling in my gut that it wasn't the first time.

That Darius goes drinking with Otto a lot.

My stomach twists. How many times have they drugged her? How many times have they done that?

I watch as he's talking, as he's working his charm on the two women in front of him. We're at another event, a hastily prepared one that is meant to give calm. Meant to reassure. It feels like everyone here is pretending that the city isn't descending into chaos as we speak.

I can't stay like this.

I can't continue like this.

I have to do something to bring him down myself.

I steal my breath because I tricked Roman didn't I? I played the judas well that time. It wouldn't take much effort to do it here. It really wouldn't.

I just need to plan it right, to ensure that when I make my move, Roman is ready, that Ty passes on the message and then we can end this properly.

"Rose."

I jump just a little as Katie smiles at me kindly.

"I didn't mean to startle you." She says quietly.

"It's okay." I reply. I was too fixated on Darius, too fixated on escape to be paying attention to what was going on around me. I need to be smarter.

She narrows her eyes slightly. "You look like shit." She says.

I let out an exhale. I have enough makeup onto rival a cosmetics store. I'm wearing Valentino and I'm covered in diamonds. I do not look like shit.

"It's your eyes Rose." She murmurs. "They give you away."

"They better not." I reply. God, if they do, if Darius sees, he'll punish me for that too. He won't let me back out until I've learnt to pretend better.

"What the fuck is he doing to you?" She asks.

I bite my lip, forcing back the tears. My mask feels like it's so damn fragile, like any minute my perfect façade will shatter and all I've been through will be for nothing.

She tilts her head running her eyes over me then stares at my broken fingers that I've been so careful to keep from view.

"Did he do that?" She says. "Did he hurt you?"

"It's not me you should concern yourself with." I say. "I can handle it. But Sofia, Sofia has it so much worse."

Her eyes widen, she glances across the room to where Otto is stood thankfully with his back to us. Sofia isn't here. She's never allowed out. Beyond the funeral and the Cuckoo Club I've never seen her in public but I guess I know why now.

"She's in the same situation." She guesses.

"Worse." I say. "So much worse."

"Give me something, give me something I can use."

I gulp. Is this it? Is this my chance? I want to believe her but what if she's a plant? What if this is a test, that Darius has paid her off and right now he's playing me?

I turn my back, facing the wall. I don't know what to do. On one hand I have to do something but if I Darius finds out he will make me pay big time.

"Rose…" She murmurs.

"Alright." I hiss as quietly as I can. I have to take this chance, I have to try. Even if he breaks my bones for it. "He rigged the vote."

"What?" She replies.

"He fixed it. I don't know how. I don't have any evidence beyond him telling me but he cheated to make sure he was re-elected."

She shakes her head slightly. "I can look into it. It'll take time though. I'll need to have proof before I dare print such an accusation."

"He says he controls the press too." I state and I see the wince that tells me she knows more about that than I do.

"I can get around it." She reassures me. "Leave it with me."

"He's selling people." I don't even know how to explain it. How to explain all the fucked up shit that Darius is up to. "He's got a compound where he keeps them and he sells their organs."

She gives me a look like I can't be serious.

"I'm not lying." I state. "I think Ro…" I collect myself, not wanting her to know Roman is alive. I don't know why he's still pretending to be dead but he must have his reasons. "Someone attacked it. They destroyed it. But I was there. I saw it myself. I saw dozens of people locked in cages."

"Okay." She says nodding. "I'll find out what I can."

"He sent Lara away." I add. "He sent her away, can you find out where she is?"

"Lara is your daughter?"

I nod. "She's at a boarding school somewhere in the city. She's only six."

"Leave it with me." She says before passing over a glass of champagne and her whole expression seems to change. "That sounds like a lovely idea." She adds simpering to me.

I take the glass in my good hand and she clinks hers against mine.

"Governor." She says brightly to the man I know is now stood right behind me.

Darius looks between us, in the same sort of fashion he did the last time he caught us talking.

"Rose." He murmurs wrapping his arm around my waist.

"I hope you don't mind…"I say leaning into him. "But we agreed to do that article remember, after the wedding, about what it's like to be First Lady."

He blinks clearly trying to recall.

"Katie wants to come round tomorrow, to discuss the details, and I thought we could share some wedding photos seeing as we got them back." I state.

Darius's lips curl. "That sounds like a good idea."

"Perfect." Katie says beaming. "I'll get onto our editor now. He's been bugging me for weeks and he'll be just as excited as I am about this."

I smile before sipping more of my champagne. I can do a fake article. If anything I hope it will convince Darius that I'm giving in.

He leads me away, introduces me to the commissioner and some other leads for the charity Darius and Carter selected as this week's bit of good news to cover the nearly daily shit storm. I fight the feeling of disgust as they touch me, as they lean in and kiss my cheek, while their hands feel like they linger for far too long.

And I laugh too. At all the jokes Darius makes.

He catches my eye as we find ourselves alone for a brief moment and I can see he's trying to figure this out in his head.

"Rose…" He murmurs.

I blink back, my lips curled in expectation, as if I hang on every word he utters. As if I'm so in love with this man that only he matters.

And then his phone buzzes. Everyone's phone buzzes. He pulls it out glancing at the screen and I dare to steal a glance.

My heart freezes. I can see it, the news alert. Someone has breached whatever embargo Darius put in place. It's out. It's official. Everyone now knows my mother is MIA.

His face turns into something deadly. I'm quick to drop my eyes, to not let him know that I know.

"We're done here." He says, taking my wrist, making for the exit.

"Governor?" Someone asks holding their phone out for us to see. "What is this?"

Darius stops, a big smile on his face. "I'd say it's exactly what it looks like. Somebody's idea of a joke."

The man nods glancing at me and then back at Darius.

"I'm afraid we have another appointment to get to." Darius says smoothly before continuing on.

When we get to the car I climb in quickly. Darius slams the door shut, barks at the driver to go and then turns his full attention on me.

"What was that?" He half growls.

"What was what?" I reply.

He runs his eyes over me. "You seem far more compliant today."

I wince, glancing at the window, playing this carefully because I can't simply act like I suddenly want him and expect him to believe it. "Maybe I'm too tired now." I half whisper.

"Too tired of what?"

"Fighting." I say looking back at him. "Besides you've made it clear what happens when I do."

He smiles leaning in and I put my hand on his chest, acting like I need to say my piece first.

"I don't want you to do to me what Otto is doing to Sofia." I state.

He tilts his head at that, scrutinising my face. And internally I fight my guilt. I'm using her situation to my advantage, acting like seeing that, witnessing that has put the fear of god into me, when in truth it's just spurred me on, made me more furious, more determined than before.

"Maybe I should have done that to start with then." He murmurs. "Maybe I should have taken you there, let you see how much worse you could have it…"

I gulp, nodding, shutting my eyes as another horrific image flashes before me.

He grabs me pulling me into his lap and his hands grab my hips. "If this is you submitting I want you to do it fully."

"What does that mean?" I ask.

He grins leaning back into the seat more. "Prove it now. Take off that dress, fuck me like you love me. Come on my cock like it's the best thing you've ever felt."

My heart hammers in my chest. My stomach twists.

I can't deny him. I have to do this. To play this game better than I have before, better than I've done my entire life. I nod sinking to my knees before him because the roof of the car feels far too close to my head.

I slide my dress off, keeping my eyes on my movements and not the man in front of me and then I'm reaching up, undoing his tie first, then easing his suit jacket from his shoulders. He sits there, so fucking smug as I do it, as I undo each button, as I reveal his chest, as I undo his belt and free his cock.

He grabs my face, shoving it into where he's already so hard he's practically throbbing. I run my tongue along him, playing the obedient whore and he groans.

"There's a good slut."

I look up at him, take him into my mouth and suck like I want him, like I enjoy him.

He groans harder, clearly enjoying the show before he pulls me up and all but rips my thong from my body. "Ride my cock Rose." He says.

I sink onto him, at least my saliva has lubricated his cock, so it's not as brutal as normal. He pushes me back so that he's got a good view of where he's penetrating me and I do it, I fuck him, just as he asked. I act like this is a thing of love. I act like I want him. Only I won't pretend this is Roman, I won't sully any last remnants of those precious moments by doing that.

He thrusts into me, gripping my hips, driving his own pleasure.

And then I commit the worst betrayal yet. I put my fingers on myself. I touch myself as he watches, and I make myself come.

I make myself give in entirely.

Feeling the twist of the knife, feeling my last bit of who I was severing as I do.

He holds me to him, he groans as my body clenches so hard around him.

"Fuck." He gasps. "You feel so good, so fucking good."

I don't reply, I just continue the pretence, continue the moans, as he pumps into me and then he's pulling my face to look at him and he's smiling like he really has won the world. Like someone's handed him the keys to the world.

I stare back, I can feel my cheeks flushed, I can feel my shame sinking in deeper than before but I don't show it. I just meet his gaze as it feels like my heart freezes over forever.

They turned me into a whore, they made me this, and now that I've accepted that there's no pieces left of me to take, I'm turning the tables.

And that's how I'll get my revenge.

That's how I'll beat him. I'm going to pull the very rug out from beneath his feet. I'm going to slip a knife into his chest right when he's least expecting it.

ROSE

I think he's starting to buy it.

He certainly seems more relaxed in my presence.

And it's been days since he's hurt me, days since I've felt his hands on me as a form of punishment.

But the news alert did cause some shit. Especially after what's been going on in the streets. He and Carter spent the rest of the day and half the night trying to figure out who was behind it and how to counteract it.

This entire week he's been there, locked in his office, working later than usual and while I relish the freedom from him, hiding in this room won't get me any closer to escaping it forever.

So I wait until I hear Carter leave and then I slip down, into the main house, tapping lightly on his door before I open it.

He looks up, his eyes devouring me as I step into the light.

"You've not come to bed." I say.

He looks tired. He actually for once looks like he's had to do something.

He leans back in his chair. "I had work to do." He states.

"Are you all done now?" I reply.

He gets up out of his chair and the leather squeaks but his phone rings right at the same time. "Give me a second." He says picking it up, turning his back to me.

I take the moment, stepping forward, casting my eyes over his desk. He's always been messy. He's always had papers strewn everywhere and I seize the opportunity to get something, anything that might help us, help Roman.

When I spot the scrawled note I want to smile so badly.

Only I don't.

Instead I take a step back. Silently. Returning to the same spot I was stood in and make sure my eyes are dropped to the floor. I don't want him to get any inkling of what I'm up to. I don't want him to have a clue.

He grunts into the phone. Then shouts out about wanting the bloody job done already before he hangs up.

When he turns back to look at me I take a millisecond longer than I need to lift my gaze, to ensure that he sees I've not snooped.

"You sound stressed." I say.

He snorts. "I'm Governor of this city of course I'm fucking stressed."

I hate myself for the words I speak, hate myself for the acts of betrayal I'm about to commit but it's necessary. All of this is necessary.

So I step closer, wrap my arms around his neck and murmur. "Maybe you should let me help you destress then."

He frowns with a ghost of smile on his lips. I take his hand and he lets me lead him out of the office, up to our room, to our ensuite where I've already made sure to have a hot bath waiting.

His eyebrows raise when he sees it.

"You need to relax more." I say moving to undo the buttons on his shirt.

He stands there, watching me undress him, watching every move I make before I motion for him to get in.

And then I pass him a glass of bourbon, with one cube of ice, just the way he always asks for it.

"I'm liking this." He says.

"Liking what?" I ask as I move to knead his shoulders, easing out the muscles, and all the while I'm imagining what it would look like to drive a blade into his back.

"You. Being nice."

I plant a kiss on his skin. "I can be nice." I say.

He groans again before sipping his drink. "Keep this up and I might just give you a reward."

"I don't need rewards." I reply. I'm not going to ask for anything. I want him to believe that just this peace between us is enough now.

"Not even seeing your daughter?" He murmurs.

I freeze for a millisecond. The temptation to say yes is so great. But I won't do it. I know if he takes me to her he'll turn it into some sort of test. He certainly won't leave me alone with Lara. And I don't want to have to pretend, to see the hurt and the pain and the look of betrayal on her face when she sees how I am now. When she believes it too.

No, I won't do that to her. I won't betray her in such a way. I'd rather not see her at all and spare us both that pain.

"No, just, promise me you won't hurt me anymore." I say instead.

He lets out a low breath. "Don't give me a reason too."

"I won't." I say quickly. "I'll be good."

He nods. "Fine then. Be the perfect wife and I'll be the perfect husband to you Rose."

I smile, planting another kiss on his back. "That's all I want." I say. Each word a lie. Each word a piece of blasphemy on my tongue.

But it doesn't matter now. I'm as twisted as they are. And every moment I can convince Darius that I've broken, that I really have given in, is a moment closer I am to getting my revenge.

IN THE MORNING WE EAT BREAKFAST TOGETHER. LIKE THE PERFECT picture of matrimonial bliss.

He plants a kiss on my lips when he goes to leave and I make sure I pout my lips, that I cup his cheek with my hand and kiss him back like he really is the love of my life.

When he's out the door I catch Ty's face from where he's stood narrowing his eyes, trying to figure out why my behaviour's suddenly done a complete one eighty.

I glance at the guards who Darius is still keeping around me during the day time, and then I get up walking out to the balcony beyond.

Ty takes the hint to join me there and for a moment we stand looking down to where the side of the street is just visible over the great walls designed to keep everyone out.

"What's changed?" He asks quietly.

I look at him sighing. "Nothing."

"You're acting like you're suddenly okay with this." He states.

I shake my head, my anger rising so quickly. Does he think I'm as fickle as that? "I'm not okay with any of this Ty. I'm playing a game just as you are."

"Yeah? You seem to have changed the rules then."

"Maybe I have." I snap. "Maybe I can't take it anymore. Maybe after seeing Sofia…"

"What?" He asks stepping nearer me.

I drop my gaze, my eyes threatening to spill over as the images, as the sounds, the horror of what I witnessed once more fills my head.

"What the fuck is happening with Sofia?" He growls.

"They're drugging her." I say. "They're pumping her full of GHB and they're…" I look away, I can't even meet his eyes but I know he gets what I'm trying to say. That they're gang raping her. Otto, Darius, all of them.

He gasps like he's been mortally wounded.

"You have to tell Roman. You have to help her." I state.

"I will." He says. "I'll get her out."

"And Lara?" I say. He knows what schools she's at. He knows exactly where she is. If Roman is going to save Sofia then I need him to save her too or she'll be a sitting duck when Darius decides to make his own moves.

"She's safe." He says.

"Safe how?" I reply.

"Roman got her out."

I gasp, my heart leaps. "She's with Roman?" I whisper.

"Yes. She's safe Rose. You don't have to worry about her now. Just focus on you."

"And you can focus on Sofia." I say.

He shudders. "I'll get her." He replies.

"Good. And tell Roman there's a drop, a new delivery of drugs coming in this week. It's coming through the ports. Darius is making sure there's a big security detail because he's nervous after all the attacks."

He nods but I can see he's not okay. I can see there's something there, something breaking in him too.

"Ty?"

"Leave it." He growls.

Only I won't. I grab his arm forcing him to look at me. "Why the fuck are you so wound up?" I ask.

"Sofia…" He murmurs.

I screw my face up. What the fuck does she have to do with Ty? I don't think their paths have ever even crossed. He's only muttered her name in the past to spit insults.

"I love her Rose alright." He snaps.

"What?"

"I love her." He growls. "I fucking love her and they're…" He trails off turning his back on me before turning straight back around. "I asked Darius, I begged him to give me her. I wouldn't have touched her, I would have protected her, kept her safe. Only he wouldn't. He said he'd promised Otto he could have her. Promised his cousin first dibs as if she's a fucking piece of meat."

He slams his fist into the balustrade.

"Does she know?" I ask.

He doesn't reply. He just stares out, looking like he's cursing the entire world right now.

"Ty, does she know?" I ask grabbing hold of him.

"No." He says. "She doesn't have a fucking clue."

"Then how can you love her?" I ask.

He scowls at me. "That's coming from you? You, who slept with Roman Montague, you who had a secret child that no one even knew about?"

I don't know how to reply to that. I don't know what to say.

He slumps. And for a minute I think he might even cry. "I can't leave her like that. I won't fucking leave her like that."

"Then get her out." I snap.

He looks at me with an awful look on his face. "Your dear loverboy won't let me."

"What?"

"He doesn't want to blow his cover. He's got some sort of plan and he's sticking to it come what may."

My heart sinks. I trust Roman. I really do but he can't be that inflexible. Not when his sister's life is on the line.

"Then tell him that you're doing it. Force his hand." I snap.

He shakes his head. "I can't…"

"If you love her then you would." I say playing the only card I have.

I need them to get Sofia out, I need them to rescue her. Not only will it help relieve my guilt but once that's done I can focus better on me, focus on bringing Darius down without worrying how Otto might take revenge on Sofia if I am successful.

He throws me a look like he wants to punch something, like he wants to seriously fuck someone up and I've got a good idea of exactly who.

And then he turns, walking away, clearly doing everything he can to act calm.

ROMAN

I stare at him. For a second I think this is another dream. Another fucking nightmare like the ones I keep having about Rose.

Only I know I'm awake.

And I know all this right now is my fault.

"Rose told you this?" I say.

Ty nods. "We have to get her out."

Ben looks like he's ready to do it already, to take half the damn arsenal, start shooting and not stop until she's free.

Koen looks between us. "Want me to create a distraction?" He says.

I shut my eyes, palm them with my hands. My whole plan right now hinges on the fact everyone thinks I'm dead. If I do this, how soon will it be before Darius puts two and two together and realises that's not the case?

"Rose is fine." Ty says.

I shoot him a look. She's not fucking fine. She's literally sleeping in the same bed as the devil.

But Sofia, Sofia, my poor innocent sister, she's only caught up in this because of me. Because of my stupid belief that I could simply contain Darius through blackmail alone.

"Alright." I say. "We get Sofia."

"Otto takes her to the Cuckoo Club…" Ty says.

My heart practically stops at that. He fucking takes her there? Is that where they're assaulting her?

"We can ambush him on the way." He states.

"It's too risky." Ben replies.

"She doesn't leave his house beyond that." Ty states. "That's our only chance."

"I don't know." I murmur thinking it over.

"There's a tunnel near to his house, we can come up, ambush them, get the girl and be gone before anyone even sees us." Koen states.

I look between them. It's not a bad plan but it's barely a thought out one.

"We don't have time for anything else." Ty snaps. "They're drugging her and raping her. I'm not just going to…"

"I get it." I say. He doesn't need to convince me, this is my sister we're talking about. "When are they next hitting the club?" I ask.

Ty lets out a low breath. "They go at least twice a week. Thursdays are his favourite."

"Today is Thursday." Ben points out.

There isn't time. Not to plan this properly. But if Ty is right, and I know he is, then I won't leave Sofia to endure this for another day.

"We go tonight then." I say.

Ty meets my gaze and nods. "I'll do whatever you need." He states.

"I need you out of the way." I say. I don't want him seen, I need him as my spy, on the inside, not revealing what he's really up to and fucking this all up.

"I'm not just…" He begins.

"We'll get her Ty." I state cutting across him. "But I need you to hold up your end. I need you to help me to help Rose. She's still there remember?"

He shakes his head, screws his hands up and mutters before storming out, leaving the door to slam behind him.

Ben watches him go and then he turns to look at me. "I want to be the one to gut Otto. I want to make the bastard suffer."

I smile back. "We'll form a queue." I say. "But Sofia gets the final shot."

He nods. "Yeah I guess that's fair."

"How about you get her out first, then you can decide who's cutting Otto's cock off." Koen growls.

We both look at him.

"I'm going to need your help." I state.

"Standard." He replies getting to his feet. "I'll have our best soldiers on it, no half measures. We'll get your sister back. And then we'll make an example of Otto fucking Blumenfeld."

I'M SAT IN THE TRUCK, AT THE CROSSROADS WAITING FOR THE ACTION to start, trying not to think of all the reasons we should be calling this off.

We've got a lookout stationed on a bike outside Otto's house, then one at every damn junction, literally following them through the city. As they get caught at the lights just before us I swear you can hear a pin drop. All of us, all five pairs of eyes are focused in the direction of where the Mercedes will come from.

And when the vehicles start moving again I hold my breath.

One of our trucks cuts right across the junction, cutting off the front of Otto's convey. The cars brake, swerving hard not to crash into it. The Mercedes makes a sharp right turn as if they know, as if they've practiced this event over and over.

Our trucks race to catch up, race to corner him. A swarm of bikes manoeuvre themselves into position.

One of ours rams his and it sends the vehicle spinning around before it smashes into a wall.

But there's another car right behind it. Men seem to pour out, shooting everywhere, not caring who gets caught in the crossfire. Not giving a damn.

We fire back. We don't stop firing until the sound of bullets finally stops.

I jump out of the truck, sprint across the street to where the damaged vehicle is, wrenching the door open.

Otto looks up at me and his eyes widen. "No…" He begins but I punch him hard before he can say anything further.

And then Sofia looks at me. She frowns, her eyes unfocused like they've already pumped her full of drugs.

She tries to stand and her legs give way.

I reach out scooping her up and she physically freaks out at the contact. She starts screaming, fighting, jerking in my arms as if I'm the monster here.

"It's okay." I say. "Sofia, it's me. It's your brother."

She shakes her head, her eyes darting wildly. Her hands slapping at me and I stupidly put her down.

And then she is running, or trying to, she stumbles to her knees, crying out, then all but crawls away from the scene.

I move to grab her but suddenly more bullets are spraying at us and I'm forced to duck, using the now fucked up Mercedes as cover. But as I do I see Otto running for Sofia. Running to get her back.

I pull my gun, taking aim and shoot out his ankle. He howls landing in a heap barely metres from where she is now curled up, whimpering, with her eyes so tightly shut as if this is all just a bad dream.

I can hear sirens now, I can hear what I don't doubt is the militia on its way to us.

This whole thing is turning into a complete shit show, just as I feared it would.

I get up again, trying to get to her and clearly my movements give me away. Someone starts shooting again. How they miss me this time I don't know.

From our truck Ben and the others shoot back but I'm immobilised. Unable to do a damn thing.

I stare at my sister, at where she's shaking so hard with fear. I have to get to her, I have to save her before the militia arrive and this whole thing is done for.

I try to move and a bullet almost takes my hand off.

And then I see Otto going for her again.

She screams as he grabs her but almost in the same instant a body is colliding with them both.

It's Ty.

Fuck me. It's fucking Ty.

I want to curse him. I want to lose my shit over the fact he disobeyed me but right now he's punching the living shit out of Otto.

Ben and the others take the opportunity to start shooting again and I take the chance to cross the distance to get to Sofia.

I scoop her up, even as she slams her fists into my chest.

"I'm so sorry." I say but I keep moving, keep heading towards the waiting truck.

A bullet whistles past my head from behind. I turn without thinking and he's there stood, with a gun pointed right at us.

"Give me my wife back." Otto snarls.

"The fuck I will." I say.

He takes a step, narrowing his eyes, pointing the gun not at me but at my broken sister in my arms. "Give me Sofia or I'll blast her fucking head off and you'll be left with just her corpse."

I hear the yell, I see the movement of Ty jumping onto him, bringing him back down.

"Go." Ty yells at me.

I step back, my eyes focused on the two of them now caught in this damned fight.

And then the gun goes off again.

"Roman." Ben yells at me.

I realise I'm stood here, out in the open. Exposed. With my sister still in my arms.

"Fucking go already." Ty yells before landing another punch.

"Roman." Ben yells again.

And this time I respond. This time I run, back across the street, back to the truck. Koen takes Sofia off me before I can do anything. I clamber in, sliding the door shut and all but scream for us to go already.

And just as the sirens turn to screaming point, we speed off in the other direction.

I sink into the seat palming my face, taking a moment just to breathe. I don't know what happened to Ty. I don't know if he managed to kill Otto but I hope he did. I hope he made him fucking suffer too.

But if he didn't, if Otto is still alive, then he'll tell Darius exactly what he saw. That I'm alive and most certainly kicking and that they didn't kill me after all.

I know that will put Rose in way more danger. Jesus, this whole house of cards is crumbling right around us.

"We got her." Ben murmurs patting my back, like that's where my head is at.

I look up, seeing my sister in Koen's arms.

She's no longer fighting. No longer screaming either.

256

She's just lying there, limp, in a dress that's barely worthy of the name. As I take her in all I can see are the bruises, the burns, the way her ribs poke through her skin with how the cut outs of the fabric expose her body.

She used to be curvy, she used to have muscle too. Now she barely looks more than a bag of bones.

"Is she conscious?" I ask.

Koen looks up at me. "No." He replies.

She must have passed out as soon as we got into the truck. I don't know whether to be relieved by that fact or not.

But his eyes are blazing. He looks like he's about to lose his shit too.

I glance at Ben who meets my gaze but doesn't say anything. Only I can see it written on his face. What he's thinking, what he's feeling in this moment. The woman he loves, the woman he's always loved is lying here, close to death, and yet another man sacrificed himself to save her.

And right now, another man entirely is holding her like she's the most precious thing in the world.

ROMAN

T he beeping of the monitor seems to be the only noise in the room.

I'm sat here, staring, feeling fucking useless as the doctor checks Sofia over. Ben is sat the other side, face in his hands, and Koen, he's pacing back and forth like a typhoon about to go off.

I watch him from the corner of my eyes but I don't let him see.

I'm certain he's never met my sister before, certain they've never even uttered one word to one another so why the fuck is he acting like this affects him too?

"She's severely malnourished." The doctor states like we don't know that, like we can't see that with our own eyes. "I'm putting her on a drip to get her vitals up. We have to do this slowly though because she's at high risk of refeeding syndrome."

"What is that?" I ask.

"Essentially if we give her too much too soon it will overwhelm her system." She explains. "Her brain will go catatonic and she'll go into multi-organ failure."

"So how do we make sure that doesn't happen?" I reply.

"We do this slowly. She's at the critical stage but over the next week she stood stabilise."

I look back at Sofia, she's still unconscious, though this time I know it's partly to do with the meds. She looks so fragile. So broken.

"Are all the drugs out of her system?" I ask.

The doctor glances at Sofia then back at me. "We're doing a full toxicology report now so once that's back we'll be able to determine that and if we have to do anything further…"

"What does that mean?" Koen growls.

She flinches a tiny bit at his tone. "She might have withdrawal symptoms. We don't know though. We'll only know that once we see what we're dealing with."

He looks at her then at my sister. "I want updates. I want to know every time her situation changes. I want to know hourly."

The doctor nods, while internally I want to tell him to fuck off. That that's not his place, that he has no relation to Sofia.

"Me too." Ben says. Only his tone is completely different. He sounds hollow. Like he's as broken as she is.

"Focus on my sister." I say to the doctor. "Get her better, do whatever you need to do."

She nods and I get up, leaving them to it. I can't sit here, I can't think in her presence because the guilt is overwhelming.

I did this. I left her with Otto. Knowingly left her with a monster. What else did I expect? What other outcome would there be but this?

I stalk back down the corridor, clenching my fists. We need to work out next steps. We need to…

"Daddy?"

I pause seeing Lara poking her head around the door. She's in her pjs so she's clearly woken up with all the commotion going on.

"You okay Sweetpea?" I've not been spending as much time with her as I'd like. I sat down, explained it, explained that I had to work to get mummy back. I know she understands but that doesn't make it any better.

Tia's sister has been watching over her, babysitting her. I'm grateful for her help and I resent it all the same. It should be me, me and Rose, looking after our daughter together.

Every night I can, I sleep with her curled up in my arms. Most night she wakes from the nightmares and I'm there to soothe her and make it better. She's starting to laugh now. She's starting to come back but I don't doubt she's going to need some sort of counselling, as Rose most likely will as well.

"They're saying Aunty Sofia is here." She says.

"Who is saying that?" I ask.

She chews her lip. "I heard them daddy. Is she back? Can I see her?"

"She's resting Sweetpea. She's not very well so she needs to sleep for a bit."

"Did they hurt her too?" She asks.

I wince at how normal she makes it sound. As if any of this is normal. I scoop her up into my arms. Yeah she is getting heavier and I'm relieved to feel it.

"She'll be okay Lara. She just needs a little time. Just like you did."

She nods before leaning against my shoulder.

"Shall we get a snack? A midnight treat?" I ask.

"Cake?" She says hopefully which makes me laugh.

We don't have all that much cake. At least not the fancy ones we had back at home. Here it's mainly Victoria sponges and pudding. Things that are easy to whip up and make on mass.

I carry her into the canteen, put her onto a bench and then go get something from the counter.

Even this is starting to feel normal, that living in some sort of commune is how we've always been.

I grab two bowls, treacle pudding and custard. Extra sugar I guess but I know Lara won't complain.

When I put it in front of her, her eyes literally light up. "This is a big snack daddy."

"Yeah?" I smile. "Wanna see if you can manage it all for me?"

"I will do my best." She says picking up the spoon that looks so big in her hand.

I plant a kiss on her head at those words. "You always do."

She smiles at me before tucking in and for a minute I let myself just enjoy this moment, enjoy the fact that my child is safe, is with me. That we got her out before Darius could seriously hurt her.

"Roman."

I look around as Holden walks up to me with a look I definitely do not like. I know it's got nothing to do with Sofia so that helps.

"What is it?" I ask infinitely aware that my daughter is here and I don't want her to hear anything that might traumatise or scare her further.

"Everyone knows." He says.

"Knows what?" I reply.

"That you're not dead."

"Of course daddy isn't dead." Lara says looking between us. "He's my daddy, he can't die."

It's hard not to react to that statement, I can even see Holden who's the toughest bastard I know melting at her words. Yeah she'll have that effect on you mate, she'll melt even the blackest of hearts.

"How do they know?" I ask quietly.

"Someone recorded the whole thing on their phone. It's all over social media." He replies.

"Show me."

He pulls his phone out, brings up an app and flicks through until we both see it, the action replay of everything that went down.

I can see myself, in the streetlights it's hard to make out that it's me unless you know my face well. But the thing that damns us is Ben, when he hollers 'Roman' not just once, but twice. If they don't put it together then they have to be an idiot.

"Fuck." I murmur.

"Daddy that's a bad word." Lara admonishes me.

"Sorry Sweetpea." I say.

And I am sorry. I'm sorry this has been viewed over a quarter of million times already.

I'm sorry of what the consequences will be.

That Rose is there, and that ultimately Darius will make her pay for all of this.

"What do you want to do?" Holden asks.

I shake my head slightly as I think. I need to do something. I need to do something big. Darius knows, there's no use making small gestures anymore. No use simply poking the dragon.

I have to make a statement, I have to kick the hornets' nest and fight with everything I've got. Fight for Rose now, fight because both our lives depend upon it.

"We blow the whole thing open." I say.

"What does that mean?" He replies.

I give him a grin, before planting a kiss on my daughters head. "You'll see."

ROMAN

I type fast. My fingers striking the keys one after another as I work away.

Tia sits behind me, peering over my shoulder. She's been watching me work, trying to learn from me. In her lap Lara is dozing. I know I should have tucked her into bed first, that it's way past her bedtime but I didn't want to leave her to sleep alone.

And more importantly, I wanted her to witness this. To realise what this will mean for us.

"You sure about this?" Holden murmurs.

He's been stood cross armed watching me as well but he doesn't have a clue about technology beyond anything weapons based.

"It's time." I reply, not taking my eyes from the screen. No wanting to pause for a second.

It is time. It's more than bloody time.

"What about your girlfriend?" Tia asks quietly.

I blink for a second. "She's not my girlfriend. She's my fiancée." I state. "And if we do this right then she'll be safe."

"And if you don't?"

I can't think like that. I have to do this because Rose is in danger right now. There's a chance that when everyone realises what's really going on that will save Rose. That they will turn to the streets, that they will march on the Governors House and Darius will realise all of this is over.

I don't divulge Rose's secret. I don't divulge the fact that Darius forced her into this relationship, that he forced her hand. I don't know how she would feel about the world knowing her business.

Besides Darius has enough other shit going on that I don't need to.

So instead I post evidence, all the evidence about the organ trade, about the human trafficking, about the fact that Darius has been running the gangs, running the drug trade. I put up so many faces, all people he's indirectly murdered, all victims that men like Collin King have paid thousands to steal their organs.

I reveal the whole lot.

That Verona is not a glistening city of gold. But one of blood. One of corruption. That law and order doesn't exist the way they think it does, but that every citizen, every person living here is caught in the whims of a despotic leader who they didn't even elect, no, he faked that too. He rigged the vote to ensure he would maintain his grip on power.

It takes little over an hour to get it all up. I hack into every news station, every paper, every journalist's social media account. I don't care whether they're sports journalists, or fashion, or economics. I put the same posts out. All of them repeating the same thing.

The truths about this city and the man in charge.

When I'm done I sit back staring at my handiwork, seeing the comments already growing, seeing the stories already going viral.

"What now?" Holden asks.

I look across at my daughter, at Lara now fast asleep in Tia's arms. "We go to the streets." I say. "We make sure this becomes an uprising. I want every man and woman who lives in Verona marching on his house. I want uproar. I want fury."

"In that case we'll need numbers." Holden replies.

"We should set off at different junctures. We take the city street by street." I state.

"Whatever you need you have it." Koen says and we all turn seeing him stood in the doorway watching us.

"What about you?" I ask. Surely he's not planning on staying here, on hiding underground now that everything he's been work-ing for is finally coming into fruition.

He meets my gaze before grinning. "I'm going for Otto." He growls. "I'm going to skin the bastard alive."

ROSE

I'm awoken to the sound of doors slamming and yelling too.

I don't move. I stay where I am, huddled in the darkness.

Darius went to the club tonight. He didn't say that was where he was going but I could tell. I just knew from the way he was acting.

And I did everything I could to try and make him stay here. I didn't want to inflict anything more on Sofia that could be avoided.

But he just took what I offered and left anyway.

I guess I should have seen that move. And a part of me is more disgusted with myself, that I so willingly offered myself up, spread my legs, and yet I got nothing from it. I didn't save Sofia.

I rub my eyes, looking at the clock on the bedside table. It's barely midnight.

I don't know why he's back so early but from all the noise it must be something to do with Roman. That he's done something else.

He's escalating. It feels like every day he's twisting the screw and Darius is getting more and more volatile.

It's taking all my charm now to keep from his beatings despite our newly established ceasefire.

The door slams open. Light from the hallway streams in. I cover my face with my hands but I'm already being dragged out of the bed.

"What's going on?" I gasp.

They don't reply. It's not Darius. He's sent his guards to come get me.

And that makes me panic more.

I'm hauled down the stairs. My feet don't even make contact. I'm held up purely by my arms.

And then I'm thrown into the centre of the room, onto the cold wooden floor.

My face slams into it before my hands can stop the impact. I lay for a moment, just taking in breaths, steeling myself for what is undoubtedly coming next.

When I look up I don't see Darius.

I see Ty.

My head tilts, I frown as I take him in. He's covered in blood. One of his eyes is so swollen up it's black with bruising. He looks like he's lost teeth, there's blood smeared from his mouth and his hands, they've broken his fingers, every single one is at a horrific angle.

"What have you done to him?" I gasp, crawling, reaching out to cradle him.

Darius snarls, grabbing my hair, pulling me back as I yelp.

I blink up, playing the same part I've kept up these last days. "Darius?"

He smirks before glancing at my cousin and then to Otto who's stepping out of the darkness clearly beaten up too. He's limping.

His nose looks broken and his lip is split. He turns his head, stares at Ty and then kicks him so hard in the head.

I scream trying to throw myself over him and once more Darius holds me back.

"Why are you doing this?" I ask as my tears begin streaming down my face.

"Why don't you ask your cousin that?" Otto replies. "And while you're at it, ask where my wife is."

He slams another boot into him. This time I can hear as his bones break. Ty lets out a deep groan as he curls up into himself.

"Stop." I gasp. "Please stop. You're hurting him."

"That's the point Rose." Darius says. "Your cousin thought he could switch sides, thought he could double cross us."

"What are you talking about?" I say screwing my face up.

He lets out a laugh. "Oh please, you think we haven't checked? There's footage of it all over the internet. Ty here decided to play knight in shining armour and rescue Sofia only he wasn't quick enough to not get caught."

My face reacts, I look across at Ty who is clearly now in severe pain. Please tell me he didn't decide to save her all by himself? It would be a suicide mission.

He meets my gaze then drops it.

"Ty?" I whisper.

"Sofia is safe." That's all he manages to say before Otto is on him again. Slamming his head into the floor till he's spitting blood.

"Sofia is my wife." Otto shouts. "She belongs to me."

"No she doesn't." Ty shouts. "She was never yours."

I get to my feet, my legs are shaking but I won't let my fear get in the way of what I have to do. I place my hands on Darius's chest, playing my part as always.

"I don't understand what's going on." I say. "But he needs a doctor. He needs medical help."

"Yeah?" Darius replies. "Guess he's not gonna get that is he?"

I screw my face up before I can stop myself. They're going to kill him. I know they are. "Please, he's my cousin, please don't hurt him."

Darius laughs before shoving me so hard I fall backwards onto the floor. "You can stop the pretence now Rose. Your little trickery is over."

"What?"

"You think we didn't speak to the guards, you think we didn't ask them about his comings and goings? Turns out he's been visiting you a lot. Turns out the two of you keep having little secret conversations."

I gulp, my stomach reeling as I realise this whole charade is collapsing around me. That both of us are utterly screwed in this moment.

"What were you discussing huh?" He continues. "What little plan were you coming up with?"

"I…" I gulp. "I was asking after Lara. He knows where she is. I just wanted to make sure she was safe. That she was okay."

"Sure you were Rose." He replies. "Just like you were making sure Sofia would be safe too."

His hand hits me before I see the movement. I'm sent flying to the floor and I cry out as my body slams into it.

As I lay stunned he grabs my hair wrenching my head around to look at him.

"Your daughter is gone. Roman's already seen to that. Guess you were last on the list. Bottom of his give-a-shit pile."

I stare back at him, biting my tongue. I won't goad him further now. There's no point.

He drags a chair over and shoves me into it. As I try to move he grabs my right wrist holding it in place as someone wraps tap around and around, fixing it to the arm. Then he does the other with my left wrist as I struggle so hard to get free.

"What I want to know is why you turned tail?" Otto says grabbing Ty by the throat. "We all know Rose is a whore but you, what's in it for you? What did the Montagues promise that was so great?"

Ty glares back at him. "They promised me nothing."

"That's a fucking lie." Otto snaps before kneeing him in the chest.

"Stop." I cry but he doesn't.

"I love Sofia." Ty gasps. "I love her and you were killing her."

"Yeah?" Darius says before wrenching my head at an angle by my hair. "What about Rose? You consider the consequences for her in all this?"

I gulp meeting Ty's gaze. Trying to tell him that I can handle it. Whatever they throw at me. Whatever they do. I can take it.

"Where is he?" Darius asks.

"Where is who?" Ty replies.

Otto says the name, as if Darius can't even speak it. "Roman Fucking Montague."

"I don't know." Ty states.

They both laugh at that.

"Let's see if we can jog your memory then…" Darius murmurs looking over to the guards and jerking his head as some sort of signal. I hear the footsteps, the pounding as someone struts out of the room.

"Darius…" I try again and he backhands me before I can even get the word out.

The guard comes back and when I see what's in his hand I let out a whimper. Darius smirks at me as if my fear is amusing him now, as if this entire situation is a comedy for him.

"This is how this is going to go…" Darius says pointing the cattle prod at me while Otto tapes Ty to a chair the same way I am. "You claim to have amnesia, you claim to have conveniently forgotten where Roman is hiding which is fine, so to help get your memory back we're going to play a game…"

I gulp staring at the thing, at where it's so dangerously close to me. I think I'm grateful that I don't know where Roman is, that I can't divulge that information, because I don't know long I'd be able to hold out.

I'm not resilient.

I'm not strong.

I'm a coward.

A weak, pathetic person who couldn't even save themselves.

I look across at Ty. He's shaking his head. I can see he's so torn, that he might just admit what he knows to spare me and I can't have that. I can't have come this far, have endured this much for it to all fall apart again.

"Don't." I say as firmly as I can. "Whatever you know, don't tell…" My words turn to screams as Darius shocks me.

My body goes rigid, solid, as if every cell in me has turned to concrete, and yet I can feel it, white hot searing agony as wave after wave of electricity hits me. My back arches and it's only the tape holding me in place, fighting to keep me from tearing apart.

And then it stops. Everything stops. I slump back into the chair, my breath sounds ragged, my heart thumps as if I'm on the verge of a heart attack.

"Ty…?" Darius murmurs.

I open my eyes, look across at my cousin and shake my head.

I can do this. I can endure this. I have to.

"I, I don't know…" Ty says.

And once more my screams override everything.

My toes curl up with the pain, my fingers scrunch into fists so tight that my broken bones feel like they've snapped even more.

"I don't know."

I hear Ty shouting it over and over.

And then the pain goes and Darius is there soothing me, stroking my cheek as if he wasn't the one inflicting this torture in the first-place.

"It's very simple Tyrone." Otto says.

I can't even form words. I feel like my tongue might have swollen, that my body is no longer under my control. How I haven't pissed myself I don't know.

"I don't know." Ty yells. "I only ever met him one place."

My heart sinks, I whimper opening my mouth to say something and Darius covers it with his hand. Ty barely speaks more than a sentence, giving away what sounds in truth like a nonsense piece of information.

Otto tilts his head like he's not convinced.

And Darius stands back up before shocking me again.

I scream. With each new sound my voice grows more hoarse, my throat feels like daggers are slicing it open.

When the pain ceases, when I slump back into the chair, I see Otto whispering into Ty's ear, no doubt taunting him, trying to get him to break.

And then Carter storms into the room looking between us. He doesn't even flinch when he sees us both tied up so I guess he's been informed of tonight's adventures.

"You have to see this." He says.

"What?" Darius snaps.

Carter hands him a phone and I study his face as his eyes widen.

"Who's seen this?" Darius growls.

"It's everywhere. They hacked into the news stations, they've hacked into every tv station too. Everyone in Verona will know before the sun is up."

Darius lets out a snarl. "Fine sort it. Do whatever is necessary."

Carter nods, turning on his heel and stalks back out. For a second Otto just stares down at Ty and then he shakes his head looking across at Darius with a look I know only too well.

"Don't." I beg. "Please don't."

But Otto is already pulling out his gun, wrenching Ty's head back and shoving it right under his chin. When he pulls the trigger I scream like I've finally given up. Like they really have broken me now.

"Shut the fuck up." Darius says to me.

I don't respond beyond shutting my eyes. I'm shaking now, my tears are streaming once more and I can feel it mingling with the dirt and blood on my face.

"I'll sort the militia." Otto says. "We'll have the city back in our control before the sun is up."

Darius grunts back but his gaze is fixed on me still. He clearly knows everything. He clearly knows Roman is alive. That he has Lara.

The only thing he has now is me and I wonder what new horrors he's going to inflict before this day is out.

ROSE

They leave me here. In semi-darkness. With Ty's body still opposite me for what feels like the entire rest of the night.

I try to get my wrists free. I try to manoeuvre my hands to loosen the tape but it's too tight and all it does is rip at my skin.

My body keeps shuddering, as if I'm enduring aftershocks from the electricity, though I don't know if that's a real thing or it's just in my head.

All I can think about is that Roman is coming. That this all awful situation is finally coming to an end.

I can feel my tears falling. I can feel my nightdress getting wetter as they drip from my cheeks but I can't stop now that I've started.

Ty is dead. They murdered him like his life meant nothing. But I could see the way his eyes met mine, I could see the acceptance just as Otto pulled the trigger. I think in his heart he was happy to do it, happy to sacrifice himself for Sofia but that doesn't make it okay. None of it is okay.

I'm shivering so much it feels like the very chair is shaking. I don't know what happens if it gives way. I don't know what happens if it overturns. Will they come back to see what the noise is? Will they think I did it deliberately in some attempt to get free and then punish me more?

I don't care now. They can hurt me as much as they want because Roman is coming. Roman is going to save me. I just have to do what he says and keep myself alive. I just have to be brave for a little longer.

The door opens. I blink rapidly as the light pours in.

I don't know how long I've been down here or what the time is.

Darius walks up to me, squats in front of me and brushes my hair from my face. I try to jerk my head away but I can't escape his touch.

"All you had to do was play nice Rose." He says. "All you had to do was be obedient. Except you wouldn't do that would you?"

I bite my tongue, glaring back at him.

"I'm going to kill Roman. You do realise that don't you?"

I cast my eyes beyond him, to the open doorway and the men who seem to be moving rapidly around.

"I'll give you his head as a gift." He continues. "I'll have it mounted the way they mount a stag's and I'll hang it over our bed, so you'll know every moment you're awake that it's over. That I won."

He grips my jaw, forcing my attention back to him.

"Are you listening to me Rose?"

I roll my eyes before I can stop myself. I'm too tried now, too exhausted, and in truth, I'm sick of playing a part. I want to look Darius in the eyes and for him to know that he doesn't scare me anymore. That nothing he can do will hurt me. I want him to see everything I feel for him, I want him to feel it, my contempt, my hate, my desire to pick up a knife and drive it into his beating heart.

"Even now we're taking back control of the streets." He continues. "This little protest will be over by lunchtime."

"Sure it will." I spit.

He tilts his head, his lips curling. "You think I'm that stupid? You think I haven't planned for something like this?"

"I know you didn't." I say back. "You thought Roman was dead. You believed it all these months…"

He lets out a laugh that cuts right through me. "God you're naïve." He replies. "You think I didn't know? You think I wasn't more than aware that he was still out there? I had men hunting for him."

I narrow my eyes. I can't tell if he's pretending or not.

"…We didn't find his body after all, so what else could it mean?" He continues.

I gulp at those words. "You knew you weren't burying him."

"No." He grins.

"But you said to me…"

"I lied Rose. I lied to make you understand how utterly pointless your fighting was."

"Who did you bury instead?" I scream remembering what he'd done to me, how he'd violated me over what I believed were Roman's remains. "Who did you stuff into his coffin?"

He laughs more then. "Just some random homeless man. Provided more use in death than he ever did in life."

I fight the ties then. I physically jerking as I try to get free.

He watches with amusement until I stop. Until I give up realising that it's just a pointless waste of my energy. I can't get free. He's ensured that.

"How about you come watch the rest of this play out Rose?" He taunts.

"How about you fuck off." I spit back.

He smacks me and because of how I'm tied my whole body takes the full impact and the chair topples onto its side.

I spit blood as I realise he's split my lip. Though I don't that's the last injury I'm going to suffer today.

He crouches down, cuts through the tape, and hauls me up. My feet slide in the blood pooled on the floor. He drags me out the room, out along the corridor to the main living space which right now feels like the command centre for a damned army.

He plonks me into a seat and I'll admit I'm grateful to be out of his hold, to not have to depend upon him to not collapse onto the floor. Now that my wrists are free I can feel my blood flooding back to my fingers and they're tingling unpleasantly with pins and needles.

"Watch the show." Darius says.

I glare at him and he grabs my jaw wrenching my head around to where the massive TV is projecting what I imagine is the streets of Verona right now.

It looks like some sort of battle. I gulp as I watch it play out. People with scarfs tied around their faces hurl what look like Molotov cocktails at the Militia who stand behind their bulletproof shields before taking pot shots where they can. And along the bottom the news channel is streaming more and more alarming headlines.

That the Militia have opened fire in two different districts.

That ten people are confirmed dead and dozens more wounded.

"You have to stop this." I whisper.

Darius shakes his head. "Not until I have Roman."

"You're killing people." I hiss.

He smirks more. "Have you not been paying attention Rose? I don't give a fuck about other people."

"You're the Governor of this city. You're meant to protect it."

He shakes his head. "I protect those who deserve it. These people…" He jerks his head at the TV. "These people deserve everything they get for coming up against me."

"You like some despot. Some sort of dictator." I spit.

He doesn't reply. He just fixes his gaze on the screen and with a horrible sinking feeling I watch as it plays out. As slowly, minute by minute the Militia gain the upper hand and this tiny part of the protest is extinguished.

"You can't beat me Rose." He states. "You can't stop me. I have too much power to simply be overthrown in such a manner as this."

I shut my eyes. I don't want to believe him. I don't want to see that this is true but with every image it's showing the same thing.

The riot is dying out.

The Militia have control.

Roman hasn't won this.

ROSE

He forces me to watch, forces me to sit here, and witness as what feels like another bitter defeat is played out.

Carter comes in, glances at me, then whispers something in Darius's ear.

He grins then. His eyes sparkling.

He turns to me and I brace myself for whatever horror he's about to announce but the voice from the TV gets all our attention.

"…We're getting reports that Otto Montague has been killed in the riots. That his body has…" The reporter pauses, looking at her notes then at the screen, her face looking like she can't quite believe the words in front of her.

"What the fuck is this?" Darius growls picking up the remote, switching channel.

My stomach flips at the new, more horrific image now displayed in full HD. Otto hasn't just been killed. He's not simply been caught in the crossfire. The footage is clearly amateur. But the image is as clear as day.

Otto is hanging from a balcony, like he's been crucified.

His body has been stripped. He looks like he took one hell of a beating before he was finally offed. And though they've tried to blur the offending part, it's more than obvious that someone cut his dick off. That he was castrated. Tortured too.

I smirk before I can stop myself. I don't know if Roman did this, or whether it was some other person working for him but it gives me some satisfaction that the bastard suffered before he met his end.

A fist to the side of my head knocks the smile right off my face.

Darius stands over me and then his head turns back to the screen. My eyes dart to it barely believing what they're now saying. That the protestors are back. That there are more now than ever, and that they're marching on the Governor's House.

My eyes meet Darius's and I can see it, the uncertainty of what next steps to take.

"They're coming for you." I taunt.

"Shut the fuck up." Carter snarls.

I glance at him grinning more. "You think they'll leave you alone Carter? You think they won't get their revenge on you too? Roman knows everything you've done, and he's going to make you pay…"

Carter steps into no doubt hit me and Darius blocks him. "That's enough." He says. "We don't have time for this shit."

"Then what do you suggest we do?" Carter snaps.

"Get the chopper. Get it ready to go. We leave now."

My eyes widen. I look between them both. No fucking way am I being taken from this house. Not now, not when I'm so close to getting free.

Carter talks into his earpiece, passing on the instructions. Darius wrenches me up by my arm and I take the chance to fight him. Hitting him with both fists.

He takes my blows as if they're nothing and then he throws me over his shoulder and carries me as I jerk so violently trying to force him to put me down.

I guess he gets tired of my fighting. I guess he just expects me to acquiesce and he pulls me back to my feet then slams my head so hard into the wall that I all but pass out. My body goes limp, I can't focus. I slump against him and this time, when his disgusting hands scoop me up I can't do a thing to stop it.

He picks up speed then, all but running through the house to where the helipad is located. When we get outside I can feel it, the freezing cold air. It's afternoon, now. The sky is thick with grey stormy clouds. We've been inside watching this riot play out for almost the entire day and I'm still in the damned nightgown I was dragged out of bed in last night.

I can hear the chopper. I can hear the sound of the blades going round and round.

Darius gets in, plonking me into the seat opposite him.

Carter climbs in beside Darius and I stare out, over the wall, at the mass of people, at the tsunami of rage headed right for us. I can see them now. I can see the thousands of people marching on the house. Even with the forces we have, there's no way we could hold that mass back.

And I know if Darius gets me away from here, I know Roman won't be able to track me. Darius has too much money, too many connections. I'll be even further from help than ever.

My heartrate picks up. My adrenaline is spiking even more than my fear. I'm utterly exhausted but I can't not fight. I can't just let this happen. Not this time.

The chopper starts to take off. Something comes hurtling at us threw the air and Darius ducks as whatever it is smashes against the window.

But he hasn't shut the door. It's still wide open and right now, I'd take a broken leg over a lifetime stuck with Darius.

Without hesitating, without considering the consequences further, I hurl myself out the door.

Except, I'm not the only one who moves.

Carter moves with me. He's got a gun in his hand and he wraps his body around mine, as if his weight can pull me back but the momentum is too much and instead of keeping me in the helicopter we both fall from it.

We slam into the concrete below. Somehow in the milliseconds it took to fall we spun around so that I land on top of Carter, with his body cushioning the impact. But that doesn't make it hurt any less.

I meet his furious eyes and then we're both scrambling for the gun he had. Only in the fall it's too far from both of us. I pull my head back slamming it with all my strength into his face and then take the moment to grab the knife I know he keeps in his belt.

Despite the blow, he's not even dazed and his hands wrap around mine. He's shouting something. But the noise of the chopper above us is too much. And the sound of protest is getting louder and louder.

We both struggle for control, both desperately fight for ownership and as I sense a brief moment of advantage I take it, driving the blade into his stomach.

He groans as it slides in. But his grip remains just as firm around my hand and I know I've not stabbed him nearly hard enough to do any real damage.

"Easy now." He says.

I shake my head. My rage, my fury, my complete and utter desperation taking over in this moment.

"Come on Rose. We both know you don't have it in you." He says.

I grip the blade harder and with all the strength I can muster I force it back, back into his flesh, back into his stomach.

His hands try to push me off. He grapples for dominance and I become rabid, screaming, as I drive the blade into his abdomen again, then into his chest, and finally, I drive it right into his throat where it remains lodged.

When I'm finished I'm covered in blood and panting like we've been fighting for hours when in truth it couldn't have been more than a minute of frenzy.

As my body slumps beside him I stare up and realise the helicopter is still there. Darius is still there. He stares at me and in a split second I reach over, grabbing Carter's discarded gun and I start shooting. Aiming for Darius. Aiming for the helicopter. Not caring who I fucking hit.

He yells out, the chopper makes a sharp turn away and then it's climbing, gaining altitude so quickly.

I keep firing. I keep pulling the trigger until I'm all out of bullets and then I lay there, on the freezing cold concrete as my adrenaline drops and the pain of everything I've gone through really starts to hit me.

ROMAN

We walk through the house. It's completely empty. Deserted. As if everyone has already abandoned it.

And that gets my nerves up.

Because what if Darius has fled? What if he's taken Rose with him? Taken her and gone to ground.

If he has it could take months to figure out where the fuck he is and even longer to get Rose out.

"In here." Someone yells.

I pick up speed, gun still in my hand, and sprint through the rooms. There's a massive TV still on, flashing images of the riots, images of this house now with it's gates half hanging off from where a vehicle drove into them at force, but what it keeps returning to is the image of Otto.

Of him hanging there.

Dead.

I wasn't the one to do it though I wish I had. I wanted to gut him and look my sister in the eyes, to tell her he was dead by my hands, only I won't get the honour now.

Because Koen did it.

He took three men with him. Three assassins. Together they stalked the streets and, right when the new stations were spreading fake news about how the militia were back in control, they made their move. They got Otto. They butchered him.

And they made sure everyone saw the results of it by hanging him from the Courts of Justice, right where everyone could see him.

I pause as I reach the room. As I see the men stood outside waiting for my reaction. I can see the body beyond, I can see the pool of congealed blood around it.

"Ty." I murmur.

So they did capture him. I let out a sigh at the knowledge. I was hoping he'd escaped. I was hoping that somehow he had gotten away.

I walk up to where he's slumped in a chair. He looks like he took a beating, like Otto and Darius made sure he suffered before they blew his brains out.

His body is cold when I touch him, telling me that he's been dead for some time but as I drop my gaze I see it, bare footprints in the blood. Small smears too from where someone was clearly dragged away from him.

Rose.

She was here. She witnessed this.

My eyes fall on the other chair, an empty one with tape cut where wrists had been held in place. I clench my fists at the thought of her being dragged in here, forced to watch as they no doubt tortured and then executed Ty.

"Roman?" Holden says behind me.

Only we both freeze as we recognise what that sudden sound is.

"He's got a fucking chopper." I yell. That's where he is. He's fleeing as we speak and I know he has Rose, that he's taking her hostage.

I run back through the house, smashing into someone and sending them flying, but I don't stop to apologise. I don't have time. The helipad is out to the side, it's a good few minutes from the main house. My legs are killing me from the force at which I'm forcing them to go but I won't slow down. I can't slow down. Not now, not when I'm so close to reaching her.

As I get outside I hear all the commotion, all the noise and chaos of the riot I set in motion. The sound is deafening but above it, I can hear that hum of the rotor blades.

And then I hear gun shots. A lot of them.

I run faster, force my body on, so fearful now that I'm too late. That once again, Rose is slipping away, being stolen again right when I'm convinced this might all be over.

I shout her name. I scream it over and over until my lungs feel like they have no oxygen left.

The sound of helicopter seems to be getting dimmer, it sounds like it's already disappearing.

I fight back the tears, fight the anger too as I make the final turn to where the damned helipad is.

And then I freeze, staring at the scene before me.

Rose is here. She's lying there, propped up on her elbows, gun pointed right at me but that's not what gets my attention. I don't care right now if she does pull the trigger because she's covered in blood, utterly soaked in it.

I blink, taking in her body, she's in nothing more than a damned slip of fabric. The silk clings to her and I can see from the way her body is trembling that she's absolutely freezing and utterly petrified as well.

"Rose." I murmur.

She tilts her head, that gun still dangerously blocking any movement on my part.

Behind us the crowd seems to burst through like a damn finally giving way.

She spins around, her eyes so wide with fear, pointing the weapon at this new threat. I take the chance to close the distance, crouching down when I get close enough, putting my jacket around her to get her warm.

"It's okay." I say quietly, wrapping my hand around the metal.

She whimpers, shaking her head, as if this gun is the only thing that can save her right now.

"It's okay Rose, I've got you." I state.

She gulps, her tears are now streaming back down her cheeks. I prise the weapon from her hands and suddenly she's collapsing into my arms, sobbing into my chest.

"I knew you'd come." She says. "I knew you wouldn't leave me here."

I clasp her head in my hands. "I'll never leave you Rose. I promised you. Whatever happens, wherever we end up, we'll always be together."

She cries harder then. I try to soothe her but I'm infinitely aware of all the people swarming us. All the crowd that seems to watch us like this is some sort of performance put on for their entertainment.

I raise my head, glaring at them, daring them to come closer because I swear to god I will kill anyone that goes near Rose right now. And then thankfully I see Holden making his way, with half a dozen of my men too. They're clearing a path, giving us a safe route out of this damned place.

"It's time to go." I say to Rose.

"Go where?" She whispers.

"Home." I say back before lightly kissing her forehead. "And back to our daughter."

She bites her lip, trying to force some sort of composure but she's too far gone for any of it. She looks like she's in a trance, she looks like she's almost delirious. I wonder if Darius drugged her too. I guess we'll find that out when we get her to a doctor.

As I help her to her feet, I can feel how unstable she is and realise she can barely walk so I scoop her up into my arms. She's so light. She's lost so much weight. She feels fragile now, not the strong, powerful woman I last held.

Her eyes drop to the bloodied body we've both been ignoring this entire time.

"I killed him." She says. "I had to kill him."

"It doesn't matter." I reply.

She grabs my face, her grip so hard and her eyes suddenly flash. "Yes it does." She snarls. "It does fucking matter."

I don't know what to say. I don't know how to respond to that but as she slumps back into my shoulder I guess she's not looking for any reply.

So I carry her out, past all those onlookers, past every one of my men too. I know Holden has a car already waiting and I'm so relieved once we're in it. Once we're speeding away.

ROMAN

The doctor checks her over.

I want to stay in the room, I want to hold her hand but I can see as every second passes she's freaking out more.

Her eyes keep darting around like she's expecting someone to jump out and attack her. She keeps whimpering, rocking, trembling so hard the very bed creaks.

When I try to soothe her she freaks out even more, screaming, clawing, completely losing it until the doctors all but force me from the room and lock the door so I can't get back in.

I stare in through the window, my heart breaking as I see how traumatised she is, how changed. And then they draw the curtain, cut even my vision of her off, and though I want to smash down the door, to kick it off its hinges and storm back in, I know that won't help. That won't make things better. It will only make it worse.

I walk into Sofia's room, where she's still there, barely conscious, her eyes dazed from all the meds they've put her on. There's a pump by her bed, feeding some sort of liquid in through her arm. I try not to look at it because for some reason this turns my stomach more than anything else.

"Daddy?"

I turn at the timid call of my name.

"You okay Sweetpea?" I reply. She's not meant to be in here. I didn't want her seeing Sofia like this but clearly she's found a way in when we were all out rescuing Rose.

"Aunty Sofia won't talk to me." She says.

"She's resting Lara." I say. "She needs time that's all."

She nods like she understands it and then she's lifting up her arms, and I pick her up, holding her against me.

"It's okay. Everything will be okay." I say.

"Did you find mummy?"

I give her a smile. "I did."

Her eyes widen. She bites her lip in the same way Rose always does when she's happy and doesn't know how to contain the emotion.

"Can I see her? Please daddy, please let me."

I frown pulling her in. I want to say yes. God, more than anything I want to carry her into Rose's room and hope that the mere sight of our daughter will cure everything.

But I'm not that naïve.

Right now Rose is clearly lost in her trauma. Processing whatever the hell has happened to her. If I let Lara see her like this, it won't help. If anything it will scar them both more.

"How about we go watch a movie?" I say. It's not what I want to do, but I know Koen and his men are in control, and I know Holden is with them now.

Besides, with Darius gone there's nothing left for me to do.

I got my child, I got my sister and now finally I have Rose safe as well.

She winces like she wants to say no but that urge to keep my happy, to appease everyone around her takes over. It's the same way Rose behaves, that same conditioning and I make a mental note to work on that, to ensure in the future they both put themselves first.

"Okay." She whispers.

"Come on then." I murmur turning to leave but as I do I hear the voice, the quiet timid, fearful word.

"Roman?"

I spin around. "Sofia?"

She looks at me and for the first time I think she's actually seeing me. "Roman?" Her face screws up. She looks so confused. She looks at Lara and then back at me. "I don't understand." She says. "I, I thought you were dead."

I put Lara down, rushing to the bed. "It was a lie."

"You're, you're alive?"

"I am." I say. "And Ben is too. And Holden."

"How?" She tries to sit up, she tries to move but she's still so weak she just crumples into the pillows.

"Wait a moment." I murmur glancing at my daughter. There are so many things I have to say to Sofia, so many things I need to tell her but I know I can't do that with Lara here. I can't speak about it because she's too young, too innocent.

"Daddy?" Lara whispers.

"Can you go find Uncle Ben for me?" I ask her.

"But I want to stay. I want to be with Aunty Sofia." Lara pouts.

"I know Sweetpea." I say gently. "But we need to talk. And…"

Lara bursts into tears and my heart sinks. I wrap my arms around her, hugging her so tightly. "I'm sorry Lara. I'm so sorry."

"I don't want to leave. Please don't make me." She cries.

I look over at my sister and shut my eyes for a moment. "Okay. But I need to talk to Aunty Sofia." I say. "Can you sit by me and try and sleep?"

I can see she's exhausted. I don't think she's slept a wink since this all kicked off and her tiny body is not used to it. If I were a better parent she wouldn't have to live like this. She'd be warm right now. She'd be tucked up in bed, somewhere safe, in a room with all her toys around her and her mummy and daddy there, reading her stories, showing her how much we care.

She nods so quickly.

I take her hand sitting down with her curled up beside me.

Sofia watches her for a moment as if she knows what I'm thinking too. And sure enough, after a few moments Lara drifts off, with my arm wrapped around her front and her back pressed into my chest.

"How is she?" Sofia asks quietly.

I shrug. "She's traumatised. She doesn't understand any of it. I've tried explaining some but…"

"She's six." Sofia says. "She's thankfully too young to get it."

I nod seeing the pain in her eyes. "Christ Sofia, I am so sorry."

"For what?"

"For Otto, I had no idea, I was so damn stupid."

She opens her mouth to argue and I cut across her. "It's my fault. I should never have let you play that part, should never have let you anywhere near him."

"I knew what I was doing." She says. "I mean, I thought I did."

I feel my stomach turn at what Otto did to her, what I allowed to happen.

"It was my decision Roman." She says. "Besides, you didn't know it would end this way."

"I should have." I snap. I won't let her excuse it, I won't let her simply brush it off. What I did was unforgiveable.

She shudders folding her arms over herself. "I wanted to help. I…" She shakes her head, looking like she's forcing back the tears. "They buried you. They held a funeral. I thought you were dead."

"I know. But it was all fake."

"And Rose, did you get her out? Is she okay?"

I wince. "She's alive." I reply. "Darius has fled."

"And Otto?" She half whispers. "What about him? Is he dead? Please tell me you killed him Roman."

"He's dead." Koen growls.

We both turn staring at the man who's suddenly stood in the doorway.

Sofia frowns looking at me then back at him. "Who are you?" She says so quietly.

He smiles, a genuine, soft smile I could barely believe possible. "I was the one who made him pay."

She binks, her face going from confusion to fear. "Who, who are you?" She asks again but as he takes a step into the room she seems to panic more, and he sees it, he registers it, and he glances at me before walking back out and leaving us alone as if he'd never even been here.

She turns her head away, shutting her eyes and I place my hand over hers. "No one is going to hurt you now." I say.

"Who is he?"

"His name is Koen. He's been letting us hide out here. He's been helping us too. Helping us fight Darius."

"Koen Diaz?" She gasps.

"Do you know him?" I ask. God, it would certainly explain a few things if she did, though I can't imagine how their paths have crossed.

"No." She says. "I mean, we all know of him don't we? But I've never met him, I've never…"

"It's okay." I say hearing the strain in her voice, the panic too. "You need to rest, you need to get your strength back." I don't add that she needs to get clean too. That they injected her with meth. That though she herself is not technically an addict by choice, her body is being weaned off it nonetheless.

"Where's Ben?" She asks. "Is he alive?"

"He's alive. I can get him for you."

She shakes her head. "No, I don't…" Her shoulders slump. "I just needed to know he was okay that's all."

"Sofia," I begin but she shakes her head cutting me off.

"I need to sleep. I, please." Her eyes fill with tears, as though she's in pain and then I see it, the way her body is trembling.

"I'll get a doctor." I say quickly.

She nods, biting her lip. "I need to be alone." She whispers it but I still hear the shame.

"Sofia, you have nothing to be ashamed of." I state.

She whimpers shutting her eyes. "Please, just go, just go."

I want to argue, I want to say something, something healing, something that gets through but I can see the way she's crumbling that right now what she needs is alone time. So I pick Lara up, say goodnight, and walk away.

Once more feeling utterly useless. Utterly helpless.

ROSE

It feels like a blur. I know I'm out of the house. Away from him and yet it's like my mind can't register it, like I can't process anything.

A doctor checks me over. Beyond a few nasty bruises and a facture of my arm I've escaped relatively unscathed.

Only it doesn't feel like that.

Every time I blink I see his face, that look, that acceptance. And then the gun goes off and his face is blown away and all that is left is a wound so big and so horrific I keep screaming.

I can't stop screaming.

They give me something to calm my nerves and though I know it's meant to help that scares the shit out of me more, that they're drugging me, sedating me, taking away some level of my control. I fight them, I lash out, sending a drip stand crashing to the ground.

But the needle gets in anyway.

And that awful drug slips into my blood and while I'll admit I do feel calmer, I can feel that panic still there, that fear that any minute someone is going to come storming in, that Darius will find me and I'll be too weak to stop it.

They give me sympathetic looks, as if they understand what I'm going through and then, once I've convinced them that there's nothing psychically more they can treat they tell me to get some rest. To try to recover. As if it's as easy as that.

There's a bathroom attached to the room. I manage to function enough to wash myself, to wash off the dirt, and blood, trying to ignore the way the water streams so red and puddles around my feet. And then I pull on the pyjamas that are left and crawl into the bed.

I don't know where Roman is. I don't know if he's left simply to give me space or because he finds me repulsive now. If after everything I've endured he no longer loves me.

And that thought breaks my heart.

In my head I thought it would end, that as soon as I was free, I believed all the fear would be gone.

But that's not what's happened.

Instead it's like it's multiplied. It's like my brain is so used to suffering now that it can't register when the pain is no longer there.

I curl up, pulling the covers over my head, hiding beneath them and weep until my tears no longer fall, until I'm so exhausted I do sleep.

I WAKE TO MY OWN SCREAMS. TO THE HOARSE, HORRIFIC SOUND OF my own fear as one nightmare merges into another, and another in my mind.

It's so dark. I don't think this room has any windows and it feels more like a prison than a reprieve. But beyond my own breathing there is nothing. Just a silence that seems to hang in the air, seems to sound otherworldly.

I shut my eyes, too exhausted to move, too exhausted to function.

But the bed is warm, the bed is soft. And the fabric surrounding me feels comforting.

When something moves beside me I freeze. Ice fills my stomach. A whimper escapes my lips because I don't know what it is, it doesn't feel human, and yet what else could it be?

It moves around, sniffing, and then suddenly I realise who it is. "Bella?"

She nuzzles into my face. I let out a cry of joy.

She's not dead. She's not dead. Carter lied then. But how is she here?

"Mummy?"

I spin around. My heart is beating so fast now I can barely breathe.

"Lara?" I half sob her name.

The weight of the bed changes as my daughter clambers on and her arms wrap around me.

"Lara." I gasp again, pulling her around, holding her so tightly. "Lara." I repeat it again. I whisper it. I sing it. I refuse to let her go in this moment.

And we lay here, the three of us, me with my daughter in my arms and Bella snuggled in between us.

But I still don't know where Roman is. I still don't understand why he isn't here with me.

"I missed you so much." Lara cries.

"I missed you too baby." I say. "But I knew you were with Daddy, that he was keeping you safe."

"But no one was with you." She says. "No one was keeping you safe." She's sobbing now, crying into my chest and I realise suddenly that I'm crying too.

"It's over." I say. "It's finally over."

"Is he dead mummy? Did you kill him too?"

I want to say yes. God, I want to say yes so badly but I can't. I won't lie to her. I won't tell her false truths. Instead I kiss her head, take a deep breath and breath her in. I have my daughter back. I have her back.

"The only thing that matters is that I have you." I say.

ROMAN

I watched as Lara crept into her room and so much of me wanted to join them, to see them reunited. To hold them both in my arms and never ever let them go again.

But I have to protect Rose. That's my first priority.

And right now we've got the new Police Chief calling for her head. As if she's a criminal and not a victim in all of this.

I sit beside Koen. Both of us glaring at the man who right now sees himself as some sort of hero. Only he wasn't here when we needed him. He wasn't the one on the streets, fighting for Verona's very freedom.

"It's very clear…" He begins.

"No, it is not." I snap back.

"She was his wife. She is complicit in everything he…"

I stand up, flexing my hands, itching to wrap them around his throat. "Have you not heard a word I just said?"

His lips curl just enough to tell me he doesn't believe a word of it. That he thinks Rose is the gold-digging whore Darius made her to be.

"She was blackmailed." I state again. "He kidnapped our daughter…"

"That's as maybe." Chief Ambrose cuts across me. "But until we establish the facts…"

"She jumped out of damned helicopter to escape him." I half yell.

The footage of that has been doing loops on social media. The press are having a field day over it. It's been on repeat so many times I don't know how they've not grown bored of analysing it.

He sits back in his seat. "Mr. Montague, whatever you believe, she is not above the law."

"Meaning?" I ask.

"We have actual footage of her attacking a man, of murdering him."

I shake my head as my fury rages. "You mean the man who helped hold her captive? You mean the man who had a gun to her head? I'd say that was the very definition of self-defence wouldn't you?"

"That's for a jury to decide not for the likes of us."

"That's not actually true is it?" Koen says leaning forward, and for the first time I see the man flinch. "You decide who you prosecute in all of this, after all half the city rose up, you want to arrest them, arrest hundreds of thousands of people and charge them with inciting violence?"

"Not all of them are murderers." He states.

"And not all of them were held hostage for months on end." I snap back.

He shakes his head getting to his feet, staring out the window of the sterile hotel room we agreed as a meeting place. "The law is the law." He says. "We cannot pick and choose what bits we wish to abide by."

"Tell that to Darius." Koen growls.

"We would if we knew where he was." Ambrose says before fixing his gaze back on me. "Maybe Rose can give us that information."

"She doesn't know." I state. I don't know if that's actually true but right now I won't give him anymore reasons to want her in his possession.

"You know that for certain?" He replies.

A knock at the door stops my retort. We turn to look as a man in a suit more expensive than the damned ones Darius used to strut around in, appears.

"Governor Hastings." Ambrose says with a smug tone to his voice.

I stiffen but Koen doesn't react at all.

He's so different from Darius. He's red hair is balding. He doesn't have the charm, the charisma that Darius exudes and yet there's something about him that tells you he will fuck you up if you cross him.

And that puts me on edge.

He looks at us all and gives a curt nod.

"We've just been discussing Rose Blumenfeld..." Ambrose begins.

Hastings eyebrows raise. "And where is she?"

"That's exactly what we're asking." Ambrose says looking pointedly at me.

"And as I said." I growl. "I'm not telling you."

"If you refuse to cooperate then we will have no choice but to arrest you." Ambrose states.

"Enough." Hastings says. "We have enough to deal with without adding additional drama."

"But he knows where she is and he's refusing to disclose it." Ambrose snaps.

Hastings eyes flash and for a minute I can't tell what is going on in his head. I know he's been brought in to take charge. To clear up the entire shitshow that Darius has left. The city has declared a state of emergency after Darius fled and the President is on every news channel trying to instil calm. He personally picked Hastings, personally sent him here to sort the whole situation out.

"There's an article circulating in the press." Hastings says. "A journalist claims she was working with Rose, that Rose was passing on information, that she was whistleblowing despite the very real danger to her and her child."

My eyes widen. I hadn't heard that. I don't even know what journalist he's talking about.

"Is it true?" He asks fixing his gaze on me.

"Rose was being blackmailed." I confirm. "Darius kidnapped our daughter. He was threatening her life unless Rose did exactly what he wanted."

"A daughter nobody seems to know anything about." Ambrose says but Hastings acts like he hasn't even spoken.

"I see." Hastings says crossing his arms. "And your sister, what about her?"

"Otto forced her into marriage." I reply. "He was drugging her, assaulting her…" I trail off because even now the thought sickens me.

"Otto paid for that." Koen growls with a smirk.

Hastings looks over at him. "I know who you are. And though I don't condone your actions, right now I have bigger fish to fry."

"Meaning?" Koen says.

"Meaning, keep your head down and out of my way and I won't look for you." Hastings replies.

And that makes me pause.

We all know Koen is technically a wanted man. A murderer too. He'd make a damned good trophy to wave around if Hastings wanted some instant kudos from the new job but to be saying what he has suggests he isn't that way inclined.

"I won't give you Rose." I say. "She is as much a victim as every person Darius cut up and sold."

"I'm inclined to agree." Hastings says.

"What?" Ambrose half shouts, his face is the colour of beet-root as he cuts across Hastings.

"At present Rose is not a person of interest but she is a witness." Hastings states. "When she is ready I want to speak to her myself."

"And until then?" I ask.

He lets out a sigh. "Until then she can remain where she is. Wherever that is. As long as it's within the confines of this city."

"Thank you." I murmur.

He inclines his head. "I'm sweeping through the city. We're arresting anyone we find who is out beyond the curfew, looting, or breaking the peace."

"Noted." Koen says.

"Make sure we don't find your people because I will not be lenient if I do." Hastings says.

"You're, you're letting them go?" Ambrose splutters.

"I have the entire country in uproar. I have a man on the run who by all accounts was not only trafficking people but selling their organs. And best of all, half the rich of this city seem to have been in on it, seemed to have profited from it. I have a city on the verge of collapse, I have very little electricity and even more limited water and food, and the President wants this all fixed in the next week."

For the first time I see Hastings lose his cool just a little.

"If you wish to remain Chief of Police then you will do exactly what I tell you. You will focus on what I tell you. And right now, your focus is law and order. Returning these streets to calm."

Ambrose shakes his head but he doesn't argue further.

And I take that as my cue to leave. To get back to the Tunnels. Back to my family.

Only Hastings pulls me aside, right as I walk out the door.

"I heard a rumour." He says quietly. "That you have a certain Ignatio Capulet in your possession."

I meet those brown eyes, not showing anything, not revealing my hand.

"I want him. Unlike his daughter he will be held responsible for his actions." He states. "Give me Ignatio and all of Rose's sins will be forgiven."

I pull my arm free, hearing clear message that if I don't play ball, if I don't give him this he will change his mind of the whole 'Rose only being a witness' thing.

"I'll see what I can do." I murmur.

His lip curls a tiny bit. "I'll be waiting then."

ROMAN

I slip into the room.

It's still dark.

With no windows and no lights on, only the strips from the hallway illuminate the space through the curtains, making it feel otherworldly.

I can't tell if they're awake.

For a moment I just stand there, frozen, listening. I can hear Bella snoring softly. I can hear someone breathing slowly. It could be Rose. It could be Lara.

As quietly as I can I sink into the chair. I don't want to disturb them. I don't want to wake them. And most importantly I don't want to alarm Rose.

The drive back to the tunnels was awkward to say the least. I wanted to speak to Koen, to ask him what the hell his deal was with Sofia, but when I broached the subject he told me under no uncertain terms to leave it alone.

I checked on Sofia first. Checked she was okay but she was fast asleep so I left her to it.

And now I'm here, practically paralysed as I watch my family because I don't know what to do. I don't know how to fix this.

So instead I sit here, in silence, praying that maybe it's just sleep they need, that maybe everything will just sort itself. But maybe that's just wishful thinking.

Maybe.

It's her whimpers that make me move, that make me get up.

I lean over, seeing her face screwed up in what looks like pain. Lara is still out for the count so thankfully she hasn't heard it.

I brush her hair back before I can stop myself and her eyes snap open. For a second I see it, her fear, her terror, and then she's blinking, registering who I am, where she is.

She shifts, moving Lara enough to be able to sit up.

I don't speak. I don't say a word. In truth what the hell could I say? What words would help right now?

"Where have you been?" She murmurs.

"I had to see the Governor." I reply just as quietly. She flinches at the word I know is a trigger. "He's a stand in." I add. "The state issued a state of emergency."

She nods. Not blinking. Not taking her eyes from me.

"Rose…"

"Why did you have to see him?" She asks cutting across my words. Her voice sounds flat. Devoid of anything that makes her *her*.

I chew my lip for a second. "They want to know where you are. They have questions for you."

"Did you tell them?"

"No." I reply. "But when you're better, when you're recovered…"

"What do they want to know?"

She sounds so serious. So harsh. As if she's locked all her pain and sorrow up and her heart is no longer there. That she's just a cold, hard creature now.

It makes my own heart twist. It makes me want to grab her and not let her go until I feel the old her, the soft her, return.

"They want to know where he is." I say. I won't say his name. She's not stupid. She knows exactly who I'm talking about.

"I don't know." She says dropping her eyes.

"You jumped from the helicopter."

She sighs. "I couldn't, I wasn't going to..." She stares at Lara for a moment. "They killed Ty."

"I know. We found his body."

"They tortured me to get him to tell them where you were."

"What?"

My growl makes Lara stir. Only for a second but it's enough to kick my ass into getting control of myself.

Rose's lip trembles, her eyes seems to glisten as she meets mine and then she swallows it down. Swallows all of that trauma. "He didn't tell them. He kept it secret."

"Rose..."

"You've looked after her." She says dropping her gaze again, stroking Lara's hair. "You took good care of her."

I nod. "I did the best I could. But she wanted you. She never stopped asking for you."

She looks way, shuts her eyes, lets out such a sigh that I can feel the pain inside her. "I couldn't protect her."

"That's not true."

"I tried so hard." Her voice breaks, finally I hear that hard exterior crack.

"Rose."

"You weren't here." She states. "I woke, and you weren't here."

"I'm so sorry."

She whimpers, those tears streaming down her face. "I kept seeing you. I kept dreaming about you. I thought I was betraying you."

"You did no such thing." I say climbing onto the bed taking her into my arms as best I can while she's still holding onto Lara.

"I thought you were dead. I thought I'd lost you. That we were stuck forever and I didn't know how to save Lara, how to do any of it without you."

"I'm so sorry." I say. "I got shot. I was in a coma. But from the moment I woke all I could think about, all I did was to get you both out."

She buries her face into my neck. "I couldn't save Sofia. I tried so hard…"

"It's okay." I say, cupping her face with my hand. "And you did save her. You made sure we rescued her."

"I didn't realise what they were doing, you have to believe me, if I'd known, if I'd witnessed it sooner…"

"What do you mean by witnessed it sooner?" I ask quietly.

She flinches. "Darius took me there, to that club. I think he did it to prove a point. To show how much power he had and to humiliate us both."

"Did they…" I trail off unsure how to even ask the question in my head but I have to know. I have to. "Did they do that to you too?"

She shakes her head but she looks so ashamed anyway. "No, but…"

I wipe her tears with my thumb. I can see whatever the hell she's been through she's not ready to talk about it.

"I love you Rose." I say feeling like she needs to hear the words. Like she needs me to confirm it. "I've always loved you. And I will never stop loving you."

She lets out a sob. Her body seems to heave against me.

"Mummy?" Lara whispers looking up half asleep.

"It's okay baby." Rose says reassuring her. "You're safe. Mummy and daddy have you."

Lara snuggles in, falling back to sleep, and I tighten my hold around Rose as she leans into me.

"Sleep Rose." I murmur. "I've got you. I've got you both."

And she does. Her body seems to relax at those words. She lets out a sigh and she drifts off once more.

ROSE

I can feel arms around me. I blink opening my eyes and the space is so dark.

For a second I think I'm back. In that room. With Ty's body still there.

And it's Darius holding me. Darius who has me trapped.

I kick out. A cry escapes my lips but the voice that cuts through my confusion is not the one I'm hearing in my head.

"It's okay."

"Roman?" I whisper his name, fully expecting a fist to come flying at my face the way it always does when I say it out loud. Fully expecting pain. Punishment. Only it doesn't come.

"I'm here." He says.

"I thought…" I gulp the rest of that sentence down, registering suddenly that my child is in my arms and I don't want her to hear what I was going to say. She's been through enough. She's seen enough. She doesn't need to know about all the death and destruction that happened after she left.

And then I register the damned rings on my finger. That awful, gawdy diamond that Darius forced on me. It's still there. Taunting me. I yank them both off like their cursed, throwing them as hard as I can and they clatters as they hit the floor.

I can hear his breathing. I know he's staring at where they landed, we both are, as the diamond glints in the poor light.

God, it feels good to get it off. I want to smash it to pieces. I want to melt it down. To destroy it completely.

"It's just us." Roman says gently stroking my hair reassuringly. "The three of us."

"And Bella." Lara says.

I let out a giggle at her indignant tone and it helps relieve some of the tension.

"And Bella." Roman concedes.

"Where did you find her?" I ask.

"Back at the house. We cleaned her up." Roman says.

"And I've been looking after her for you mummy." Lara says.

I can't help the smile that creeps across my face. She sounds so proud. She sounds like the old Lara.

I sit up, looking around the strange room. There are no windows. No form of natural lighting at all. "Where are we?" I ask.

"In the tunnels under the city." Roman replies. "We hid out here the entire time."

"Are we still hiding here?" I ask.

Roman's lip curls just a tiny bit. "No. We can leave. Though we should have guards just in case."

I nod understanding his unspoken meaning. That Darius is out there. That he may well take an opportunity to attack if we let him.

"Is there some sort of kitchen down here?" I ask.

"Are you hungry?" Roman replies.

"I want cake." Lara says and we both laugh cracking the tension that is still there, still festering.

"Breakfast would be good." I say though I've no idea what the actual time is.

Roman gets out of the bed, helping Lara out. I watch the two of them, seeing that old familiar trust between them. At least that is still there. At least Darius hasn't stolen that from us.

"I'll give you a moment." Roman says quietly before leading her outside.

I frown confused and then I realise what he's getting at. That I need to get dressed. That I have to get out of these pyjamas and he's giving me the space to change, to get dressed alone.

My arm is in a cast. My fingers have been re-strapped up. I pull the jeans and jumper on as best I can but I can't do the zip and button up no matter how hard I try.

My face flushes with shame when I open the door. Roman is outside, combing Lara's hair, carefully easing out a knot. He looks up at me and when our eyes meet I feel that same flip of my heart that I've always felt.

"I…" I swallow, feeling my cheeks burning. "I need your help."

He tilts his head before murmuring to Lara to wait a moment and then he walks up to me.

"I can't do them up." I half whisper.

His eyebrows raise a tiny bit. "It's okay." He says before quickly doing it, acting like this is all perfectly natural. Taking so much care not to touch me, not to do anything that could be misconstrued, that might make me panic.

I mumble my thanks and he gives me a smile that makes my knees feel weak.

"Can we get cake now? I'm starving." Lara says.

"Come on Sweetpea." Roman replies taking her hand. "We'll get you the biggest slice they have."

Lara all but pulls him along and Bella races at their feet. For a moment I just stand there watching them, wondering if I'm hallucinating. Wondering if I'm dreaming.

I have them back. I have them both back.

Roman glances back at me and I see it, that reassurance in his eyes.

I need to pull myself together. I need to get a grip. I've been given a second chance. No way am I going to let myself ruin it this time.

WE SIT ON A LONG BENCH. THE ROOM RESEMBLES SOMETHING OF A high school cafeteria. I can't stop looking around, taking in the bright lights, the high ceiling, everything that is so normal, and yet we're underground.

"Here you go." Roman says putting a tray of food in front of me. "It's lunchtime so I got the things closest to a breakfast."

I give him a small smile back. He got me bread, and cheese, and bacon too. My stomach rumbles as I look at it and I dig in without complaint, ignoring the cutlery entirely and just using my thumb and index finger to pick it up like I'm some sort of savage. I can't remember the last proper meal I've had. It feels ages ago.

Lara is sat beside me, wolfing down a plate piled just as high as mine.

And Roman is sat across watching us, not taking his eyes off of us for a minute.

"It's okay." I say quietly. "We're not going anywhere."

A micro-expression shows his pain. He opens his mouth to reply but Ben is suddenly there, stood behind him.

"Rose." He says quietly. "It's good to see you."

I give him a weak smile. "It's good to be seen."

"Everything okay?" Roman asks.

Ben glances at me then back at him. "He's in her room." He says quietly.

"Who is in whose room?" I ask.

Roman narrows his eyes, his focus on his friend, not me. "It's her decision."

Ben's eyes flash. "She's too weak. She's…"

"Stop." Roman says. "I've seen her. I've spoken to her." He shakes his head like he doesn't know how to continue that sentence and I realise then exactly who he's talking about. Sofia.

"Is she okay?" I ask.

Roman winces. "She will be."

I look at Ben and he looks like he's about to go on a rampage.

"Roman." Someone half growls.

We all look up at the new voice. I don't know who the hell this man is but he's huge, muscular, covered in tattoos.

"Koen." Roman says getting to his feet, glancing at Ben like he's making a point of telling him to shut up, to control himself.

"The Capulet bitch has been spotted."

"What?"

I gasp it while Roman snarls. I'm on my feet now and for some reason I'm trembling.

"She's still missing?" I say.

Roman nods. "For now." He mutters before looking at Ben. "I want you on it."

"Too late. My men are already hunting her down." Koen says.

"I guess I'll check on Sofia then." Ben states.

And this man, this stranger narrows his eyes like he wants to tell him no.

"Take Lara with you." Roman says. "It will cheer Sofia up."

"You're sure?" Ben asks glancing between us.

Roman nods before I can say anything. Before I can object.

Lara gets up, grabs his hand in her left and in her right, she's got a doughnut that's dripping jam down her wrist but she doesn't seem to notice. "Is she awake Uncle Ben?" She asks. "Yesterday she was so sleepy."

"So were you Sweetpea." Roman murmurs.

Lara flashes him a grin before Ben leads him away.

And then it's us, me, Roman, and this stranger just stood here.

"Who are you?" I ask.

He meets my gaze with eyes darker than Roman's. "Your boyfriend didn't tell you?"

"Tell me what?" I ask.

Roman steps between us just a little as if he's protecting me almost. "This is Koen Diaz."

My eyes widen, I take a step back and almost stumble over my own feet.

Koen Diaz? What the fuck are we doing interacting with a man like him? I look at Roman questioningly and I can feel my heart pumping in my chest, I can hear my breath suddenly so ragged.

"He's been helping us Rose." Roman says. "He's the reason we've been able to take down Darius."

"I don't understand…" I begin.

"We gave your boyfriend and his mates bed and board. We gave your daughter shelter too. And your dog."

I gulp looking from one man to the other. I don't know why I'm reacting like this. Roman wouldn't put me in danger. I know this. I know him. And yet I can feel my palms are so sweaty. I can feel my body's fight or flight response kicking in.

"He won't hurt you." Roman says quietly. "No one is going to hurt you."

"And Sofia?" I ask because clearly there's some shit going on there.

Koen's eyes react. I see it in his face. She means something to him.

"No one is hurting my sister." Roman says and then he turns fixing Koen with a look that makes me jaw drop in shock. "Whatever the fuck is going on, you stay away from her until she's well enough to make up her own mind."

Koen tilts his head, his eyes flashing bloody murder. "You think I would hurt her?" He growls. "You think after everything I've witnessed that I would do that?"

"She's twenty one." I say, though I don't know why. I'm not even sure what difference it makes.

He looks at me and I swear it feels like a bucket of ice has been poured on me.

"You have no idea what you are talking about. Either of you." He says. "But if it makes you happier, if you both will sleep easier then I'll stay away from your precious sister. But you can't stop me protecting her. You can't stop me from making sure she's safe."

Roman opens his mouth to say something but I cut across him. "That's all we want. All any of us want. Sofia safe and happy too."

He narrows his eyes and then stalks off.

And I think my bravery leaves me then. I sink onto the bench seeing my hands trembling and feeling my throat constrict the same way it keeps doing when I feel like I'm spiralling out of control.

"Rose?" Roman murmurs.

I run my hand over my chest, taking slow breaths. "I…" My face heats with shame. "I'm not strong." I whisper it. "Not anymore."

He shakes his head, taking my hand, and I hate the way I flinch at his touch.

"Yes you are." He says like he can't feel it, like he hasn't noticed it.

My heart is hammering. I feel dizzy.

"Do you need a doctor?" He asks.

I shake my head. "No. I just, I just need a moment. I need to calm myself."

He gives me such a look of concern that it seems to reset whatever is going on in my head. I blink, focusing on his pain in this moment.

"Why did you let Lara go with Ben?" I ask.

"You'd rather she stayed?" He replies.

"I don't like her being out of my sight." I admit.

He sighs. "I should have realised that. I'm sorry."

"It's okay." I say and then I deliberately change the subject. I don't want to dwell on it. I don't want him to overthink it. "So my mother?"

He narrows his eyes. "We tried to capture her but she got away."

"Carter had someone watching her." I state. "They were under orders to kill her if you tried to take her."

His eyes widen at that revelation.

"She knows something Roman." I say. "She knows something about Darius."

"Do you know what?"

I shake my head. "No, but it's clearly something big if he feels the need to kill her."

"Maybe your father will know."

I bite back the grin. I'd forgotten that. That Roman had him. "Please tell me he's still alive then?"

He grins back at me. "I've been having some fun with him Rose." He says. "But I thought you had more right than I did to kill him."

I don't know how to react to that. Yes I want him dead. Yes I have now killed people. Murdered two men. And yet both of them I did in blind rage. In response to my environment.

I pull my gaze from his, looking at the room around us. It's filling up with more people. More strangers. As a few look our way I feel myself getting more and more on edge. What's to stop Darius from sending someone in here? What's to stop him from bribing someone to kill me, to kill Lara, to kill any of us?

"What is it?" Roman asks.

"This place. How safe is it?"

He frowns glancing around too. "It's safe."

"You don't know that." I reply and even I hear the snap in my voice. The way my fear coils around my words.

He pauses as if he's trying to understand my headspace.

I can't even explain why I'm feeling like this. Afterall Roman has lived here, existed here for months and nothing has happened to him. And yet the thought of it, of being here makes me feel like I'm losing control. Like I'm in danger.

There are too many people here. To many strangers.

"We can eat back in your room from now on."

"That's not what I meant."

His eyebrows raise. "You want to leave, leave?"

"Is that possible?" I ask.

He shrugs. "Technically yes. The new Governor has said you're not a person of interest."

"So we can leave Verona?"

His face falls a tiny bit. "No. Not yet. That was made clear."

I try to hide my disappointment but I know he sees it. I know he can tell. God, what I would give to be able to leave, to really get away from all these people, to disappear, to go somewhere where no one even glances our way.

But I guess that's not an option. Not yet anyway.

"Let me see what I can do. Let me find somewhere, in the city. Somewhere safe for all of us."

"For Sofia too." I say. "And Ben, if he wants."

He nods in agreement. "I'll find somewhere, somewhere new, where can start afresh."

ROSE

I don't ask for it but he lets me sleep, lets me have some alone time. I need to clear my head. I need to clear the horrific thoughts out.

But every time I close my eyes I see either Sofia in that place, or I see Ty. I see him tied to a chair, begging for his life.

And then I see Darius, laughing, mocking me, mocking my pitiful attempts to beat him, before he pulls the trigger over and over and over again.

I wake in a cold sweat. I have a clock in the room now so at least I know what the time is.

Lara must be with Roman because she hasn't returned but Bella is here, curled up on the bed beside me.

I get up, all but crawl into the bathroom and turn the shower on. I know it's just the trauma. On some level I get it. I understand it. But I need it to stop. I need to stop.

I want to be me again. I want to be able to laugh, to smile, to look at Roman, to let him hold my hand and not feel some deep sickening repulsion at the feel of his skin against mine.

I clamber into the cubicle. The water is cool but I don't have the energy to reach up and turn the temperature up.

I've got a plastic bag wrapped around my left arm, protecting the cast. Somehow I managed to remember it but my right hand is uncovered and the tape holding my fingers together is unpleasantly wet.

I sit here, scrubbing what feels like all the blood still marring my skin, only I know that's also in my head. That it's not actually there.

And then I break down entirely. Sobbing, crying, letting it all out as the water pours down.

I did this. I caused this. I got Ty killed.

If I'd kept my mouth shut, if I'd kept quiet, he'd still be alive.

But then Sofia would still be suffering wouldn't she? And perhaps none of this would have happened, that the city wouldn't have risen up, that I would still be with Darius. At his mercy.

I wail again, hating the fact that in so many ways I had to choose, I had to decide, even though I didn't know it at the time.

I never liked Ty, not growing up. He was always mean to me. Not as mean as Tybalt. But still.

And now, all that resentment, all those old memories twist in my head.

I can see it, the time he pulled my hair when I was six. The time he spat in my food when no one was looking. And when he and Tybalt pushed me into the mud and then my mother lost her shit when she saw me all dirty and beat me so hard for it because she thought I'd done it on purpose.

I cry harder. Hating that I hated him. Hating that I never told him how grateful I was. How much at the end, his help, his words, his moments of kindness were what got me through each day.

I never even said thank you.

Not properly. Not enough.

I let him die. I sat there, seeing that gun, seeing that smirk on Otto's face and if I admit it, I hate that he accepted it, I hate that he didn't fight. God, I wish he'd blamed me. Why didn't he blame me? Why didn't he say that I'd tricked him, that I was the traitor. Hell, he could have said anything, he should have said anything.

But he didn't. He just took it. He took that bullet like he deserved it. When in reality I was the one who should have died. I deserved it. After everything, after every stupid mistake, every moment in my life that I allowed myself to be outmanoeuvred. I deserved that bullet for becoming the weak creature they all think I am. I deserved it. Not him.

"Rose?"

I don't look up. I don't even acknowledge him.

I'm sat here, naked, pathetic, sopping wet and covered in tears.

He climbs in, ignoring the fact that the water is still cascading down and that he's fully clothed. And he wraps a towel around me to cover my body, and holds me so tightly in his arms.

"It's okay." He murmurs.

"No it's not." I sob. It's not okay. None of this is okay.

He doesn't reply. He doesn't answer me. He just stays there, letting me cry, letting me wallowing, letting me have this moment.

He must be drenched. He must be absolutely soaked. But he doesn't turn the water off. He just sits there like this is all perfectly normal behaviour.

When I've cried myself out, I'm the one who reaches up and turns the water off, but beyond that I don't move. I stay there, listening to his heart beating in his chest, soothing myself with a sound that I'd believed I'd never hear again.

"Where's Lara?" I whisper.

"She's tucked up in bed."

My eyes widen? I don't want her to see my like this. I don't want her to witness me so broken. I need to protect her.

"She's in my bed." He says as if he can read my thoughts.

"Oh."

He brushes a tendril of my wet hair from my face. "I thought you might want to sleep there, with her."

"And you?"

He pauses. We both can hear the nervousness. The hint of something in my voice. That I'm not ready for that.

"I'll sleep on the floor." He says gently.

"You don't have to." I say quickly.

He smiles. "I want to. I'll be able to watch over you both. Keep you safe."

"I need to get dry first." I mumble.

"Good thing I bought some more clothes then." He murmurs.

I look away as he gets up. His shirt is sticking to his chest and I can see the outline of every muscle he has.

When I get to my feet I pull the towel so tightly around me. I don't know how to reconstruct who I was, who we were before, and who we are now.

He walks into the bedroom and I toss the sopping wet towel, replacing it with a dry one.

He's put some clothes on the bed. I snatch at them before fleeing back to the bathroom once more. I yank on the leggings. They're fleece lined and my body is immediately grateful for the warmth of them. And then I pull the hoody over my head. It's Roman's I realise. It's his hoody. I can smell him. I shut my eyes, welcoming that scent, feeling the relief as it spreads over me.

And then I walk back out.

He's tossed his shirt, tossed his trousers, and pulled on some sweatpants. But he's topless. Completely naked from the waist up.

I stare at him, all but gawp. His body looks leaner. Like he's lost weight but he still looks so strong.

And then my eyes find a scar, a mark on his chest that wasn't there before.

His fingertips brush at where I'm looking. He draws in a low sigh.

"That's where they shot you?" I murmur.

He nods. "They missed my heart by a few millimetres."

I bite my lip realising how close I was to losing him. "How did you get help so quickly? How did you survive?"

He shrugs. "I don't know. I don't remember. Ben saved my life."

I step up to him, my heart feels like it's hammering in my chest so loudly. I want to hold him, I want to touch him, to kiss him too and fix all his pain but I know that's too far. Way too far.

"I guess you two are even then." I murmur.

His lips curl. "Yeah I guess we are."

We walk back to his room in silence.

I feel like there's so much I need to say, so much I need to explain and yet I have neither the words, nor the energy to do so.

His room is small. Utilitarian. The biggest thing in there is the bed. There's a clothes rail against one wall and all his belongings seem to hang off of it. It's a far cry from the millionaire lifestyle that either of us are used to.

Lara is curled up in the bed. Bella jumps up and immediately snuggles into her.

"She really helped." Roman murmurs.

"Lara or Bella?"

"Bella." He says. "Having her here, giving something for Lara to focus on, to take care of."

I give him a smile. I can't even put into words how happy I am that he had Bella, that he kept her safe. I know in many ways I got Bella as a substitute, as a comfort to try to mitigate the grief of losing Lara, and I think he realises that too.

"I found somewhere." He says.

"What?"

"A house. It's big. Big enough for all of us. And it's got enough of a garden for Lara to be able to explore without feeling like she's constrained but she'll be safe."

"Where is it?"

"In the bay district." He says. "Not far from your old house. It's a similar style too."

I smile then. I loved that house. I loved what it had represented before they tore it away from me.

"When can we leave?" I ask.

"In a few days, if you want?"

"And Sofia, will she come too?"

"She will." He says in a way that I think means he had to persuade her.

I open my mouth to ask and he shakes his head a tiny bit. "Let's talk more in the morning. You need to sleep. You need to recover."

"I've slept most of yesterday and most of today." I reply.

He tucks my hair behind my ear. I freeze at the contact. My body instantly locking up and my stomach twisting in a way that makes me feel sick.

I can see in his eyes that he's seen it. That he knows.

"You need to rest." He says gently.

I look away, feeling my own eyes welling with tears.

"I'm afraid." I whisper.

"Of what?"

"Sleep. When I close my eyes I see Ty. I see what they did to him."

His face morphs into one of sorrow, or sympathy. "What can I do?" He asks.

I don't know the answer to that. I want him to hold me, I want him to hug me, to wrap his arms around me and tell me nobody will ever hurt me again. But I can't let him do that. I can't bear the thought of him touching me right now. Of anyone touching me right now.

I shut my eyes, shaking my head.

He lets out a low sigh before slipping down the wall, sitting on the floor. "Do you remember that first night?" He says. "When we both crept into her room. Do you remember how we sat there, both watching her sleep, both amazed by what we'd created."

I nod, feeling my tears threatening to spill again.

"Sit with me Rose." He says quietly. "If you can't sleep, if you're afraid, then just sit here, and I'll be with you, by your side, in the dark."

I sink down beside him, silently sobbing, silently heaving as so many tears fall again.

He puts his hand on the floor between us. Not touching me. Not trying too. But it's there, like a signal, telling me in his way that he loves me. That he cares. And that I only have to reach out and he'll be there, giving me what I need, whatever I need.

ROMAN

She falls asleep halfway through the night. I lift her up, carry her so carefully over to the bed and wrap the covers around her.

She doesn't wake. She doesn't even register that I've done it.

And I sink back down, taking a new position, closer to them both.

When a nightmare half wakes her, I'm there, soothing her without actually touching her, and soon enough she falls back asleep.

And I return to my guard.

I don't know when I drift off. I don't know when sleep takes me, but I wake with a crook in my neck and an a stiffness in my bones.

I rub my eyes, seeing the pair of them still out for the count.

I got a clock in my room that illuminates with the daylight hours. It helps to keep track of the day seeing as we're underground and don't have any windows to do that job for us.

I get up, walk silently into the bathroom and wash.

When I come back out, Rose is awake. She's sat up, all but waiting for me. Her eyes wide like she's still expecting an attack at any minute.

I don't ask her how she slept. We both know she had a terrible night.

"Are you hungry?" I ask instead.

She nods.

"I'll get some food." I say.

"I can come." She says quickly.

"Stay. Watch over Lara." I reply.

By the time I get back Lara is awake too. She gives me the biggest grin as I put the tray of food down for them.

"Breakfast in bed?" Lara says.

"Only the best for my girls." I reply.

Lara giggles and Rose's lips curl.

I watch as they dig in. As hey both devour their breakfast. I guess that's where Lara gets her appetite from, I just never noticed until now.

"What?" Rose murmurs fixing those beautiful eyes on me.

I smile, shaking my head. "Nothing."

I leave them alone to wash, to get dressed. Lara is chatting away, already coming more out of her shell, returning back to the daughter we'd both found at the beginning.

I have things to sort, things that need to be put into place if we really are leaving.

But first of all I want to check on Sofia. To see how she is.

WHEN I KNOCK ON HER DOOR I'M RELIEVED TO SEE SHE'S ALONE. That neither Koen nor Ben are here.

She's laying on her side, staring off at a patch of the wall.

"Hey." I murmur quietly but I still make her jump.

"Hey." She says pulling the covers up, even though she's in a hoody. One sleeve is tucked up where the drip is still in her arm but she looks better. A little better.

"How you doing?"

She shrugs. "Been better."

I sink into the same chair I sat before. "I saw the new Governor. Governor Hastings."

"Oh?"

"He's sorting out the city."

"Right." She looks as disinterested in this conversation as I am. To be fair it's a lame topic but I don't know what else to say.

I let out a sigh. I've never struggled with Sofia before, we've never not gotten on. Sibling rivalry for us was just never a thing.

"How's Rose?" She asks.

I smile. "She's okay. Or as okay as she can be. I found a house, so we can get out of here, get somewhere above ground and try to get back some normality."

She doesn't respond to that. She just keeps staring.

"Ben can come too." I add.

Her eyes react. They widen just a little as she registers what I'm saying. "You mean all of us?"

"Yes." I reply. "It's big, there's ten rooms, you can have your pick."

She shudders. "I don't think that's a good idea."

"Why not?"

I can see the tears pooling in her eyes. "Roman, please…"

"Do you want to stay here?" I ask gently though I'm afraid of that answer. Afraid she will say yes. That somehow Koen has gotten into her head.

She shakes her head. "No."

"Then come with us. We can heal together. All of us can."

Her lips tremble. "I can't."

"Sofia…"

"You don't know what it's like." She hisses. "You don't understand."

"Tell me." I say more forcefully than I mean.

Her eyes flash. She looks not in pain right in now but in fury. "I can still feel them. I can still see them. They might have drugged me but I was still there, I was still there." She hisses. "And I'm not free even now, even with Otto dead. All I can think about, all I can focus on is my next hit."

Her tears stream down her face. She scratches her arm almost manically. I get up wrapping my arms around her and she flinches before she relaxes into my hold.

"I'm so sorry." I say. "I'm so fucking sorry."

"I can't be there, I can't let Lara see me like this, I don't want anyone seeing me like this."

"You have nothing to be ashamed of."

"Yes I do." She cries pushing me off. "Yes I do."

"They did this to you Sofia." I reply. "But you don't have to accept it. You don't have to endure this alone."

"What if I want to be alone?" She whispers.

My shoulders slump. I feel defeated and yet I won't give up on her. "I won't let you do this alone. I won't."

She looks away, shaking her head but she doesn't argue. Like she's too exhausted, too spent to fight anymore.

ROSE

I sneak away. I sneak out of his room.

He thinks I'm with Lara, that we're both sleeping.

Only I can't sleep. I can't even shut my eyes.

I creep down the hallway, if that's what you can call it. My eyes dart around taking in the rooms, taking in the odd lighting, and the people that are already evacuating, already seeking their own emancipation.

I don't know how long some of them have been living down here and though it's as well equipped as any house above ground, it still feels claustrophobic. It still feels, wrong.

When I bump into Ben he does a double take.

"Rose?"

I draw myself up, suck in a breath of air through my teeth. We've never really spoken all that much. I knew he knew about me and Roman all those years ago. He even caught us once, and made it clear what he thought of it, what he thought of me.

But, as he frowns at me now, I wonder how much has changed. How much better he now understands me.

"Where is he keeping my dad?" I ask.

His eyebrows raise. "If he hasn't…"

I step closer, into his personal space, though I won't touch him. I don't want to touch him.

"You know what this feels like." I reply. "You know what it is to suffer. To see someone else suffer…"

His face is so hard. Like he doesn't want to give anything away but I'm not a fool. I know how he feels, I've seen how he's looked at Sofia, how he's pined over her.

"If you had a chance, if you had an opportunity to make Otto pay…"

"This isn't about revenge." He states.

I let out a laugh. "Of course it is." I reply. "It's exactly that. That man sold me, sold Sofia too. He used us like bargaining chips to further his power. Don't tell me you think otherwise."

"He might know something." He argues.

"Why do you think I want to talk to him?" I say as sweetly as I can considering my heart is racing at a hundred miles an hour.

"He hasn't…"

"I'm his daughter." I cut across him. "I know how to make him talk better than anyone."

"Roman won't like it."

"Roman already said I can kill him." I reply. I'm sure he said that. He insinuated it anyway back in the cafeteria.

He narrows his eyes. Clearly thinking it over.

"Ben, please, we've never been friends, not really, but I need you to help me. I need you to give me this."

He lets out a low sigh, jerking his head, and mutters for me to follow him.

I don't say anything, I'm so fearful that any minute he might change his mind so I shadow his steps down deeper into the tunnels, away from all the activity, away from all the people.

When we reach the door I can see the huge bar across it. It's rudimentary, like something from a medieval castle but I guess it does the job.

He pulls off the bar and it creaks as it opens.

I want to say thanks, I want to say something, but my heart is beating so loudly and right now all I can focus on is that in this room is the sole source of all my pain, all my daughter's pain, all Roman's pain too.

He doesn't follow me in. I don't look to see where he goes, I just step inside, shutting the door staring at the man who was meant to love me, meant to protect me, meant to be an actual parent.

But I guess all that pain, all that questioning about why I wasn't good enough for him to love has gone. It's been erased. Replaced.

I've realised the question isn't about me and my supposed failings as a daughter. You see I've always judged him by my own values only he doesn't have them does he? He doesn't view the world the way I do. He doesn't look at people, and see them the way I do. As people, and not things to be used. To be manipulated. This whole time I realise it's been about him, about his ineptitude, about his fucked up perspective that valued power and money over morals.

I was never going to win his love, no matter what I did. Because he wasn't capable of it. Neither he nor my mother were. I was a thing to be used, to be capitalised.

Not a person in my own right.

And now that I finally realise it, now that I've finally accepted it, it's like some deep, dark grief inside me goes. Like something that's been coiled and fisted around my heart for so long seems to finally dissipate.

I draw in another breath and instantly regret it.

It stinks. It absolutely stinks.

I can see him, taped to a chair the way I was. His shirt is drenched in sweat and blood too. He's pissed himself. Soiled himself.

It's disgusting. He is disgusting.

And yet when his eyes meet mine I can't help the grin.

He looks shocked, surprised, I bet he never thought he'd see me like this, in this situation, that either he would die here or Darius would win and he'd be there lauding it up over me again.

"Hello father." I say softly. Teasingly. As if this is all some silly prank.

He narrows his eyes, that same look of disdain he always kept aside just for me.

I walk over to where someone has laid a cain that is bloodied, a knife that looks blunt as hell, and some other instruments that could cause a delightful amount of pain.

I pick up the chain. It's heavy, each of the five loops are the size of my hand and I know it will take an effort to swing this but hell, it will certainly hurt when it makes contact, it will break bones. With my fingers still bound together it's definitely a lot easier to grip than a knife and I know it will be satisfying to swing it, to see the damage it causes. I wrap the chain around my hand, anchoring it with my grasp.

"Do you know what he did?" I ask. "Do you know all the disgusting ways he hurt me, how he abused me, how he tortured my body?"

He doesn't reply. He just looks at me like I'm the traitor.

"You all thought I was so weak. You all thought I was just a thing you could use…"

"We thought you were a whore." He spits.

I let out a laugh then. "I was." I reply. I'm okay with that word now. Even that doesn't bother me I realise because I don't care what people think. I'm beyond it now. Finally too, that need to be loved, to be accepted is gone. "You made me that, first for Paris, and then for Darius."

"You were a whore long before that, you became one the day you fucked that Montague bastard…"

I swing the chain smash it into his jaw, cutting off the insult before it can even properly form on his lips. His teeth are already broken and they cut into his tongue as he reacts.

"You made me the whore." I shout. My voice echoing off the cold sterile walls. "You."

My chest is heaving, my heart is thumping but while I can feel the fear there, I can feel something else, something deeper.

"You tried to break me, all of you did, you thought I'd simply take what you dished out, but what you didn't realise is that I was stronger than you, stronger than all of you."

"You're not strong. You're weak. Pathetic…"

I smash the metal into his body and this time he cries out which I'll admit gives me all the satisfaction I want in this moment.

"If I am weak then why are you the one tied to a chair?" I taunt.

"It won't be for long…"

"No?" I reply. "Darius has lost, you have lost, the entire city has risen up against you."

"Darius would not…"

I laugh then. He thinks so highly of him, doesn't he?

"He left." I state. "He flew away like a coward, leaving you to face the consequences."

His face reacts, he shows his confusion then, albeit briefly.

I toss the chains, letting it crash to the concrete floor. And then I pick up the knife. My fingers fumble but I manage to keep my grip. I want to have the intimacy of this, I want to pinpoint the exact moment I puncture his flesh, I want to feel the blade sliding into his body, cutting him piece by piece.

As I stalk towards him that foul stench gets even worse.

"God," I murmur. "You really did shit yourself."

He spits at me but he misses.

"At least when they tortured me I didn't do that." I state. "I still kept some dignity."

He tilts his head his eyes darting to the blade and back to my face. "Who tortured you?"

"That dear man you forced me to marry." I reply. "He wanted to get Ty to talk, only Ty refused."

"Ty is not a traitor."

I laugh, feeling my pain, feeling my grief once more. "He was working with Roman. He was helping him."

"He'd never…"

"He loved Sofia." I state. "He loved her and you all were killing her."

"Yeah? That fucking bitch deserved it." My father spits.

I snarl, driving the blade into his arm, stabbing right through his flesh, into the wood of the chair. "She was barely more than a child." I hiss.

He cries out, snarls, as I yank the blade back out and his blood spurts.

"But what I want to know is why Darius had a hit on my dear mother?" I state.

"What?" He says, panting, glaring at me like some beast.

"You heard. He sent someone to do her in. Why is that?"

The look on his face says it all. For the minutest of seconds I can see the confusion, the way he's trying to see if I'm the one bluffing or not. And then that smirk cuts across his lips.

"Why would I tell you that?" He says.

I shake my head, hearing the lie, knowing him too well now to believe it.

"You don't know do you?" I retort.

He leans back in the chair, glancing at the gouge I've left. "I know Rose but you won't get me to talk. The only way I'll tell you is if you get me out of here. Get me away from them."

I laugh. It's so pathetic. The way he's trying to control this situation now. The way he thinks he can outsmart me. Manipulate me. As if I'm that same girl he fucked over six years ago. That same stupid, naïve idiot I was before.

"For so long I feared you." I say. "For so long I allowed you to dictate my life, control it, use me as some sort of instrument but not anymore."

"No?" He muses.

"No." I repeat. "You don't have that power anymore."

He laughs. The bastard laughs.

But I see red, I see all my pain, every agonising moment of my life that he has been the cause of, that he has inflicted on me. I grip the knife, all but throwing myself at him.

And I stab. Over and over, slicing through his flesh, slicing through his arms, his hands, his stomach, his legs. I drive the blade in over and over, feeling his blood splattering me, hearing not only his cries of pain but my own screams as I lose myself in a pain so deep and agonising that I have to exorcise it like a demon.

I have to get it out.

The door crashes open. I don't look around. I'm too lost in the frenzy of my attack. In the bitter twisted emotions that I'm finally getting out.

"Rose."

Someone yanks me back, pulls the knife from my hand, and it's so slick with blood I can barely fight it.

I stumble, only just keeping on my feet. I'm drenched. Soaked. I'm covered from head to toe.

I blink, staring at my father, seeing his body slumped, seeing his shirt completely crimson with blood.

"Rose?"

I turn my eyes looking at Roman. I'm not ashamed. I don't regret a second of it. But I'm waiting for him to admonish me. To state all the reasons why I shouldn't have just done what I did.

Only, instead of admonishment he cups my cheek and I feel that warm blood pooling between our skin.

"He's dead." Someone says echoing the same scene, what feels like months ago, when I killed the man who'd hurt Lara, when I'd beaten him to death.

I glance back at him, at where there's two men crouched down, cutting him free, making sure the bastard really is gone.

"Let's get you cleaned up." Roman murmurs.

I let him lead me from the room, let him guide my arm and I'm curious to know what he thinks about this, what he thinks of me now.

Does he see me as a monster? Does he see all the darkness that's twisted inside?

He meets my gaze, doesn't even seem fazed as he guides me into a bathroom and turns the shower on.

ROMAN

She's covered in blood.

Drenched.

On one hand I'm pissed that he's dead, that we haven't even been able to question him but I understand that need, that drive to make him pay. It matches to the same deep need in myself. It matches to my very soul.

We're in a bathroom. Not mine. I couldn't exactly bring her back to my room with Lara there. I couldn't let our daughter see her like this.

"He doesn't know." She says cutting through the silence that's hung between us since I all but dragged her out.

"Know what?" I ask.

"What my mother knows, why Darius wanted her dead."

"You're sure?"

She nods. "I asked him, he lied, he tried to pretend but I saw the look on his face."

I let out a sigh. I promised Hastings he could have Ignatio, how the fuck am I going to explain this? That Rose has murdered someone else.

Will he arrest her for this? Will this be the thing that finally condemns her? I don't even know how to save her from it, how I could even go about it.

"What?" She says looking at me, tilting her head like she's ready to fight me.

I frown for a second but she's slamming her fists into my chest. "What?" She screams.

"Rose."

"I had to kill him. I had to. After everything he did, everything he put me and Lara through. And you too."

"I'm not disputing that." I reply.

"Then why aren't you saying anything? Why are you just standing there?"

"I promised Hastings." I say back. "I promised him he could have your father, that he would be put on trial."

Her jaw drops. "You what? How could you do that?"

"I did it to save you. I did it so that he wouldn't come after you."

She blanches, leaning back against the wall. "Why would he come after me?" She half whispers.

"Because you killed Carter." I state. "They have the footage. Everyone has seen it."

Her head spins, she folds her arms, but she's clearly not giving up. "He deserved it." She spits. "He deserved to die after everything he did."

"I'm not disputing that." I say.

"So what, I'm a criminal now, is that it?"

I can't help but curl my lips at the haughty way she puts it. Fuck even in this moment she's still the most beautiful woman I've ever laid my eyes on.

Her lips curl too. She looks up at my face and starts laughing. "I am a criminal. I'm a murderer."

"So am I." I reply.

"Yeah but I'm Verona's sunshine princess." She laughs more. "And now I'm a serial killer."

I don't know how to respond to that. I guess technically she is, technically we both are.

"Are you angry at me Roman?" She asks more seriously.

"No." I reply tucking a strand of her hair behind her ear and ignoring the blood that's tangled up in it. "I've never been prouder."

"You mean that?"

I nod. "Do you feel better for it?"

"Yes." She doesn't hesitate. "I had to do something, I had to get some of this anger out."

"Is there anything I can do, anything else…"

She places her fingers on my lips and I freeze. She hasn't touched me, hasn't made any moves to. It's always been me holding her, soothing her. Just the feel of her skin against mine sends a shiver through me, sends a bolt right to my dick.

She steps closer, brushes her lips against mine and just as I react, just as I move to kiss her she pulls away and her eyes well. "I can't." She whispers so quietly. So sadly.

"It's okay." I say. It's going to take time, we both know that. But that's what we have now, we have all the time in the world.

She strips the hoody off, strips off her leggings too and then her underwear, discarding it in a pile. I stare wide eyed at her as she steps into the water, as it streams down her body. I tried to keep my eyes averted when I found her the other day. I tried to give her some sort of dignity. But now I can see all the bruises, all the marks, the burns where something was pushed into her skin.

Before I can stop myself I'm reaching out, touching, putting my fingertips on the damage, ignoring the water now covering my sleeve.

She whimpers a tiny bit as I do it.

"They burnt you?" I half growl.

"The cattle prod." She whispers. "That's what he used on me to try to get Ty to talk."

My anger flares, it takes all my control not to flip out. They fucking tortured her with a cattle prod?

"Hold me." She murmurs so quietly. "Just hold me Roman. I want to feel safe."

"You are safe." I reply before pulling my own clothes off. "You will always be safe with me."

I step into the shower, feeling the heat of the water and I'm so aware of how naked we both are, how she's trembling though she's trying to hide it.

Despite her words I know if I try to hold her right now she'll panic.

So instead I grab the sponge, pour a load of soap onto it and slowly, carefully, I wash her clean.

ROMAN

Two days later we leave. We move into this new house. All of us, me, Rose, Lara, Ben, Sofia, and Bella.

I've got enough guards around the place and enough cameras that we'll know when even a bird flies into the garden. But I won't take any chances.

Bella runs through the garden like she's forgotten what the feel of grass is beneath her feet.

The air is cold. Clearly winter is setting in and I make a note to ensure we all have enough warm clothes, and hats.

Lara chases after Bella, laughing, skipping, acting the way a six year old should.

And Rose stands on the veranda, looking out, watching her, smiling in a way that makes my heart melt.

But Sofia disappears, she retreats into herself, keeping to the room furthest from us, all but hiding in it except for dinner when she comes down, plays nice but as soon as the meal is done she's gone, up the stairs and into the darkness.

Ben sits outside her door, not wanting to push enough to actually enter but I can see he's torn about what to do. We all are.

And then halfway through the first week Hastings comes knocking.

I did my best to put him off. I did my best to tell him that Rose needed more time. I'm half minded to tell him where to stick it when I open the door but from the look on his face I realise I don't have a choice.

He follows me into the study. His eyes scanning the place, taking in the marble floors, the double heighted ceilings and vintage Persian rugs. All of it décor that's far more old money than new. Far more Montague vibes than Capulet.

In the study there's a huge chesterfield desk with a green leather top so similar to the one my father owned. I sit behind it and Hastings takes the seat to the left.

"I came to speak with Rose." He says pointedly, like he thinks I don't know it.

"She'll be down in a minute." I say.

He sits back into the chair, assessing me, one leg resting over the other by his ankle.

"Drink?" I ask.

"Scotch if you have it." He says, his eyes already spotting the decanter on the side.

I get up, pour two glasses, feeling like I could do with one myself, and put the other in front of him before I sink back into my chair.

And then the door creaks open and she's there, drawing in a deep breath, looking both beautiful and on edge. Like a wild creature caught in the crosshairs, trying to figure out whether to fight or flee.

"Rose." I murmur.

She gives me the smallest of smiles before looking at the new Governor and her face becomes that hard mask I'm so used to seeing now. I can't tell if I prefer it to the fake sunshine smile or not.

"You're Hastings?" She says carefully.

"I am." He replies.

She flexes her hand, no doubt enjoying the movement now that her fingers are free of the bindings though her arm is still in the cast. It'll be at least another month before it comes off.

"Do you want a drink?" I ask her.

She shakes her head but I get up and pour one for her anyway. I know she will want the distraction.

"I need to ask you some questions." Hastings says as she takes a seat.

She doesn't respond. She just sits there waiting, like she's on trial again.

I can tell Hastings doesn't quite know how to take her. She's not the sunshine princess he was expecting. She's not the perfectly coiffed, perfectly manicured creature Verona knows.

She's only got enough makeup on to hide the dark circles under her eyes. Her hair is pulled up into a messy bun. She's the girl I'm used to seeing, the low maintenance, carefree one I fell in love with. Only she's not so carefree anymore.

She's wearing a long jumper dress. It's grey, cashmere, loose enough to highlight her body without looking intentionally sexy.

"You've been in a relationship with Darius for six months and married for two?" Hastings begins.

"Yes." She says wincing at his name.

"And he was blackmailing you the entire time?"

"Yes."

"How long have you been aware of your husband's illegal activities?"

"He's not…" She trails off, shutting her eyes, scowling. "Don't call him that." She says.

"Legally you are still married." Hastings replies.

"And legally a marriage made under duress does not stand." She snaps back angrily.

His lip curls just a little. Like he likes her riled up. Like he likes that reaction.

"Rose is still recovering." I say fixing him with a look that could kill. "If you do anything that upsets her I will toss you out of this house myself."

"I don't need you to defend me Roman, I'm perfectly capable of looking after myself now." Rose says jutting her chin up, staring me down.

Fuck, it's hard not to react to that. Not to reach across the table and kiss her.

Finally she's showing the side I know has been in her this entire time. She's not that subservient, submissive charm of a woman anymore. She's the real Rose. The fiery Rose. The one who says what she actually thinks and will do whatever is necessary the consequences be damned.

"Clearly." Hastings says. "Seeing as we can attribute at least one man's death to your hands…"

"In self-defence." I state.

"He bloody deserved it." Rose hisses. "He'd been torturing me for months."

Hastings eyebrows raise. "He tortured you?"

"Psychologically. Darius was the one who actually hurt me physically, who beat me, who assaulted me, who inflicted the real torture."

I can see Hastings face react. I can see him thinking 'what the fuck'.

"They murdered my cousin. They murdered Ty." Rose says and I can see she's reliving it, that she's spiralling again, the way she does every time she thinks of that moment, that memory.

"It's okay." I say reaching across taking her hand, trying to ground her back in this room, in this moment not the horrific one playing in her head.

"No, it's not." She snaps. "They stole my daughter. My father did it first and then Darius learnt from him. I've been nothing but cannon fodder, nothing but a thing to be used. Of course I killed Carter. That's what any animal does when it's been caged, when it's been abused. It lashes out. It fights back."

"You think of yourself as an animal?" Hastings says.

She draws herself up. "I've not been treated as a human being have I?" She retorts.

He inclines his head for a second and then takes a sip of his drink.

"Talking of your father, where is he?" Hastings says looking at me.

"He is no longer with us." I say.

"What?" Hastings growls. "I thought I made myself more than clear…"

Rose opens her mouth but I cut across her. I won't have her taking the fall for this. I won't have her being punished for something she had every right to do.

"He tried to escape." I say simply. "He was injured when we recaptured him and he died of his wounds."

"I would like to see his body. To confirm that."

"That will not happen."

"How do I know you're telling the truth?" He asks.

"My father is not the one you want." Rose says getting his attention.

"Then who is?" He asks.

"My mother. She's the one with the information. She's the one who knows about Darius."

"Knows what?" He asks.

She shrugs. "I don't know. But that's what he said. He told Carter he'd rather she was dead then caught."

His eyes register that. He looks at me then back at Rose. "Do you know where she is?"

"If I did she wouldn't still be there." She says curling her hands into fists.

"I see." He says. "Then let me make this perfectly clear, if you do find her I want her handed over. No excuses. No accidents. I'll let the incident with your father pass only if I get Carla instead."

Rose narrows her eyes and I can tell she doesn't like it. That she's as determined to make her mother pay as she did her father.

"Agreed." I say before she can say anything. If that's the price then I'll pay it. I'll face her wrath if it means she gets away with it.

Hastings grunts, reaches into his suit, pulls out some photos and lays them on the desk. "I want you to look at these faces. Did any of them ever come into contact with your husb... with Darius? Did they come to the house, did he meet them somewhere?"

She frowns staring one by one at the six images and when she gets to the last one she freezes. Her face goes so pale, like she's seen a ghost.

"Him." She whispers, pointing to the average looking man in the ridiculously priced designer jacket.

Hastings narrows his eyes. "You're certain?"

"Positive."

"How positive?"

Her face goes so cold, her looks like she might just murder him. "Because I was in the room when he violated Roman's sister." She snarls.

I'm on my feet before I can stop myself, snatching that photo up and staring at the bastard.

"Roman."

Both Hastings and Rose say my name but I look at her.

356

She looks ashamed, she looks heartbroken, she looks like she still believes it was her fault, that she could have done something to stop it.

"Who the fuck is he?" I growl.

"His name is Nicholas Austin-Reed." Hastings says.

My stomach knots, I know that name, I've heard it before.

"He's the President's stepson." He adds.

"What?" Rose gasps.

Hastings tilts his head. "I don't want a word of this to leave this room you hear me?"

"You think I'll agree to that?" I growl. "You think I'll let you bury it? Let him get away with what he did?"

Hastings shakes his head. "You misunderstand me Roman. I'm not burying it. The President chose me as Governor for a reason. He believed Nicholas was involved, he believed he was tied up in a lot of Darius's shit. But he can't let that get out. He can't let the masses know…"

"So his reputation is worth more than justice?" Rose scoffs.

"No one said anything about not giving justice." Hastings says. "There will be justice. By estimation it's more of the kind that you two seem to favour."

"Meaning?" I ask.

He reaches forward, downs his drink. "I'll be in touch. I need to speak to the President…"

"And then what?" I snarl.

He smiles at me, getting to his feet. "Then you will understand exactly who the President is and why he is best suited to dealing with Nicholas."

"He deserves to die." Rose says.

Hastings meets her gaze. "He does." He agrees. "And believe me he will."

He sees himself out while I'm just stood, seething, feeling my blood boil. I knew Darius's reach went far but I didn't believe he had a direct line to the President. A direct link.

"Do you trust him?" Rose asks me.

I blink, realising she's stood in front of me, her body so close to mine. I can see those frown lines on her face, I can see the dark circles under eyes still. She's been through so much. She's endured so much. I lift my fingers tracing her skin, tracing her lips and she shuts her eyes, trying to control herself in this moment.

"He could have had you arrested." I murmur.

"You wouldn't have let him do that." She says back, her lips brushing against my tips as she replies.

She's right. I wouldn't have. If that's what it took, I would have taken Hastings on, taken the President on. Taken everyone on. I fought for six years to get back to her, fought for months to save her and my child.

I'm not going to back down now.

I'm not going to stop until this is ended. Until Darius is taken care of.

And until everyone who wronged us has paid their dues.

ROSE

Being in this house feels like a transformation.

Lara seems to come to life. Being outside, being out of the tunnels, and being around us both.

I get up each morning, and she and Roman are already downstairs, eating breakfast, and she's chatting away.

My heart swells when I see them. It feels normal. It feels right.

Roman and I are technically sharing a room, though he's doing his best to give me space. I want him there, next to me, holding me, cuddling me and yet whenever he gets closer my head panics and I can't stop the fear taking over.

Each night he sleeps beside me in a bed so big we can both lay out without touching.

I swear neither of us has gotten a decent night sleep because of my nightmares but he doesn't say anything about it, he just acts like this is normal, like he expected it.

Only I didn't. In my head, as soon as I was free this was all meant to stop. It was meant to be like it was before, in the Montague house. For those few precious weeks we had before everything collapsed around us.

The first week here goes in a blur. That is after the shock of Hastings visit and what we discovered. We spend our time making this house ours, moving furniture around, buying things, ensuring that Lara's bedroom in particular is how she wants it, though more often than not she's sneaking into ours to sleep after her own nightmares wake her up in the night.

When I wake and dress on the eighth day here I come down to find the scene outside completely white.

"It's snowed." Lara says with the biggest grin on her face.

"I can see that." I reply. Thank god Roman got us all warm clothing, that he made such a big deal about it while I thought he was just being overprotective.

Roman meets my gaze with a smile.

I almost kissed him this morning.

He doesn't know that. He doesn't realise. But when I awoke and he was there, asleep, looking more irresistible than ever I wanted to lean over and kiss him so badly.

But I didn't. I just lay there instead, and then he opened his eyes and Lara bounced into the room and the moment passed.

"Shall we build a snowman?" I ask Lara.

She frowns looking from me to her dad. "What is that?" She asks.

My eyes widen, I swear my jaw drops.

"You don't know what a snowman is?" Roman says quietly.

Lara shakes her head looking at us like she's trying to figure out if we're pulling her leg or not.

"I think this is the perfect opportunity to show her." I say.

Roman gets up, walks out of the breakfast room and comes back with a handful of coats and scarves in his hands.

Lara is still looking like she has no idea what is going on so I put her coat on, wrap a thick woolly scarf around her neck and then get myself ready.

"You look snug as a bug." I say feeling my heart thumping so loudly. This was what I wanted, what I'd thought about over and over.

Roman takes my hand, squeezing it, as we walk towards the huge doors onto the veranda.

It's so cold outside I can see my breath. I huddle up more in the thick white coat, pulling the collar up against my neck. Lara walks tentatively out into the snow. Her feet sink a good few inches into it and she squeals as the cold clearly drips into her shoes.

I can't help but let out a laugh. "Come on baby." I say to her. "Let's make our first snowman together."

She nods but she's still clearly got no idea, so I'm the one who scoops up the first bit, showing her what to do. It's hard to do it with my arm still in the cast but thankfully the coat protects it from the damp and I've got a ridiculous sized mitten on to at least make my hand usable. To say I'll be happy when it's off is an understatement.

"How is this a snowman?" Lara half scoffs when I've built it. It's not the best. It's wonky, veering off to the right. Roman disappeared inside and came back with a bunch of carrots and I push one into its face.

"You think you can do better?" I tease.

She tilts her head like she's trying to work out how best to let me down.

"How about a competition?" Roman says. "Whoever builds the best snowman gets a prize."

"What's the prize?" Lara asks.

I bite my lip at that. She's so like him, she wants all the details before she commits herself.

"If you win then you can choose Sweetpea." Roman says.

She half pouts before turning her face to the perfect snow laid out in front of her.

"First one to build one wins." She half yells before rushing to scoop up as much snow in her hands as she can.

"Hey!" I say pretending to be outraged. Only I'm not, I'm loving every minute of this.

It takes less than ten minutes for us to finish them. I let her win. And it turns out she's a terrible winner because she keeps gloating, jumping up and down, cheering delightedly at the fact that she's beaten me.

Movement in the window makes me look up but Sofia is gone before I can see her. Only I know she was there. I'd put money on it being her.

"You okay?" Roman asks seeing the way my face falls.

"It's nothing." I lie. I don't want him to know. I know he's worried about her enough. I don't want to make it worse. She needs time. She needs a lot more time than even I do and in truth, I'm not all that convinced that being here is helping her. Though I don't speak that thought out loud.

She's Roman's sister. He's doing what he believes is best. And maybe he is right. Maybe her being here is helping. I guess only time can tell on that front.

When Lara is all cheered out we go inside for hot chocolate and we sit in front of the fire feeling as the warmth slips back into our feet.

Out the window I can already see more snow falling. Great blobs of it coming thick and fast. It's like something out of a movie. Something out of a picture postcard.

"Maybe we'll have snow for Christmas." I say hopefully. It's not uncommon in Verona. But the thought of it makes me feel so content.

"What's Christmas?" Lara says quietly.

My eyes dart to her. Roman shifts in the seat opposite me.

I'd never considered the fact that she might not know what Christmas is. I mean, why would she? They barely spent more than a dime on her existence before we got her out. Why would they have made any effort to celebrate it? To buy her presents?

My eyes well with tears. I can feel my lip trembling. "Lara." I half whisper and she frowns even more in confusion.

She gets up, walking towards us. "What is Chrismus?" She even mispronounces the word like she's not sure how to say it.

"It's a festival." Roman explains. "Families celebrate it together. We give presents and eat nice food, and spend time together."

She gulps looking from me to her daddy. "Can we, can we do that?"

I get up pulling her into a tight hug. She's the only one I can touch properly without flinching and thank god for that. "We will baby." I say. "We'll get decorations, and a tree…"

"We can pick one together." Roman says coming up behind me, cupping her cheek.

"A tree?" She repeats looking even more confused.

"You'll see baby." I say. "We'll make sure this Christmas is all about you."

"About us." Roman adds. "About our family together."

My tears spill over at that. I fight the wail that wants to escape my lips but I lean back, into his chest. I'm finally going to get it aren't I? I'm finally going to have that one thing I dreamed of over and over.

When I look up, when I meet his gaze I feel my whole body seem to flush. Perhaps this is what he was planning by bringing us here, perhaps this was what I subconsciously knew would happen, that us creating a home, creating this environment would be enough to heal, enough to forget, at least to begin to sow those seeds.

ROSE

Ben and Sofia are there at dinner. Once again Sofia doesn't speak beyond a few words here and there and there's a smile I know she puts on solely for Lara's benefit.

It breaks my heart to see her like this and it makes me angry that she feels she has to even pretend.

The doctor came around while we were outside and from what I can tell she's now completely med free. Completely clean.

She should be celebrating. She should be happy. But she looks just as broken as always.

Ben sits next to her, like he's some sort of protector but he's careful not to overwhelm her. He's more a shadow than a person when she's there.

Lara chats away, she talks excitedly about the snow and the prospect of Christmas now that she's getting her head around it.

And I keep glancing at Roman. I can't seem to stop. It's like some part of me has finally woken up from my grief and realised that he's here, he's alive, and that I have him back.

But my fear is still there, my nerves. I feel like two people split, conflicted, caught up in a twister of emotions that keep flitting from relief, to panic, to joy, to love, to utter desolation.

I don't know what to do. I don't know how to get past this.

Sofia slips away as soon as the dessert is done. Ben takes Lara off as if he can sense we both need some alone time.

And for a moment we just sit there, at the formal dining table not speaking, not even looking at each other until the tension breaks.

I get up, I walk past him, knowing he's going to follow me and praying that he does.

When I get to our room he pauses like might be reconsidering whatever this is.

"Roman." I murmur his name, almost intoxicated by the fact that I can say it, that I can speak it once more without dire consequences.

He comes up behind me and I can feel the heat of his body. I know in normal circumstances he would be touching me, putting his hands on my shoulders, brushing his lips against my neck, and perhaps the fact that he isn't doing any of that is driving me more mad.

"I want you so much." I whisper. "I want what we had. I want everything we had."

"We will get that back." He says quietly. Confidently.

I let out a half laugh at the way he believes it. The way he doesn't even question it.

And then I turn, facing him, meeting those beautiful brown eyes.

He tilts his head, his own dropping to stare at my lips as if he wants to catch them with his. Before he can, I put my finger across his mouth.

"I want to try something." I murmur. My hearts fluttering like a flame in the wind, it feels like I'm about to jump off a cliff, take a risk part of me doesn't need to but so much of me is desperate for.

"What?" He asks.

"I…" I gulp, feeling the heat rise in my cheeks. I feel like that inexperienced girl again, caught with a man she shouldn't be with only this time it doesn't feel exhilarating, it feels daunting, like a mountain I suddenly need to scale. "Lie on the bed."

His eyebrows raise, his lip curls and then he's doing it, sitting so that he's resting against the headboard.

"I don't like being touched." I say, pulling off my jumper. "I hate the thought of someone else touching me, of their skin against mine, of that lack of control."

A micro-expression of something crosses his face but whatever thoughts he has, he keeps them to himself.

I drop my jeans, but I keep my t-shirt on, keeping my top half covered with it. And then I walk to the dressing room, pull the tie free from the silk robe that's hanging there.

When I come back he's exactly where I left him. Still fully clothed too.

He eyes the turquoise band in my hands but he doesn't say anything.

I let out a ragged breath. I can do this. I can control this. And if I can get past this, then maybe another piece of me will not only be fixed but will be restored. That I will be another step closer to the new me, the improved me.

I get on the bed, straddling him before I can talk myself out of this and I tie one end to his left wrist before twisting it around the headboard and then securing his right.

"You're tying me up." He murmurs.

I bite my lip. "I figured that this will give me more control. That this way I can touch you, but it will feel safe."

His eyes narrow. "You're always safe with me."

I blink back at him. My heart is racing so loudly, I can feel that adrenaline fluttering inside me and there's a voice screaming at me inside my head. But I can feel something else too, that need, that want, that hunger that was always there, that was always present inside me from the moment I'd first laid eyes on Roman.

"I love you." I say. "I love you so much."

He shifts, clearly fighting the urge to lean forward and kiss me. "I love you too Rose."

And that's when I decide to do it, to lean down, to kiss him, to stop letting all those bastards continue to beat me. To beat us.

It's slow, hesitant. My lips press into his and while he mimics my movements he doesn't take over, he doesn't fight for dominance. I let out a moan, a gasp as my eyes prick with tears and then I push myself more, slipping my tongue into his mouth, deepening that kiss even further.

He growls out. His arms shift against the ties but he still lets me have this, lets me control this.

When I pull away I feel breathless. I feel like I've just had the biggest high.

I can feel him beneath me too. I can feel how his body has responded. How his dick is hard.

I draw in a breath, keeping my eyes focused on him, making sure that in this moment I don't get myself confused, don't panic into thinking this is someone else.

I reach forward, undoing his shirt button by button. My fingers are trembling, my body is too. When I pull the fabric back I stare at his chest, at the scar where he was stabbed so long ago, at the bullet wound that stopped him from coming for us sooner.

I lower my mouth, planting a kiss on him. Then another.

I can hear his breathing. I can see the way he's watching me with those eyes that he wants to devour me whole. As I shift down my body pushes against his dick and he tenses more.

"Rose." He half growls, half murmurs, as if he's trying so hard to be passive in all this.

I gulp, feeling that fear twist inside me, only I won't give in. Not yet.

I run my hands over his skin, trace a pattern with my fingertips. I'm putting off what I really want, buying time, trying to get a hold on my nerves.

"Rose." He murmurs again, softer, as if he can tell I'm right on the cusp of fleeing the room, of turning back into a messy, crying wreck once more.

I shut him up with my mouth. I press my lips to his, not kissing him, not really, our lips are closed, my face feels wet with my tears but my hands are reaching down, undoing his belt, his jeans, freeing his dick.

His fists his own hands, forces his body to be still. Letting me take what I want. Letting me do what I want. Giving me all the control.

I've still got my underwear on, I'm still in a bra and t-shirt, his t-shirt technically, but I'm wet. Not much. But I am wet. I slide my thong aside, raising my hips and then I lower myself onto him.

He groans. He growls deep in his throat. I don't move, I just sit there, holding him inside me, trying to fight the memories as they all seem to come crashing down like an avalanche and I'm suddenly drowning under the weight of them.

"Undo the ties." He says quietly.

I shake my head. I can't move even if I wanted too. In this moment I feel paralysed. Torn between my fear and my trauma.

"Let me hold you. Let me touch you." He says.

"I can't." I half whisper.

He tilts his head, pulls one hand free and then the other and I realise then that he's been pretending the whole time, that I clearly didn't do the knots anywhere near tight enough to restrain him.

I think if I could I would laugh at that. At my own folly.

His hands wrap around me. I'm shuddering, whimpering, trying not to let this spiral further down the path we're already headed. One of disaster. One of pain. One I know will hurt us both more.

"Open your eyes." He says. "Look at me."

I blink, releasing more tears, but I do it.

His face is right there, his beautiful features, his chocolate eyes, his stubble, everything I've missed for so long. I can smell him, I feel him. I'm surrounded by him, engulfed by him. Completely intoxicated by him again.

His hands trace up, under the t-shirt, up my back, his touch is so light, so gentle. I let out a gasp as my body finally gets the message that this is Roman.

"You're always safe with me." He says.

I let my tears fall then, I stop trying to pretend but I'm raising my hips all the same, slowly, carefully allowing that need to take over.

He holds me to him, he cradles my body as we move. It feels like we're rediscovering one another, it feels like we're both re-learning how our bodies connect.

I can feel myself getting wetter and wetter. I can feel my release building. I shut my eyes, fighting the words, fighting the whispered taunts that echo in my head.

"Stay with me." Roman says softly. "I'm right here with you. I've got you."

I let out a wail. There's no physical pain, there's no physical trauma like there was when I was with Darius and yet it feels like I'm back there, hearing every disgusting thing he said to me, feeling his fingers digging into my body, feeling him violating me, and the way I allowed him to do it, the way I pretended at the end.

"Roman." I gasp his name. I dig my hands into his forearms. Desperate for those memories to go. Desperate to replace them. To erase them. To just be over it all.

"I've got you." He says again.

ROMAN

I can feel how her body is trembling. I can feel how close she is to freaking out.

"I've got you." I say brushing her hair back from her face, cupping her cheek in my hands.

She's got her eyes shut. She's screwed her face up as if she's fighting some internal battle with her own head.

I twist us around, laying us on our sides, but I keep myself inside her, I keep us connected.

She's so warm. She feels incredible. It reminds me of how long it's been since we've had this, since we've felt this, since I've claimed her in this way.

She's still wearing my top, she's still in her underwear and I'm still in my jeans and shirt. I take the moment to pull them off, to free myself of my clothes and be able to move better.

I want her to feel me, I want her to know that it's me touching her, me loving her.

She whimpers again and I soothe her quietly. Her breathing sounds ragged, I can see how much she's shaking. A part of me wonders if we should stop but I know if we do, it will haunt us, it will haunt her. And she'll be afraid to take this step again, she'll overthink it even more.

"Open your eyes." I say.

She does as I ask and I hold her gaze. I make sure this time she doesn't look away.

I raise her leg more, tucking it around me and I start to thrust into her.

She's wet. Her body is aroused even if her head is conflicted.

"You're so beautiful." I murmur.

"Don't." She says cutting across me. "Don't say that."

The way she reacts, the hiss in her voice tells me that he used to say that, that he used to say the same words. That it's another trigger for her.

I let out a sigh. Maybe my words alone can't help, but my actions can. I can show her my love, I can show her how safe she is with my body.

I hold her hip, keeping her gaze and continue those slow sensual thrusts, fighting every groan, every urge in my body to be ploughing into her. She feels incredible. She feels every bit as perfect as she always has.

Her hands cling to me. She buries her face into my chest taking deep breaths but she's raising her hips, meeting my movements, echoing them.

And slowly, I can hear her moans. She's whispering them like she's ashamed to be making the noises, like she's ashamed to be enjoying this.

"Don't hold back." I say. "I love the way you used to moan for me. I loved the way you always let me know how good it felt for you."

She flushes, her cheeks going so red. I thrust into her, deliberately pushing into her body in a way I know she'll enjoy.

And she lets out such a moan.

"There's my good girl." I say.

She bites her lip, her eyes darting down to where we're connected, to where I'm so deep inside her.

"Fuck me Roman." She says. "Fuck me properly. I can take it now."

I scan her face trying to figure out if those are just words or if she actually means it. She's spent her whole life appeasing other people, putting their wants above her own. I have to be sure this is what she actually wants.

"Roman." She says leaning in catching my lips. "Make me yours again."

I kiss her back, hungrily. I take her mouth and this time I don't hold back. I'm ferocious as I claim her, as my tongue swirls with hers.

"You were always mine." I say breaking off. "Nothing has ever changed that."

And then I am thrusting into her, driving both our need. She rocks her body, she meets my thrust with such urgency, as if this moment here is her freedom. As if this moment here will fix all that pain.

I can feel her body clenching. I can feel her getting so close. Once more she whimpers like she doesn't want to do it, like she's afraid of the consequences.

And then she's toppling over, screaming, digging her nails into my skin and writhing like a creature half mad. I groan, burying myself inside her. Her muscles are holding me so tight I think my dick might snap.

"Fuck Rose." I gasp. "You feel so good. You feel…" I trail off as my own orgasm hits me. As I pour into her.

I didn't think to use a condom. Maybe if we'd planned this better I would have. But as she slumps into my arms and I lay there buried inside her I don't care about the consequences anymore.

She nuzzles into my chest. Her t shirt has ridden up enough that I can see her stomach. I run my hand over her skin, revelling in the fact that we're here, tangled up, exactly where we belong.

"I didn't mean it to go that far." She whispers.

"You didn't want to come?" I ask.

She shakes her head. "I wanted you…" She trails off clearing her voice like she can't quite get the words out. "I wanted you to but not me."

"Why not?"

She shuts her eyes, palms her hands into them. "He was fixated on it. He'd taunt me about it. He tried to make me but I couldn't and then in the end, I stopped fighting. I pretended I'd given in and I…"

Somehow I know what she's going to say. That she acted the part that they made her. That she played the whore.

"It's okay Rose." I murmur. "Nothing you did was out of choice."

"But I chose to do that, I chose to give him that."

I cup her cheek, understanding now where some of that conflict came from. She made herself come for him, that's why she doesn't want to feel that pleasure now. Because he tarnished it. "You have nothing to be ashamed of. Nothing to explain. You're alive because you did what was necessary. You're alive because you fought. You fought for Lara and you fought for me and most importantly you fought for yourself."

She drops her hands, placing one on my chest. "You're not just saying that?"

"No." I reply planting a kiss on her head. "You've been incredible. Everything you've been through, everything you've faced."

"I want everyone to know." She says.

"What?" I frown.

"I want everyone to know we're together. I want Verona to know about Lara. I want to make it so that no one can separate us again. That no one can pretend that we aren't in a relationship."

"That won't happen." I state. "But if you want to go public, we can."

She nods. "I know a journalist…"

"The one you were speaking with before?"

She looks surprised. "How did you know…?"

"Hastings told me. She went to him, she told him what she knew. She told him you risked your life."

"It wasn't like that."

I place my hand on her lips. I don't want to dwell on it. I don't want her to keep denying what she went through. "We can do whatever you want Rose. Whatever makes you feel safe."

"You make me feel safe." She says pulling my arms tighter around her like now that she can tolerate it she doesn't want to let me go.

She runs her hands up my chest, feeling my muscles. "You lost weight." She says quietly.

"It's muscle wastage." I reply. Though I've been building it back I'm still not as strong as I was but I guess it takes time.

She leans into me more. "Perhaps we can work out together? Get stronger together?"

There's a gym in the basement. It's fully equipped with every-thing you could imagine. There's a pool too and I've been looking forward to teaching Lara how to swim from the moment she told me she couldn't.

"Would you like that Rose?" I ask grinning. "Me perving on you while you do your squats?"

She chuckles softly. "I was thinking that I need to get stronger."

"Why?"

She fixes me with a fierce determined look. "Because when we find Darius I want to be able to match him. I want to be as strong as I possibly can be."

I narrow my eyes, my hand moving to hold her chin. "You sure about that?"

She nods. "I need to do it. I need to prove that he didn't break me."

"You don't need to prove anything Rose." I state. "But if you want to do it, do it for yourself, not for anyone else."

I won't stop her. I won't tell her no. Refuse her anything. But if this is what she wants them by god will I make sure she has the skills to do it. Because this time, when we face him, it will be us the victors. Us who come out on top.

I know that fight is coming. I know Darius hasn't simply slinked off into obscurity. He'll want his revenge. He'll be planning something even now. He'll be coming up with a way to kill us both.

ROMAN

I leave Rose only to put Lara to bed. Ben put a Christmas movie on for her to watch and I got downstairs to see she'd fallen asleep next to him.

I carried her up, tucked her in, and then went back to our bed.

Only Rose isn't in it.

I frown, glancing around the room and then I hear her moving in the bathroom. She's run a bath. She's lit candles. She seems like some great stress has finally been lifted.

"Hey." I murmur leaning against the doorframe.

She turns, giving me a smile. "Is she asleep?"

"She was watching movies with Ben." I say. "She was already out so I carried her up."

My eyes glance at the tub. It's filled, with bubbles and everything.

"You wanted a bath?" I ask.

"I thought we could have one together." She says.

I tilt my head. She sounds nervous. Like she's suddenly unsure of everything again.

"Alright." I say walking over to where the damned bag is for her arm. I think we'll both be more than glad when the cast is off.

She holds her arm out, pulling the baggy silk sleeve of the robe she has on, out the way. I slip it in place and secure it while she pulls an annoyed face.

"You'll be free of it soon." I state.

And in truth we're lucky she didn't have more injuries. She did jump from a helicopter after all.

She slips the silk robe off and it pools at her feet like water. I blink feeling my dick react as I realise she's naked. She looks down at herself, wrapping her arms in a way that tells me she's more insecure than she used to be.

I want to tell her how beautiful she is. I want to reassure her but as I go to speak the words I remember her reaction last time. That he obviously said that. That he told her that.

I let out a sigh, pulling my own clothes off as she turns and steps into the water.

"How is it?" I ask.

"It's perfect." She says running her hands through the bubbles.

I could sit opposite her. The bath is certainly big enough for me to do so. But instead I slide in behind her, pulling her body into my chest.

"We've never done this." I murmur.

She sighs, relaxing enough to tell me she's okay with me being this close, that she can tolerate my touch again.

"That's why I thought of it." She replies. "I wanted new memories. New moments."

I plant a kiss on the side of her head. "That's all we will have from now."

She places a hand on my thigh, letting out a low breath. "Thank you."

"For what?" I ask.

"For being you. For being so understanding, for not..." She shakes her head.

"Of course I am." I say. Like hell I would behave any other way. She's always been my world, and nothing has changed that.

She shifts her hand, drops it between our bodies and I let out a deep groan as she starts to fondle me. I'll admit I wasn't expecting that, in my head I thought we'd sit here, that we'd talk, that after earlier she might need some time out before we went anywhere near the sex situation again.

But I guess I was wrong. Not that I'm complaining.

"Will you, will you touch me again?" She says.

It feels like the air tenses. Like she's waiting for my response. As if I would turn her down. As if I would ever deny her a thing.

She's already got me riled up, she's already got me fighting myself to not sink my cock into her.

My hand slips around, onto her leg as she sits between mine. She must feel my own reaction, she must feel how hard I already am.

"Do you want me to?" I ask.

"I need you to." She says.

"I need you do something as well." I say running my hand up, feeling how soft her skin is, feeling her stomach, her ribs, and the underside of her breasts as she takes in one heavy breath after another.

"What?" She asks.

"I need to know what he said. I need to know what words, what taunts, all of it."

She gulps. "I can't..."

"You can." I reply taking her nipple in my hand, twirling it between my fingers as her back arches. "Tell me Rose. Tell me what he did and I'll erase every moment of it."

She shifts further into me. Her hips grinding just enough to tell me I've got her worked up. That right now, I can use her lust against her, though in truth I want to know not because I want to torture either of us with the knowledge. Far from it. I want to know so I cannot say anything or do anything that triggers her. I need to know what the boundaries are to protect us both.

"He…" She gasps as I tease her breasts more. As I fondle them both. "He called me a slut. And a whore."

I guess that was obvious. It certainly wasn't very inventive was it? I run my lips down her neck. "But you were always *my* slut weren't you Rose? My trouble?"

She nods. "I couldn't come for him. No matter how many times he tried. So he…" She shudders as I pinch her nipples, as I tease those hardened buds, giving her a hit of pleasure that right now she needs more than oxygen.

"He what Rose?"

"He used a vibrator." She states. "He forced me to come."

I feel my anger flare. If she wasn't in my arms, if I didn't need to have complete control right now I swear I would flip.

"But when I did, I said your name. Every time I said your name he would hurt me. But that time…" Her words turn to moans as I manoeuvre her body around enough to suck her nipple. "Oh god Roman."

"That's right." I say looking at her, at how she looks like she might just come for me right now. "Say my name Rose, scream it for me."

I suck again, I swirl my tongue over her, I nibble enough that her legs kick out and she is moaning more, moaning my name.

"Roman." She groans. "Don't stop."

I snake my hand down her front. I know I'm pushing this but I want to get her back to what she was, I want her as she was, I want to prove to her that her pleasure is not something they can take. That these moments here are not affected by what he did.

As my hand cups her pussy she freezes. She stills.

"What else did he do?" I ask.

She whimpers. "He…"

I slide my fingers between her lips, teasing her but making sure not to touch her most sensitive part. I want her to want it. I want her to be desperate for it.

"Tell me Rose."

"He.." She swallows, whimpering at what my hand is doing to her. "Please Roman."

"Tell me what else he said." I say like I'm not probing her entrance, teasing in every way except the way she wants.

"He would call me beautiful. He would tell me how soft my skin was. He would say how perfect my body was." She half cries. "And he would groan, he would groan and go on about how tight I felt, how I was gripping him so well."

I shut my eyes, storing that information, I've already said similar to her without meaning to. "You are beautiful." I say, circling her clit so lightly, giving the reward I promised. "You're so beautiful but it's not just your body Rose. It's you, you as a person. As the mother of my child. As the love of my life."

She rocks her hips, she rubs herself against me as I tease her. "I can't stop." She says. "I want you to make me…"

She rolls her head back and I sink two fingers into her. She is tight. Her muscles are gripping me so perfectly though I don't voice it.

"Roman." She gasps.

I squeeze her breast with my other hand, massage it as I begin to thrust.

Her own hands fumble for me but I shift to block her off using my elbow. "This is about you Rose." I say. "This is about you remembering your pleasure."

"But I want you. I need you."

"And you have me." I say running my face against hers. "You always have me."

"I need more."

My lips curl. I thrust my fingers into her, curl them as she arches her back.

"That enough?" I taunt before I can stop myself.

"I need you Roman. I need to feel you. I need you in me."

"Tell me then. Tell me the last of it."

She shudders, her tears are streaming and I can't tell if it's from her need to come or her want to keep the worst bits from me.

I pinch her clit. Not hard. But the way I know she likes. She jerks, she spreads her legs wider, rocking her hips. "Make me come. Please Roman. Please."

"Tell me and I will."

She looks up at me, and for the first time since I started this I see real sadness, regret.

"He kept saying he wanted me pregnant. He wanted me to have his children. He kept saying that if I did then I would give in and love him."

I tilt my head, dropping my gaze to her belly, remembering the taunt that her father said before. About how much Darius was fucking her non-stop. They would have tested her surely? She would have said if she was carrying his child. There would be signs.

"I'm not." She says. "I'm not pregnant. And I never was."

I let out a deep exhale. If she was, if she was carrying his child then would have dealt with it. We would have figured it out together. She would have been the one to decide if she wanted to keep it, she would have had that call and whatever action she took I would have supported her.

But I guess we don't have to worry about that do we?

"Roman?" She asks quietly.

I curl my fingers, teasing deep inside her and that concern turns back to pleasure. Her face melts as she sinks back into me.

"The only child you've had is mine." I say.

She nods, putting her hand on top of mine, joining in with how I'm manipulating her body so deliciously.

"And if you want another, if you want more, then it will be my children you grow fat with." I state.

"Only yours." She says breathlessly.

"My Rose." I grow. "My woman to love, my woman to touch. And nobody else's."

"Yours." She says kicking out, writhing, splashing water everywhere as she topples over.

As soon as she comes I pull her hips up, slide myself into her with her back pressed into my chest. She moans as my full length spreads her wide and her muscles shift to accommodate me.

"So fucking perfect." I say.

She grabs my hand, puts it back on her clit and, as if my fingers were a toy, she uses them to tease herself. "He would do this too." She states. "He would try to make me come, only he doesn't know my body like you do."

I smile, thrusting into her sending the water cascading over the sides once more. I can still feel the after effects of her orgasm, I can feel the way she's clenching around my cock.

"That's because your body was made for me Rose." I state. "Nobody knows your body like I do. Nobody understands how to pleasure you like I do."

"I've never come for anyone else." She says. "Even when I was pretending, even when I forced myself to for him, it was you I was thinking of, you I was imagining."

Her tears slide down her cheeks. I kiss them away. Every last one.

"I've never loved anyone but you." I reply. "I've never needed anyone the way I need you Rose."

She puts my other hand on her stomach, where once she was swollen with our child. "If you want more children then…" She begins.

I crash my lips into her mouth silencing those words. I've seen enough from her reactions to know that's a trauma point, a trigger.

When I pull apart I rest my head against the side of hers.

"One day." I say. "When you want to. If you want to. And only if you want to."

She leans into me, rolls her hips, gyrates, as I bring us both back to climax.

ROMAN

The scream rips through the house. Even with the size it is. Even with us being here, in the orangery and Sofia being right at the other end.

Rose's eyes widen. Lara drops the colouring pen that's been staining her fingers bright pink from where it's leaking.

"Sofia." Rose says like I don't know.

I spring to my feet just as Ben does the same but when I get to the door I freeze looking back at my daughter.

"Shall we go outside?" Rose says already understanding exactly where my head is at. "Shall we play with the snow a bit?"

"But," Lara frowns. "Aunty Sofia is upset."

"It's okay baby. She'll be okay. Daddy is going to go check on her."

"Can I…"

Rose shakes her head gently pulling her from the chair. "Let's go outside for a bit. Let's see if we can build an even bigger snowman than last time."

I don't wait to watch, I race through the house, up the stairs, along the corridor that feels like it's going on forever and when I get into her bedroom I freeze.

Ben is already there. Stood. Staring at Sofia.

She's shaking, curled up in a corner. Half the space has been trashed. Furniture is on its side. The clothes we bought her for the winter weather is in a pile on the floor, dumped.

She's always been such a neat freak. She was always the tidy one growing up, putting everything in its place. Every teddy bear had their own spot. Even when she was a teenager she had all her makeup and jewellery organised in a way that was Instagram worthy.

But this room here, it looks like a train wreck. It looks like a disaster area.

"Sofia." I murmur.

She doesn't look up. She just stares blankly at the floor beyond her feet.

I don't understand what's brought this on. She seemed like she was doing okay. She seemed like she was being more herself, at least at meal times.

"Sofia." I say loudly.

She blinks, looking up, like she's only just realised we're here in her space.

Her lip trembles, her eyes well. "What, what do you want?" She asks.

"You were screaming." I say quietly. "We came to see if you're alright."

She stares back at me in confusion. "I wasn't…" She gulps. "I can't do this."

"Do what?" I ask.

She gets up, her legs are shaking, and she using the window sill to prop herself up. "I want to go."

"Go where?" I ask.

She throws her head back in frustration. "I told you. I told you from the start but you wouldn't listen. This isn't helping me. None of this is helping me."

"But it is…" I begin only she cuts across me.

"I want to go."

"No." I snap.

She shakes her head, her arms are wrapped so tightly around herself. "Please Roman."

"You belong here. With your family." I state.

She draws herself up. Clenches her fists. "If you loved me then you would let me go."

"It's because I love you that I won't." I snap back.

"You're keeping me like a prisoner." She screams. "You're forcing me to be here, to pretend, to…" She trails off as I step up to her, as I grab her arms and pull her into my chest.

"I'm trying to protect you." I say.

"You can't protect me from my own head." She replies.

"We can get through this together Sofia, let me help you."

"Let me go. Let me have space. Let me have freedom."

My heart twists. The last thing I wanted was for her to feel like I was trapping her here. I wanted to help. I wanted to fix her but everything I'm doing is wrong.

"Let me go." She says.

I meet Ben's gaze expecting him to be backing me up, only he's not. He's nodding. Agreeing with Sofia.

"Where will you go?" I ask.

She shrugs for a second. "The Four Seasons."

"You're not staying in a hotel." I snarl.

"It's my decision." She says.

"It won't be safe." I state.

"It's no less dangerous than being here. Besides I can have security. And I'll have space."

I want to say no. I want to come up with so many objections as to why this is a shit idea but I can see from her face that she's desperate. That she needs this. And ultimately it's not my decision is it? She's her own person. And from the sounds of it I've been suffocating her by forcing her to live like this.

"Will Ben go with you?" I ask.

It's not my place to know what's going on between them though I suspect there is still nothing. It's still platonic and I'm starting to wonder if that's all it will ever be on my sister's part.

She shakes her head. "I want to be alone. I want to process this alone. I need space."

"Okay." I say. "But if you need anything, anything at all."

She blinks back tears thanking me like I've done her a favour when in reality I've created this situation haven't I?

"I'll call a cab…" I begin.

"No, you won't." Ben says stepping out of the shadows. "I'll drive you. I'll make sure you're okay and then I'll go."

She nods glancing around the room. "Okay, just give me a moment to pack."

We step outside, into the corridor, Ben keeps his eyes averted and all to soon she's there, with a suitcase that he's taking from her and she's kissing my cheek, murmuring that she'll be in touch, not to worry, and then they're gone.

She is gone.

I walk back into her room. It's not as big as mine and Rose's. I gave her first pick and she chose the smallest, most out of the way one which should have been a sign if nothing else was.

Fuck I'm an idiot.

But then I was trying to fix this. Trying to fix her.

Only I'm the reason she's broken in the first place. I'm the cause of it. I put her in that situation. I caused all of this shit.

If I'd simply killed Darius that first time, if I'd done my research better, realised what was really going on with Rose, all of this would have been avoided.

I slam my fist into the wall, hearing the way my bones crunch and I grunt at the pain.

But my eyes register a movement, something that shouldn't be there.

I stare out the window, down to where Rose and Lara are. They're completely unaware. They're completely oblivious.

She's right behind them and neither of them have a damned clue.

I let out a shout, sprinting from the room, racing down the hallway.

How the fuck she even got inside the perimeter I don't know but I don't have time to consider it now. I have to stop whatever the fuck is about to happen.

I have to ensure that Carla motherfucking Capulet does not get anywhere near either of them.

ROSE

I wrap Lara's coat around her as quickly as I can. I don't know what's going on but clearly something's happened and I want to spare both my daughter and Sofia any further trauma.

She's still trying to argue, still trying to say that she wants to see her aunt but I shake my head, take her hand and pull her outside.

I haven't even put my own coat on. I've stuck my bare feet into the boots in my haste and I can feel them already starting to freeze.

"Mummy."

"Come on baby." I say. "Sofia is just having a bad moment. She just needs a little space right now." I don't want to lie to her. I don't want to pretend this isn't happening. She needs to understand at least enough of what this is.

The cold wind hits my face and I regret not putting on more layers. I'm not sure how long we'll be out here but I fight the shiver, forcing a smile and continue on out down the veranda, into the garden.

"What can I have for Christmas?" Lara asks.

I squeeze her hand, loving that she's that she's getting in the spirit, that she's behaving the way a normal child would.

"What would you like?" I ask back.

She frowns. "Daddy bought me a pony. Can I have my pony back?"

I'd forgotten about that. Bramble was it's name. It was a tempestuous shit of a Shetland. Thank god Roman had only loaned it so in all likelihood it's still alive, unharmed even.

"Shall we ask daddy?" I say.

She nods. "And can I have some new toys?"

She's already had a room full of toys as it is. "How about we go to a shop, we can pick them together?"

"Can we?" Her eyes widen so much. I've never been shopping with her. I know Holden has taken her once, back before everything got fucked up.

"Yes." I say giving her a hug. "And we can buy you some more clothes too. We can make a day of it. Eat out for lunch too if you'd like."

Her face lights up so brightly at my words. "Will daddy come?"

I doubt he'd want to miss it though I know how he feels about shopping. "I'm sure he will." I reply.

We walk a little further. I bend down picking up a handful of snow and roll it into a ball. As hard as I can I launch it at one of the trees and it smacks into it exploding into nothing.

Lara laughs copying me and for a minute she seems to forget everything.

When she turns back around her face is red, she's grinning from ear to ear but I can see a glint in her eye that says she's up to mischief.

"There's something else I want mummy. For Christmas."

"What is it?" I ask. I'm sure I'll agree. Whatever she wants, this year she gets it, even if she is spoiled, even if I'm creating a situation any normal parent would know better to avoid.

"You and daddy getting married."

I freeze, frowning. Does she even know what that means? "Lara…"

"If you marry then no one else can split us." She says.

I bite my lip seeing that defiant look in her eyes and the flash of trauma. Roman and I have talked about getting someone, a counsellor, not just for Lara but for me too. I hate the idea of it. Of telling a complete stranger everything that I've been through. Everything that I've accepted and allowed to happen in my life.

But I keep wondering how it might help Lara. How, at such a young age she needs someone professional to ensure she doesn't get as fucked in the head as I am.

"Come here baby." I say wrapping my arms around her. "No one is going to split us up this time."

"He's not dead though is he?" Lara murmurs into the thick fabric of my coat.

No. He's not. And while that plays on my mind, that Darius is out there, that he is almost certainly planning something, I don't voice it. I won't put anymore fear and anxiety into my child's head.

I bend down, feeling the cold sink in through my jeans and to my skin. "We're going to let everyone know Lara." I say. "Me and your daddy. We're going to tell the world we're together and that we have you."

"Will that help?" She asks.

"It will." I say. "It will mean there are no more lies. No more pretending."

She nods but I'm not sure she really understands it.

I glance back at the house. We've not heard a peep since we got out here. In truth I'm not sure if we even would. It's too big, and we're too far. But my fingers are getting numb and I'm starting to shake despite my best efforts not to.

"Shall we go back inside?" I say. "We can get a hot chocolate and warm up by the fire."

"Well doesn't that sound idyllic."

My whole body seems to react to that voice. I spin around, my heart suddenly stopping as I lay eyes on her. *What the fuck?*

"What a picture perfect life you've gotten yourself Rose." My mother spits.

I grab Lara pulling her behind me, protecting her.

She's got a knife in her hand. She looks half manic. Her usually immaculate hair has twigs and knots and god knows what else in it. She's shaking and I can't tell if it's from the cold or from her own anger. She looks like a rabid dog about to attack.

"What are you doing here?" I ask.

She glances down and I know she's staring at my daughter, staring at Lara who's peeping out from behind me.

"What do you think Rose?" She says taking a step towards me. "You really thought that it would all just end? That you could simply walk away and we'd let you?"

"It is over." I state. "Darius is gone."

She tilts her head and that manic smile spreads. "You were never good enough for him." She says. "I told him that. I told him over and over but he wouldn't listen."

"If you're just going to…"

She launches herself at me. Only I'm quicker. I push Lara out of the way, grabbing my mother's wrist where that knife is pointed so dangerously.

She's screaming, snarling. She really is rabid.

I kick up, kneeing her in the groin and she bends over double but she's still not relinquishing the knife.

"You stupid bitch." She says. "You could have had everything. You could have had it all."

I slam my body sideways into her and we fall, both of us into the snow.

She starts thrusting the blade, it's so close to my eye, so close to blinding me. I jerk my head back only she's got my hair holding me in place.

"Mummy." Lara screams.

I don't look at her. I don't dare too. Instead I curl my fist and slam into her face. Her noses crunches. She howls and I snatch the blade, scrambling to my feet.

Lara runs to me and I grab her pulling her once more behind me as the sound of running feet hits my ears.

My mother tries to get up and I step onto her, forcing her back into the freezing ground, pointing the knife right in her throat. By the look of it I broke her nose, again.

"Rose."

I smirk at Roman as he comes to a stop. Half the security are here now. I step back as they haul her to her feet, kicking and screaming.

"Are you hurt?" Roman asks checking Lara over and then me.

"We're fine." I say.

"Mummy saved us." Lara says.

I let out a laugh that feels more weighted than it should. I've still the knife in my hand, the one my mother no doubt planned on gutting me with. I guess the tables have turned now haven't they? I look up at Roman and he's watching me like he expects me to go feral again. Only I won't. I'm beyond that now. Yes I want my revenge, but this time I want more than that.

I want answers too.

"Take her to the basement." I say to the guards.

They look at Roman for confirmation and he nods.

"Let's go inside." I say to Lara, handing Roman the knife in a way that our daughter can't see. "I promised you hot chocolate didn't I? You must be freezing."

ROSE

We sit by the fire, Lara and I sipping our drinks with extra marshmallows and cream while Bella is laid out on the rug and Roman is stood watching us, watching me like I've lost my mind.

I can't help but smile at him.

He thinks I'm being weird. But I'm not. I want Lara calm. I want her reassured. Besides, my mother is safely secured right now and I've made sure she's already suffering.

Lara goes to the bathroom and Roman walks up to me and sits down like he's got the world on his shoulders.

"How's Sofia?" I ask.

He tilts his head. "She left."

"What?" I gasp.

"She said she needed space." He states.

"Where has she gone?" I ask.

He sighs. "The Four Seasons. Ben has taken her there. He's making sure she's okay."

I nod. Maybe this is what she needs. Space. Not being forced to watch me and Roman play happy families now. Not forced to pretend that she's okay for Lara's sake. She can heal in her own way, in her own time too.

I sink back into the chair and then a thought hits me.

"Roman, how did my mother get through our security?" I ask scanning his face.

"I'm looking into it as we speak." He says.

"Maybe you need to do more than that." I reply. "If Sofia is at a hotel you need to make sure she's safe. That no one has gone after her."

His eyes flash as it sinks in what I'm getting at. He gets to his feet and pulls his phone just as Lara comes back.

"You okay baby?" I ask.

She nods but I can see she's not. That my mother's attack has made her panic, has made her retreat once more.

"How about we watch a movie?" I say. "The three of us."

She blinks confused and I can see Roman can't figure out what I'm up to either. I get up, leading her into the cinema room and Roman walks behind us clearly having finished whatever phone call he made.

Lara sinks into the massive chair, pulling a blanket up. I snuggle in beside her and Roman sits beside me. As the film starts he pulls me closer, murmuring into my ear. "What are you doing?"

"She needs calm." I say quietly back. "She needs us right now as parents."

"And your mother?"

I smirk. "Does anyone else know she's here?"

He shakes his head which is what I guessed.

"Then we have time on our side." I state.

"Meaning?" He asks narrowing his eyes.

"We promised Hastings could have her right? I want information first."

"What are you planning Rose?"

I smile more. "She's made my life a misery. I think a few days of doing the same is justified don't you?"

He tilts his head, his eyes glinting in a way that says he agrees.

I plant a kiss on his lips before whispering, "Trust me."

"I do trust you." He replies. "Even if right now I'm unsure whether to be scared of you or turned on."

My eyes widen but I can't deny the heat that hits me at his words.

He tucks my hair behind my ear, pulling me in to rest against him. "Watch the movie Rose." He murmurs. "Before I carry you to our bed and forget we even have a daughter to take care of."

WE LEAVE MY MOTHER LOCKED IN THE BASEMENT. FOR TWO DAYS.

I'm itching to go down there, to start beating the shit out of her and get some answers but I know that's not the way to play it. She's the brains of this operation. She was the one behind it all. She's smarter than I gave her credit for and I'll be damned if I'll let my anger rule my head.

I need to weaken her. I need to beat her down mentally and thanks to Darius I've got a good idea of how to do that now.

We've kept Lara away, kept her distracted. Ben came back hours after he left, telling us that Sofia is in the penthouse suite, that she's okay and that Koen's men turned up and are now watching over her.

Roman didn't seem surprised by that information and, when I questioned him later, he said he was the one he'd called. That he knew Koen would keep her safe.

I decide then not to get involved. It's none of my business. The only thing I want is Sofia happy and healthy again and if it that means Koen is in her life then so be it. It's not my decision to make.

We tuck Lara into bed, say goodnight and leave Ben to watch over her in case she wakes up to find us not in our room.

Roman and I walk down the steps into the basement together. We had her locked in what was once a storage room at the far end.

As I go to walk in Roman grabs my arm, yanking me back. "You can't kill her." He says.

I roll my eyes at him. "I know that. But I can make sure it still hurts."

I don't look for his reaction. I just walk past as my patience finally snaps and my need for revenge takes over.

The room is bright. We've kept her here in constant brightness, not allowing her to sleep, not allowing her to sit still. Keeping her awake the entire time.

She looks even more of a wreck than she did outside.

The blood from her broken nose has smeared down her face. She's got no makeup on and though her face is filled with botox and fillers, nothing can hide the haggard skin.

I smirk before I can stop myself. Sleep deprivation's a bitch isn't it?

Two guards have been hauling her around, dragging her around in circles for hours. They've been working shifts, four hours on, four hours off, to ensure the bitch never gets a break. I jerk my head to them and they let her go, stepping to the side.

She falls in a heap, whimpering.

I crouch down, squatting over her. "Guess this wasn't how you planned this to go huh?" I murmur.

She looks up at me and narrows her bloodshot eyes.

"Tell me mother." I say. "Was it just me you planned on killing or were you going to murder my daughter as well?"

She spits, muttering about Lara being a bastard before her eyes fall on the man stood behind me.

"Hello Carla." Roman says in a way that should terrify me.

She forces her body up and tries to launch herself at him. I slam my fist into her stomach bringing her back down before she has a chance.

"Don't bother." I say. "It's over."

"No it isn't." She says. "Darius won't let it end like this."

I laugh so loudly. "Darius doesn't give a fuck about you. He told Carter to have you killed. He wanted you dead mother."

She lies on her back shaking her head. "He would never. He would never."

"What do you know?" Roman snaps. Apparently his method of questioning is far more direct than mine. I'll admit I'm curious to see which one of us wins.

She looks at him with contempt. "You'll get nothing from me."

I let out a fake sigh. "That's a pity." I say. "I was really rather hoping you'd cooperate. Mainly because you stink and I don't want to get any closer to you but if you won't play ball..." I let my voice trail off as I walk over to where we already laid out a few torture items. I had them placed for psychological effect, but I'm not opposed to using them to rough her up.

I pick up the screwdriver and turn back around.

She eyes it in my hand then juts her chin. "You don't scare me Rose."

"No?" I smirk but Roman catches my arm giving me a look. Another warning.

I pull myself free muttering that I'm not an idiot. Besides I've been Darius's plaything long enough to know how to delve out pain without causing any life-threatening injuries.

"Trouble in paradise?" My mother taunts.

"Not at all." I reply. "We couldn't be better thanks for asking."

She sneers and her eyes fix on the screwdriver again.

She's not restrained, not tied down in anyway. Roman walks past me hauling her into a sitting position in the creaky old chair and securing her arms with zip ties.

"Let's keep this simple." I murmur. "You're going to tell me everything you know about Darius. Every horrible thing he's done. Every little secret. And if we think you've been honest enough we might stop hurting you."

She scoffs. "You're his wife Rose, one would expect you to know all his secrets."

I shake my head. "I was never his wife." I say before driving the blunt end into her forearm.

She snarls. Screams so loudly. It's so blunt it takes a lot of effort to puncture her skin and the wound it leaves is horrific.

She jerks in the ties, jerks in the chair and one of the guards steps up to hold it so she can't flip it over.

"Tell me." I say.

She shakes her head. "Fuck you."

I attack her again. This time making two more puncture wounds. She screams louder and then she slumps into the chair like she's fallen unconscious.

Roman steps up slapping her around the face. "You won't get a reprieve that way." He states.

"Fuck you." She snaps at him. "You turned my daughter into a whore."

"You were the one who did that." He says back. "First with Paris and then with Darius."

She looks at me, her head hanging low onto her chest. "I just wanted you to have what I never got."

"And what's that?" I snap.

"To be a Blumenfeld. To call yourself that."

I frown confused. What the fuck is she talking about?

I open my mouth to speak and she cuts across me.

"I had every right to do it. You were my daughter. My flesh and blood. I created you." She rolls her head back, then looks directly at me. "You were never good enough for him. I told him that. I told him but he wouldn't listen."

"I was your daughter." I spit. Like it makes a difference because clearly to her it didn't.

"And it should have been me." She screams. "Me that he married. Me that he acknowledged. Only he wouldn't do it. He needed Ignatio too much and by the time he didn't, it was too late."

"What?" I snap. What the fuck is she talking about?

"He had a plan. He knew he could never marry me, that Verona would never accept it, that our parents would never accept it."

My stomach twists. For a moment I wonder if she was like me and Roman, that their love was as forbidden as ours. But she wasn't fighting to be with him. She didn't do anything to make that happen. She forced me into a relationship instead, so what the fuck was she doing?

"I had to marry Ignatio. I had to ensure Darius had enough support to be Governor."

"What are you talking about?" I snarl.

She licks her lips, her eyes darting about like she's actually lost her mind. "I'm so thirsty."

We haven't given her anything to eat or drink. We can hear her belly rumbling. Roman jerks his head and the guard that isn't holding the chair gives her some water. Only a mouthful though. Only enough to wet her mouth.

"Our parents wouldn't allow it." She repeats.

"Why not?" I ask.

She draws in a deep breath looking around the room with disdain. "Because of who we were. Because his father and mine were the same."

My eyes widen. I stumble back. "What?"

"His father had an affair. He slept with my mother. Darius and I are half brother and sister." She says smiling like she's so proud of that fact.

"And you wanted to marry him?" I gasp disgusted.

"I deserved the Blumenfeld name." She cries. "I had as much blood as Darius did. I deserved to be treated the same. To be able to walk through life, treated like a Blumenfeld. Just because my mother wasn't married to his…" She shuts her eyes then forces them open again. "We didn't care that we were related. It didn't matter, not to us. But his father found out, he caught us at the cabin, and they made me marry Ignatio. He argued it was for Darius's sake…"

I can't listen to it. Not right now. If she's Darius's sister then that makes me his niece. I can feel the bile churning in my stomach. I married my uncle. I had sex with him…

"Rose." Roman steps back, reaching out for me and I put my hand to stop him.

"You married me to him." I snarl at my mother. "My own uncle."

She looks at me and snorts. "I would have sold you to the devil if it got me what I wanted. My blood mixed with his."

I slap her so hard across the face her head snaps back.

"You fucking bitch." I hiss.

She spits the blood from where I've split her lip. "You think I didn't have him? You think after he married you that he didn't still fuck me? You think you satisfied him that much Rose?"

"You're just as fucked up as he is." I say clenching my fists.

She laughs. "No Rose. It was me that set it up, me that suggested to him that you became his wife. Everyone in Verona loves you so much, the great sunshine princess." She spits again. "He needed that. He needed it. You should have been thanking me. You should have been grateful. I gave you the love of my life. I gave you the man I wanted, the man I deserved, only instead of him you went for this scum."

She looks at Roman, goes to spit again but his fist in her face shuts her up.

"You piece of shit." He growls. "You evil, conniving, bitch."

She laughs as blood drips down her mouth. Her teeth are cracked. She looks like a horror show.

I let out a deep sigh. My anger is blinding me right now. I'm falling right into the trap I said I wouldn't. I'm so close to losing it, to going feral and ripping her throat out. My hands shake, something is screaming in my head.

"Tell me where he is." I say.

She shakes her head.

"So you do know then." I reply.

She runs her eyes up and down me. "You should have had his children. He deserved that. After what he did for us…"

"What did he do?" I ask.

She smiles more glancing at Roman. "Did you never wonder why your parents fell from grace? Did you never wonder why your mother had to die?"

Roman tenses. "What are you talking about?"

I narrow my eyes, my adrenaline racing at what she's implying. His mother had a heart attack. They found her in Sofia's nursery, dead on the floor with Sofia crying in the cot.

"She found out about us." My mother says. "About me and Darius. She was always a nosey little bitch. Always one for gossip. She put it together and realised what we were."

"She knew you were related." Roman states.

She looks so smug. She looks so proud.

I'm itching to wipe that damned smile off her face. "Silly little Lizzie." She taunts. "She was so gullible. So naïve."

"What did you do?" I ask.

"We did what was necessary." She says.

"You murdered her." Roman replies.

"What else could we do?" My mother laughs. "Silly bitch had found out everything. Of course we got rid of her. No one even batted an eyelid. No one even cared."

Roman reacts, his fist slams into her face and this time the man holding the chair can't keep it upright. She falls back, slamming into the concrete.

"You murdered my mother." Roman bellows.

I jump in, pulling him back, and he swings his arm narrowly missing my face. His eyes widen. He blinks, realising how close he was to hurting me and then he's pulling me into his arms, holding me so tightly, apologising, like he has any need to.

"How does it feel?" My mother taunts. "How is it holding her, knowing that she was Paris's wife and then Darius's?"

I tense, not wanting to react, hating that I do.

"...Knowing that she willingly fucked them both."

I try to turn my face away but Roman doesn't let me, he cups my cheeks in his hands, silently telling me that he loves me, that none of her taunts are affecting him.

"She knelt there." My mother says. "Sucking his cock while they defiled your sister. While they raped her."

I tremble. My legs give me away but Roman doesn't let it me go. Was she there? Was she at that club and I didn't see? Or did Darius tell her after? Did he gloat about it? About what he'd done. What he'd made me do?

"It wasn't like that." I say blinking back the tears. "He threatened Lara, he…"

He kisses me, silencing my excuses.

And then he looks at where my mother is still tied, on her back, sneering at us.

"Nothing you say can change what I feel about your daughter." He says. "I love Rose despite everything you put her through, everything you forced her to do."

"And what about Lara?" She hisses. "What about the fact Rose wanted her aborted?"

I go for her then but Roman pulls me from the room, slamming the door shut, putting his hand on it to stop me from going back in. "Enough." He says. "We don't need to hear it. We don't need anything else from her."

"She knows where Darius is." I say.

He cups my cheek, shaking his head. "It's not worth it. She is not worth it."

ROMAN

She lets me lead her away. She's shaking, she's so close to falling apart.

When we reach our bedroom she stops, facing me like this is a battle she has to get over with. "I didn't want her aborted. I never wanted that." She says.

I tilt my head. "I didn't believe it for a second." I state.

"I was trying to run, after I found out I was pregnant. I had some money, I was going to leave Verona. I thought you'd abandoned us and I was going to go somewhere far away and raise her alone."

"It's okay Rose." I say cupping her cheek. I know what she's been through. I'm not stupid enough to believe the hateful words her mother has said because it's obvious what she was trying to do. She was shit stirring. Trying to drive a wedge between us. Only that's not going to happen.

She shakes her head. "Carter was the one who caught me. He was the one who dragged me back."

"Rose."

"I did suck his cock. I did." Her words don't even sound like her now. She sounds like a ghost. Like she's spiralling so badly out of control. "I tried to stop him going back too, I did everything I could to stop him from being there, from hurting Sofia."

"Rose." I say placing my hands on her shoulders. The thought of her being there, of both of them in that situation makes my blood boil. "You are not responsible for what happened."

"I should have fought harder."

I shake my head, unsure how on earth I can get through to her.

"I saw the needle. I watched Otto drugging her. I watched…"

"Stop." I growl slamming my fist into the wall and she flinches as she falls silent. "You didn't do this. You are not responsible. You need to stop carrying this guilt. Stop fooling yourself that you could have prevented it."

"But I should have…" Her voice trails off as she cries.

I grab her, pulling her into my chest. "You did everything you could." I state. "You saved Sofia, you are the reason we rescued her. You are the reason we even found out about it."

She wraps her arms around my neck. "I just want it to stop hurting."

I carry her to our bed, laying her down. She's got herself so worked up she's sobbing. I walk to the bathroom, get her a glass of water and come back.

"Drink this." I say.

She gulps it down and then looks at me.

I don't speak. I just wait for whatever it is she needs to get off her chest. Whatever words are still stuck in her head, haunting her.

"How can you love me?" She whispers. "After everything my family has done to yours?"

My lips curl. "That's easy." I reply. "You are not them. You are nothing like them."

"But they killed your mum."

I flinch burying that pain. In truth I'd long suspected her death wasn't what my father said. The way he reacted after, the way it broke him, like he was carrying some deep dark secret that he couldn't do anything about.

"You are my family now. You and Lara." I state.

She nods, shifting to sit right in front of me and I brush her tears away with my thumb. She drops her gaze, staring at my lips, and I swear I feel the tension between us tighten.

"Lara asked me something. When we were out in the snow. She said she wanted a specific Christmas present."

I pause, confused as to why now of all times she would bring this up.

"Whatever she wants she can have it." I say.

"You mean that?" She half whispers.

I nod.

She tilts her head. "Don't you want to know what it is?"

"I'll buy whatever it is." I say.

She bites her lip. "It's not something you buy Roman. At least not in the traditional sense."

"What is it?" I ask.

She gets to her feet standing in front of me. "She wants her mummy and daddy to get married."

My eyes widen.

She drops to her knees in front of me, looking up with those angelic eyes. "She wants us to be married so that no one can separate us."

"No one will." I growl, grabbing her jaw.

"Roman." She whispers. "Will you marry me?"

My lips curl. I lean down capturing her lips in a punishing kiss that I want her to feel. "Did I not ask you the same thing six months ago?"

"I was worried you might have changed your mind."

"Why would I?" I say pulling her back up to her feet, scooping her into my arms and spinning her around so that she's flat on her back on the mattress. "I told you before Rose. I've told you many times. You are mine. Mine to touch. Mine to love. Mine."

She nods, gasping as I kiss her once more.

"Make me mine again Roman. Make me feel it in a way that nothing will ever have me doubting that."

My eyes narrow. I grab at her trousers, undoing the button, yanking the zip down, pulling them off.

"You doubt it?" I say.

She blinks instead of replying. The little minx is toying with me. Riling me up.

I pull my own clothes off, tear my shirt from my chest, and all the while she's laid there, on the bed waiting like a good girl.

"Spread your legs Rose. Let me see all of you." I murmur and she does. She widens her legs letting me see how wet her underwear is.

I pull it to the side, running my finger right through her folds. "Such a needy thing." I taunt.

She moans arching her back.

I reach up and shove her top above her bra. Her chest is heaving, she's practically gasping with her need.

"Make me yours." She says.

"You want me to mark you is that it?" I reply.

She looks up at me, her eyes widening as she clearly comes up with an idea. She rolls away, disappearing into the bathroom before coming back with something between her fingers.

I narrow my eyes giving enough space for her to sit back down in front of me.

When I see what's in her hand I frown more. "You really want that?"

She nods placing the razor blade into my hand.

"This will hurt." I state.

She gives me a strange grin. "I've been hurt before Roman. Besides, I like the way you hurt me."

I catch her lips, force my tongue into her mouth and she wraps her arms around my neck deepening it further.

When I pull away I stare down at her body, pushing her down onto the bed.

"Hold still." I say spreading her legs wide again.

She nods, gripping the sheets. As I begin to cut she whimpers, but she doesn't move. She takes every stroke, breathing through the pain. When I'm done she stares down at where the blood is pooling, where it's running down her thigh. I get up, grab a plaster and put it in place. I made sure to only cut as deep as was necessary. The scar will be fine. The letters small. But they are there.

My name is there.

Etched into her skin.

She's got the blade in her hand and then she looks at me.

I take in a deep breath, already knowing what's in her head. Taking her hand, I rest the blade below the scar on my chest, indicating exactly where I want her to mark me.

She doesn't hesitate. She doesn't flinch. She cuts into my skin, carves her name into me, and I revel in every twist of the blade, every slice she makes.

When she's done my own blood is trickling down my chest. I take the blade, toss it into the sink in the bathroom and clean my own mark.

And then I walk back in, pushing her back onto the bed, claiming her mouth, devouring her as something primal takes over.

She moans, wrapping her body around mine, writhing, telling me that her need is matching mine.

I rip her top off her, toss it away and then unhook her bra. She digs her nails into my scalp, she rubs herself against my hardened cock.

"Fuck me Roman." She gasps.

I tear her underwear off, hearing her whimper as the fabric pulls her skin.

When I sink into her she's so wet and warm I think I lose my head. I thrust all of me inside not giving her time to adjust and she claws at my back in a way I know will leave scrapes.

"My Rose." I gasp. "My woman."

She buries her face into the space between my shoulder and my neck. I pick her up, push her into the wall, fucking her like a mad man. She throws her head back, she arches her back, her muscles inside grip me so tightly it steals my breath.

"I'm yours Roman." She says. "I've always been yours."

My thumb reaches down, massaging her clit and her body jolts as she cries out.

"Come for me Rose, come like you love me."

She shudders, blinking, opening her eyes and catches my face in her hands. "I love you." She says over and over. Screaming it as she falls apart and as I pound into her until I'm so lost in my own pleasure that when I finally come it feels like I really have died and gone to heaven.

ROMAN

I leave Rose sleeping.

It's the early hours. Too early to be awake but my mind is working something out. The clogs are turning and I can't shut them up.

Any ordinary day I'd wake Rose up and spend the next god knows how many hours easing that tension out of myself in the best way possible.

But right now I need it. I like it. I want it.

I walk into the office, turning the laptop on, and pour myself a drink.

Carla said something. Something that stuck more than anything else. That she got caught with Darius at a cabin. That her father had caught them there.

Carla married Ignatio when she was seventeen. Her parents had to give permission because she was technically underage.

If she and Darius were hooking up before that then they needed it to be somewhere close, somewhere they both could get to without being absent too long.

But a cabin? Nowhere in Verona fits that description. It's all skyrises and duplexes. Even back then every piece of real estate was being developed. Anywhere that didn't fit the bill was either pulled down and redone or sold and turned into mansions.

So it couldn't have been in the city. It had to be somewhere else. Somewhere discreet too.

My mind keeps going to the mountains. To where a few hours' drive from here are chalets used for skiing in the winter and hunting in the summer. Is that where she meant? Did Darius have a chalet there?

I do a search of his properties, of his companies too and their holdings. It comes back with nothing, just as I expected.

I do a search of the Capulets and that too draws a blank.

A cabin would make sense. A cabin would be a logical place for Darius to slink off too. To regroup. He's not the kind of person to flee too far and besides, we checked where the helicopter went from the flight logs. Officially it made five stops. We know most of those were bogus but three were in remote areas, away from prying eyes, and two were close enough to the mountains to be logistically possible.

I sink back into my chair, taking another gulp of my whiskey.

The answer is here, I just can't quite work it out.

An hour goes by, an hour of searching through every cabin, every owner, every tiny possible clue as I get more and more frustrated.

Just as I'm about to throw the damned computer out the window I see a breadcrumb.

I smirk as I realise how damned obvious it was.

Darius didn't own the chalet. Neither did Carla. And neither did Robert Blumenfeld, their father. It was her mother. Francis

Herlington-Bach. The second generation immigrant whose father had come to Verona seeking his fortune and was lucky enough to strike it rich with his timing.

Franz Bach started off with small fry businesses, nothing too glitzy but he made enough money to marry into the moderately respectable Herlington family. And it was their money that enabled him to make them all big time.

He bought his wife the chalet as a holiday home years before Carla was born. Bought it through one of his companies so the ownership is more of a puzzle than it should have been.

I wonder how many times Robert Blumenfeld would visit Francis there. How many years their affair went on for. She had other children too. Two boys. Only they looked spitting images of her husband so I guess they got smarter after Carla was born.

When her husband died, Francis was free to marry Robert. Only clearly she wasn't a big enough name for him to tie himself with. Everyone knew he was philanderer, that he'd slept with half of Verona. Did it come as a shock to her that he didn't overlook her poor origins? Was that why she told Carla who her father really was? Or did Carla only find that out after she'd slept with Darius?

Clearly it didn't bother them. From what she insinuated they continued the relationship after they found out they were half-siblings but I doubt Darius would ever have married her even if his father hadn't had been the one to force Carla down the aisle to Ignatio.

No, she too was small-fry. She too didn't have enough clout for the Blumenfeld glamour.

But a Capulet was different.

Carla in siding with Ignatio took herself from the middle ranks to the big time. I wonder how much Robert paid to set up that match, to get her safely dealt with. I don't doubt Carla worked her charm. That though she wanted Darius she wasn't so stupid as to let something like love turn her head. No, Ignatio could give her power, and prestige, and a status in this city far above her own.

And Rose, being who she was, was enough to get Paris's attention. Enough to get Darius's too.

And I bet Carla loved and hated every minute of it.

I let out the snarl, downing the last of my glass.

The chalet is rural. Completely isolated on the side of a mountain far from anywhere. There's a track road that in summer would lead right up to it but in winter I don't doubt it's completely cut off.

Darius must be stewing there. Waiting out the snow and the cold until the spring thaws and he can rise up again.

Only this time I won't let him.

This time we're going to take the fight to him.

I pull up some altitude maps, making a plan. Access won't be easy. Surrounding it won't be easy either. No doubt he'll have traps. He'll be prepared. I bet he's dug in and made himself a little fortress.

I just need to figure out exactly how to pop the box open and get to the treasure inside.

Walking through the house it feels quiet, more empty without Sofia. She messages me, daily. One liners saying she's okay.

I tried calling and she picked up but didn't speak. She just sat there and all I could hear was her breathing.

I had to call Koen. I hated that I did it and yet I had to put my pride aside and ensure my sister was safe.

We don't know how Carla got through our defences. Maybe it was luck. Maybe she's being hiding down the bottom of the garden for a while. It's certainly big enough for her to have done it.

Tomorrow Hastings is coming to collect her and the bitch will finally be out of our hair.

I let out a sigh as I reach our bedroom. If I could I would gut her myself, I would tear the very flesh from her skin for every hateful word she spoke. But that won't save Rose.

And besides, I meant what I said. She isn't worth it.

We've given so much of our lives. Lost so much in this. I'm not willing to sacrifice anything more than I need to now that we can finally see the end.

"Roman?"

I look up seeing Rose sat up, leaning against the headboard, frowning through the darkness at me.

"You're awake." I say.

"Where were you?"

I wonder if she thinks I'd gone back down there, if I went to the basement to finish the job after all.

I walk up to her, sit down and take her hand. "I did it." I say.

"Did what?" She asks her voice betraying her concern.

"I found out where he is."

Her eyes widen. Her breath increases. "You're sure?"

"Absolutely certain."

She draws herself up like she's ready for a fight right this instant. "When can we go?"

"You still want to?" I say. I won't stop her if she does but I wondered if, after what she found out, that she and Darius and uncle and niece, that she wouldn't want to see him again, that she wouldn't want to face him.

"I want this over." She says. "And the only way I know it will be is when Darius is dead."

"Hastings won't like it." I tease. I don't give a fuck what he thinks. I'm going to make sure this doesn't trace to us. Besides, he won't let us have that Austin fucker, so why would we give him Darius?

She leans in, kissing me. "I thought you didn't care what other people think about you?"

I grin. "I thought you don't either?"

She draws in a breath, pulling me down beside her. "Katie is coming tomorrow."

"The journalist?" I reply.

She nods. "I figured we'd celebrate my mother's capture by going public about us and Lara."

I smile. "That sounds fitting."

ROMAN

Hastings arrives at eight am on the dot. Carla is bound, gagged, and despite this she's still making one hell of a racket as we hand her over.

Rose watches her go with a look on her face that is half vindication, half regret.

"She'll pay." I say taking her hand.

"She better." Rose replies.

Hastings walks up to us both and smiles. "I have to admit, I wasn't convinced you'd do it."

"Hand her over?" I say.

He nods looking at Rose. "I thought you'd have other ideas."

Rose shakes her head slightly. "I want my freedom more than I want her dead."

"Well you have that now." He says pulling out some paperwork.

"What is that?" I ask.

He passes it to Rose and she frowns, opening it up.

"Just making it official." Hastings says.

"You're clearing me of all charges." She says scanning the document.

"Read the next piece. I'm sure you'll like what that says more." He replies.

She glances at me before flicking the page. Her eyes widen as she scans it and then she steps back, covering her mouth as she composes herself.

"I keep my promises Rose." Hastings says.

"What is it?" I ask keeping my eyes on her.

"My marriage." She says passing the paper for me to see. "He had it annulled."

"A marriage made under duress doesn't count." Hastings says folding his arms. "You're officially Rose Capulet again."

She leans into me letting out such a sigh of relief, as she's been caged and is finally free to fly again.

"I had the lawyers draft it. I've also been informed that the bank has unblocked your account. Your money has been returned."

"What money?" Rose asks.

"Your inheritance from your first husband."

Fuck. I'd forgotten about that. By the look on her face Rose has forgotten about that too. Her jaw drops and she murmurs something incomprehensible under her breath.

Hastings looks at me. "After your prematurely announced demise your estate was transferred to your sister. Her husband has had full access to it, however, that works both ways. Seeing as Otto is dead, all his wife's money has been returned to her and his wealth has been split. Sofia inherits a third of it along with his daughters."

"Have you told her?" Rose asks.

Hastings shakes his head. "No. We are aware she is staying at the Four Seasons and we have patrols stationed there to keep an eye on her but she is not being forthcoming with me in any capacity…"

"She needs time." I growl.

Hastings sighs. "Then it's a good thing her husband is dead. It means she doesn't need to testify about any of it."

"What about everyone else?" Rose replies. "What about everyone else Darius and Otto let near her?"

Hastings winces. "Those we know of will be held accountable."

"And the rest?" I ask.

He shrugs. "Without her testimony we have nothing to go on."

I snarl. I know what he says makes logical sense but I won't put her through that, I won't have her forced to relive it in any capacity.

"We are still trying to locate Darius." Hastings says fixing us with a look. "If either of you have an inkling…"

"We don't." Rose says lying better than I can in this moment.

"Fine." He says looking annoyed. "I'll speak with your mother, perhaps she has an idea what part of hell he has crawled to."

"Good luck with that." I mutter.

Hastings turns to go and but Rose lets go of my hand and quickly follows after him. She murmurs something to him. He pauses, frowning like he doesn't get what she's saying. When she repeats it, he gives her a look of sympathy and then he nods.

"What was that about?" I ask when she returns but she just shakes her head changing the subject to Lara, to how she will be hungry and wanting breakfast.

WHEN KATIE ARRIVES, IT'S CLEAR THERE'S SOME TRAUMA THERE TOO. Some bonding as well. Katie hugs Rose and I'm shocked that Rose hugs her back like she's a friend.

"You were so brave." Katie says.

I narrow my eyes looking between them. I didn't see one article. I didn't see a damn thing she did to help Rose and yet apparently she knew what was going on?

"It's okay." Rose says looking at me, clearly seeing the expression on my face and already knowing where my head is at.

"You didn't do anything." I say to Katie.

She winces. "I know. I had my hands tied. I needed proof and I was getting that when everything kicked off."

"What proof?" I snap. There was enough proof. There was more than enough evidence.

"He controlled the media." Rose says. "He controlled everything."

"And yet I got around that." I snap.

Rose mutters under her breath shaking her head.

"I'm sorry." Katie says. "I think about it, about what else I could have done…"

"You did enough." Rose replies. "You gave me hope when I needed it."

Katie gives her a tight smile like she's not convinced.

"Not everyone has your tech skills." Rose says to turning to admonish me. "You can't be such an arse…"

"No, it's alright." Katie says cutting across her. "It's nice to see someone has your back, especially after everything that went down."

"I do have her back." I say. "I will always protect Rose."

Katie pulls a recording device and puts it on the table. "How about we start at the beginning? About how you met, about what happened six years ago."

I turn my head, letting Rose lead this. She's far more savvy in this department than me. She knows how to be the media's darling, and besides it feels more her story to tell, she has more secrets, more trauma than me and it's her decision how much she wants the world to know of.

I add bits here and there. My side to some of the anecdotes. And I keep hold of Rose's hand, though I'm concerned that might be misconstrued. That this journalist might read more into this, that she might think I'm controlling Rose, exerting my influence.

Halfway through Lara interrupts us. She comes running up, throwing herself into my arms and I catch her just in time to stop her colliding with the table.

It seems to break the tension, it seems to put me at ease so instead I focus on my daughter, on making sure she's comfortable with this. That she understands what we're doing.

When Katie leaves she tells us that the story will go live tomorrow. That everyone will know what was really going on, though they've agreed already what details Rose will divulge and what she won't.

Everyone will know she was forced to marry Paris and forced to marry Darius.

That her parents are good for nothing pieces of shit.

They'll know about us, about Lara, about how we met at a party and fell in love, but they won't know the sordid details. The parts that make this story salacious, that makes this story depraved.

I slip away once she's gone. I sit in my study coming up with a plan on how to take on Darius. It's a risky one, one that could backfire but I can't see how else we can work it.

When the door opens I know it's Rose stood there before I even look up.

She smiles awkwardly at me and I frown.

"You were very offish today." She says walking towards me.

I let out a sigh. "I didn't mean to be. I'm just sick of meeting people who knew what was going on and did nothing."

She shakes her head. "It is what it is."

"You're okay with that? With forgiving people?" I half snarl.

"It's not for me to forgive." She states. "And this time tomorrow we will control the narrative. We will have protected ourselves in a way we haven't been able to before."

I nod leaning back in the chair. "What was it you said to Hastings earlier?"

A micro-expression crosses her face. "I needed to know something. I needed to check something."

"What?" I ask.

She gulps, leaning against the desk. "My mother and Darius were in a relationship long before I was born. I needed to know that I wasn't his daughter."

My eyes widen. How the fuck had I never thought of that? How had that thought never crossed my mind?

"I'm not." She says. "I had him run a DNA test. He doesn't understand why but he fast tracked it for me."

"But you are his niece?" I say.

She nods and something flickers across her face again. "Yes." She spits.

"I'm so sorry…"

"Don't be." She says as her eyes flash. "I'm done feeling sorry. I'm done wallowing. I want my vengeance and I know you have a plan Roman so tell me what it is."

I smile, wrapping my arms around her, pulling her to sit in my lap as I bring up the map on the screen. Quietly I explain what's in my head. What I'm thinking. How exactly we are going to bring the bastard down.

ROSE

I'm nervous. Jittery. On edge.

I expected to be calm. I expected to have that same confidence I had when I brought down my mother.

Only today it feels very different.

I'm armed, with a gun in my hand and a knife strapped to my ankle. I feel like an assassin as we make our way through the snow, up the incline to where the bastard is hiding.

We've got enough men around us to feel like we're an invading army.

And yet there's something niggling in my head.

Maybe it's just my past, maybe it's my own headspace expecting failure, conditioned to believe that I can't win.

My feet crunch under the snow. None of us are talking. We're all moving as quietly as we can. I've got an earpiece in.

Roman already has something in place to scramble all the comms. Any cameras, any radar, anything that might pick us up has been disabled. It was a risk we gambled on. If we did it Darius might know we were coming. But if we didn't, and he was monitoring it then he'd get the alert anyway.

We had to make a call.

As his voice murmurs in my ear, calming me, I tell myself that we made the right one.

We had one final conversation about whether I should go. Roman wasn't trying to tell me not to. I think he just wanted to make sure I was comfortable, that I was certain, and that the decision really was the one I was happy with.

Once I'd confirmed it he spent time training me, teaching me how to shoot, how to actually hit something and, if worse came to worse how to kill someone with a knife. When I pointed out that I didn't think I need any tips in that he gave me a look that said he didn't find it funny but he kissed me anyway and murmured that I really was trouble.

We've been walking for an hour. We knew the hike would be bad. That the road would be blocked and besides we didn't want to give any signs we were coming, any giveaways.

I'm cool but not cold. My boots are big enough and my clothes thick enough to keep the chill out, and my adrenaline is definitely helping.

My hand grips the gun, it's got the safety on just in case but it's reassuring to be in my hands. Reassuring that I have it if anything goes down.

"Ten more minutes." Roman murmurs into my ear. "Then we'll reach basepoint."

Basepoint. Where we get out first glimpse of the cabin.

I nod enough for him to see. We're spread out, with the trees as they are we could hardly walk beside one another. Roman is a good twelve metres from me but I can feel it every time his eyes look over to where I am.

As we breach another mini hill the sun hits my face and it's so bright I have to throw my hand up to block it.

Someone shouts.

It's not one of us.

Not any of us.

I freeze, pressing myself into the nearest tree, just as we trained.

All I can hear now is my own breathing. No one is moving. No one is making a sound. I turn my head searching for Roman but he's too far off and all I can make out is the outline of him in the distance.

As carefully as I can I slip the safety off the gun. Maybe I don't need it. Maybe this is nothing but I sure as hell am not taking the risk.

Beside me I see something move. A flicker of light. It's barely noticeable and yet I know it's there.

As my eyes lock eyes with someone my fear lurches. He's not one of us. He's dressed in winter camos. Whites. Like some sort of abominable snowman. Some sort of monster. I lift the gun, pull the trigger and though it's got a silencer on, I hear the thwoop as the bullet flies through the air.

He cries out, slamming into the ground.

And then all hell goes off.

Shots fire from all directions. I sink down into the snow, I burying my body as tight to the tree. I don't know what direction to even look in.

I can hear Roman shouting through the earpiece. I shout back. But we can't make out anything. I can't make out any coherent words.

As a body rams into me I scream shooting once more and though the gun goes off I know I don't hit him, I see the bullet ricochet into the tree. I see the bark splinter.

I slam back into the ground, groaning as my head seems to take all the impact and I see stars.

But my arms are flailing. Instinct is taking over and though I'm losing focus I'm kicking, punching, thrashing as hard as I can.

I'm picked up, slammed into the ground once more and it feels like something explodes behind my eyes. All my fight goes out of me. My body goes limp.

I look up, blinking at the person staring down at me, and then they smile, smirk, reaching down before they haul me over their shoulder and I pass out.

65

ROSE

Someone lays me down. I blink, my eyes not registering anything but shadows around me and the brightness of the place they've carried me to. They step away and I hear the sound of muffled talking and then it fades off.

Whoever it is retreats and I lay here. Limp. Pathetic.

My body is heavy. I can feel every single step that I've climbed, every mile that I've trekked. I'm damp, wet. My clothes are sodden from the snow, I'm missing my jacket, but, as I realise that, I also register that I'm warm.

I'm inside.

I shift my head looking around, feeling my fear spiking. The cabin is big. Really big. I can see a room beyond the one I'm in where it looks like there's a kitchen. There's a mezzanine layer above me with a glass balustrade.

I'm on a couch. Laid out. Beneath it is a great fur hide and above me a chandelier is glinting with what I'd guess are actual diamonds. It's more luxurious than I imagined. It's far more glamourous.

"My slut of a wife is awake."

The cry escapes my throat before I can stop it.

Darius tilts his head from where he's sat across from me, his eyes narrowed.

I sit up, making slow movements. I don't have the knife or the gun. They've clearly stripped them from me.

My eyes dart to the front door. It's shut. Locked. Too far to get to from where I am.

"You're not getting out that way." He says.

I swallow my bile, looking back at him, acknowledging him for the first time, fighting the urge to shut down, fighting the panic that is rapidly taking over all logical thought.

"Why am I here?" I say.

"You think I didn't know you'd come?" He smirks. "Have you learnt nothing about me?"

"I wish I knew nothing." I spit and the bastard laughs.

He gets up crossing the space and sits down in the small space I've created by sitting up. I take in a ragged breath, inhaling that awful scent, and everything, every horrific moment he inflicted washes over me and I tremble so hard.

"Darius…"

"What did you say?" It's Roman's voice, in my ear. The relief I feel when I hear it is indescribable. He's still alive then. He's still out there.

Once again, I just have to play this safe, survive, until Roman gets me.

Darius runs his hand up me and I jerk.

"Don't fucking touch me." I snarl.

He laughs again. "You're my wife Rose. I can do whatever I want with you." He says grabbing my throat, squeezing it enough to make his point.

"I'm not your wife." I reply half choking. "Our marriage was annulled."

He smirks. "It makes no difference to me. You're not going anywhere from now on."

"Roman is coming." I taunt.

"I know." He replies. "I'm ready for him."

"You can't stop him this time."

He pushes me back, straddles me, and lowers his mouth right to my ear, right to where the mic is only it's so tiny he can't see it.

"I've got a surprise planned for him." He states. "I've rigged all of the ground around us."

"Rigged it with what?" I ask.

He runs his face up against my cheek. I grimace, pulling away, at least trying to but I don't get far. He makes sure of that.

"Something that will make a nice big bang." He murmurs.

"Explosives?" I gasp.

He smirks. "Anyone who walks through that door will be blasted off the mountain unless they have the signal to deactivate it."

"And what about us?" I ask.

He meets my gaze with those watery eyes I hate more than anything else about him. "Do you think I'd risk you and me Rose? Do you think I'd do anything that would mean we would end?"

"There is no 'we'." I snarl. I don't know if what he's saying is true. I don't know whether to believe him or just pray that he's bluffing but I hope Roman heard. I hope he knows and he's careful.

His hands begin to grope me as I whimper. "We both know that's not the case." He states.

I jerk, I kick out, I slap him and he grabs my wrists pinning them back above my head.

"Even if that happens. Even if you blow everyone else up there's nowhere left to hide." I state. "You've lost Darius. You've lost everything."

He laughs at that. "But I have you don't I? And I have enough funds to disappear. To go wherever I want, taking you with me."

"You won't take me anywhere." I snarl.

"No?" He muses. "Maybe we'll haul up here, hide out into the snow passes." He runs his eyes over me licking his lips. "I'm sure we'll find a way to entertain ourselves while we wait."

I screw my face up, ignoring the bile that is so close to coming up.

"I know what this place is." I say. "I know you and my mother used to meet here."

He pauses, his lips curling with amusement. "Did she tell you that?"

I nod.

His eyes drop to stare at my breasts. Thankfully he hasn't stripped me beyond my jacket but I still feel indecent.

"Carla and I used to have a lot of fun here." He murmurs. "Perhaps we can recreate some of it…"

"You sick bastard." I scream. "I know what you are. What you and she were."

He sits back on my thighs then, letting my arms drop as he appraises me. "So she told you?"

"She told me everything." I snap as I wrap them around myself like some sort of protection. "She told me you have the same father."

He doesn't even looked ashamed. He doesn't even look that bothered.

"You forced me to marry you." I snarl. "Knowing we're related…"

"What does it matter?" He says shrugging. "You think that's the worse thing I've done? I've killed people Rose, cut them into pieces and sold them."

"I'm your daughter." I cry saying the words out loud that I haven't even admitted to myself. That I've pretended are not true. That I lied about.

He runs his hands over me and I slap him so hard across his face. He grabs my throat, pinning me against the couch once more.

"I wanted you." He states. "That's all that matters."

I spit at him. And he lowers his mouth kissing me as I jerk and kick and buck with as much movement as he will allow.

"Fuck I missed this attitude." He murmurs. "I realised I like the way you fight me, I like the way it feels when I take what I want and make you break."

I shake my head, shutting my eyes, praying that whatever Roman is doing he hurries the fuck up.

"You were more fun when I forced you. More fun when you cried and begged me to stop." He continues. "Though I'll admit the feel of you coming around my dick was worth all your pretence."

"You piece of shit." I snarl slamming my body, rolling it into his to try to get him off me.

He smacks me so hard in response I blank out. When I come back around he's gotten off me. He's just left me here.

My face feels lopsided, I lift my hand, whimpering at the bruise that's already forming there.

In a heap I roll off the couch, biting back the groan as I hit the rug. I can hear him moving about. I can hear him looking for something.

I get to my feet, my eyes searching about, looking for something that might help. But I feel dizzy, I feel like I don't have any control over my body. I put my hands out in front of me and I can see them physically shaking, blurry, like I've drunk too much and I'm seeing double.

"It's kicking in."

I cry out as Darius leans against the doorframe watching me.

"Wh, wh, what is?" I stammer.

He grins. "The GHB."

My eyes widen. *He didn't. No fucking way.*

"I gave you a hit while you were out. I'm curious to see if you react the same as Sofia does."

"You pppiece of shittt." I mumble.

He laughs. "You know the first time we fucked her she cried the entire time."

I stumble back, stumble towards the door but it feels so far away. He walks to where I am, grabbing my arm, spinning me around before pushing me back and it takes all my effort not to trip over my feet.

"Otto went first of course, seemed fair considering, and then when he was finished we all lined up, one after another…"

"You sick fuck."

He grabs my hair wrenching my head back. "We should have done that to you too." He spits. "You deserved it for what you did."

"Roman is going to kill you."

He laughs in my face. "You really haven't learnt. I win Rose. Every time."

I shut my eyes, trying to ignore the way my scalp is on fire from how he's holding me. He pushes me down, forces me to my knees and squats over me, pressing his body against me.

"Maybe I should strip you down, let him see the way I treat you."

"Don't you fucking dare." Even I can hear my words are so mumbled now, that I can't pronounce half the syllables.

He starts yanking at my top, pulling it up only it gets stuck over my head so he starts ripping the fabric off me. He's so focused on it that he doesn't seem to notice what I'm trying to do. Where I'm headed.

I try to crawl away. He kicks me enough to make me double over and then he's on top of me, pushing my body down, grabbing at my trousers to wrench them off.

"Maybe I'll fuck your ass this time." He groans.

I reach out grabbing at the pen. It's not the best weapon. In truth it's not a weapon at all but it's all I have in this moment. As fast as I can I spin my arm around burying it into his eye.

He screams out. Howls. Rolls off me onto the rug as blood spurts everywhere.

I kick him away, fighting the grogginess that is rapidly taking over everything.

I can see the control system now. I can see all the monitors. The buttons. Maybe he did rig the place with explosives but I don't know how I'd even make it safe. How I'd begin to go about it.

His body collides with mine.

I scream out landing on the floor.

His hand is over my face, his nails digging into my skin.

"You fucking bitch." He snarls.

I don't know how he isn't dead. I thought putting a pen through his eye would be enough but clearly I didn't reach his brain.

He holds me down one handed, I don't know how I'm still even fighting. His other hand yanks at the belt, then the button, before he starts wrenching my trousers down.

The front door slams open. Cold air rushes in.

If they've been shooting, if they've been fighting their way up here, I haven't heard it.

Darius turns his head, meeting Roman's gaze and for the tiniest of seconds he shows his shock before he recovers, before he grins like he's never been happier.

ROMAN

I don't know where they come from. One minute it was just us and then suddenly we're surrounded.

I flatten myself into the tree, avoiding the bullets as they come flying, taking aim at whoever the fuck was shooting at me.

At us.

Someone slams into me, bringing me down. I use the butt of the gun straight to their face and they slump.

They're dressed in winter camo. Clearly Darius was waiting for us and that thought gives me no comfort.

I stare around trying to see where Rose is and another man launches themselves at me. His bullet misses my head by the smallest of margins. I slam my fist into his face, breaking his nose and his blood spurts out all down his face.

But another replaces him. *Fuck, how many men are here?*

I kick, I fight, but they're overpowering me.

And then suddenly they slump. One after another. I groan as I take the weight of both of them making me infinitely aware of how much strength I still need to get back.

I roll the first off and then the second.

A shadow falls on me and I reach out to grab my gun, to take aim.

"No need to shoot me."

I look up seeing Hastings stood there and I frown.

"What the fuck?" I say.

"You need to be careful who your friends are." He replies.

"What does that mean?" I snap.

He holds his hand for me to take. "You had a breach in your security. The same breach that allowed Carla to get into your house."

"And you knew?" I spit getting to my feet.

He smirks. "Come on Roman, don't be so surprised. We've both been playing games. Did you think we wouldn't be watching you? Did you think I actually believed you both when you said you didn't know where Darius was?"

I don't know what to say to that. If we had a breach then Darius knew hours ago that we were coming which certainly explains how they managed to overpower us.

I snarl slamming my fist into the tree. We had a plan. A good plan. A logical plan and now all of it has gone to shit.

My eyes scan the space around us. Half my men are dead. All of Darius's are too. But I can't see Rose. I can't see her anywhere.

My heart races, I starting walking, rolling bodies over, staring into dead mans faces. "Where the fuck is she?"

"He has her."

I turn staring at Hastings. No. No Fucking way.

"One of his men got to her before we did." He states. "They carried her off before we could stop them."

"We have to get there. Now."

Hastings tilts his head, grabbing me, like he thinks I'm an idiot. "She's in the cabin. We get her when we get him."

"He'll hurt her." I reply.

He turns his back on me, starts barking orders and for a second it feels like my world collapses. I stare at the blood covered snow. He has her. I promised her and once again I've left her in danger.

I shut my eyes, focusing on the ear piece. I don't know if it still works. I can't hear anything because there's too much fucking noise now.

"Shut up." I snarl letting my fury out and everyone turns to stare at me.

I press my hand to my ear. I can hear her. I can hear her voice.

My heart sinks as she says his name. So she is with him. But what else did I expect?

"Give me that…" Hastings walks up to me and I look up at him for the first time really wanting to claw his fucking face off.

I shake my head.

"Give me that earpiece now or I will rip it from your ear."

"What did you say?" I snarl.

He slams me into a tree, wrenching the device out.

"It won't help you. Not right now." He says.

"We have ears inside." I reply.

He shakes his head pocketing it. "No. Not like this. This will only distract you."

"Distract me?"

"If you want to save her you have to go in level headed. Hearing what he's doing won't achieve that, it will only make you reckless."

I blink, my rage threatening to overwhelm me. Make me fucking reckless? Darius has her. Right now he could be doing anything to her.

But he's right. Hearing it won't help. I need to be there. I need to get up there and stop it.

"Then let's go." I snarl.

"Wait." Someone else says making us all turn.

"What now?" Hastings growls.

The man bends down, swiping at the snow and we all freeze as we see what he uncovers. It's a fucking IED. He's got the place rigged.

I meet Hastings gaze and his is as cold with fury as mine.

"Please tell me you bought someone who can clear them?" I say.

He grunts. "Do you think I was born yesterday?"

It takes what feels like forever. We make slow progress, walking in a line, keeping low, ensuring we only cover the ground that's been cleared and is safe.

Two men are ahead clearing each patch of snow inch by inch. If we lose them I don't know what the fuck we will do.

But Darius is waiting for us. I know that much.

I clench my fists, staring ahead, keeping my eyes fixed on the horizon and slowly, so fucking slowly the cabin comes into view.

It's built in the Swiss style. All wood and glass. In truth, if I didn't know what had gone on here, it would be beautiful.

My heart picks up. I grip the gun tighter. She's in there. She's in that fucking place with Darius.

As we make it to the front, we pause. No one has shot at us. No one seems to be making any attempt to stop us now and it feels odd.

The two explosive guys inspect the building, and all to soon their confirming what I already suspected; that the place is also rigged. That it's a set up. If anyone tries the door they'll be blasted into fuck knows where.

Hastings grunts at them to sort it and I crouch there, waiting, clicking the safety on and off, slowly losing my mind.

But when they announce it's safe I don't hesitate. I spring up, I slam my body into the door not caring who is following me, not caring if this is Hastings plan.

The door crashes into the wall. Warm air hits my face.

I scan the room desperate for any sign of her and when I see her my heart lurches.

She's under him, she's in her bra and he's clearly in the midst of ripping her trousers off. I can see where he's hit her, where her cheek is blackening with a bruise. Darius turns his head. One of his eyes is bloodied like it's been half gouged out, whatever the fuck has happened it's clear he can't see out of it.

But he grins at me. The bastard actually grins.

"We were just about to get started." He says. "Want to watch me fuck her? I know how much you Montagues enjoy sharing."

Any self-control I have left dies. Hastings says something behind me but I don't hear it. I don't hear anything. I throw myself at him, slamming my body into his.

Rose collapses, dragging herself out the way as Darius and I fight.

I slam his head into the floor. His hands wrap around my throat, trying to choke me. I push my thumb into his good eye and he howls kicking out, jerking, trying to throw me off.

"You fucking bastard." I yell.

He can't reply. He's too busy fighting me to get any words out.

I throw one punch and then another. But he swings right back at me and we fall back onto the floor, rolling on top of one another, delivering blow after blow.

He manages to get on top of me and he pins me down, choking me once more.

I snarl trying to throw him off. I'm not going down like this. I'm not losing like this. This bastard stole my fiancée, he stole my daughter, and he raped my sister.

As I curl my fist once more he freezes.

His whole body stiffens.

And then blood starts pouring out of his mouth.

His hands release their grip, he slumps just enough to tell me I can beat him now. That whatever fight he has is gone.

I kick him off and he falls onto his side with a knife buried into the back of his neck.

I look across and Rose is there, on her knees, covered in his blood.

She's trembling, she looks like she doesn't have full control of herself. I move to grab her and she collapses into my arms.

"Rose."

"GHB." She mumbles the letters but I know what's she saying. That he drugged her.

My gut twists. I shout out, screaming for a medic. Screaming for a doctor. But as I look around I can see other men, shooting, fighting Hastings' men. Where they came from I don't know but I drag her out the way, drag her into a corner where I can keep her safe.

It takes barely more than a minute before it's over. Before the guns stop and silence finally rings out.

A man rushes to us, pulling Rose free from me, lying her down, checking her vitals.

"Tell me she's okay." I say.

He looks up at me and nods. "She's breathing."

I shake my head, feeling my fear ease a little. But just because she's breathing doesn't mean she's going to make it.

"He drugged her." I state.

"Do you know what with?" He asks.

"GHB." I murmur staring down at her, at where she's unmoving with her eyes shut. Her chest is rising slowly, her upper body is almost entirely exposed. I hate that's she's on display like this and I pull my jacket off wrapping it over her, covering her.

"Roman."

I turn looking across at Hastings and he pulls me away, forces me to leave her, muttering about how the doctor has it sorted.

I scowl at him but he doesn't seem to care. Instead he walks to where Darius is lying dead, but his blood is still seeping out.

"I guess you got your wish." He murmurs.

"And what is that?" I reply.

He looks up at me. "Revenge."

I shake my head. Yes I wanted that, yes I needed that but I hadn't planned on it going down this way. I hadn't planned on Rose ending up like this.

"I'm taking it from here." He says quietly.

"What does that mean?" I ask.

He looks back at Rose. At where she's still laid out. "I understood your intentions, your drive, but this is the end. No more backstreet justice you hear me? I'm Governor now. This ends my way."

I narrow my eyes stepping in front of him, blocking him from her. "What more do I need?"

"Sofia?" He says. "You don't want justice for her?"

I gulp. "Maybe if I was a better brother I would have done that." I state. "I would have hunted everyone who hurt her down and made them pay. But ultimately Darius was responsible, he was the one who fed her to the wolves."

He lets out a sigh dropping his gaze back to Rose. "He was a sick son of bitch especially considering who he is, who they are to one another."

My stomach lurches. I don't know why. It shouldn't matter and yet it feels like another betrayal. Another of Rose's secrets laid bare for everyone to pick over and enjoy.

"You figured it out then." I reply. She did ask him to run the DNA, I guess he got curious as to who's it was.

He shrugs. "I had to know who his daughter was."

My eyes widen. My stomach drops at the word.

Daughter?

He narrows his scanning my face, clearly confused by my re-action. "You didn't know?"

"She told me they weren't..." I trail off staring at where the doctor is shining a light in her eyes.

"Maybe she didn't want you to know." Hastings murmurs.

"Why the fuck would she hide that?" I growl. Why would she hide anything from me?

He tilts his head. "Would you want the man you love knowing you fucked your own father? That you married him?"

I don't know how to reply to that. I don't think I have any words.

"No one else will find out." He says quietly. "No one else will know. I've already destroyed all the records so there's no evidence of it."

I nod feeling numb. Feeling so damn confused. He pats me on the back then walks away, leaving me to my own thoughts. Leaving me stood here, useless.

I crouch down beside her. She's still out. I get the feeling she won't be conscious anytime soon. God knows how much he dosed her with.

"Is there nothing you can give her?" I ask.

The doctor shakes his head. "It's safer if she sleeps it off. She's not in any danger now."

I scoop her up, ignoring his objections. "If she's not in any danger then I'm taking her home." I growl carrying her out, carrying past all those faces, all those people watching us.

I want her home.

I want her to wake up in our bed and know that she's safe.

That it's finally over.

She killed the bastard. *She* did it.

And as I stare down at her in my arms I couldn't be any prouder

67

ROSE

I know I'm in my bed. Our bed.

I know it as I roll my head over, as I smell the pillows, as I blink and recognise the bedside lamps.

For a moment I don't move. I just lay there, in the semi-darkness, warm, content, taking this tiny bit of peace before I have to face the man waiting so patiently for me. Before I have to look him in the eye and face the last of my shame.

He crouches down, brushes the hair from my face and I reluctantly open my eyes.

"How are you feeling?" He asks gently. Lovingly.

And if anything that makes it so much worse.

I wince, sitting up. My body still feels like lead. I have a raging headache as if I drank the entirety of the alcohol cupboard. God, I wish that was what had happened.

"Like shit." I murmur.

He lets out a snort wrapping his arm around me. "It's over Rose. He's dead."

I look up feeling a mixture of emotions. I expected to feel joy. I expected to be dancing from the rooftops at those words and yet now I feel hollow.

"Did he hurt you?" He asks scanning my face as if he knows my reaction right now is not right.

I shake my head. He did, but it was nothing compared to what he'd done before. Nothing I couldn't take.

"I fought him off." I murmur looking away.

He cups my cheek, forcing me to look back at him, and I see something there, something in his eyes that makes me freeze. That makes me feel like I'm back out in the snow, that I'm buried in it.

"You didn't tell me the truth Rose." He says. "You lied to me the other day."

I gulp, trembling, shaking my head, and suddenly my tears are streaming down my face. It's like a dam breaks, like the last horrors of everything finally hits me.

"I couldn't." I gasp.

"You know you can trust me. You know I will always protect you." He states.

I shove my face into my hands, burying my eyes into my palms. "Not with this."

"Rose..." He murmurs.

"You would despise me."

"I would not." He snaps.

I take in a deep breath forcing myself to look at him as my disgust and anger coil into one unrelenting wave of anguish that it feels like I'm drowning in.

"How could I ever admit that?" I spit. "How could I ever tell you that?"

He pulls me into his chest and I bury my face into his neck while he's rubbing my back in a way that is so soothing. "You didn't choose that Rose. You didn't have a clue."

That doesn't make it right though does it? That doesn't make any of this right?

"No one else knows." He says quietly. "And no one will know."

"What does that mean?" I ask.

"Hastings has destroyed the records. As far as anyone is concerned Ignatio was your father and no one knows your mother and Darius were related."

I should feel relief at that. I should feel better. It really is over. I should be jumping from the damn ceiling and yet all I want to do is curl up into a ball and hide in my shame and my disgust.

I don't understand how he can even touch me right now, how he can even bear to be in my presence. I'm disgusting. I'm repulsive.

He lets out a snarl, pulling the covers off and I shiver at the sudden loss of them. He grabs my legs wrenching them wide open.

"What are you doing?" I gasp.

He stares down, his eyes flashing as his hand moves and for a second I think he's going to touch me, that he's about to pull my thong aside. Only instead he pulls the plaster off, twisting my leg around at an angle for me to see.

"Remember this?" He says. "Remember how you asked me to mark you?"

I nod, trembling. He's so angry right now and I know it's my fault. I caused this. I created this.

"You are mine Rose." He growls. "I carved my name into your skin." He pulls his top off and I see the bloodied outline where I did the same, where I sliced into his chest. "Your name." He states taking my hand, running my tips along it, feeling the raised edges. "Nothing changes that. Nothing alters that."

"But I'm disgusting." I whisper it.

He snarls more, putting his hands either side of my head, pinning me into the headboard. "Stop saying that. You're not disgusting. To me you're the most beautiful person I've ever met. You're the love of my life."

My tears stream down my face. I wish I could feel that. I wish I could believe that. But I fucked my own dad. What kind of person even does that?

He cups my face, careful not to put any pressure on the bruising of my cheek. And then he's capturing my lips in a kiss that's so punishing I know my lips will swell. When he pulls away he holds my chin up, refusing to let me break our gaze.

"I will never stop loving you." He states. "I will never stop wanting you. Nothing that they did will change that."

I let out a shudder.

"Don't let them win. Don't let them beat us. Not now."

"They haven't." I whisper it.

He's right. I know he is. I just have to get my head around this. I just need to process it and then move on. Only that feels so much easier said than done.

His lips curl. He kisses me again softer than before and this time I kiss him back, I wrap my arms around his neck and pull him into me.

"Roman." I gasp.

"It's over." He murmurs.

I wrap my legs around him, I pull him down, pull us both down into the bed.

He opens his eyes scanning my face as if he's assuring himself of what he thinks I'm looking for, as if he wants to check what signals I'm giving off, like he doesn't know my body better than I know myself.

"Fuck me." I say. Not because this moment is sexy, not because I'm turned on exactly, but because I want him to prove it, to claim me, to override my stupid thoughts with his body and just get lost in the physical pleasure of this for a bit.

He tangles his right hand in my hair. He kisses me again as his left slides under my t-shirt and then he's cupping my breast, teasing my nipple before he pulls the fabric up entirely and he's capturing it with his mouth.

I let out a moan. I rub myself against his hardened cock and I run my own hands down his chest to where the elastic waistband of his sweatpants are.

He groans as I take him in my hands and as I run them up and down his shaft, turning him on more.

And then he's pushing me onto my back, ripping my underwear off, and opening my legs so wide. I arch my hips, I arch my back, ready for the deep delicious feel of him.

His fingers spread me open. His hot breath hits me right at my core.

He plants a kiss on my clit and I feel myself leaking out more arousal.

"Roman." I gasp opening my eyes staring down at him.

His face is right there, he's studying my most intimate part like I'm a piece of art, a sculpture.

"I'll never get sick of this view." He murmurs before running his tongue so lightly up me.

I shudder, raising my hips. "Fuck me. Please." I beg.

He tilts his head looking back up at me.

I don't want this foreplay, I don't want him taking his time, I want him in me, buried so deeply. I want to lose myself as he fucks the very breath out of me.

He smirks like he's amused and then he's dragging me further down the bed, lining himself up and thrusting all of his dick inside me.

I let out a cry so loud I don't doubt the entire house hears.

"Is this what you wanted?" He taunts sliding out before thrusting all the way back into me.

"Yes." I gasp, clawing at him, digging my nails into his skin. "I need you too…"

"Need me to what Rose?" He says doing it again and I swear I lose my mind.

I wrap my legs around his waist, I gyrate my hips, welcoming every inch he gives me, every merciless thrust.

"Tell me Rose, tell me what you need and I'll grant it."

"You." I cry. "I need you."

He slides out, and I physically deflate at the loss of him. But he's rolling me onto my front, lifting my hips up, realigning himself and thrusting back into me.

"Fuck you feel incredible." He groans, pausing as if it's almost too much for him to take.

I raise my hips higher, rock them, encouraging him more.

He lets out a chuckle, planting a kiss onto my back. "So needy." He murmurs.

And then he starts sliding so much deeper into me and I swear my eyes roll back. The sound of our skin slapping against one another fills the air. The sounds of my moans gets higher and higher pitched.

I shudder, I clench around him, coming so hard I think I might pass out.

He pulls himself out, picks me up, places me so I'm straddling him and then he buries himself inside me again.

I'm covered in sweat. My tears are falling, half from pleasure half from how my heart is breaking. He kisses them away, thrusting so deliciously into me and I meet each one, I drive us both to our release while he tells me how beautiful I am, how much he loves me, and how proud he is of me.

When we slump into each other once more, he curls us up in the bed. Stroking my hair, watching me so intently.

"We're free now." I murmur. "Free of all of them."

He smiles, nodding. "We can get our own home, we can put proper roots down."

I glance around. "Why can't we stay here?" I ask. "Why don't we buy this house?"

"The owner may not want to sell it." Roman replies.

I let out a laugh. "I'm sure we can offer him enough money to. I have Paris's fortune. I still have all his properties as well." What better way to get my revenge than by turning all those old memories into new, happier ones? I'm sure he'd happily swap this one for Paris's monstrosity of a mansion in the Hamptons.

His lips curl. "You want this place as our home?"

I tilt my head. "Don't you?"

He looks around nodding.

"We can be a family here, continue living as one." I say.

He wraps his arms tighter, murmuring about what future he wants, about everything he's ever dared to imagine for us. Each tiny part.

It's a future we fought for.

A future we have killed for.

A future we've ensured that we can have now.

EPILOGUE

ROSE

Lara's squeal rings out as she races towards the massive pile of presents in the middle of the room practically throwing herself at them all.

"Careful." I say knowing that at least some of them are breakable.

Ben smirks. Sofia is sat, holding a mug of tea like she needs the warmth of it to get through this day.

"Happy Birthday Daddy." Lara says as Roman walks in.

He stops, taking in the scene and then looks at me.

"What's all this?"

"You think we wouldn't want to spend our first family birthday together?"

He lets out a chuckle walking over to where Lara is eyeing up the presents like we haven't bought her enough new things already.

"There's a lot here." Roman says.

"There are daddy." Lara says grinning like she knows what he's about to say.

He kneels down beside her. "You know, I might need a hand unwrapping them all."

"I can help." Lara says bouncing up, springing at the first one and ripping the paper off before anyone can say another word.

Roman and Ben laugh out loud. Even Sofia is laughing.

She passes it over to him and he looks at it before putting it to the side. "Which one next?"

"This one." She says manhandling a box like one.

He nods helping her tear the paper off when in truth she doesn't need any help.

"What is it Daddy?" She asks frowning.

He looks at the side then across at Ben. "A watch winder?" He teases.

"You have enough watches to put it to use." Ben replies.

"Christ, you are getting old." Sofia says and we both snigger.

"Open the next." Roman says to Lara before getting up and moving to sit beside me.

This is the first birthday any of us have had together. It feels like another turning point. Another memory we can store away. A happy one. A one we can think back on when we're old and decrepit and can smile.

We have this. We have our happy ending.

"Stop looking like that." Roman murmurs into my ear.

"Like what?"

"Like you're thinking this can't be real."

"But it is."

He cups my face, kissing me lightly. Too lightly. "One day you'll actually believe it."

Lara lets out a whine and Ben goes to help her, clearly seeing me and Roman are now distracted.

I lean back into him as he wraps his arm around me, giving me another heart melting kiss.

It's been almost six months since everything ended. Since Darius died. Since every arsehole who tried to break us up got their rightly deserved comeuppance.

Hastings is still Governor. Although he's no longer an interim. He decided to stay, to make Verona Bay his home and I'll admit I was relieved when he told us he was running in the elections.

I know he supports us, that he has our back. But he's also made it more than clear everything from now on has to be above board. No more vigilante tactics, no more talk of revenge.

I guess for me everyone who wronged us has been held accountable but for Sofia that's not the case. Sure Otto is dead, just as Darius is, but there were others.

Hastings came to us a month after everything settled and showed us the video evidence of what happened to Nicholas Austin-Reed. Sofia watched it without saying a word and then she got up, left, and never mentioned it.

I don't know if it helped. I don't know if it gave her peace but I hope it did.

The two of us have grown so close, I guess our shared trauma has bonded us. I'm as protective of her as I am of Roman and Lara. To me, she's just as much my family as they are.

She's doing okay. She's still staying at the Four Seasons. But she comes over every Sunday for lunch, putting on a big bright smile when she visits and this entire city thinks she's good but I know better, and I think deep down Roman does too.

What she needs is time. What she needs is space. And as a family we will do whatever we can to support her.

Koen came to our house two days after Darius's demise was publicly announced. He told Roman that his debt was paid, that he owed him nothing, and then he walked out leaving us both dumbfounded. Afterall who turns down twenty million?

We haven't spoken about him. Not one of us have. We haven't even mentioned his name to her.

I still don't know what is going on between Sofia and him. Or Sofia and Ben for that matter. We don't discuss it. We make it clear it's none of our business.

But he's stayed away from Sofia, just as we asked, though I know he's still looking out for her, making sure she's safe from a distance.

Roman and I got married just before Christmas. Only Ben, Sofia, and Lara were there. We didn't want anyone else there. We didn't need anyone else.

I'm now Rose Montague and to say I couldn't be happier is an understatement.

As I stare down at the simple gold band beside my vintage engagement ring my heart does a leap. It turns out Darius didn't toss the ring Roman gave me, he stashed it away, no doubt as some sort of trophy. Guess the jokes on him because this ring to me is worth so much more than the awful diamond he forced on my hand.

In so many ways Verona hasn't changed. It's still golden on the outside, filled with people who seek fame and fortune, but for me everything has changed. I have changed.

I've learnt how to fight, how to stand up for myself, how to stop allowing my circumstances to force me into situations I don't want to be in.

And my mother is finally learning a few things too. They had a big trial. She managed to get some hot-shot lawyer to defend her but nothing could explain the things she'd done. The people she'd murdered, all the ways she aided and abetted Darius.

Of course no one knows their real relationship. Hastings was as good as his word on that front. No one knows what Darius really was to me either. But I took the stand, I testified, telling the world all the twisted things she did in pursuit of money and power.

She's now locked away in a high security prison. Locked away in solitary confinement because all the other prisoners have already tried to gut her more times than I can count.

She'll never get parole.

She'll never get released.

And that thought alone puts a smile on my face every night I go to bed.

We bought this house, we made it our home, and now that everyone knows Roman and I are married, nothing can ever separate us. Lara has started therapy, she also attends a school a few days a week. We're easing her in but every day she seems to blossom more. She's not shy, she's no longer afraid. My daughter is growing into the happy person she deserves to become.

Beside me Roman checks his phone.

"Are you late for something?" I tease.

He grins back at me. "She's got at least another dozen presents to unwrap."

"And?"

He takes my hand. "Even once she's unwrapped them I say we'll have a good half hour."

"Half hour for what?"

He just grins.

"You mean..?"

"It's my birthday Rose." He murmurs getting silently to his feet. "How about you give me a birthday treat."

I bite back the shocked laugh but I'll admit his words have already made me flush with need.

"What treat is my husband thinking of?" I ask as we sneak away, out of the room, though I know both Sofia and Ben will take note of our sudden absence.

He runs his fingers over my lips. "We don't have much time."

"We have half an hour by your reckoning."

"Not enough to satisfy my wife." He states.

I smirk at those words because we both know that's not exactly true. He knows exactly how to make me come almost on command, he just likes to take his time, to drag it out, to torture me in the most delicious ways possible.

"I want your mouth on me, Rose. I want you showing me how much you love me."

I wrap his finger around my tongue, staring back at him and then I pull off with a pop. "Take what you want Roman. Use your wife the way she wants you too."

He undoes his belt and trousers as I sink to my knees.

"I love you so much." He says cupping my cheek.

I smile back at him. "I love you too, Roman." And then I slide him into my mouth, hearing that way he always groans, feeling the way my body always responds to him.

My Roman. My husband. We're bound together now. Till death us do part.

THE END

RECKONING

BLURB

**They broke me. Abused me. Treated me like
trash and left me to die...**

I SURVIVED EVERYTHING THEY PUT ME THROUGH AND WHEN MY
brother came back from the dead, I thought it was over.

I thought I could move on.

Except they're still here, in Verona, they're still living free and
with every day that passes I feel that insult more and more.

And my abusers aren't just going to trust I'll keep my mouth
shut. They start stalking me, start trying to turn my own family
against me and then it's game on.

They think I'm still some broken little thing. They think I'll
just roll over and die.

Except I've got claws now. Long f*cking claws.

I will have my revenge. I will have my vengeance.

Even if I have to make a pact with the devil to achieve it. Even
if I have to sell myself to Koen Diaz himself.

SNEAK PEEK
RECKONING

SOFIA

I shouldn't be here. That's the thought that keeps echoing in my head.

That I have to stop. That I need to stop.

Turnaround Sofia. Turnaround you utter fool.

Only I don't. I just keep my pace, creeping through the darkness like I'm some sort of avenging angel.

But that's not what I am is it?

I'm not anything remotely close to angelic anymore. Not after what they did to me. Not after what they put me through. I used to be a good person, considerate, despite how my family and I suffered, I still believed that the world was a good place.

And then Otto Montague happened.

I grit my teeth burying the wave of emotion that rises up at the mere thought of that man's name.

Ahead a street lamp flickers. I pause, watching as my would be target comes to a stop and I press myself flat against the damp brick of a building.

I had to take this chance. I didn't know when I would see the bastard again. If I would see him. I didn't even know his name, we'd never been introduced. After all, who makes introductions in the kind of situation I was forced in? No, I wasn't going to let him slip through my fingers. Wasn't going to let him continue to live his life like none of it happened.

As soon as he starts moving so do I. Around the corner, into the yard of some construction company.

It's hard not to smile. It's hard not to let out a laugh because I couldn't have picked a more perfect place if I tried. It's away from the street. Away from any would be bystanders. Would be witnesses.

I grip the knife firmer in my hand. My eyes fix on him. One firm strike will be enough to bring him under my control and after that I can take my sweet time. The way he did with me. The way he brutalised and tortured my drug addled body as my monster of a husband stood by and laughed.

I take a bigger step. Then another closing the distance. Just as I get within striking distance he turns and our eyes connect.

He must recognise me. He must.

Only he doesn't speak. He just stares at me, running his eyes over my body before fixing on the blade.

Footsteps echo behind me. I drop my focus on the man in front for a millisecond and someone behind me laughs.

"Did you come for another round?" The man in front taunts. "Drop the knife and we'll all have some more fun."

"Fuck you." I spit raising it instantly, pointing it right at his face.

They both laugh. The one behind stepping closer, making this feel like this was all done as a set up. That they knew.

My heart rate turns erratic. Sweat starts to moisten my palm and it feels like the handle of the knife is suddenly so slick.

I've lost the element of surprise. I've probably lost this entire fight and I know it's not going to end well but then, it never has for me, has it?

I charge, without hesitating. If I can gut one of them, kill one of them, just do something before I once again lose then maybe this might ease the incessant, continuous, all-consuming pain inside me.

Maybe it might make the voice in my head shut up.

Maybe, just maybe I might be able to look at myself in a mirror and not feel disgusted with what I see.

The man's eyes widen. He makes a grab for my wrist and I knee him in the balls before jabbing wildly with the knife. The other man grabs me trying to pull me back but I'm manic now, feral. I lash out, I thrash in their arms, slicing the blade through the air not caring where I cut, where I hurt, just as long as I make contact.

And I do.

I feel the knife hitting something solid over and over. The handle no longer just wet with sweat but with blood.

One of the men fall. He collapses and I realise I've actually hurt him.

My heart leaps.

I can do this. I can kill them both.

The other man wraps his arms around me locking my body against his and as his smell washes over me I get a flashback, a memory so vivid I lose sense of myself.

I let out a whimper, trying to fight it but the trauma is overtaking me. I can't focus. I can't do anything.

"Stupid fucking whore." The man spits swinging me around, throwing me forward.

My eyes widen as I see more men surrounding us. So this *was* a setup.

"Drop the blade or we fuck you with it." One of them says.

I shake my head. I'm not that stupid.

"Little bitch wants another lesson."

Every voice, every man here I look at makes a new vision echo in my head. One of pain. One of violation.

"It's been a while Sofia." One of them says stepping closer. "I'll admit I missed your cunt but I missed the way you cried as I was fucking you more."

I snarl, holding the blade out like my life depends upon it but I guess in a way it does.

They all start moving, closing in on me and I turn swinging the blade, trying to force them to keep away but I can't hold five men off. I don't stand a chance.

But just as that thought hits me I see more. They're rushing in, only they're not joining this sick soirée, they've got bats, wrenches and they're attacking the men who seconds ago were all but attacking me.

I stare about, not understanding what the hell is going on and someone grabs me, trying to use me as some sort of human shield. I scream, I flail, instinct taking over as I bury the knife over and over and the man slumps releasing his grip while I'm covered in his blood.

He falls to the floor, blood now gurgling from his mouth but he's not who I'm staring at. Not who I've got my attention on.

All I can see are the pitch black eyes of a man so big, so domineering it feels like this entire world would bend to fit him.

He stares back at me but there's no brutality in his eyes right now. There's something so much softer.

"Sofia."

The way he murmurs my name feels wrong. My body shouldn't react to it, shouldn't respond the way it does.

This man should petrify me more than every other and yet he does the complete opposite.

I shake my head, dropping my eyes and for the first time take in the blood that's covering me. It's soaked my clothes, it's all over my skin.

My breath hitches.

I killed him. I killed that man. I know it's what I intended, but now that I've done it, it feels so different. It feels too real.

I have to get it off. I have to get his blood off me.

Koen steps closer to me, not touching me but it still feels like he is.

"Sofia." He says again, more softly, as if he can tell I'm about to break completely.

I shake my head, shut my eyes. I don't want to be here. I don't…

"Carlos." Koen growls and a man crosses the space, running to us. "Get her out of here."

"Yes boss." The man says.

I shake my head once more. I don't want to leave, I want to see that every one of those bastards are dead but I can't stand here. My legs are shaking, my body is losing itself in the trauma and I can't focus on anything.

I let out a whimper, my head feels too dizzy, my heart is beating too rapidly. I take a step back but it feels like my feet aren't even on the ground anymore and as I start to slip into darkness I know it's Koen's arms that catch me.

That it's him who carries me away. Not the man he called. Not one of the five men who raped me so long ago.

And worse than that, I don't fight him, I don't even try, I just let the darkness take me and let this man carry me away, trusting that he won't hurt me. Trusting that he will keep me safe.

OUT 17 NOVEMBER 2023

VENGEANCE WILL BE HAD

RECKONING

A TWISTED LOVE STANDALONE NOVEL
- ELLIE SANDERS -

ALSO BY ELLIE SANDERS

ABOUT THE AUTHOR

ELLIE SANDERS LIVES IN RURAL HAMPSHIRE, IN THE U.K. WITH HER partner and two troublesome dogs.

She has a BA Hons degree in English and American Literature with Creative Writing and enjoys spending her time when not endlessly writing exploring the countryside around her home.

She is best known for her series of spy erotica novels, 'The BlackWater Series', as well as standalone novels including Good Girl, and Vendetta: A Mafia Romance.

For updates including new books, please follow her Instagram, TikTok, and Twitter @hotsteamywriter.

AUTHOR'S NOTE

THANK YOU SO MUCH FOR READING THIS DUET. I HOPE YOU ENJOYED it as much as I enjoyed conjuring up all the twists!

Look out for Sofia's story where some of those loose ends will finally be tied up!

If you enjoyed this book, why not subscribe to my newsletter where you'll be the first to hear about new releases and any give-aways I'm running.

I would be eternally grateful if after reading this you left a review. Reviews really are an author's lifeblood, not just because it helps beat back the crazy amount of imposter syndrome we all have but because it helps us get noticed / builds our community on places like amazon and ensures we can continue creating more stories for you to read and indulge in.

Made in the USA
Las Vegas, NV
13 February 2024

85719157R10262